Scarlet Wils[illegible] never stopped. She'[illegible] years, trained as a n[illegible]rks in public health [illegible]th her fiance and th[illegible]s and contemporary romances is a dream come true for her.

Barbara Wallace can't remember when she wasn't dreaming up love stories in her head, so writing romances for Mills & Boon is a dream come true. Happily married to her own Prince Charming, she lives in New England with a house full of empty-nest animals. Readers can catch up with Barbara through her newsletter. Sign up at www.barbarawallace.com

Brenda Harlen is a multi-award winning author for Mills & Boon True Love who has written over twenty-five books for the company.

A New Year Bride

SCARLET WILSON
BARBARA WALLACE
BRENDA HARLEN

MILLS & BOON

First Published in Great Britain 2019
by Mills & Boon, an imprint of HarperCollins*Publishers*
1 London Bridge Street, London, SE1 9GF

Special thanks and acknowledgment are given to Scarlet Wilson for her contribution to the *Maids Under the Mistletoe* series.

Special thanks and acknowledgment to Brenda Harlen for her contribution to the *Montana Mavericks: What Happened at the Wedding?* continuity.

ISBN: 978-0-263-27998-6

1219

MIX
Paper from responsible sources
FSC™ C007454
FSC
www.fsc.org

This book is produced from independently certified FSC™ paper to ensure responsible forest management.

For more information visit: www.harpercollins.co.uk/green

Printed and bound in Spain
by CPI, Barcelona

CHRISTMAS IN THE BOSS'S CASTLE

SCARLET WILSON

This book is dedicated my favourite little people, Taylor Hyndman, Noah 'Batman' Dickson, Lleyton Hyndman and Luca Dickson. Let's hope you're all on Santa's 'nice' list this year!

CHAPTER ONE

GRACE BRUSHED THE snow from her shoulders as she ducked in the back door of the exclusive Armstrong hotel in Chelsea, London. It was just after six in the morning, the streets were still dark and she could see her footprints in the snow outside.

Frank, the senior concierge, came in behind her. A wide grin lit up his face as he saw her looking at the snow outside. 'Finally,' he muttered as he shook the snow from his coat and started to sing the words to *It's Beginning To Look A Lot Like Christmas.* The words of the song floated from his lips. He gave her a nudge. 'You're too young to remember this one.'

She raised her eyebrows. 'Frank, you should know, I know every version of every Christmas song that's ever existed.'

They walked into the changing room. 'What version do you want to go for? Johnny Mathis, Frank Sinatra, or Michael Buble?' She started singing alongside him as she wound her long brown hair up into a loose bun and tied on her white chambermaid's apron over her black shirt and skirt.

Christmas was her absolute favourite time of year. It brought back great memories of the Christmases she'd spent with her grandmother in the little flat they'd shared in one of the poorer parts of London. But what they didn't have in wealth, they'd certainly made up for in love. This would be her first Christmas without her gran and she was determined not to be sad and gloomy—her gran would never have wanted that for her.

Frank slid his arms into his dark green and gold jacket and started fastening the buttons. 'I swear this thing shrinks every night when I put it into my locker.'

Grace laughed and closed her locker, walking over to Frank and pulling his jacket a little closer across his wide girth, helping him with the buttons. He kept singing the whole time. She finished with a sigh. 'I wish those words were true.'

Frank frowned as he glanced at his reflection in the nearby mirror and straightened his jacket. They started walking down the lower corridor of the hotel together. She shrugged. 'I wish it was beginning to look a lot like Christmas.' She held out her hands. 'Because it certainly isn't in here.' She gave a shake of her head. 'I don't get it. All the other big hotels in London have huge Christmas trees in their reception area and garlands and holly wreaths everywhere.'

The Armstrong hotel was part of a luxurious chain across the world. Locations in London, Paris, Tokyo, Rome and New York were regularly used by statesmen, politicians, rock stars and Hollywood celebrities. They were the epitome of glamour, renowned for their exclusivity, personal touches and attention to detail. It was a far cry from the small flat that Grace lived in and over the past few months she'd secretly loved seeing how the other half lived their lives. She knew one pop star that never laundered their underwear and instead just threw them away. A politician who had a secret interest in romance novels and a statesman that only ate red-coloured candy.

They reached the stairway up to the main reception. Frank held the door open for her and pressed his lips together. But now Grace had started, she couldn't stop. 'I mean, I know this place is exclusive, but the minimalist Christmas decorations?' She gave another shake of her head. 'They just look—well…cold.'

Frank sighed as he headed over towards his granite-topped desk. He spoke quietly as he glanced around the reception area. Everything was sleek and shades of black or grey. 'I know.' His eyes took in the small black and glass sign on the main reception desk.

The Armstrong wishes you
a Merry Christmas.

It was the only concession to Christmas on show. He checked the ledger on the desk in front of him and handed Grace an envelope. 'The Armstrong used to have beautiful Christmas decorations and lights. All exclusive. All extortionate. But they added colour to the place. Vibrancy.'

Grace started to automatically open the envelope with her day's assignments. She glanced upwards. 'So, what happened?'

Frank paused for a second before finally answering. Her gaze narrowed. Although she'd only been working here a few months, Frank had been here for ever. He was thoroughly professional, good at his job and for the guests who returned time after time—a most welcome sight. 'They had a rebranding,' he said finally.

Grace frowned. She wanted to ask more, but, like most good concierges, Frank had always been the soul of discretion. It was unlikely she'd get any more out of him.

She waved her assignment at him. 'I wish they'd let me do the rebranding around here. I could sprinkle some Christmas fairy dust.' She held out her hands and spun around. 'Some silver lights up here, some red ones over there. A tree near the glass doors. How about some garlands at the reception desk? And a huge pile of beautifully wrapped presents in the little alcove, just as you go through to the bar.' She stopped spinning, closed her eyes and held her hands to her chest. For a few seconds she could actually see in her head what this place could look like. The welcome. The warmth. The festivities.

Frank let out a wry laugh. 'Keep dreaming, Grace.'

Her eyelids flickered back open. Grey. Sleek. Blackness everywhere. She leaned forward across Frank's desk. 'I could even make this place *smell* like Christmas. Cookies. Cinnamon sticks. Cranberries. Pine trees and Christmas spices. And *not* from some tacky candle.'

Frank arched an eyebrow and leaned over towards her. 'There's a lot to be said for candles. And I'm sure we've got a whole host of those things packed up in the basement somewhere.' He shook his head. 'But I doubt very much we'll ever see them again.' He gave her a careful nod. 'You should take some home with you. Make good use of them.'

She gave a half-smile. He knew. He'd heard from some of the other girls that she was on her own. Grace didn't like people feeling sorry for her. But Frank had only the best of intentions. She knew that. So, she couldn't be offended by his good intentions. In fact, she was quite sure that some time, some place he might actually dress up as Santa.

Truth was, while The Armstrong hotel was opulent, its biggest asset was actually the staff. There were no 'bad pennies' as her gran used to call them.

Everything here was luxurious. From the bed sheets, to the furnishings, the Michelin-starred restaurant, even the heavy-duty stationery that her daily work assignment was printed on.

It was a world away from what she'd been brought up in. Working with the Maids in Chelsea agency had been a blessing in disguise. When her grandmother had died almost a year ago after a long battle with cancer, Grace had realised it was time to stop putting her own life on hold. Her gran had been the biggest part of her world. For a few years she'd only managed to take temporary part-time jobs that fitted in around being full-time carer for her gran. Working as a chambermaid might not be many women's dream job, but the salary was good and her work colleagues had turned into the best bunch of friends a girl could have.

As it was one of London's exclusive hotels, work at The Armstrong varied. There were a few guests that stayed here permanently. Some of the city's big businesses always had rooms on hold for their overseas visitors. A few of the suites seemed to be permanently vacant. Then, there were the celebrity guests.

In the space of a few months Grace had seen enough scandal and impropriety to keep the tabloid presses in headlines for the next year. But confidentiality was part of the contract for Maids in Chelsea—and she would never have breathed a word anyway.

Today's assignment was a little different. She headed over to the reception desk. 'Anya, can I just check? I've to clean the Nottingdale Suite? The penthouse? No one has stayed there in the whole time I've worked here.'

Anya checked the computer system. 'Yes, it's going to be used later. We're expecting the guest around five.'

'Who normally stays there?'

Anya smiled. 'I'm not sure. I did hear a rumour it was the reclusive tycoon who owns the whole chain.'

Grace tried not to let her mouth hang open. 'Really? Is it a man or a woman? What's their name?'

Anya held up her hands. 'You tell me. You've worked here longer than I have.'

Grace shook her head. 'I haven't paid that much attention. And I've never been in the penthouse.' She winked at Anya. 'This could be fun.'

* * *

The morning flew past. And it was fun. She cleaned a few rooms. Made a few special request orders for guests. Unpacked seven giant cases for a guest who was staying for only two nights. Then spent nearly an hour with Mrs Alice Archer, her favourite long-term guest who was eighty-nine going on twenty-one. Mrs Archer needed special soft sheets for her bed due to a long-term skin condition that affected her back, legs and arms. Grace was happy to give her a hand applying cream to spots she couldn't quite reach and helping her into whatever fabulous outfit she'd picked for the day. Alice's walk-in wardrobe was every girl's fantasy. It was full of original nineteen-forties clothes—all completely immaculate. Gorgeous full skirts, waist-cinching jackets, gingham dresses, a rainbow array of neckerchiefs, fitted sweaters and a few rarely worn satin evening gowns. There were a handbag and shoes to match every outfit.

Alice Archer had her hair styled twice a week, was fastidious with her make-up, favouring bright red lipstick, and drank lemon tea that Grace prepared for her most mornings, once she'd been helped into her clothes. In a way she reminded Grace of her grandmother. Oh, her grandmother had certainly never had the lifestyle that Alice had experienced. But both had the same quick wit, sharp minds and big hearts. Grace finished fastening Alice's shoes as she sipped her lemon tea.

'What are you doing today? Lunch or afternoon tea?'

Alice patted her hand. 'Thank you, Grace. It's Thursday. So it's afternoon tea at the Ritz. I'm meeting an old colleague.' She nudged Grace. 'He proposed to me once, you know.'

Grace looked up. 'He did? Now that sounds interesting. Why didn't you marry him?'

Alice let out a laugh. 'Harry? Not a chance. Harry was

a cad. A man about town. He would have broken my heart. So I had to break his first.'

Grace blinked. It was the throwaway way that she said it. There was a trace of something else behind those carefully made-up eyes. Did Alice regret her choice?

She hoped not. A man about town. Definitely not the type of guy that Grace was looking for. She'd never want a relationship with a man who only wanted a fling, or something meaningless. She'd suffered rejection enough. It was pretty much the worst thing in the world to be abandoned by your mother; hers had moved to another continent, married another man and created the family she'd really wanted, instead of the unexpected teenage pregnancy she'd ended up with.

Grace had always been determined that would never be her. She wasn't prepared to hand her heart over to anyone. Least of all a man that wouldn't value and respect her. She wanted everything: the knight on the white horse, the total commitment and someone with eyes only for her.

Hence the reason she was still on her own.

She rested back on her heels and looked up at Alice. 'Well, I'm sure that you couldn't have broken his heart too much, or all these years later he wouldn't still be meeting you.'

Alice sighed and leaned back in her chair. 'Or maybe we're the only ones left,' she said wistfully. Grace reached up and put her hand over Alice's frail one, giving it a gentle squeeze. 'I bet he'll be delighted to see you.'

After a second Alice seemed to snap out of her thoughts. 'What do you have planned? Tell me you've finally decided it's time to say yes to one of those nice young men that keep asking you out.'

Grace felt her cheeks flush. Alice's favourite hobby seemed to be trying to pair her off with a 'suitable' young man. She wasn't quite sure any of the men that had asked her out recently would be Alice's definition of suitable though. Lenny, the biker, had been looking for somewhere cheap to stay and thought asking Grace out might solve his problems. Alan, the banker, had earned another nickname in her head—as soon as darkness had surrounded them he'd turned into the eight-handed octopus. Ross from college had merely been looking for someone who might do the shopping and make him dinner. And Nathan? He'd seemed perfect. Handsome, hard-working and endearingly polite. But when he'd leaned in for that first kiss they'd both realised there was absolutely no spark.

She was still searching for her knight on a white horse.

In a way it made her sad. Her friends at Maids in Chelsea seemed to be pairing off at an alarming rate. Emma had just reunited with Jack—the husband nobody had known she had. Ashleigh seemed to have fallen under the spell of her gorgeous Greek, Lukas. Even Clio, their boss, had just announced her engagement to her old boyfriend Enrique and was currently planning an intimate New Year wedding. Then two nights ago her fellow singleton Sophie had mysteriously disappeared. Grace was beginning to feel like the inevitable spare part.

She shook her head at Alice and stood up. 'No men for me, I'm afraid. Maybe we can make a New Year's resolution together to try and find some suitable beaus.'

Alice let out a laugh. 'Now, that would be fun.' She glanced at the clock. 'What are you doing next?'

Grace glanced at the clock too and gave a start. Where had the time gone? 'Oh, I'll have to rush. I'm going to make up the penthouse suite—the Nottingdale. I've never even been in it before. I heard it belongs to the owner.'

Alice stared at her for a second with her bright blue eyes.

'What? Do you know him? Or her?'

Alice pressed her lips together. She seemed hesitant to

speak. Finally she gave a little smile. 'I've stayed here a while. I might know *him* a little.'

Grace grinned. She was instantly intrigued. 'Go on, then. Tell me about him. He's a bit mysterious. No one seems to know much about him.'

Alice shook her head. 'Oh, no, Grace. Sometimes mystery is good. I'm sure you'll meet him in good time.'

Grace narrowed her eyes good-naturedly as she headed towards the door. 'Alice Archer, I get the distinct impression you could tell me more.' She shook her head. 'But I'd better get on. Have fun with your afternoon tea.'

She closed the door behind her and took out her staff key for the elevator to the penthouse.

The elevator didn't just move. It glided. Like something out of the space age. It made her want to laugh. The rest of the hotel used the original elevators and Grace actually loved them. The little padded velvet love seat in the back, the panelled wood interior and the large brass button display inside. This private elevator was much like the front entrance. Shades of smooth black and grey. So silent that even her breathing seemed to disturb the air. When the doors slid open she almost jumped.

She stepped outside pulling her little trolley behind her. The entrance to the penthouse was different from the rest of the hotel. Usually the way to guest rooms was lined with thick carpet. The entrance way here was tiled, making the noise of the trolley bumping from the elevator echo all around her.

There was a huge black solid door in front of her with a pristine glass sign to its right: 'The Nottingdale Suite'.

She swallowed. Her mouth felt dry. It was ridiculous. She was nervous. About what?

She slid her staff card into the locking mechanism at the door. An electronic voice broke the silence. *Grace Ellis, Housekeeping.* She let out a shriek and looked around. In the last few months that had never happened anywhere in the hotel. It took a few seconds for her heart to stop clambering against her chest. Her card had actually identified her?

She pulled it out and stared at it for a second. Her befuddled brain started swirling. Of course, her staff card probably identified everywhere she went in the hotel. That was why she had it. But it had never actually said her name out loud before. There was something quite unnerving about that. Something a little too futuristic.

Hesitantly, she pushed open the door. It swung back easily and she drew in a breath. Straight in front of her were the biggest windows she'd ever seen, displaying the whole of Chelsea—and lots of London beyond around them. Her feet moved automatically until her breath misted the glass. The view was spectacular.

Kings Road with its array of exquisite shops, Sloane Square. If she looked in the other direction she could see the Chelsea embankment with Battersea Park on the other side and Albert Bridge. The view at night when everything was lit up must be spectacular.

Beneath her were rows of beautiful white Georgian town houses, mews cottages, streets lined with cherry trees. Houses filled with celebrities, Russian oligarchs and international businessmen. Security at all these houses probably cost more than she earned in a year.

She spun around and began to tour the penthouse. The still air was disturbing. Almost as if no one had been in here for a long time. But the bedroom held a large dark travel case. Someone had been here. If only to drop off the luggage.

She looked around. The bed was bare—waiting to be made up. It took her a few minutes to find the bedding—concealed inside a black gloss cupboard that sprang open as she pressed her fingertips against it. It only took a few minutes to make up the bed with the monochrome bedding. Underneath her fingertips she could feel the quality but the effect still left her cold.

She opened the case and methodically unpacked the clothing. It all belonged to a man. Polished handmade shoes. Italian cut suits. Made-to-measure shirts. She was almost finished when she felt a little lump inside the case. It only took a second to realise the lump was from something hidden in an inside pocket.

She pulled out the wad of tissue paper and unwrapped it carefully as she sat on the bed. The tissue paper felt old—as if it had wrapped this item for a number of years. By the time she finally peeled back the last layer she sucked in her breath.

It was gorgeous. A sparkling Christmas angel, delicately made from ceramic. Easily breakable—no wonder it was wrapped so carefully. She held it up by the string, letting it dangle in the afternoon light. Even though it was mainly white, the gold and silver glitter gave it warmth. It was a beautiful Christmas tree ornament. One that should be decorating a tree in someone's house, not being hidden in the pocket in a case.

Her heart gave a little start as she looked around the room. Maybe this businessman was having to spend his Christmas apart from his family? Maybe this was the one thing that gave him a little hint of home?

She looked around the cold, sleek room as ideas started to spark in her brain. Frank had told there were decorations in the basement. Maybe she could make this room a little more welcoming? A little bit more like Christmas?

Her smile spread from ear to ear as her spirits lifted a little. She didn't want to be lonely this Christmas. She certainly didn't want anyone else to feel that way either.

She hurried down to the basement. One thing about The Armstrong, it was super organised. She checked the ledger book and quickly found where to look. Granted, the room she entered was a little cluttered and dusty. But it wasn't impossible to find all the cardboard boxes. The tree that once stood in the main entrance was twenty-five feet tall. How impressive it must have looked.

She found some more appropriate-sized decorations and put them into a box to carry upstairs.

Two hours later, just as the sky had darkened to shades of navy blue and purple, she'd finally achieved the effect she wanted.

Tiny white sparkly lights lit up a tree in the corner of the main room. A gold star adorned the top. She'd found other multi-coloured twinkling lights that she'd wrapped around the curtain pole in the bedroom. She'd even strung a garland with red Christmas baubles above the bathroom mirror.

Each room had a little hint of Christmas. It wasn't overwhelming. But it was cute. It was welcoming. It gave the room the personal touch. The thoughtfulness that could occasionally be missing from even an exclusive hotel like this.

She walked around each room once again, taking in the mood she'd created. The Christmas style potpourri she'd found added to the room, filling it with the aroma of Christmas spices and adding even more atmosphere. She closed her eyes for a second and breathed in. She just loved it. She just loved everything about it.

Seeing the sky darkening with every second and snow dusting the streets outside, she gave a little smile.

Just one more touch.

She lifted the Christmas angel from the tissue paper and gently placed it on the pillow in the bedroom. She hadn't felt this good in a long time.

'Perfect,' she whispered.

'Just what do you think you're doing?' The voice poured ice all over her.

* * *

Finlay Armstrong was tired. He was beyond tired. He hadn't slept in three days. He'd ping-ponged between Japan, the USA and now the UK, all while fending off concerned phone calls from his parents. It was always the same at this time of year.

When would they realise that he deliberately made things busy at this time of year because it was the only way he could get through the season of goodwill?

He'd already ordered room service in his chauffeur-driven car on the journey from the airport. Hopefully it would arrive in the next few minutes then he could sleep for the next few hours and forget about everything.

He hadn't expected anyone to be in his penthouse. Least of all touching something that was so personal to him—so precious to him.

And the sight of it filled him with instant anger.

He hated Christmas. *Hated it.* Christmas cards with happy families. Mothers, fathers and their children with stockings hanging from the fireplace. The carols. The presents. The celebratory meals. All yearly reminders of what he had lost.

All reminders of another year without Anna.

The tiny angel was the one thing he had left. Her favourite Christmas decoration that she'd made as a child and used to hang from their tree every year with sentimental pride.

It was the one—and only—thing that had escaped the purge of Christmas for him.

And he couldn't even bear to look at it. He kept it tucked away and hidden. Just knowing it was there—hidden in the folds of his bag—gave him a tiny crumb of comfort that others clearly wouldn't understand.

But someone else touching it? Someone else unwrapping it? The only colour he could see right now was red.

Her head shot around and her eyes widened. She stepped backwards, stumbling and making a grab for the wall. 'Oh, I'm sorry. I was just trying to get the room ready for you.'

He frowned. He didn't recognise her. Didn't recognise her at all. Her shiny brown hair seemed to have escaped from the bun it was supposed to be in with loose strands all around her face. There was an odd smear across one cheek. Was she dirty?

His eyes darted up and down the length of her body. An intruder in his room? No. She was definitely in uniform, but not quite *his* uniform. She had a black fitted shirt and skirt on, a white apron and black heeled shoes. There was a security key clipped to her waist.

'Who are you?' He stepped forward and pulled at her security badge, yanking it from the clip that held it in place. She let out a gasp and flattened against the wall, both hands up in front of her chest.

What? Did she think he might attack her in some way?

He waved the card. 'Who on earth are the Maids in Chelsea? Where are my regular housekeeping staff?'

She gave a shudder. *A shudder.* His lack of patience was building rapidly. The confused look on her face didn't help. Then things seemed to fall into place.

It was easy to forget how strong his Scottish accent could become when he was angry. It often took people a few seconds to adjust their ears to what he was saying.

'Maids in Chelsea is Clio Caldwell's company. I've worked for her for the last few months.' The words came out in a rush. She glanced around the room. 'I've been here for the last few months. Before that—I was in Knightsbridge. But I wasn't here.' She pointed to the floor. 'I've never been in here before.' She was babbling. He'd obviously made her nervous and that hadn't been his intention.

He pointed to the angel on the pillow. He could hardly even look at it right now. 'And is this what your work normally involves? Touching things you have no business touching? Prying into people's lives?' He looked around the room and shook his head. He couldn't help himself. He walked over to the curtains and gave the annoying flickering lights a yank, pulling them so sharply that they flickered once more then went out completely. 'Putting cheap, tacky Christmas decorations up in the rooms of The Armstrong?' The anger started to flare again. 'The Armstrong doesn't do this. We don't spread Christmas tat around as if this were some cheap shop. Where on earth did these come from?'

She looked momentarily stunned. 'Well?' he pressed.

She seemed to find her tongue again. 'They're not cheap. The box they were in said they cost five hundred pounds.' She looked at the single strand of lights he'd just broken and her face paled. 'I hope that doesn't come out of my wages.'

The thought seemed to straighten out her current confusion. She took a deep breath, narrowed her gaze at him and straightened her shoulders. She held up one hand. 'Who are *you*?'

Finlay was ready to go up like a firework. Now, he was being questioned in his own hotel, about who *he* was?

'I'm Finlay Armstrong. I'm the owner of The Armstrong and a whole host of other hotels across the world.' He was trying hard to keep his anger under control. He was tired. He knew he was tired. And he hadn't meant to frighten her. But whoever this woman was, she was annoying him. 'And I take it I'm the person that's paying your wages—though I'm not sure for how much longer.'

She tilted her chin towards him and stared him in the eye. 'I'd say it's a pleasure to meet you, Mr Armstrong, but we both know that wouldn't be true.'

He almost smiled. Almost. Her dark brown eyes were deeper than any he'd seen before. He hadn't noticed them at first—probably because he hadn't been paying attention. But now he was getting the full effect.

He still wanted to have something to eat, crawl into bed, close the curtains and forget about the world outside. But this woman had just gained his full attention.

The tilt of her chin had a defiant edge to it. He liked that. And while her hair was a little unkempt and he still hadn't worked out what the mark was on her cheek, now those things were fading.

She was quite beautiful. Her hair must be long when it was down. Her fitted shirt showed off her curves and, although every part of her body was hidden, the white apron accentuated her slim waist and long legs.

She blinked and then spoke again. 'Clio doesn't take kindly to her staff being yelled at.'

'I didn't yell,' he replied instantly.

'Yes, you did,' she said firmly.

She bent down and picked up the broken strand of lights. 'I'm sorry you don't appreciate the Christmas decorations. They are all your own—of course. I got them from the basement.' She licked her lips for a second and then spoke again. 'I often think hotels can be a little impersonal. It can be lonely this time of year—particularly for those who are apart from their family. I was trying to give the room—' she held up her hands '—a little personality. That's all. A feeling of Christmas.' It was the wistful way she said it. She wasn't trying to be argumentative. He could tell from the expression on her face that she meant every word.

His stomach curled. The one thing he was absolutely trying to avoid. He didn't want to feel Christmas in any shape or form. He didn't want a room with 'feelings'. That was the whole point of being here.

He wanted The Armstrong to look sleek and exclusive. He'd purposely removed any sign of Christmas from this hotel. He didn't need reminders of the time of year.

For the first time in a long time he felt a tiny pang of regret. Not for himself, but for the person who was standing in front of him who clearly had demons of her own.

She pressed her lips together and started picking up the other decorations. She could move quickly when she wanted to. The red baubles were swept from above the bathroom mirror—he hadn't even noticed them yet. She stuffed the small tree awkwardly into the linen bag on her trolley. The bowl with—whatever it was—was tipped into the bin.

Her face was tight as she moved quickly around the penthouse removing every trace of Christmas from the room. As she picked up the last item—a tiny sprig of holly—she turned to face him.

'What is it you have against Christmas anyway?' She was annoyed. Upset even.

He didn't even think. 'My wife is dead and Christmas without her is unbearable.'

No one asked him that question. Ever. Not in the last five years.

Everyone tiptoed around about him. Speaking in whispers and never to his face. His friends had stopped inviting him to their weddings and christening celebrations. It wasn't a slight. It was their way of being thoughtful. He would never dream of attending on his own. And he just couldn't bear to see his friends living the life he should have with Anna.

The words just came spilling out unguarded. They'd been caught up inside him for the last five years. Simmering under the surface when people offered their condolences or gave that fleeting glance of pity.

'I hate Christmas. I hate everything about it. I hate seeing trees. I hate seeing presents. I hate seeing families all happy, smiling at each other. I don't need any reminders of the person missing from my life. I don't need any at all.

I particularly don't need some stranger digging through my belongings and taking out the last thing I have of my wife's—the only thing that I've kept from our Christmases together—and laying it on my pillow like some holy talisman. Will it bring Anna back? Will it make Christmas any better?' He was pacing now. He couldn't help the pitch of his voice. He couldn't help the fact that the more he said, the louder he became, or the broader his Scottish accent sounded. 'No. No, it won't. So I don't do Christmas. I don't want to do it. And I don't want to discuss it.'

He turned back around to face her.

She looked shell-shocked. Her eyes wide and her bottom lip actually trembling. Her hand partially covering her mouth.

He froze. Catching himself before he continued any further.

There were a few seconds of silence. Tears pooled in her eyes. 'I'm s…sorry,' she stammered as she turned on her heel and bolted to the door.

Finlay didn't move. Not a muscle. He hadn't even taken his thick winter coat off since he'd arrived.

What on earth had he just done?

He had no idea who the Maids in Chelsea were. He had no idea who Clio Caldwell was.

But he didn't doubt that as soon as she found him, he could expect a rollicking.

CHAPTER TWO

ONCE THE TEARS started she couldn't stop them. They were coming out in that weird, gasping way that made her feel as if she were fighting for every breath. She stopped in front of the elevator and fumbled for her card.

No! She didn't have it. He still did.

She looked around. Fire exit. It was the only other way out of here. There was no way she was hanging around.

As soon as she swung the door open she started upwards instead of down. Her chest was tight. She needed some air and she must be only seconds away from the roof. The grey door loomed in front of her. Was everything in this place black or grey? She pushed at the door and it sprang open onto the flat roof.

The rush of cold air was instant. She walked across the roof as she tried to suck some in.

She hadn't even thought about the cold. She hadn't even considered the fact it might still be snowing. The hotel was always warm so her thin shirt was no protection against the rapidly dipping temperatures on a late December afternoon.

But Grace couldn't think about the cold. All she could think about was the man she'd just met—Finlay Armstrong.

The expressions on his face. First of anger, then of disgust, a second of apparent amusement and then the soul-crushing, heart-ripped-out-of-his-chest look.

She'd done that to him. A stranger.

She'd caused him that amount of pain by just a few actions—just a few curious words.

She shivered involuntarily as the tears started to stream down her face. He'd implied that he'd sack her.

It was Christmas. She'd have no job. How could she afford to stay in the flat? As if this Christmas weren't already going to be hard enough without Gran, now she'd absolutely ruined whatever chance there was of having a peace-filled Christmas.

Her insides curled up and tumbled around. Why had she touched that angel? Why had she thought she had a right to decorate his room? And why, why had she blurted out that question?

The look on his face…the pain in those blue eyes. She shivered again. He'd lost his wife and because of that he couldn't bear Christmas. He didn't want to celebrate, didn't want to be reminded of anything.

The little things, the little touches she'd thought he might like, the tree, the decorations, the lights and the smells had all haunted him in a way she hadn't even imagined or even considered. What kind of a person did that make her?

She knew what it was like to find Christmas hard. A hundred little things had brought tears to her eyes this year—even while she was trying to ignore them. The smell of her gran's favourite perfume. The type of biscuit she'd most enjoyed at Christmas. Even the TV listing magazine where she used to circle everything she wanted to watch. But none of that—none of that—compared to the pain of a man who'd lost his wife.

Her gran had led a good and long life. His wife? She

could only imagine how young she must have been. No wonder he was angry. No wonder he was upset.

She squeezed her eyes closed. She hadn't managed to find someone she'd made that special connection with yet. Someone she truly loved with her whole heart. Imagine finding them only to have them ripped away. How unfair must that feel?

The shivering was getting worse. Thick flakes of snow started to land on her face. She stared out across London. The views from the penthouse were already spectacular. But from the roof? They were something else entirely.

It was darker now and if she spun around she could see the whole of Chelsea spread out in front of her. The Armstrong's roof was the highest point around. The streets below looked like something from a Christmas card. Warm glowing yellow lights from the windows of the white Georgian houses, with roofs topped with snow. There were a few tiny figures moving below. People getting excited for Christmas.

The tears flowed harder. Battersea Power Station glowed in the distance. The four distinctive chimneys were usually lit up with white lights. But this time of year, the white lights were interspersed with red—to give a seasonal effect.

Every single bit of Christmas spirit she'd ever had had just disintegrated all around her.

Perfect Christmas. No job. No family. A mother on the other side of the world who couldn't care less. And probably pneumonia.

Perfect.

The realisation hit him like a boxer's right hook.

What had he just done?

There was a roaring in his ears. He didn't behave like

this. He would never behave like this. What on earth had possessed him?

All thoughts of eating, pulling the blinds and collapsing into bed vanished in an instant.

He rushed out into the hall. Where had she gone? Her chambermaid cart was abandoned in the hall. His eyes went to the panel above the elevator. But no, it wasn't moving. It was still on this floor.

Something cut into the palm of his hand. He looked down. The plastic identity card. Of course. He'd taken it from her. She couldn't use the elevator.

He strode back into his room and picked up the phone. He hadn't recognised the new receptionist. Officially—he hadn't even checked in.

The phone answered after one ring. 'What can I do for you, Mr Armstrong?'

'Frank? Who are the Maids in Chelsea?'

There was a second of silence. The question obviously caught the concierge unaware.

He could almost picture the way Frank sucked the air through his teeth when he was thinking—he could certainly hear it.

'Staff from the Maids in Chelsea company have been working here for the last four months, Mr Armstrong. There were some…issues with some of our chambermaids and Mr Speirs decided to take a recommendation from a fellow hotel.' Frank paused and then continued, 'We've had no problems. The girls are excellent. Mrs Archer, in particular, really loves Grace and asks for her whenever she's on duty.'

He cut right to the chase. 'What were the issues, Frank?'

The sucking sound echoed in his ear. He would have expected Rob Speirs to tell him of any major changes in the way his prestigious hotel was run. But Speirs was currently in hospital after an emergency appendectomy. That was part of the reason that he was here at short notice.

'There were some minor thefts. The turnover of staff was quite high. It was difficult to know where the problem lay.'

'And Rob—where did he get the recommendation?'

'From Ailsa Hillier. The Maids in Chelsea came highly recommended and we've had no problems at all.' There was another hesitation. 'Mr Armstrong, just to let you know, I have something for you.'

'What is it?'

'It's from Mrs Archer. She left something with me to pass on.'

Now he was curious. 'What is it, Frank?'

'It's a Christmas present.'

Frank was silent for a few seconds. Just as well really. Every hair on Finlay's body stood on end. Of course, he'd received Christmas presents over the last few years. His parents and sister always sent something. But Mrs Archer? This was a first.

Frank cleared his throat again. 'Mr Armstrong, is there anything I can help you with?'

This time it was Finlay that paused. He liked Frank. He'd always liked Frank. The guy knew everything that happened in his hotel—including the fact that his manager had used a company recommended by their rivals at the Corminster—interesting.

'Keep a hold of the present, I'll get it from you later, Frank.' It wouldn't be good to seem ungracious. Then he asked what he really wanted to know. 'Have you seen Grace Ellis in the last five minutes?'

'Grace? What's wrong with Grace?'

Finlay really didn't want to get into this. He could already hear the protectiveness in Frank's voice. He should have guessed it would be there. 'Nothing's wrong, but have you seen her?'

'No, sir. Not in the last hour at least.'

Finlay put down the phone. She could easily have run out but he had the strangest feeling that she hadn't.

He walked back outside, leaving the penthouse door open behind him and heading towards the stairs. When he pushed the door open he felt a rush of cold air around him.

The roof. She'd gone to the roof.

He ran up the stairs, two at a time, pausing when he reached the top.

She was standing at the end of the roof, staring out over London. She wasn't thinking of…

No. She couldn't be. But the fleeting thought made him reluctant to shout her back in.

He crossed the roof towards her. As he neared he could see she was shivering—shivering badly.

He reached out and touched her shoulder and she jumped.

'Grace? What are you doing out here? You'll freeze.'

She must have recognised his voice but she didn't turn towards him. Her arms were folded across her chest and more wisps of her hair had escaped from the bun.

He walked around slowly, until he was in front of her, blocking her view.

Her lips were tinged with blue and her face streaked with tears.

Guilt washed over him like a tidal wave.

Him. He'd caused this. He'd made this girl cry.

Why? After five years he'd thought he was just about ready to move on. But Christmas was always the hardest time for him. He was frustrated with the rest of the world for enjoying Christmas when it only brought back what he had lost.

Thank goodness he still had his coat on. He undid the buttons and shrugged it off, slipping it around her shoulders.

She still hadn't spoken to him. She was just looking at him with those huge brown eyes. The ones that had caught his attention in the first place. The ones that had sparked the reaction he should never have had.

Why was that? He'd always kept things locked inside. His friends knew that. They knew better than to try and discuss things. They spent their lives avoiding Anna's name or any of the shared memories they had of her.

'I'm sorry,' he said hoarsely. 'I should never have shouted at you.'

She blinked. Her eyes went down to her feet. 'I should never have decorated the room. I'm sorry,' she whispered.

He shook his head. 'No, Grace. You were trying to do something nice. Something sweet.' The words made his insides twist a little. Was it really so long that someone had done something sweet around him?

She blinked again. The shivering hadn't stopped yet and he could tell why. The wind was biting through his thin knit black jumper. It didn't matter he had a shirt underneath. It had been a long time since he'd felt this cold.

She bit her bottom lip. 'I… I sometimes forget that other people don't like Christmas. I should have been more sensitive. I should have thought things through.' A tear slid down her cheek. 'Did you come up here to fire me?'

'What? No.' He couldn't believe it. That was the last thing on his mind right now.

She looked confused. 'But you said…you said—'

'Forget what I said,' he cut in. 'I was being an idiot. I'm tired. I haven't slept in three days. I'm sorry—I know it's no excuse.'

'I'm sorry about your wife,' she whispered.

It came out of the blue. Entirely unexpected.

Sweeping through him like the brisk breeze of cold air around him.

It was the waver in her voice. He'd heard this a thousand times over the last few years. Most of the times the words had seemed meaningless. Automatically said by people who were sometimes sincere, sometimes not.

This woman—Grace—hadn't known his wife at all. But there was something about her—something he couldn't quite put his finger on. It was as if she knew mourning, she *knew* loss. It was probably the sincerest he'd ever heard those words spoken and it twigged a little part inside him.

He stepped back a little. He stepped back and sucked in a breath, letting the cold air sear the inside of his lungs. She was staring at him again. Something about this woman's vulnerable eyes did things to him.

He wanted to protect her. He wanted to make sure that no one hurt her. There was something else. It wasn't sympathy in her eyes.

He couldn't stand the look of sympathy. It only filled him with rage and self-loathing.

A tear slid down her cheek and the wave of protectiveness that was simmering beneath the surface washed over him completely.

He couldn't help himself. He reached up with his thumb and brushed it away, feeling the coolness of her smooth skin beneath the tip.

He stepped closer again. 'Don't,' he said quickly, his voice rising above a whisper. 'I'm sorry I made you feel like this.' He wanted to glance away—to have the safety of looking out over the capital's skyline—but Grace's chocolate gaze pulled him in. His hand was still at the side of her face. She hadn't pulled away. 'I meant what I said.' He pressed his lips together. 'Christmas brings out the worst in me. It just brings back too many memories. And I know… I know that not everyone feels like that. I know that maybe…just maybe I should be able to get past this.' A picture swam into his head and he let out a wry laugh. 'As for the Christmas decorations in the hotel? They might be a little on the sparse side.'

It was the oddest situation. The most bizarre he'd ever found himself in. The irony of it almost killed him. If someone had told him twenty-four hours ago that he'd end up on the roof of his hotel, in the snow, with a strange, enigmatic woman who was causing the shades to start to fall away from his eyes after five years, he would have laughed in their face.

He wasn't joking about the sparseness of the hotel. Rob Speirs had emailed to say some of the guests were complaining about the lack of Christmas spirit. Rob had also dropped a few hints that it was bad for business.

Grace's eyebrows arched. The edges of her lips turned upwards. 'You think?'

He put his arm around her shoulders. 'It's freezing out here—and only one of us has a coat. Let's go back inside.'

She hesitated for the tiniest second then gave a shiver and a nod as they started walking to the door. 'So you can fire me in comfort?'

'Less of the firing thing. Are you going to bring this up all the time?'

She nodded. 'Probably.'

He pulled open the door. 'How about we go downstairs for some hot chocolate and you can tell me more about Maids in Chelsea? I have it on good authority you've got a fan in Mrs Archer.'

Grace nodded. 'I thought you were tired. You said you hadn't slept in three days. You don't need to talk to me. We can just call it quits and I'll go home now.'

He shook his head as they stepped inside and walked down the stairs. 'Oh, no. You don't get off that easy. We have things to discuss.'

'We do?'

She sounded surprised. He swiped a key fob next to the elevator and the doors swished open. He gestured with his hand for her to go inside. 'You don't want to have hot chocolate with me?'

He made it sound light-hearted. He wanted to try and make amends for his earlier behaviour. But the truth was his curiosity was piqued by Grace.

She gave him a cheeky stare. 'Only if there are marshmallows and cream. I get the impression you might be a bit of a cheapskate.'

He laughed as she walked into the elevator and for the first time in five years something happened.

It had been so long he almost didn't recognise it.

His heart gave a little leap.

Grace wasn't quite sure what to make of any of this. One minute Mr Film Star looks was firing her in his gravelly Scottish voice, the next minute he was apologising and making her heart completely stop when he touched her cheek.

It was the weirdest feeling. She'd been beyond cold—but the touch of his finger on her cheek had been like a little flame sending pulses around her body.

They stood in silence as the elevator moved silently to the ground floor. Frank caught sight of them as they walked out into the foyer, but Finlay didn't give them time to talk. He ushered her through to one of the private sitting rooms, speaking to a waitress on the way past.

They sat down on the comfortable black velvet-covered chairs. She ran her hand over the material. 'Black. Nice,' she said as she watched his face.

He shook his head. 'I feel that you might be going to make me pay.'

The strange wariness she'd felt around him had seemed

to vanish. She'd seen something up on that roof. Something she'd never seen in another person.

For a few moments it had felt as if she could see right into his soul. His pain. His hurt. His bitterness.

He seemed to be at a point in his life that she couldn't even begin to understand.

'Me? Make you pay? Whatever makes you think that?'

He put one elbow on the table and leaned on his hand. He did still look tired, but there was a little sparkle in those blue eyes. When Finlay Armstrong wasn't being so businesslike and generally miserable, he showed tiny glimmers of a sense of humour.

The good looks were still there. Now she wasn't so flabbergasted she could see them clearly. In fact, in the bright lights of the hotel his handsome features might even be a bit intimidating.

But there was something about that accent—that Scottish burr—that added something else to the mix. When she'd first heard it—that fierceness—its tone of *don't ever cross me* had had her shaking in her shoes. Now, there was a softness. A warmth about the tone.

He held out his arms to the room they were sitting in. 'I chose black and grey deliberately. I liked the smoothness, sleekness and no-nonsense look of the hotel. White would have been clinical. Any other colour just a distraction that would age quickly. Black and grey are pretty timeless colours.'

'If you can call them colours.'

The waitress appeared and set down steaming hot chocolates, adorned with marshmallows and cream, and long spoons. The aroma drifted up instantly. After the coldness of outside the instant warmth was comforting.

Finlay spooned some of the cream from his hot chocolate into his mouth and gave a loud sigh. 'I'm guessing you don't like my interior design selections.'

Grace smiled and tried to catch some of her marshmallows before they melted. 'I bet they cost more money than I could earn in ten years.'

He stopped stirring his hot chocolate and looked at her.

She cringed. Did she really mean to say that out loud?

The marshmallows-and-cream assortment was all sticking together inside her mouth. Any minute now she would start choking. She took another quick sip of the hot chocolate in an attempt to melt some of the marshmallows before she needed emergency treatment. Seemed as if she'd brought enough attention to herself already.

'How would you like to earn some more money?'

Too late. She coughed and spluttered everywhere. Did he really just say *that*?

As quickly as the words left his mouth and Grace started choking, Finlay Armstrong started to laugh.

He did. The guy actually started laughing. He leaned over and started giving her back a few slaps, trying to stop her choking. He was shaking his head. 'I didn't mean that. I didn't mean anything like that. It's okay, Grace. You don't need to fake a medical emergency and escape in an ambulance.'

The choking started to subside and Finlay signalled over to one of the waitresses to bring some water. He was still laughing.

Her cheeks were warm. No, her cheeks were red hot. Between choking to death and thinking completely inappropriate thoughts she couldn't be any more embarrassed if she tried.

Because she had thought inappropriate thoughts—even if it had been for just a millisecond.

She hadn't had enough time to figure out if she was mortally offended and insulted, or just completely and utterly stunned.

A bartender in a sleek black dress came over with a

bottle of water and some glasses with ice. She shot Finlay her best sultry smile as she poured the water for them both. Grace got a look of disdain. Perfect.

The water-pouring seemed to take for ever. She could almost hear some sultry backtrack playing behind them.

Finlay was polite but reserved. The bartender got the briefest of thanks, then he turned his attention back to Grace. It was hard not to grab the glass and gulp the water down. She waited until the water was finally poured, then gave her most equally polite smile and took some eager sips.

She cleared her throat. 'I didn't think that, you know,' she said quickly.

Finlay laughed even harder than before. 'Yes.' He nodded. 'You did. My bad. The wrong choice of words. I didn't mean that at all.'

She gulped again. Now they were out in public his conduct seemed a little different. He was laughing but there was more of a formality about him. This was his hotel and right now he was under the microscopic view of all his staff. He had a reputation to uphold. She got that. She did.

And right now his eyes didn't show any hint of the vulnerability she'd glimpsed upstairs. Now, his eyes seemed like those of a worldly-wise businessman. One that had probably seen and done things she could only ever dream of.

All she knew about Finlay Armstrong was the little he'd told her. But Finlay had the self-assured aura that lots of self-made businessmen had.

The knowledge, the experience, the know-how and the confidence that a lot of the clients she'd met through Maids in Chelsea had. People who had lived entirely different lives from the one she had.

She set down her water and tried to compose herself

again. Heat had finally started to permeate into her body. She could feel her fingers and toes.

She finally shook off Finlay's coat. She'd forgotten it was around her shoulders. That was what the bartender had been staring at.

She tugged at her black shirt, straightening it a little, and put her hand up to her hair, trying to push it back into place.

Finlay was watching her with amusement. 'Leave it—it's fine. Let's talk about something else.'

Grace shifted a little on the velvet chair. What on earth did he want to talk to her about?

His hands ran up and down the outside of the latte glass. 'I'd like you to take on another role within the hotel.'

She sat up a bit more. Her curiosity was definitely piqued. 'What do you mean?'

He held out his hands around the room. 'You mentioned the lack of Christmas decorations and I think you might be right. Rob Speirs, my manager, mentioned there's been a few complaints. He thinks it could be affecting business. It might be time to have a rethink.'

She tilted her head to the side. 'You want me to bring up the stuff from the basement?'

He shook his head. 'No. I don't want any of the old decorations. I want new. I want you to look around and think of a theme for the hotel, something that gives the Christmas message while keeping the upmarket look that I like for the hotel.'

Grace's mouth fell open. 'What?'

He started a little. 'And obviously I'll pay you. A designer fee, plus a company credit card to cover all the costs and delivery of what you choose.'

Grace was having trouble believing this. He'd pulled the few decorations she'd put up in the penthouse down with his bare hands. He'd called them tacky. Now, he wanted her to decorate the whole hotel?

She couldn't help the nervous laugh that sneaked out. 'Finlay, do you know what date it is?'

He wrinkled his nose. 'The sixteenth? The seventeenth of December? Sorry, I've crossed so many time zones lately I can't keep track.'

She shook her head. 'I don't know for sure, but I'm guessing most of the other hotels decided on their Christmas schemes months ago—and ordered all their decorations. They've had their decorations up since the middle of November.'

Finlay shook his head. 'That's too early. Even the first day of December seems too soon.'

Grace leaned across the table towards him. 'I'm not sure that what you have in mind and what I have in mind will be the same thing.'

'What do you mean?'

She sighed and tried to find appropriate words. 'Less than half an hour ago you told me you hated Christmas and everything about it. What's changed your mind?'

The hesitation was written all over his face. Just as she'd done a few seconds earlier, he was trying to find the right words. She could almost see them forming on his lips. She held her breath. Then, just when he looked as if he might answer, he leaned forward and put his head in his hands.

Now she definitely couldn't breathe. She pressed her lips together to stop herself from filling the silence.

When Finlay looked up again, it wasn't the polished businessman she'd been sitting opposite for the last twenty minutes. This was Finlay, the guy on the roof who'd lost his wife and seemed to lose himself in the process. What little oxygen supplies she had left sucked themselves out into the atmosphere in a sharp burst at the unhidden pain in his eyes.

'It's time.' His voice cracked a little and his shoulders sagged as if the weight that had been pressing him down had just done its last, awful deed.

She couldn't help herself. She didn't care about appropriateness. She didn't care about talk. Grace had always had a big heart. She always acted on instinct. She slid her hand across the glass-topped table and put it over his.

It didn't matter that the word no had been forming on her lips. It didn't matter that she felt completely out of her depth and had no qualifications for the position he wanted to give her. She squeezed his hand and looked him straight in the eye, praying that her tears wouldn't pool again.

He gave himself a shake and straightened up. 'And it's a business decision.' He pulled his hand back.

She gave him a cautious smile. 'If you're sure—and it's a business decision,' she threw in, even though she didn't believe it, 'the answer is yes.'

He leaned back against the chair, his shoulders straightening a little.

'I have to warn you,' she continued, 'that the picture you see in your head might not match the picture I have in mine.'

She glanced across the room and gave him a bigger smile. 'I can absolutely promise you that no matter how sleek, no matter how modern you think they are—there will be no black Christmas trees in The Armstrong hotel.'

The shadows fell a little from his eyes. 'There won't?'

There was the hint of a teasing tone in his voice. As if he was trying his best to push himself back from the place he'd found himself in.

'My Christmas could never have black trees. I'll do my best to keep things in the style you like. But think of Christmas as a colour burst. A rainbow shower.' She held up one hand as she tried to imagine what she could do. 'A little sparkle on a gloomy day.'

Finlay nodded in agreement. . 'I'll get you a credit card. Is there anything else you need?'

She licked her lips. Her throat was feeling dry. What had she just got herself into?

Her brain started to whizz. 'Use of a phone. And a computer. A space in one of the offices if you can.'

Finlay stood up. 'I can do that.'

It seemed the businessman persona had slotted back into place. Then, there was a tiny flicker of something behind his eyes.

He smiled and held out his hand towards her.

She stood up nervously and shook his hand.

'Grace Ellis, welcome to The Armstrong Hotel.'

CHAPTER THREE

'WHAT'S WRONG WITH you today?' asked Alice.

Grace was staring out of the window, lack of sleep making her woozy.

She turned her attention back to Alice. 'Nothing, I'm sorry. I'm just a little tired.'

Alice narrowed her gaze with a sly smile on her face. 'I've seen that kind of distracted look before—just not on you.'

Grace finished making the bed and turned to face Alice. 'I don't know what you mean.'

The last thing she wanted to do was admit to Alice the reasons that sleep had evaded her. It would be easy to say it was excitement about the job offer. Stress about whether she could actually *do* the job. But the truth was—while they might have contributed—the main sleep stealer had been the face that kept invading her mind every few seconds.

There was something so enigmatic about Finlay Armstrong. It wasn't just the traditional good looks, blue eyes and sexy Scottish accent. It was something so much more.

And there was no way she could be the only one that felt it.

A successful businessman like Finlay Armstrong must have women the world over trying to put themselves on his radar.

She had no idea how he behaved in private. Five years was a long time. Had he had any hook ups since his wife died? Probably. Surely?

She didn't even want to think like that.

It was just…that moment…that moment on the roof. The expression in his eyes. The way he'd looked at her when he'd reached up and touched her cheek.

Grace hadn't wanted to acknowledge how low she'd been feeling up there. She hadn't wanted to admit how she was missing her gran so much it felt like a physical pain.

But for a few seconds—up on that roof—she'd actually thought about something else.

She'd actually only thought about Finlay Armstrong.

'Grace?' Alice Archer had walked over and touched her arm.

'Oh, sorry, Alice. I was miles away.'

Alice raised her eyebrows. 'And where was that exactly?'

Grace bit her lip and pulled some folded papers from her white apron. 'I've to help choose some Christmas decorations for the hotel. I was up half the night trying to find something appropriate.'

Alice gave a little smile and reached her thin hand over to look at the printouts. Grace swallowed. She could see the blue veins under Alice's pale skin. A few of her knuckle joints were a little gnarled. They must give her pain—but she never complained. Another reminder of how much she missed her gran.

Alice glanced over the pictures, her eyes widening at a few. Grace had spent hours tracking down themes and stockists for particular items. All of them at costs that made her blink.

Alice gave her a thoughtful look as she handed the pictures back. She patted Grace's hand. 'I'm sure whatever you choose will be perfect. It will be nice to have some Christmas cheer around the hotel.'

Grace couldn't help but smile. 'Christmas cheer, that's exactly what I'm trying to capture. Something to make people get in the spirit.'

Alice walked over to her Louis XV velvet-covered chair and sank down with a wince.

'Are you okay? Are you hurting?'

Alice shook her head proudly and folded her hands in her lap. 'No. I'm not sore, Grace. I'm just old. I'll have some lemon tea now, if you please.'

'Of course.' Grace hurried over to complete their morning ritual. She sliced the fresh lemon and prepared the tea, boiling the water and carrying the tray with the china teapot and cup and saucer over to the table at Alice's elbow.

Alice gave a grateful sigh. Her make-up was still impeccable but her eyes were tired this morning. 'Maybe you should have some help? Someone to give you some confidence in your decisions.'

Grace was surprised. 'Do you want to come with me? You're more than welcome to. I would be glad of the company.'

Alice laughed and shook her head. 'Oh, no. I don't mean me. I was thinking more of someone else…someone else who could use a little Christmas spirit.'

Grace had poured the tea and was about to hand the cup and saucer to Alice but her hand wobbled. She knew exactly who Alice was hinting about.

'I don't think that would be appropriate. He's far too busy. He's far too immersed in his work. He wouldn't have time for anything like that.'

She shifted uncomfortably. She had a pink shirt hanging up in her locker, ready to change into once she'd finished her chambermaid duties. Alice was staring at her with those steady grey eyes. It could be a little unnerving. It was as if she could see into Grace's head and see all the secret weird thoughts she'd been having about Finlay Armstrong since last night.

Gran had been a bit like that too. She'd always seemed to know what Grace was going to say before she even said it. Even when she'd been twelve years old and her friend had stolen a box of chocolates from the local shop. The associated guilt had nearly made Grace sick, and she'd only been home and under Gran's careful gaze for ten minutes before she'd spilled everything.

Alice Archer was currently sparking off a whole host of similar feelings.

Her eyes took on a straight-to-the-point look. 'He asked you to get him some Christmas decorations, didn't he?'

Grace set the cup and saucer down. 'Yes,' she replied hesitantly.

'Then, he's reached the stage that he's ready to start living again.'

The words were so matter-of-fact. So to the point. But Alice wasn't finished.

'It's time to bring a little Christmas magic to The Armstrong, Grace, and you look like just the girl to do it.'

One hour later the black shirt was crumpled in a bag and her long-sleeved deep pink shirt with funny little tie thing at the collar was firmly in place. She grabbed some more deodorant from her locker. She was feeling strangely nervous. A quick glance in the mirror showed her hair was falling out of its bun again. She pulled the clip from her hair and gave it a shake. Her hair tumbled in natural waves. She was lucky. It rarely needed styling. Should she redo her lipstick?

She pulled her plum lipstick from her bag and slicked some on her lips. There. She was done. She took a deep breath, reaching into the apron that she'd pushed into her locker for her array of pictures. Her last touch was the black suit jacket—the only one she owned. She'd used it for her interview with Clio some months ago and thought of it as her good luck charm.

Finally she was satisfied with how she looked. She'd never be wearing designer clothes, but she felt presentable for the role she was about to undertake.

She pushed everything else back into the locker and did her final job—swapping her square-heeled black shoes for some black stilettos. She teetered for the tiniest second and laughed. Who was she trying to kid? She pulled open the locker again and slid her hand into the inside pocket of her black bag. There. Drop gold earrings that her gran had given her for her twenty-first birthday. She usually only wore them on special occasions but in the last few months, and particularly at this time of year, she missed her gran more than she could ever say. She slipped them into her ears and straightened her shoulders, taking a deep breath.

There it was. The little shot of confidence that she needed. She glanced down at the papers in her hand and smiled.

She was going to give this hotel the spirit of Christmas no matter what.

He could hear a strange noise outside his room. Like a shuffling. After more than a few seconds it was annoying.

Finlay's first reaction was to shout. But something stopped him. Maybe it was Alice Archer? Could she have come looking for him?

He sat his pen down on his desk. 'Is someone there?'

The noise that followed was almost a squeak. He smiled and shook his head. 'Well, it's obviously an infestation of mice. I'd better phone the exterminator.'

'What? No!' Grace's head popped around the door.

Grace. It was funny the odd effect that had on him.

She kind of sidled into the office. 'I'm sorry if I'm disturbing you, Mr Armstrong.'

He gestured towards the chair in front of him. 'It's Finlay. If you call me Mr Armstrong I'll start looking over my shoulder for my father.'

She shot him a nervous smile and walked hesitantly across the room towards the chair.

He tried his best not to stare.

Grace had already caught his attention. But now, she wasn't wearing the maid's outfit. Now, she had on a black suit and stiletto heels.

Finlay Armstrong had met a million women in black suits and heels. But he'd never met one quite like Grace. She had on a pink shirt with a funny tie at the neck.

And it was the colour that made him suck in his breath. It wasn't pale or bright, it was somewhere in the middle, a warm rose colour that brought out the colour in her cheeks and highlighted the tone of her lipstick. It suited her more than she could ever know.

Her hair swung as she walked across the room. It was the first time he'd seen it down. Okay, so the not staring wasn't going to work. Those chestnut curls were bouncing and shining like the latest shampoo TV advert.

Grace sat down in the chair opposite him fixing him with her warm brown eyes. She slid something across the desk towards him.

'I just wanted to check with you.' She licked her pink lips for a second. 'How, exactly, do I use this?'

He stared down at the company credit card. 'What do you mean?'

She bit her lip now and crossed one leg over the other. Her skirt slid up her thigh and he tore his eyes away and fixed on her eyes.

Big mistake.

'I mean, do I sign—can I sign? Or do I need a pin number or something?'

'You haven't used a company credit card before?' He hadn't even considered it.

She shook her head. He could see the slight tremble to her body. She was nervous. She was nervous coming in here and asking him about this.

'Sorry, Grace. I should have left you some instructions.' He'd just left the card for her in an envelope at Reception. He scribbled down some notes. 'This is what you do.'

She leaned forward on the desk as he wrote and a little waft of her perfume drifted towards him. He'd smelled this before. When he'd been inches from her in the penthouse he'd inhaled sharply and caught this same scent, something slightly spicy with a little tang of fruit. He couldn't quite place which one it was.

He finished writing and looked up. 'Have you had some ideas about what you need for the hotel?'

She nodded and lifted up some papers in her hand, unfolding them and sitting them on the desk. She still looked nervous. 'I know quality is important to you. But, because you've left things so late this year, I can't really pre-order or negotiate with anyone for a good price. We'll have to buy straight from the retailer. So…' she pressed her lips together for a second '… I've prepared three price ranges for you. You can let me know which one you prefer and we'll go with that one.'

He waved his hand. 'The price isn't important to me, Grace. The quality is.'

Her face fell a little. Wasn't that the right answer he'd just given her—that she had no limits to her spending? Any other designer he'd ever met would have cartwheeled out of the room at this point.

She shuffled her papers.

'What is it?'

She shook her head. 'Nothing.'

There were a hundred other things he could be doing right now. But since he had worked on the plane on the way home most things were up to date. Just as well really. After his experience last night, sleep hadn't come quite as easily as he'd expected.

Oh, he'd eventually blacked out. But he'd still managed to spend a few hours tossing and turning.

Her brown eyes were now fixed on those darn papers she was shuffling in her hands and he was strangely annoyed. He reached over and grabbed them.

It didn't take long to realise what he was looking at. He started to count them. 'Nine, ten, eleven, twelve… Grace, how many versions of these did you do?'

'Well, the first one was my absolute wish list. Then, I thought maybe you wouldn't want lights, or the big tree, or some of the other ideas I had, so I made a few other versions.'

He couldn't believe it. He'd only sprung this on her yesterday. The last company he'd worked with had taken three months just to give him a *quote* for something.

He shook his head. 'How long did this take you?'

She met his gaze again. It was clear she didn't really want to answer.

'Grace?'

She pulled a face. 'Maybe most of last night.'

'Until when, exactly?'

She pulled on her game face. 'I'm not sure exactly.'

He smiled and stood up, walking around towards her. She knew exactly how long it had taken her. He guessed she'd hardly had any sleep last night.

He put one leg on the desk, sitting just a few inches away from her. 'Grace, if I gave you free rein today, where would you go and what would you buy?'

She was silent for a few seconds. Then, her head gave a little nod. To his surprise she stood up.

Because he'd changed position she was only inches from his face. From close up, he had a much better view of her curves under her suit. He could see the upward and downward movements of her chest beneath the muted satin of her shirt.

Even more noticeable was her flawless complexion. There was a warmth about Grace. It seemed to emanate from her pores. Something trustworthy. But something else, a hint of vulnerability that just didn't seem to go away.

He'd seen other little glimpses. A spark of fire when he'd obviously annoyed her in the penthouse. She'd taken a deep breath and answered him back. Grace didn't like people treating her like a fool. She knew how to stand up for herself.

His smartphone buzzed and he glanced at it. An email he should deal with. But the truth was he didn't want to.

'What's your idea for the hotel?' he asked Grace.

She blinked at the suddenness of his question, but she didn't miss a beat. She held out her hands. 'I'm going to bring Christmas to The Armstrong. The hotel is missing something. Even you know that.' She raised her eyebrows. 'And you've given me the job of finding it.'

He picked up the phone on his desk and stared at her. 'Tell me where you're going and I'll order a car for you.'

She waved her hand and shook her head. 'I can catch the Tube.'

This time it was him that raised his eyebrows. 'Aren't you going to have some purchases to bring back?'

She put her hand up to her mouth. 'Oops.'

He asked again. 'So, where do you want the car to go?'

'First Selfridges, then Harrods, then Fortnum and Mason..' She didn't hesitate.

'You really think you can do all that in one day?'

She shook her head. 'Oh, no. I can do all that in an *afternoon*. You've obviously never met a professional Christmas shopper, Finlay.'

It was the first time she'd said his name. Actually said his name. And it was the way she said it. The way it rolled from her tongue with her London accent.

He spoke quickly into the phone on his desk, put it down and folded his arms across his chest. He smiled as he shook his head. 'No, I don't think I have.'

She wrinkled her brow. 'How old are you, exactly?' She matched his stance and stood in front of him with her arms folded across her chest.

It was almost like a challenge.

He stood up to his full height and stepped a tiny bit closer. He could take this challenge. 'Thirty-six.'

'Oh, dear.' She took a step backwards and put her hand up to her head. She looked out from under her hand with a wicked glint in her eye. 'Did you play with real live dinosaurs as a boy?' Her smile broadened as she continued. 'And shouldn't we watch the time? I guess you make all dinner reservations for around four-thirty p.m.—that's when all the early bird specials are, aren't they?'

He'd met a lot of people in this life—both before and after Anna—but he'd never met anyone who had the same effect as Grace. Even though she was officially an employee, he kept seeing glimpses of the woman underneath the uniform. Whether it was fun and jokes, a little melancholy or just a hint of real.

That was what it was.

Grace felt real. She was the only person who didn't seem to be watching how they acted around him—watching what they said. He liked the fact she was teasing him. Liked the fact she didn't treat him as if he were surrounded by broken glass.

'Seriously?'

She nodded. 'Seriously.' But it was clear she was teasing.

He laughed and shook his head and countered. 'You're probably not that much younger than me. You've just found some really good face cream.'

He handed over the company credit card as his phone rang. 'On you go and have some fun buying up any Christmas decorations that are left.' He answered the phone and put his hand over the receiver. 'I look forward to seeing what a professional Christmas shopper can do.'

Sixty minutes later Finlay Armstrong didn't look happy at all. He looked as if he were about to erupt.

Grace cringed as he strode across the store towards her. She was already feeling a little intimidated. Three security guards were standing next to her. She'd understandably almost been out on the street. That was what happened when you couldn't remember the pin number for the credit card you were using or answer any of the security questions.

Finlay walked over to the counter. 'What's the problem?'

Once she started talking she couldn't stop. She'd been having the time of her life. 'I've bought a huge Christmas tree for the foyer of the hotel, along with another two large trees for the bar and the restaurant.' Then she held her hand up towards the counter and the serious-faced woman behind it. 'Well, I haven't really bought them. I got here and…'

She held up the piece of paper that he'd given her. It had managed to get smudged and the numbers on it were indecipherable. She leaned forward. 'Please tell them I really do work for the hotel. I'm not on their list and don't know any of the questions they asked me.'

Finlay's jaw tightened, but he turned and addressed the woman with impeccable politeness. 'I'm Finlay Armstrong. I own the company. I can either use the correct pin, or answer any of the security questions you need.'

The woman gave a nod. 'I'm afraid you'll have to do both on this occasion. And, Mr Armstrong, if you add another member of staff onto the card—you really should let us know.'

Grace wanted to sink through the floor. This shopping trip definitely wasn't going to plan. She was behind already.

Finlay was finished a few minutes later. 'If I give you the number, do you think you can remember it again?'

The staff member cleared her throat behind them, 'Actually, Mr Armstrong, your card has already been flagged today. You might be asked security questions if you use it again.'

Grace gulped. 'What does that mean?'

Finlay glanced at his watch. 'How much longer will this take?'

Grace glanced down at the list still in her hands. She wanted to lie and say around five minutes. But London traffic would be starting to get heavy. 'Probably another couple of hours.'

Finlay rolled his eyes. He stared off into the distance for a second. 'We need the decorations for the hotel,' he muttered. 'Okay, let's go. The car's outside.'

The cold air hit her as soon as they came outside and she shivered. 'Where's your coat?' he asked.

She shrugged. 'I just got so excited when you gave me the card and told me there was a car outside, I forgot to go and get my coat and gloves.' She shook her head. 'It doesn't really matter. We'll be inside for most of the time.'

The car pulled up and he held the door as she slid inside and he climbed in next to her. He was talking on the phone—obviously still doing business.

It wasn't deliberate. But all her senses seemed on alert.

The wool from his black coat had brushed against her hand sending weird vibes everywhere. The aroma of his after-shave was slowly but surely drifting towards her in the warm atmosphere of the car. And even though it was cold outside, she was praying her pink shirt wouldn't show any unexpected perspiration marks.

It was only early afternoon but the sky already had a dark purple tinge at its edges.

Finlay glanced at his watch. There was a tiny shadow around his jaw line. The hint of a little stubble. Mixed with those unusual blue eyes it was enough to make any warm-blooded female catch her breath.

Part of her heart was going pitter-patter. So many expectations. What if he hated her ideas? What if he couldn't see how they translated to The Armstrong?

He closed his phone and leaned forward to speak to the driver. 'How much longer?'

'Just another ten minutes,' was the reply.

Grace felt nervous. Jumpy around him. Small talk seemed like the best solution.

'You mentioned your mum and dad earlier—are you spending time with them this year?'

He frowned. She wondered if he wasn't going to answer, then he shook his head. 'No. My parents are still in Scotland. My sister is expecting their first grandchild and will probably be fussed over non-stop.'

The answer was brisk. It was clear Christmas was still an issue for him—even if he was agreeing to decorations for the hotel.

As she went to speak again, her hand brushed against his. He flinched and then grabbed it. 'Grace, your hands are freezing.' He started rubbing his hands over hers. She was taken aback. After the frown it was a friendlier gesture than she might have expected.

His warming actions brought the aroma of the rose and

lavender hand cream she'd used earlier drifting up between them. She hadn't even thought about how cold her hands were.

The car pulled up outside one of London's oldest and most distinguished department stores, Fortnum and Mason. Grace was so excited she didn't wait for the driver to come around and open the door—she was out in a flash. She waved at Finlay. 'Come on, slowcoach. Let's get started. We need Christmas wreaths and garlands.'

She walked swiftly, darting her way between displays and heading for the elevators. But Finlay's footsteps faltered. It was like...*whoosh*!

Christmas everywhere. Every display. Every member of staff. Perpetual Christmas tunes piping overhead. Grace had even started singing along. Did she even notice?

It was like Christmas overload.

It was clear he'd unleashed the monster. He hadn't seen someone this enthusiastic about Christmas since his sister was five years old and thought she might get a horse. She did—but it was around twelve inches.

He pushed back the wave of emotions that was in danger of rearing its ugly head. He'd chosen to be here. He'd decided it was time to try and move forward. The perpetual little ache he felt would always be there. But should it really last for ever?

They walked through the tea hall that was jostling with people. 'I love the Christmas shop in here. There's so much to choose from.' She kept talking as they darted between shoppers.

The lifts were small and lined with wood. He found himself face to face with her, their noses inches away from each other. In this confined space he felt instantly protective, his hand reaching up and resting on her hip.

She smiled and tipped her head to one side. 'Did you listen to a single word I said?'

He shook his head as the doors closed and the piped music continued. 'Not a single word,' he admitted.

She gently slapped his chest. 'Shocker. Well, remember only these words: *I will not complain about the price.*'

He rolled his eyes. 'Grace, what are we buying in here?'

She still looked happy. It was obvious Christmas decorations were something that she just loved. 'I told you. Christmas wreaths and garlands to decorate the foyer, the bar, the corridors, the restaurant and the elevators.' She counted them off on her fingers.

He blinked for a second. Wreaths. He'd forgotten how often they were used as Christmas decorations now. It was almost as if the world had misplaced what they actually were.

They were lucky: no one else rode to the top floor with them. The elevator pinged and she looked over her shoulder. 'This is us.' She wiggled around, her backside pressing straight into him.

Finlay felt numb. No matter how she'd joked, he was still a young guy. And like any young man, his body reacted to a woman being up close and personal—even if it was unintentional.

Grace seemed not to have noticed anything. She dodged her way through the bodies.

As soon as they stepped outside the lift Grace almost started skipping. She handed him a basket and picked up a few delicate glass and white tree decorations. Then, she walked over to the counter. 'I phoned earlier about a special order. Wreaths and garlands—you said you'd put them aside for me.'

The clerk nodded. 'They're through here. Do you want to see them before you pay?'

Finlay let Grace work her magic. She was loving this. This wasn't the vulnerable woman that he'd seen on the rooftop. This was in control and in her element Grace.

Within a few minutes he'd handed over the company credit card and heard her arrange for delivery in a few hours' time.

Grace let out a squeal. 'My favourite ever Christmas song—"Last Christmas"—let's sing along.'

He looked at her in surprise. 'This is your favourite song? It's not exactly cheery, is it?'

But Grace was oblivious and already singing along. A few fellow shoppers gave him an amused stare. She really was singing and didn't seem to care who was listening. The fleeting sad thoughts disappeared from his head again. Grace had a little glance at her lists and made a few random ticks before folding them up again and belting out the main part of the song.

The pink flush in her cheeks suited her. But what caught his attention most was the sparkle in those dark brown eyes. He wouldn't have thought it possible. But it was. He sucked in a breath. If he didn't watch out Grace Ellis could become infectious.

Grace came back and pressed her hand on his arm. 'I've seen a few other things I like. You stay here or it'll spoil the fun.' She waved her hand. 'Have a look around. I'll only be five minutes.'

He frowned as she disappeared. Fun?

He wandered around, watching people gaze in wonder at all the decorations. The garlands in store were beautiful. They had a whole range of colours and they covered walls, shelves and the Christmas fireplaces that had been set up in store. Next to them was a whole range of wreaths: some holly, some twisted white twigs, some traditionally green decorated with a variety of colours. He stopped walking.

He was looking at wreaths and not automatically associating them with Anna. Guilt washed over him. Shouldn't she always be his first thought?

But she hadn't been. Not for the last few months. It was

as if his head was finally lifting from the fog it had been in these last five years. But Christmas time was a little different. It seemed to whip up more memories than usual. It made the thought of moving on just a little more tricky.

A little girl walked into him as she stared at a rocking horse. He bent down to speak to her. She was like something from a chocolate box. A red double-breasted wool coat, a little worn but clearly loved, dark curls poking out from under a black hat. She hadn't even realised she'd walked into him—her eyes were still on the white rocking horse with a long mane decorated with red saddle. She let out a little sigh.

'Come along, Molly,' said a harassed voice. 'We just came here for a little look. It's time to go.'

He lifted his head instantly. The woman looked tired—her clothes even more so. Her boots were worn, her jacket was missing a few buttons and the scarf she had wrapped around her neck looked almost as old as she was. But it was her accent that drew his attention.

He straightened up and held out his hand. 'Hi, Finlay Armstrong. What part of Scotland are you from?'

She was startled by his question and took a few seconds to answer. He could almost see the recognition of his own accent before she finally reached over and shook his hand. 'Hi, I'm Karen. I'm from Ayrshire.'

There was something in the wistful way she said it that made him realise this wasn't a visit.

He kept hold of her hand. 'Have you been in London long?'

She sighed. 'Three years. I had to move for work.'

He nodded his head towards the rocking horse. 'Your little girl was admiring the rocking horse.'

Karen winced. 'I know. I asked for one every year too as a child.' She glanced down at her child again then met his gaze. 'But we can all dream.'

He sucked in a breath. When was the last time he'd done something good? He'd been so wrapped in his own mourning for the last five years he hadn't really stopped to draw breath. Even when it came to Christmas presents he normally gave his PA a list and told her what kind of things his family preferred. That was as much input as he'd had.

He thought about the prettily wrapped present that Mrs Archer had left for him at reception. He hadn't even opened it yet.

He kept his voice low. 'How about Molly gets what she wants for Christmas?'

Karen looked shocked, then offended. He knew exactly how this worked. He shook his head. 'I work for a big company. Every year they like us to do a few good deeds. A few things that no one else finds out about.' He pulled the card out of his pocket, still keeping his voice low. 'There's no catch. I promise. Give the girl at the desk an address and time for delivery. That's all.'

Karen sucked in a breath. 'I don't want to be someone's good deed.' He could see her bristle.

He gave a nod of acknowledgement. 'Then how about a gift from a fellow Scot who is also missing home?'

Her eyes filled with tears and she put her hand to her throat. 'Oh…oh, then that might be different.'

He glanced down at Molly and smiled. 'Good. Just give the girl at the desk your details. I'll arrange everything else.'

'I don't know what to say, except thank you. And Merry Christmas!'

He gave her a nod. 'Happy Christmas to you and Molly.'

He ruffled Molly's curls and walked away, not wanting to admit to the feelings that were threatening to overwhelm him. That was the first time he'd wished anyone Happy Christmas in five years. Five long, horrible years.

What had he been doing? Had he been ignoring people around him like Karen and Molly for the last five years?

He heard an excited laugh and Grace walked through with one of the sales assistants from another room. Grace's cheeks were flushed pink with excitement and she was clapping her hands together again.

The girl really did love Christmas.

One part of him felt a selfish pang, while the other dared itself back into life. In a way, he'd felt better sticking his head in the sand for the last few years. Some of this Christmas stuff made him feel decidedly uncomfortable. Parts of it were making him relive memories—some good, some bad.

But the thing that he struggled most with was feeling again. *Feeling.*

The thing he'd tried to forget about.

He touched the saleswoman's arm as she was still mid-discussion with Grace. 'I need you to add something to the order.'

Grace's head shot up. 'What?' Then her expression changed. 'Really?'

He gave a nod and gestured to the white rocking horse. 'The lady in the dark coat, her name is Karen. Can you make delivery arrangements with her?'

The saleswoman shot a glance from Grace, to Finlay and then to Karen, who was still standing in the distance with Molly.

'Of course,' she said efficiently, adding the purchase to the bill.

What was he doing? All of a sudden Finlay was feeling totally out of his depth. 'Let's go,' he said to Grace abruptly.

She looked a little surprised but glanced at her watch. Did she think he wanted to beat the traffic? 'Thanks so much for your assistance. I'll be back at The Armstrong for the delivery.'

She rubbed her hands together again. Something sparked into his brain. The one thing he'd thought to do back at the hotel.

He pulled out his phone and spoke quietly as they hurried back outside to the car. The light had almost gone completely now and most of London's stores were lit up with Christmas displays. The journey to Harrods didn't take quite as long as he'd imagined.

Grace gave a sharp intake of breath as soon as the gold lights of the store came into view, lighting up the well-known green canopies.

He touched her elbow. 'We need to do something first in here before we go to the Christmas department.'

She looked surprised. 'Do you need some Christmas gifts for your family?'

He shook his head. Thick flakes of snow were falling outside. 'That's taken care of. This was something I should have done earlier.'

They stepped outside as the chauffeur opened the door and walked in through one of the private entrances.

A woman in a black suit with gold gilding met them at the entrance. 'Mr Armstrong?'

He nodded. She walked them towards some private lifts. 'This way, please.'

The journey only lasted a few seconds before the doors slid open on women's designer wear. Grace frowned and looked at him. 'We need to go to the Christmas department.'

He waved his hand. 'In a few minutes. I need to get something here first.' He turned to the personal shopper. 'Do you have anything the same shade as her shirt? And some black leather gloves please, lined.'

Grace was still frowning. 'Who is this for?'

He turned to face her. 'You.'

'What?' It was a face he recognised. Karen had worn

the same expression thirty minutes earlier. 'What on earth are you talking about?'

Finlay held out his hands. 'Look at me. I've dragged you halfway across London in the freezing cold with snow outside.' He touched her arm. 'You're only wearing your suit and a shirt. You must be freezing. I feel like an idiot standing beside you in a wool coat.'

She tipped her head to the side. 'Then take it off. It's too hot in here anyhow.'

She said it so matter-of-factly. As if he should have thought of it himself.

He shook his head. 'But once we get back outside, you'll freeze again. You were rubbing your hands together the whole time we were in the last two stores. It was obvious you were still cold.'

The personal shopper appeared carrying a knee-length wool coat in the exact shade of pink as Grace's shirt. She held it up. 'Is this to your taste?'

He smiled. 'It's perfect.' He gestured towards the coat. 'Go on, Grace, try it on.'

She was staring at it as if she didn't quite know what to say. Then she shook her head. 'You are not buying me a coat.'

He took the coat from the personal shopper and held it open. 'You're right. I'm not buying you a coat. The Armstrong hotel is. Think of it as part of your official uniform.'

She slid her arms along the black satin lining of the coat as he pulled it up onto her shoulders. The effect was instant. The coat brought out the darkness of her chestnut hair and dark eyes while highlighting her pink cheeks and lips. It was perfect for her.

He felt himself hold his breath. Grace turned and stared at her reflection in a mirror next to them. Her fingers started automatically fastening the buttons on the double-breasted coat. It fitted perfectly.

The sales assistant brought over a wooden tray of black leather gloves. Grace stared down in surprise and looked up at Finlay. 'They're virtually all the same. How am I supposed to choose?'

The personal shopper looked dismayed. She started lifting one glove after another. 'This one only skims the wrist bones. This one has a more ruffled effect, it comes up much further. This one has a special lining, cashmere. We also have silk-lined and wool-lined gloves all at different lengths. Do you have a specific need?'

Finlay could tell by the expression on Grace's face that she was bamboozled. He reached out and ran his fingers across the gloves. Some instantly felt softer than others. He selected a pair and turned them inside out. 'These ones must be cashmere lined. The leather feels good quality too. Want to try them?'

He had no idea what size or length they were. Somehow he thought his eyes might be similar to Grace's—all the gloves looked virtually identical. But they didn't feel identical.

She slid her hands into the pair he handed her and smiled. 'They're beautiful…' She gave them a little tug. 'But they seem a little big.'

In an instant the personal shopper handed her an alternative pair. Grace swapped them over and stretched her hands out. 'Yes, they feel better.'

'Perfect. Add this to our bill, please,' he said. 'We're going to the Christmas department.'

'But… I haven't decided yet.' Grace had her hand on the collar of the coat.

Finlay shrugged. 'But I have—the coat is perfect. The colour is perfect. The fit is perfect and the length is perfect. What else is there to say?'

He started to walk away but Grace wasn't finished.

'But maybe I'm not sure.' Her voice started to get louder

as he kept walking, 'What if I wanted a red coat? Or a blue one? Or a black one? What if I don't even *like* coats?'

People near them were starting to stare. Finlay spun around again and strode back over to her, catching her by the shoulders and spinning her back around to face the mirror.

'Grace. This is you. This is your coat. No one else could possibly wear it.' He held his hands up as he looked over her shoulder.

Her dark brown eyes fixed on his. For a second he was lost. Lost staring at those chocolate eyes, in the face framed with chestnut tresses, on the girl dressed in the perfect rose-coloured coat.

There was a tilt to her chin of defiance. Was she going to continue to fight with him?

Her tongue slid along her lips as her eyes disconnected with his and stared at her reflection. 'No one has ever done something like this for me,' she whispered at a level only he could hear. She pulled her hand from the leather glove and wound one of her tresses of hair around her finger as she kept staring at her reflection.

'Just say yes,' he whispered back.

She blinked, before lowering her gaze and unwinding her finger from her hair. She pulled off the other glove and undid the buttons on the coat, slipping it from her shoulders.

She handed it to the personal shopper. 'Thank you,' she said simply, then straightened her bag and looked in the other direction. 'Right,' she said smartly, 'let's hit the Christmas department. We have work to do.'

She wasn't joking. The Christmas department was the busiest place in the entire store.

And Grace Ellis knew how to shop.

She left the personal shopper in her wake as she ping-ponged around the department, side-stepping tourists, pensioners, kids and hesitant shoppers.

He frowned as he realised she was picking only one colour of items. 'Really?' He was trying to picture how this would all come together.

She laid a hand on his arm as she rushed past. 'Trust me, it will be great.' Then she winked and blew into her fingers, 'It will be magical.'

She was sort of like a fairy from a Christmas movie.

He was left holding three baskets and feeling quite numb as she filled them until the contents towered. Lights. Christmas bulbs. Some weird variation of tinsel. A few other decorations and the biggest haul of snow globes. He hadn't seen one since he was a child.

'Really?' he asked again.

She picked up a medium-sized one and gave it a shake, letting the snow gently fall around the Santa's sleigh above a village. 'Everyone loves a snow globe…it's part of our theme.'

Our theme. She was talking about the hotel. Of course she was talking about the hotel. But the way her eyes connected with his as she said the words sent involuntary tremors down his spine. It didn't feel as if she were talking about the hotel.

Maybe this wasn't such a good idea after all. Maybe he should have started much smaller. Grace's enthusiasm for Christmas had only magnified as the hours increased. Was he really ready for such a full-on Christmas rush?

She tugged at his sleeve. 'Finlay, I need you.'

'What?' He winced. He didn't mean for the response to be so out of sorts. The truth was, he wasn't quite sure what he was doing here, or how he felt about all this.

Five years ago he'd still been numb. Five years ago he'd spent September and October sitting by his wife's bedside.

The year before that he'd been frantically searching the world over for any new potential treatment. On a bitter cold November day, he'd buried her.

Anna had been so much better than him at all of this. She'd been devastated by the news. Devastated by the fact no treatment had worked. But she'd been determined to end life in the way she'd wanted to. And that was at home, with her husband.

No one should have to watch the person they love fade a little day by day. But Finlay knew that every day the world over, there were thousands of people sharing the same experience he had.

Grace was standing in front of him, her face creased with lines. 'What's wrong?'

'Nothing.' He shook his head. 'Nothing. What do you need?'

She nodded to the snaking line in front of them. 'We've reached the front of the queue. I need you to pay.'

Pay. Something he could manage without any thought.

He walked to the front of the line and handed over the credit card. The personal shopper was putting all the purchases into some trolley for them to take to the car. He stopped her as she started to wrap the coat in tissue paper. 'Don't,' he said. 'Just take the tags off. Grace should wear it.'

There was a moment's hesitation on Grace's face as he handed the coat over. But after a few seconds she slid her arms back inside. 'Thank you.'

'No problem.'

By the time they got outside the air was thick with snow. It was lying on the pavements and surrounding buildings and roads.

Grace fastened her coat and slid her hands into the leather gloves while all their packages were stored in the boot of the chauffeur-driven car.

The journey back to the hotel was silent. He'd started

this afternoon with the hope of a little Christmas spirit. It wasn't that he wasn't trying. But sometimes memories flared. Tempering his mood with guilt and despair.

Grace's fingers fumbled over and over in the new gloves. She was staring at the passing shop windows. Her face serious and her eyes heavy. What was she thinking about?

When they reached the hotel he couldn't wait to get out of the car. 'I have an international videoconference,' he said as he climbed out.

'Good.'

He stopped mid-step. 'What?'

She walked around to the boot of the car. 'I don't want you to see anything until I've finished. It's better if you have something to do. I'm going to get Frank and some of the other Maids in Chelsea to help me set things up. I'd prefer it if you waited until I was finished—you know, to get the full effect.'

It was almost as if somehow she had switched gears from her sombre mood in the car. Grace seemed back on point. Focused again. Ready to complete her mission.

And right now all he felt was relief. He could retreat into his office. He could stop asking himself why he'd bought a stranger's child a rocking horse and an employee a coat and gloves that were way outside her pay range.

Two of the doormen from the hotel started lifting all the purchases from the car. One of them gave her a nudge. 'Frank says there's a delivery at the luggage door for you.'

She was busy. She was engaged. She didn't need him around.

Finlay walked back through the reception without acknowledging anyone. He had work to do.

It was finished. It was finally finished. Grime and sweat had ruined her pink shirt and black skirt. She'd swapped back from the stilettos to her lower shoes and spotted a hole in her black tights. Her hair had ended up tied in a ponytail on top of her head as it kept getting in the way. She must look a complete state.

Emma gave a sigh as she looked up at the giant tree. 'If you'd told me this was what you had in mind when you asked for a hand…'

Sophie rolled her eyes. 'As if you would have said no.'

Ashleigh was leaning against the nearby wall with her arms folded. 'I think it looks spectacular. It was worth it.'

Grace couldn't stop pacing. 'Do you think so? What about those lights over there? Should I move them?' She pressed her hands to her chest. 'What about the colour scheme? Is it too much?'

The girls exchanged amused glances.

But Grace couldn't stop with her pacing. 'I'll need to go and get him. I'll need to make sure that he's happy with it.'

Sophie walked over and put her arm around Grace's shoulder. 'Well, whoever *he* is, he'd be crazy if he didn't like this.'

Ashleigh stepped forward. 'I hope you've been paid for this, Grace. I'd hate to think this guy was taking advantage of your good nature.'

Emma folded her arms across her chest. 'Who is he, exactly? You haven't exactly been forthcoming.'

Grace hesitated. She wasn't even quite sure what to say. She tried to slip the question by giving Emma a big hug. 'Thank you for coming today. You're not even a Maid in Chelsea any more. Should I start calling you by your fancy title?'

But Emma was far too smart for that. She returned the hug then pulled back. 'I'm going to ask Jack if he knows anything about Finlay Armstrong.'

Grace shook her head—probably much too quickly. 'I

don't think he will.' She turned and looked at the finished decorations again. 'I can't thank you girls enough. I owe you all, big time.'

'I think that's our cue to leave, girls,' said Ashleigh. 'Come on. Let's get cleaned up. I'm buying the drinks.'

They all gave Grace a hug and left by the main entrance of the hotel while she went to retrieve her jacket from behind the reception desk.

Should she wait? The hotel reception was quiet. She wasn't even sure of the time. She'd asked the staff to dim the main lights a little to give the full effect of the tree.

Her stomach gave a flip-flop. He'd asked her to do this. He'd asked her. Surely he'd want to see that she was finished?

She walked slowly towards his office door, listening out to see if he was still on his conference call. She couldn't hear anything and the office door was ajar.

She gave the door a gentle knock, sticking her head around it. Finlay was staring out of the window into the dark night. His office had a view of the surrounding area—not like the penthouse, of course, but still enough to give a taste and feel of the wealth of Chelsea. It was a wonder they didn't ask for credentials before they let you off the Tube around here.

He looked lost in his thoughts. She lifted her hand and knocked on the door again—this time a little more loudly.

He jumped. 'Grace.' He stood up; his actions seemed automatic. He started to walk around the desk and then stopped, the corners of his mouth turning upwards.

'What on earth have you done with your hair?'

She'd forgotten. She'd forgotten her hair currently resembled someone from a nineteen-eighties pop video.

She glanced down at her shirt too. Random streaks of dirt.

It wasn't really the professional look she'd been aiming for.

She gave her head a shake. 'I've been busy. This stuff doesn't put itself up.' Nerves and excitement were starting to get the better of her. 'Come and see. Come and see that you like it.'

He raised his eyebrows, the hint of a smile still present. 'You're already telling me I like it?'

'Only if you have exceptionally good taste,' she shot back.

He had no idea how much her stomach was in knots. This was the guy who hated Christmas. This was the guy that had pulled down a single strand of lights she'd put in his room.

This was a guy that was trying to take steps away from his past Christmas memories. If she'd got this wrong…

She stepped in front of him. 'It might be better if you close your eyes.'

'Nervous, Grace?' He was teasing her.

'Not at all.' She made a grab for his hand. 'Close your eyes and I'll take you outside. I'll tell you when you can open them.'

For a moment she thought he might refuse. She wasn't quite sure how long she could keep up the bravado. She stuck her hands on her hips. 'Hurry up, or I'll make you pay me overtime.'

He laughed, shook his head, took her hand and closed his eyes.

His hand in hers.

She hadn't really contemplated this. She hadn't really planned it. His warm hand encompassed hers. Was her hand even clean?

The heat from his hand seemed to travel up her arm. It seemed to spread across her chest. She shouldn't be feeling this. She shouldn't be thinking thoughts like…

'Are we going?'

'Of course.' She gave his hand a tug and started walking—too quickly to begin with, then slowing her steps to a more suitable pace.

Magda at Reception raised her eyebrows as they walked past. Grace couldn't think straight for one second. This was it. This was where he would get the full effect. The effect that every customer walking into The Armstrong would get from now on.

She spun him around to position him exactly where she wanted him. Far enough away from the traditional revolving door at the entrance way to stop him getting a draught, but still with enough distance between him and the display.

She tapped his shoulder. 'Okay. Open your eyes.'

Maybe he'd been hasty. Maybe he shouldn't have made any of the suggestions about Christmas decorations. He didn't know what he was doing. He'd spent the last few hours trying to get the image of Grace in that pink coat out of his head.

He opened his eyes.

And blinked.

And blinked again.

His hotel was transformed. In a way he could never have imagined.

The lights in the main reception area were dimmed. In normal circumstances the black and grey floor, walls and reception desk would have made it as dark as night.

But it wasn't.

It was purple.

Purple in a way he couldn't even begin to find words for. He started to walk forward, straight towards the giant Christmas tree at the end of the foyer that was just pulling his attention like a magnet.

The traditional green tree was huge. It was lit up with purple lights and a few white twinkling ones. The large purple baubles and glass snowflake-style tree decorations reflected the purple light beautifully. The strange-style purple tinsel was wrapped tastefully amongst the branches. Along either wall were more purple lights. It was a strange effect. They drew you in. Drew your gaze and footsteps towards the tree. At intermittent points all along were snow globes of various sizes.

There was a choking noise beside him. Grace's face was lit up with the purple lights, her hands clenched under her chin and her eyes looking as if they might spill tears any second.

'What do you think?' Her voice was pretty much a squeak.

He couldn't speak yet. He was still getting over the shock.

Christmas had come to The Armstrong hotel.

She'd captured it. She'd captured the Christmas spirit without drowning him in it.

The tree was giant, but the effect of only having one colour made it seem more sleek and exclusive than he'd expected. The intermittent snow globes were focal points. Something people could touch, pick up and hold.

The dimmed lights were perfect. It bathed the whole area in the most magical purple light.

'Finlay?' This time there was a tremor in her voice.

He kept looking, kept looking at everything around him, before finally turning and locking gazes with Grace.

'I think Santa got everything wrong,' he said.

Her eyes widened. 'What do you mean?'

Finlay laughed and opened his arms wide. 'His grotto. Clearly, it should have been purple.' He spun around, relishing the transformation of his hotel.

He didn't just like it. He loved it.

Never, even in a million years, did he think he'd feel like this.

He picked up Grace and swung her around.

She was still in shock. She put her hands on his shoulders and let out a squeal. She was still looking for verification. She needed to hear the words out loud.

'You like it? You think it's good?'

He set her feet back down on the slate floor. 'I don't think it's good—I think it's fantastic!' He shook his head. 'I can't believe you've done this. I can't believe you've managed to capture just what I wanted for The Armstrong without…'

His voice tailed off. That wasn't something to say out loud. That was part of his private thoughts.

She stepped in front of him again. This time the tension on her face and across her shoulders had disappeared. The expression on her face was one of compassion, understanding. She touched his arm. 'Without taking you back to where you don't want to be.' She nodded. 'I wanted this to be about something new for you. Something entirely different.' She lowered her gaze. 'Not that there's anything wrong with memories. Not that there's anything wrong with taking some time.'

His heart swelled. He knew so little about Grace. This woman, that he'd almost threatened to fire, that had stood up to him, teased him, and shown him compassion and made him feel things he hadn't in years.

He was thinking things and feeling things that had been locked away inside for a long time.

He'd been so shut off. So determined not to let anything out—not to open himself up to the world of hurt that he'd felt before.

But things felt differently than he'd expected. The world

outside didn't feel quite so bad as before. He recognised things in Grace that he hadn't expected to.

It was time to start making connections. Time to start showing interest in those around him. And he knew exactly where to start.

He reached down and took her hand. 'I owe you more than a coat.'

She shook her head automatically. 'No, you don't. And that coat is beautiful. Completely impractical and the kind of thing I wear in one of my dreams. Thank you for that.'

Her dark brown eyes met his. 'Every girl should get to be a princess some time.'

There was a little pang inside his chest. 'Come to the staff party with me.'

She dropped his hand. 'What?' She looked truly shocked.

'I mean it.'

Her mouth opened and then closed again.

'Every year there is a pre-Christmas staff party at the hotel. I haven't gone for the last five years. This year—it's time for me to attend again.' He shrugged. 'I can't promise I'll dance. I can't promise I'll play Santa Claus.' He gave her a serious nod. 'But I can promise you there will be music, spectacular food and champagne. If you want to be treated like a princess, then come to the party with me.'

She still looked a bit stunned. 'I've heard about the staff party. I just wasn't sure if I was going to go. What will the rest of the staff think if I go with you?'

He waved his hand. 'Who cares?'

'I care.' She looked serious.

He shook his head and took both her hands in his. 'Grace, they will think I'm saying thank you for the way you've decorated the hotel. The way you've managed to bring Christmas to The Armstrong in such a classy, stylish way. And they'd be right.'

She glanced over at the Christmas tree and finally smiled again.

She tilted her head to one side. 'Well, when you put it like that…'

CHAPTER FOUR

ALICE ARCHER COULD sniff out a problem from forty paces away. 'What's wrong with you today, Grace? One minute you're talking non-stop, next minute you're staring out of the window in some kind of daze. All with that strange expression on your face.'

Grace started back to attention. 'What expression?' she said quickly as she hung up another of Alice's coats.

Alice gave a knowing smile. 'That I'm-thinking-of-a-special-man kind of smile.'

Heat instantly seared her cheeks. 'I have no idea what you mean.'

But Alice wasn't put off. She merely changed the subject so she could probe another way. 'The decorations are beautiful.' She leaned back in her chair and gave a wistful sigh. 'I doubted I'd ever see Christmas in The Armstrong again. But you've captured the spirit perfectly.' She gave Grace a careful glance. 'Who knew that purple could be such a festive colour?' She picked up the individual snow globe that Grace had brought up to her room this morning, tipping it over so the snow swirled around in the liquid, then setting it back down on the table and watching it with a smile on her face.

'It's nice to see things changing.'

Grace was concentrating on the clothes hanging on the

rails. She'd started arranging them into colour schemes. 'He's asked me to the staff party,' she said without thinking.

'He's what?'

Darn it. She'd played right into Alice's hands.

Alice pushed herself up from the chair and stood next to Grace. 'Finlay asked you to the party? He doesn't seem the type to do parties,' she added.

Grace turned to face her. 'He doesn't, does he?' She hadn't slept at all last night. The excitement of the day, the success of the decorations, the long hours she'd worked. The truth was she should have been exhausted and collapsed into bed. Instead, although her bones had been weary and welcomed the comfort of her bed, her mind had tumbled over and over.

Even though she'd been so busy, as soon as she'd stepped inside the flat last night a wave of loneliness had swamped her. It had been there ever since her gran had died, but this time of year just seemed to amplify it. She'd ended up texting Clio and asking for extra shifts. She couldn't bear to be inside the house herself. Keeping busy was the only thing she could think of.

She wasn't quite sure how she felt about all this. Finlay had been straight with her. He was still mourning his wife. Christmas was hard for him. He was her boss. He'd been angry with her. He'd almost fired her.

But he hadn't felt like her boss on the roof when she'd been contemplating an even lonelier Christmas than she was already facing. For a few minutes he'd felt like someone she'd connected with.

Again, when he'd held her hand and those little tingles had shot straight up her arm.

Again, when he'd given her that look as he'd stood behind her in the shop and stared at their reflection in the mirror.

Again, when she'd seen joy on his face as he'd seen the purple Christmas decorations.

But she was probably imagining it all.

What did she know? When was the last time she'd been on an actual date?

Wait? Was this a date?

'He asked me to go to the party,' she said out loud again. 'It's only a thank you for the decorations.'

Alice gave a brief nod. 'Is it?' she said knowingly.

Grace made a little squeak. Panic was starting to wash over her. 'It's just a thank you.'

Alice turned and walked back to her chair. 'I don't know that he's ever taken anyone else to the party—or to *a* party.'

'No one else has done Christmas decorations for him,' Grace said quickly, sliding the doors closed on the wardrobe.

She had to stop overthinking this. He'd been clear.

'He said we might not even stay long. And he said he doesn't dance. But the food will be good and there will be champagne.'

Alice's smile grew broader. 'So, if you're not staying long at the party, what *exactly* are you doing?'

Grace replied automatically. 'I guess I'll just go home.' Her hand froze midway to the rubbish bag attached to her cart. Would she just be going home? Or would Finlay expect them to go somewhere else?

'What will you be wearing?'

'Oh, no!' Grace's hand flew to her mouth. She hadn't even thought of that. Her mind had been too busy trying to work out what an invite to a party meant. Her stomach in a permanent knot wondering how *she* felt about everything.

Truth was, there was no getting away from the fact that Finlay Armstrong was possibly the best-looking guy she'd ever seen.

That voice, those muscles, and those blue, blue eyes…

She swallowed and stuffed the rubbish in the bin. She'd seen women looking at him on their shopping trip. She'd seen the glances that already said, *What is he doing with her?*

Her mind did a quick brain-raid of her wardrobe. A black dress from a high-street store. A pair of skinny black trousers and fuchsia semi-see-through shirt. A strange kind of green dress with a scattering of sequins that she'd worn four years ago to a friend's wedding.

Nothing suitable for the kind of party she imagined it would be.

'I have no idea what I'll wear,' she said as she slumped against the wall.

Alice gave her a smile and tapped the side of her nose. 'Why don't you leave it with me? I don't have all my clothes in that wardrobe and I think I might have something in storage—' she glanced Grace up and down '—that might just be perfect.'

'Really?'

Alice smiled. 'Just call me the Christmas fairy. Come and see me on the day of the party.'

Finlay wasn't quite sure what he should be doing. His inbox had three hundred emails. There was a thick pile of mail on his desk. His PA had left some contracts to be reviewed. A few of his other hotels had staffing issues over Christmas. He'd also had an interesting email from Ailsa Hillier at the Corminster, asking how things were working out with her recommended company, Maids in Chelsea.

She'd probably already heard about the Christmas decorations. Someone at The Armstrong seemed to tell their rivals all they needed to know. Just as well it was a friendly rivalry. Ailsa had lost her sister to cancer some years ago and when Anna had died she'd sent a message with her condolences and telling Finlay she would take care of The

Armstrong until he was ready to return. In the end, that had only been eight days—the amount of time it had taken to bury Anna—but he always remembered the kindness.

He picked up the phone, smiling as Ailsa answered instantly.

'I hear you've gone all purple.'

He choked out a laugh. 'It's a very nice colour.'

There was a moment's silence. 'I'm glad, Finlay. It's time.' Her voice was filled with warmth so the words didn't make him bristle. 'I might need to steal your designer though.'

Now he did sit straight in his chair. Ailsa couldn't possibly know about that, could she? He didn't give anything away. 'Your designer didn't pick purple this year?'

She sighed and he imagined she was putting her feet on the desk at this point. 'No. If they had then I could accuse you of copying. We are all white and gold this year and it already feels old. Tell me who you used and I'll poach them next year—after all, I did give you the Maids.'

He could sense she had a pen poised already. She was serious. And she didn't realise the connection. 'The Maids have worked out well, thank you. I'll ask Rob to have a look in the New Year about recruiting more permanent staff.' He leaned back in his chair. 'Or maybe I won't.' He drummed his fingers on the table as he thought. 'Some of our permanent residents seem to really like the Maids in Chelsea.'

'I think the truth is, Finlay, we get what we pay for. The Maids might cost more, but, in my experience, they are a polite, friendly, well-mannered bunch of girls. They want to do a good job and most of them seem to hide their light under a bushel. One of the girls I met yesterday has a degree in marketing, another has worked with four different aid agencies across four different continents. I like that.'

He liked that too. Hiding her light under a bushel

seemed to fit Grace perfectly. The work she'd done here was great. Maybe it was time to find out a little bit more about the woman he'd invited to the staff party?

'You still haven't given me the name of the interior designer,' Ailsa reminded him.

He smiled. 'Her name is Grace Ellis, but you can't have her, Ailsa, she's all mine.'

He put down the phone with a smile, imagining the email he'd get in response.

He stood up and walked through to the main reception; Frank was just waving off some guests. 'Frank, do you know where Grace is?'

Frank gestured off to the left. 'Back down in the basement. She's had some more ideas.'

Finlay looked around. Even though it was daytime the decorations still looked good. He could smell something too, even though he had no idea what it was. It reminded him of walking into one of those winter wonderland-type places as a child.

Grace was still working on this? He'd have to pay her overtime. And bonuses.

He walked down to the basement. It was well lit and everything stored was clearly labelled. But that didn't help when he walked into the room he heard rustling in and found Grace upended in a large storage barrel. All that was visible was black kicking shoes and a whole lot of leg.

'Grace?' He rushed over to help.

'Eek! Finlay! Help.' He tried not to laugh as he reached inside the barrel and grabbed hold of her waist, pulling her out.

'Finlay,' she gasped again as she landed in a heap on the floor. Blue. She was wearing a blue shirt today. Not as cute as the pink one. But she'd just managed to lose a button on this one so he might like it even more. Her hair must have been tied with a black satin ribbon that was now trailing over her shoulder.

He burst out laughing. And so did Grace.

She thumped her hands on the floor. 'Well, *that* wasn't supposed to happen.' She followed the line of his vision and blushed, tugging at her skirt.

He peered into the barrel. 'What was supposed to happen?'

She pointed to the label. 'As I left the hotel last night I realised that although it was gorgeous when people walked inside, there was nothing outside. Frank told me there used to be lights outside. I was looking for them.'

He frowned, trying to remember what the lights had looked like. They'd been made by some American company and had cost a fortune. 'We did have. Is this where they've been stored? What makes you think they even work any more?'

She shrugged. 'I figured it was worth a try. I can always check them first. Then I was going to try and order some purple light bulbs—you know, carry the theme outside.'

Wow. She thought of everything.

He held out his hand to help her up. 'Grace, can I ask you something?'

He pulled a little harder than he should have, catapulting Grace right forward crashing into his chest. 'Oh, sorry,' she said, placing both hands on his chest. She looked up at him. 'What is it you want to ask?'

He couldn't remember. Not for a second. All he could concentrate on were the warm palms causing heat to permeate through his shirt. Grace lifted one finger. 'Oops,' she said as she stepped back.

Finlay looked down and sucked in a breath. Two hand prints on his white shirt.

To the outside world it would look amusing. To him?

A permanent imprint that he was in a place he wasn't quite sure of.

What exactly was he doing here? He'd deliberately come down here to find Grace. There was no point in him denying it to himself. He wanted to find out more about her. But was this a betrayal of Anna? He now had another woman's hands imprinted on his chest. And for a few seconds, he'd liked the feel of them being there.

He was exasperated. Exasperated that he was drawn to this woman. Confused that he felt strangely protective of her. And intrigued by the person beneath the surface. There seemed to be so much more to Grace than met the eye. But how much did he really want to know?

Her hands were now clenched in front of her. He'd been quiet for too long.

'Finlay?'

He met her gaze. 'Are you free for lunch?'

'What?'

He glanced at his watch. 'Are you free for lunch?'

She looked down at her dishevelled clothing and pointed at his shirt. 'I don't think either of us can go anywhere like this.' He actually thought she looked fine.

He shrugged. 'I have other shirts.'

She shook her head. 'I only have what I'm wearing.' She bit her lip. 'But I think I might be able to borrow one of the bartender's black dresses.'

He gave her a nod. 'Five minutes, then?' He started to walk to the door.

'Finlay?' Her voice was quite serious.

'Yes?'

'Can I pick where we go?'

'Of course.' He was amused. He had no idea where he'd planned to take her. His brain hadn't got that far ahead.

'See you in five, then.'

* * *

Grace was trying hard not to breathe. The only female bartender she could find was a size smaller. She'd managed to do up the zip on the dress but there wasn't much room. Lunch could be an issue.

Why had he asked her to lunch? Did he want to talk more decorations? And now she was late. After he'd left she'd grabbed the end of the lights to check they worked. They did.

Then she'd phoned a rush order for purple light bulbs. They would be delivered in a few hours. She'd need to find out how the lights normally got up there. This could be a disaster if she needed scaffolding. Maybe one of those funny little cherry pickers would do the trick?

Finlay was waiting for her at the front door. She tried not to notice the obviously interested looks they were getting from other members of staff.

She pulled down her woolly black sequined hat. She'd got it in the bargain bucket at the supermarket and it was the least likely match for her designer pink coat and gloves. But it was all she could afford at the time.

He smiled at her. He'd changed his white shirt for a blue one. Her stomach gave a little somersault. Yikes, it just made those blue eyes bluer.

'Where are we going?' he asked.

'What do you like for lunch?'

She still hadn't quite worked out why they were going for lunch. She assumed he wanted to talk about the decorations some more. And that was fine. But she intended on doing it somewhere she was comfortable.

'I'm easy.' He shrugged his shoulders. 'What do you like?'

They started walking along the street. 'Are you okay with the Tube?' she asked.

'You want to go someplace else?'

She licked her lips. 'I don't normally eat around here.' It was best to be upfront. There were lots of pricey and ultra-fashionable places to eat around here. Artisan delicatessens where a sandwich generally cost three times as much as it should.

She veered off towards the steps to the underground. Finlay just kept pace with an amused expression on his face. She pulled out her card to use while he fumbled around in his pockets for some change and headed for the ticket machine. She shook her head. 'Just scan your credit card. It will just deduct the payment.'

He frowned but followed her lead. They were lucky—a train had just pulled into the station. She held onto one of the poles and turned to face him as the train started to move. 'I'll give you a choice of the best breakfast around or some fantastic stuffed croissants.'

He looked at her warily. 'What, from the same place?'

She laughed. 'No, silly. They're two different cafés. I'm just trying to decide which one we go to.'

'I had breakfast at six. Let's go for the croissants.'

She gave him a solemn nod. 'I warn you—you might get angry.'

'Why?'

She stood on her tiptoes and whispered in his ear. 'Because the coffee in this place is *miles* better than it is in the hotel.'

She could see him bristle. 'No way.'

'Way.' The train slid to a halt. 'Come and find out for yourself.'

There was almost a skip in Grace's step as she led him from the Tube station and across the road to a café much like every other one in London. But as soon as he opened the door he could smell the difference. The scent of coffee beans filled the air, along with whiffs of baking—apple tarts, sponge cakes and something with vanilla in it. If you weren't hungry before you entered this café, you'd be ravenous ten seconds after crossing the threshold. He'd need to remember that.

They sat at the table and ordered. As soon as the waitress left, Grace started playing with a strand of hair. 'I might have done something,' she said hesitantly.

'What?' he asked cautiously.

'I might have ordered some purple light bulbs. And some white ones. I figure that if we can get the lights up outside the hotel it will give people an idea of what it looks like inside.'

He gave a nod. 'I had a call from the manager of another chain of hotels today. She was asking about you.'

Grace's eyes widened. 'Asking about me?'

He nodded. 'She wanted to know the name of the designer I'd used because she'd heard how good the hotel looked.'

Grace leaned across the table towards him. 'Already? But I've only just finished.'

'I know that and you know that.' He held up his hand. 'But this is London, word travels fast.'

She shook her head. He could almost see her shrinking into herself. 'But I'm not a designer. I'm just one of the Maids in Chelsea.'

'We need to talk about that.'

'Why?'

Finlay reached into his jacket pocket and pulled out the cheque he'd written. 'I need to pay you for your services.'

Grace looked down and blinked. Then blinked again. Her face paled. 'Oh, no. You can't give me this.'

'Do you want to get Clio to bill me, then? I'm not sure why, though—this is different from the work you do for the agency.'

Her fingers were trembling. 'You can't pay me this much.'

Ah. He got it. It wasn't how he was paying her. It was how much he was paying her.

'I can increase it,' he said simply.

Her eyes widened even further. 'No.'

It almost came out as a gasp.

Ah. Now he understood.

'Grace, I based this on what we paid our last interior designer, plus inflation. That's all. As far as I'm aware, this is what I'd normally pay for these services.'

The waitress appeared and set down their plates. She'd caught the tail-end of the conversation—and glanced at the cheque under Grace's fingertips before making some kind of strangled sound.

Grace was looking distinctly uncomfortable. Finlay waved his hand and looked at the food in front of him. 'Take it, it's yours. You did a good job. You deserve it.'

He'd decided to follow Grace's lead. The croissant in front of him was stuffed with tuna and melted cheese. Salad and coleslaw were on the side and the waitress came back with steaming cups of coffee. She winked at him. 'Try the rhubarb pie after this, it's to die for.'

He almost laughed out loud. She'd seen the cheque and would expect a decent tip. He could do that.

'I think I might have to lie down after this,' he said, taking in all the food on the plate.

Grace was still watching the cheque as if it would bite her. He picked it up again and looked under the table, sliding it into her bag.

'Let's lunch.' He said the words in a way he hoped she'd understand. The amount wasn't open to debate. 'Where do you live?'

'What?' That snapped her out of her dreamlike state. 'Why?'

He shrugged. 'I'd like to know a bit more about the woman I'm having lunch with.'

Didn't she want to tell him where she lived?

She lifted her knife and fork. 'I live in Walthamstow,' she said quietly.

'Did you go to school around there?'

She nodded but didn't add anything further.

'How long have you worked for Maids in Chelsea?'

Her shoulders relaxed a little. That seemed a more acceptable question. 'Just for a few months.' She met his gaze, 'Truth is, it's the best job I've ever had. Clio, the boss, is lovely and the rest of the staff are like…family.'

Family. Interesting choice of word for work colleagues.

'What did you do before?'

She smiled. 'You name it—I've done it.'

He raised his eyebrows and she laughed. 'Okay, there are certain things I've never done. But I have had a few jobs.' She counted off on her fingers. 'I worked in the local library. Then in a few temp jobs in offices. I worked on the perfume counter of one of the department stores. Then I got poached to work on the make-up counter.'

'You got poached?' Somehow, he could see Grace with her flawless complexion and friendly personality being an asset to any make-up counter.

She nodded. 'But it wasn't really for me. I had to eventually give up due to some family issues and when I needed a job again Maids in Chelsea kind of found me.'

'Family issues? You have children?'

She shook her head and laughed. 'Oh, no. I'd want to find a husband first.'

He hadn't even considered the fact she might have children, or a husband! What was wrong with him? He tried to tease out a few more details. 'So, you haven't found a husband yet?'

She shook her head again. 'I haven't had time.' She looked up and met his gaze. 'I've dated casually in the last few years, but haven't really had time for a relationship.'

Due to her family issues? He didn't feel as though he could press.

'I take it you were brought up in Scotland?'

He smiled. 'What's the giveaway?'

She laughed and took a sip of her coffee. 'Is Sean Connery your father?'

'Sean Connery wouldn't have got a look-in. My mum and dad were childhood sweethearts. They lived next door to each other from the age of five.'

Grace set down her knife and fork. 'Oh, wow. That's so nice.'

It was nice. His mum and dad's marriage had always been rock solid, even when half the people he'd gone to school with seemed to have more step-parents than grades at school.

'Are they still in Scotland?'

'Always. They'll never leave.'

She gave him a fixed stare. 'Why did you leave?'

He hesitated then spoke quickly. 'Business.' There was so much more to it than that. He had a home—a castle—in Scotland that had been his pride and joy. He hadn't set foot in it for over a year. The penthouse in The Armstrong was where he now called home. He needed to change the subject—fast.

'Tell me about the Christmas stuff?'

She quickly swallowed a mouthful of food. 'What do you mean?'

He sipped his coffee. Then stopped and connected with her gaze. 'Wow.'

A smile spread across her face. 'I told you.'

He kept his nose above the coffee and breathed in the aroma, then took another sip. The coffee was different from most of the roasts he'd tasted. Finlay was a self-confessed snob when it came to coffee. This was good.

He looked over his shoulder to where the coffee machine and barista were standing. 'I have to find out what this is.'

She was still smiling. 'You'll be lucky if they tell you. The coffee in here has been this good for years. My gran and I used to come here all the time.'

Her voice quietened. He wanted to ask some more but it felt like prying. Could he really go there?

He went back to safer territory. 'The Christmas stuff. You seem to really enjoy it.'

She gave him a careful stare. Her voice was soft. 'I do. I've always loved Christmas. It's my favourite time of year.' She stretched her fingers across the table and brushed them against his hand. 'I'm sorry, I know you said you didn't like it.'

He took a deep breath. The coffee was excellent in here. The food was surprisingly good. And the company…the company was intriguing.

Grace was polite, well-mannered and good at her job. She was also excellent at the unexpected job he'd flung on her the other day. She'd more than delivered.

It was more than a little distracting that she was also incredibly beautiful. But it was an understated beauty. Shiny hair and a pair of deep dark brown eyes that could hide a million secrets. But it wasn't the secrets that intrigued him. It was the sincerity.

Grace didn't feel like the kind of person who would tell lies. She seemed inherently good. All the staff at the hotel liked her. Frank was strangely protective of her.

He took a deep breath. 'It's not that I don't like it. I know I said that—'

She touched his hand again. 'No, you said you hated it.'

He nodded. 'Okay, I said I hated it. And I have. For the last five years. But I didn't always hate it. I had great Christmases as a kid. My sister and I always enjoyed Christmas with our mum and dad.'

Grace pressed her lips together. 'I've spent all my Christmases with my gran. My mum…' She paused as she searched for the words, 'My mum had me when she was very young. My dad was never on the scene. I was brought up by my gran.'

'Your mum wasn't around?'

Grace shook her head. 'Not much. She's married now—lives in Australia—and has a new family. I have two half-brothers.' Her gaze was fixated on her plate of food. 'She's very happy.'

'Do you talk?'

Grace looked up. 'Yes. Of course. Just…not much. We have a relationship of sorts.'

'What does that mean?'

Grace sighed and gave a shrug. 'I'm a twenty-eight-year-old woman. There's not much point in holding a grudge against someone who couldn't cope with a baby as a teenager. I had a good life with my gran. And we had the best Christmases together.'

He got the feeling she was taking the conversation away from her family circumstances and back onto Christmas.

'Is that where your love of Christmas came from?'

She smiled again and got a little sparkle in her eyes. 'Gran and I used to watch lots of black and white films, and we especially loved the Christmas-themed ones. We had a whole load of handmade ornaments. Spray-painted pine cones were our favourites. We did a lot of Christmas baking. We couldn't afford a real tree every year but we always had a holly wreath and I loved the smell.' There was something in her voice. Something in the tone. These were all happy memories—loving memories. But he could hear the wistfulness as she spoke.

He'd told her the biggest event in his life. It didn't matter that he'd blurted it out in anger with a whole host of other things. Grace knew probably the most important thing about him.

Him? He knew very little about her. It was like peeling back a layer at a time. And the further he peeled back the layers, the more he liked her.

She looked out of the window. 'I love Christmas—especially when it snows. It makes it just a little more magical. I love when night falls and you can look out across the dark city and see snow-covered roofs. I always automatically want to watch the sky to see if I can spot Santa's sleigh.'

'Aren't you a little old for Santa?' Her eyes were sparkling. She really did love the magic of Christmas. The thing that for the last five years he'd well and truly lost.

It made him realise how sad he'd been. How much he'd isolated himself. Sure, plenty of people didn't like Christmas. Lots of people around the world didn't celebrate it.

But, when it had been a part of your life for so long, and then something had destroyed it, the reminder of what it could be circulated around his mind.

She set down her knife and fork. 'Finlay Armstrong, are you telling me there's no Santa?' She said it in such a warm, friendly voice that it pulled him back from his thoughts without any regrets.

He pushed his plate away. 'Grace Ellis, I would *never* say something like that.'

She wagged her finger at him as her phone beeped. 'Just as well. In that case I won't need to tell you off.' She glanced at her phone. 'Oh, great, the light bulbs have arrived.' She reached around for her pink coat and woolly hat. Her eyes were shining again. 'Come on, Finlay. Let's light up The Armstrong!'

How on earth could he say no?

CHAPTER FIVE

'I HAVE THE perfect dress for you.' Mrs Archer clapped her hands together. 'You'll love it!'

'What?' Grace was stunned out of her reverie. She'd spent the last few days in a fog. A fog named Finlay Armstrong.

He'd managed to commandeer staff from every department and they'd spent two hours—Finlay included—replacing the light bulbs on the external display. Five specially phoned-in maintenance men had hung the purple and white strips down either side of the exterior of The Armstrong.

As they'd stood together on the opposite side of the street to get a better look, Finlay had given her a nudge. 'It does look good, Grace. You were right.' He took a deep breath. 'Thank you.'

The closed-off man who apparently had a reputation as a recluse was coming out of his shell. Except Finlay hadn't been in a shell. Grace got the impression he'd been in a dark cave where the only thing he'd let penetrate was work.

He was smiling more. His shoulders didn't seem quite so tense. Since their first meeting he'd never shouted, never been impolite. Only for the briefest second did she see something cloud his eyes before it was pushed away again. Even Frank had commented on the changes in the last few days.

She nudged Finlay back. 'Just wait until next year. I'll pick a whole new colour scheme and bankrupt you in light bulbs!' She'd been so happy, so excited that things had worked out she'd actually winked at him.

Winked. All she could do right now was cringe.

But the wink hadn't scared him off. Every time she'd turned around in the last two days, Finlay had been there—asking her about something, talking to her about other pieces of interior design work she might be interested in. Getting her to sit down and chat.

They'd had another lunch together. Around four coffees. And a makeshift dinner—a Chinese take-away in the office one night.

She'd even found herself telling him about the Elizabethan-style chairs she'd found in a junk shop and spent weeks re-covering and re-staining on her own.

Last night she hadn't slept a wink. Her brain had been trying to work out what on earth was going on between them. Was she reading this all wrong? Had it really been *that* long since she'd dated that she couldn't work out the signals any more?

'Ta-da!'

Mrs Archer brought her back to the present day by swinging open a cupboard door and revealing what lay behind it.

Wow.

It glimmered in the early-morning winter light. A full-length silver evening gown in heavy-duty satin with a bodice and wide straps glittering with sequins. Around the top of the coat hanger was a fur wrap. She was almost scared to touch it.

'Don't worry,' said Alice Archer. 'It's not real fur. But it probably cost ten times as much as it should.'

Grace's heart was pounding in her chest. She'd forgotten Alice had offered to find her something for the party.

When Finlay had given her that exorbitant cheque the other day she'd almost squealed. Bills had been difficult since her grandmother had died.

Her grandmother and late grandfather had had small pensions that had contributed to the upkeep of the flat. Keeping up with bills was tough on her own. There was no room for any extras—any party dresses. She'd actually planned on going to some of the charity shops around Chelsea later to see if she could find anything to wear tonight.

'It's just beautiful,' she finally said. Her hand touched the satin. She'd never felt anything like it in her life.

'The colour will suit you marvellously.' Alice smiled. 'I had it in my head as soon as you told me about the party.'

'When did you wear this, Alice? It's just stunning.'

Alice whispered in her ear. 'Don't tell Finlay Armstrong, but I wore it at a New Year ball in The Ritz the year my Robin proposed to me.'

Grace pulled back her hand. 'Oh, Alice, I can't wear your beautiful dress. It has such special memories for you—and it's immaculate. I would be terrified about something happening to it.'

Alice shook her head. 'Nonsense, I insist.' She ran her fingers down the fabric of the dress with a far-off expression in her eyes. 'I always think that clothes are for wearing. I think of this as my lucky dress.' She gave Grace a special smile. 'And I'm hoping it will bring you some luck too.'

Grace stared in the mirror. Someone else was staring back at her. Whoever it was—it wasn't Grace Ellis. Ashleigh had come around and set her hair in curls. Sophie had helped her apply film-star make-up. She'd never worn liquid eyeliner before and wasn't quite sure how Sophie had managed to do the little upward flicks.

Around her neck she was wearing the silver locket her

grandmother had bought her for her twenty-first birthday and Emma had loaned her a pair of glittery earrings.

They were probably diamonds. But Emma hadn't told her that. She'd just squealed with excitement when she'd seen Grace all dressed up and said she had the perfect thing to finish it off.

And she'd been right. Right now, Grace Ellis felt like a princess. It didn't matter that the only items she was wearing that actually belonged to her were her locket, her underwear and her shoes.

The party was being held in one of the smaller main rooms in the hotel. The music was already playing and she could see coloured flashing lights. Her heart started beating in tempo with the music. Her hands were sweating. She was nervous.

But it seemed she wasn't the only one.

Finlay was pacing up and down outside the room. She couldn't help but smile. Just that one sight instantly made her feel better. Although the girls had helped her get ready they'd also plied her with questions.

'What's going on with you and Finlay Armstrong?'

'Is this a date?'

'Are you interested in him?'

'Do you want to date him?'

By the time they'd left her head had been spinning. She didn't know the answer to the first two questions. But the last two? She didn't want to answer them. Not out loud, anyway.

'Grace. You're here.' Finlay covered the distance between them in long strides, slowing as he reached her. At first he'd only focused on her face, but as he'd neared his gaze had swept up and down her body. He seemed to catch his breath. 'You look incredible.'

'You seem surprised.'

He shook his head. 'Of course I'm not surprised. You

always look beautiful. But…' He paused and gestured with his hand. 'The dress and—' He reached out to touch the stole. 'What is this thing anyway? You look like a film star. Should I phone the press?'

He leaned closer, giving her a whiff of his spicy aftershave. She tried not to shiver. He tilted his head to the side. 'What have you done to your eyes?'

She touched his jacket sleeve. 'It's called make-up, Finlay. Women wear it every day.' She made a point of looking him up and down too. The suit probably cost more than she even wanted to think about. But it was immaculate, cut to perfection. 'You don't look so bad yourself.'

His gaze fixed on hers. 'Grace?'

'Yes?'

'Thank you for saying you'd come with me.' The tone of his voice had changed. He wasn't being playful now, he was being serious. 'You know I haven't come to one of these in the last few years.'

She licked her lips and nodded, trying not to let her brain get carried away with itself. 'Why have you come this year?' she asked softly.

She was tiptoeing around about him—trying not to admit to the rapidly beating heart in her chest. She liked this man a whole lot more than she should. She didn't even know what this was between them. But Finlay was giving her little signs of…something. Did he even realise that? Or was this all just in her imagination?

'It was just time,' he said, giving his head a little nod.

Her heart jumped up to the back of her throat. Time.

Just as it had been time to think about Christmas decorations. What else might it be time for?

The serious expression left his face and he stuck out his elbow towards her. 'Well, Ms Ellis, are you ready to go to The Armstrong's Christmas party?'

She slid her hand through his arm as all the little hairs on her arm stood on end. 'I think I could be. Lead the way.'

The party was fabulous. She recognised lots of faces. Other chambermaids, bar staff, porters, reception staff and kitchen staff. Frank the concierge had dressed as Father Christmas and looked perfect.

There was a huge table laid with appetisers and sweets. A chocolate fountain, a pick-and-mix sweetie cart and the equivalent of an outside street cart serving burgers.

Finlay nudged her. 'What? Did you think it would all be truffles and hors d'oeuvres?'

She gave him a smile. 'I wasn't sure.'

He shrugged. 'The first year it was. Frank discreetly told me later that the staff went home hungry. After that, I gave Kevin, from the kitchen, free rein to organise whatever he thought appropriate for the Christmas party. I don't think anyone has gone home hungry since.'

She laughed as he led her over to the bar. 'Which of the Christmas cocktails would you like?' he asked.

She was surprised. 'You have Christmas cocktails?'

'Oh, yes. We have the chocolate raspberry martini, the Festive Shot, with peppermint schnapps, grenadine and crème de menthe, then there is the Christmas Candy Cane, with berry vodka, peppermint schnapps and crème de cacao—or, my personal favourite, Rudolph's Blast: rum, cranberries, peach schnapps and a squeeze of fresh lime.'

Grace shook her head and leaned her elbows up on the bar. 'You know what's in every cocktail?'

He gestured to the barman. 'We'll have two Rudolph's Blasts, please.'

He leaned on the bar next to her and leaned his head on one hand. 'Okay, that dress. You kind of caught me by surprise. Where did you get it?'

She waved her hand. 'Did you expect me to come in uniform?'

He hadn't taken his eyes off her and the smile on his face—well, it wasn't just friendly. It seemed...interested. 'Of course I didn't. But you look like something the Christmas fairy pulled off the tree.'

Her eyes narrowed and she mirrored his position, leaning her head on one hand and staring straight back. 'And is that good—or bad?'

He didn't answer right away, and the barman set their cocktails down in front of them.

She leaned forward and took a sip of the cocktail. She licked her lips again as the mixture of rum and fruit warmed her mouth. He was focused on her mouth.

And she knew it.

She ran her tongue along her lips again then bit the edge of her straw.

'I only have the dress on loan,' she said quietly. 'And I've promised to take very good care of it.'

He leaned a little closer, obviously trying to hear her above the music playing around them. Had she lowered her voice deliberately? Maybe.

As he moved a little closer she was still focused on those blue eyes. Only they weren't as blue as normal. In the dim lights his pupils had dilated so much there was only a thin rim of blue around them. Was it the light? Or was it her?

'Who gave you the loan of the dress?'

'A good friend.'

'A designer?'

Ah...he was worried she'd been loaned the dress by a male designer. She could tell by his tone. She took another sip of her cocktail. It was strong. But it was warming lots of places all around her body. 'Someone much closer to home.'

His brow furrowed. She was playing games with him.

His hand reached over and rested on her arm. 'Someone I know?'

She smiled. 'Someone you respect. Someone I respect.' Grace lifted her hand and placed it on her chest. 'I'm told it's lucky. Her husband proposed to her when she was wearing this dress.'

Something flitted across his eyes. It was the briefest of seconds but it made her cringe a little inside. That might have come out a little awkwardly. She wasn't dropping hints. She absolutely wasn't.

Then, it was almost as if the pieces fell into place. 'Alice Archer?' His voice was louder and the edges of his mouth turned upwards in a wide smile as he shook his head in disbelief, looking Grace up and down—again.

She was getting used to this.

'This was Alice Archer's dress?'

She nodded. 'This *is* Alice Archer's dress. She offered to give me something to wear a few days ago when she heard I was coming to the party.' Grace ran her palm across the smooth satin. Just the barest touch let her know the quality of the fabric. 'I had forgotten. When I walked in this morning she had it hanging up waiting for me.'

He moved closer again, his shoulder brushing against hers as he lifted his cocktail from the bar. 'Well, I think it's a beautiful dress. I have no idea how old it is, but it looks brand new.'

Her heart gave a little soar. The dress was definitely a hit. She'd need to buy Alice a thank-you present. A Christmas song started playing behind them, causing the rest of the people in the room to let out a loud cheer. The dance floor filled quickly. Grace sipped her drink.

'Do you want to dance?'

She shook her head. 'Not to this. I prefer to spectate when it's something wild. I prefer slow dances.'

She hadn't meant it quite to come out like that, but as her gaze connected with those blue eyes the expression on his face made her suck in a breath.

She could practically feel the chemistry between them sparkling. She wasn't imagining this. She just wasn't.

It wasn't possible for the buzz she felt every time he looked at her, or touched her, not to be real.

'I'll take you up on that,' he said hoarsely, before turning back to the barman. 'Can we have some more cocktails?'

His senses were on overload. Her floral scent was drifting around him, entwining him like a coiling snake. His fingertips tingled where they'd touched her silky skin. The throaty whisper of her voice had sent blood rushing through his body as if he were doing a marathon. His eyes didn't know whether to watch the smoky eyes, the tongue running along her succulent lips, the shimmer of the silver satin against her curves or the way her curls tumbled around the pale skin at her neck. As for taste? He could only imagine…

What was more, no matter how hard he tried, he couldn't shut his senses down.

It wasn't as if he hadn't spent time with women since Anna had died. On a few occasions, he had. But those encounters had been courteous, brief and for one purpose only.

There had been no attachment. No emotional involvement.

But with Grace? Things felt entirely different.

He wanted to see her. He wanted to be around her. He was interested in her, and what she thought. He didn't want to see her a few times and just dismiss her from his life.

It had been twelve years since he'd really dated. One date with Anna had been enough to know he didn't need to look any further. And right now, with his stomach tipping upside down, he wasn't sure he knew what to do any more.

Oh, he knew what to *do*.

He just couldn't picture doing it with emotions attached.

All of those memories and sensations belonged to Anna. He knocked back the last of the cocktail and lifted the Festive Shots that had appeared on the bar. He blinked, then tipped his back and finished it before turning to Grace.

Wow. Nope, nothing had changed in that millisecond. She was still here with her tumbling curls, sensational figure and eyes that looked as if they see down into his very soul.

She gave him a suspicious look as she eyed the shot glass. 'Who are you trying to get drunk, you, or me?'

He signalled to the barman again, who replaced his shot. He held it up and clinked it against her glass. 'This is only my third drink and it's only your second. Somehow, I think we can cope.'

She clinked her glass against his, then tipped back her head and downed her shot too. It must have hit the back of her throat because she laughed and burst out coughing. He laughed too and gave her back a gentle slap. 'It hits hard, doesn't it?'

She nodded as her eyes gleamed a little with water. 'Oh, wow.' She coughed again. 'Festive? More like dynamite.'

The music slowed and she glanced over her shoulder. 'Something you like?'

She tipped her head to the side as if she were contemplating the music. 'Actually, I really love this song.'

He didn't think. He didn't hesitate. He held his hand straight out to hers as Wham's Last Christmas filled the room. 'Then let's dance.'

She slid her hand into his. Her fingers starting at the tips of his, running along the palm of his hand and finishing as her fingers fastened around his wrist. His hand slid around her waist, skimming the material of the dress as they walked across the dance floor. He gave a nod to a few members of staff who nodded in their direction.

They were attracting more than their fair share of attention. He should have known this would happen. But the truth was, he didn't really care. This wasn't about anyone other than them.

Grace spun around as she reached the middle of the dance floor. Her hesitation only showed for a second before she slid her hands up around his neck.

It wasn't exactly an unusual position. This was a Christmas slow dance. All around them people were in a similar stance. If they'd stayed apart it would have looked more noticeable.

He kept his hands at her waist as they moved slowly in time with the music. Grace was already singing along with her eyes half closed. 'Hey, isn't this a little before your time?'

Her eyes opened wider. 'Of course. But I don't care. I just love it. I loved the video even more. I watched it a hundred times as a teenager.'

Finlay wracked his brains trying to remember the video. For the first time he actually heard the words to the familiar tune. 'You like this? Isn't this the video where the girl dumped him and came back the next year with someone else?'

She threw back her head and laughed, giving him a delightful view of the pale skin at the bottom of her throat. His teeth automatically ground into his bottom lip. He knew exactly where he wanted his lips to be right now.

'Yes, that's the story. But I liked the snow in the video. It looked romantic. And I like the tune.'

Her body was brushing against his as she moved in time to the music. He pulled her a little closer as he bent to whisper in her ear. 'I can't believe this is your favourite Christmas song.'

She stepped back a little, grabbing his hand and twirling underneath it, sending the bottom of her silver dress spinning out around her, with the coloured lights from the disco catching the silver sequins on her bodice and sending sparkles around the room.

Her eyes were sparkling too, her curls bouncing around her shoulders. Grace was like her own Christmas decoration. When she finished spinning her hands rested on his chest.

He almost held his breath. Would she feel the beat of his heart under her fingertips? What would she make of the irregular pattern that was currently playing havoc with any of his brain processes—that must be the reason he couldn't think a single sane thought right now?

She finished swaying as his hands went naturally back to her hips. He could see a few staff members in the corner of the room looking at them and whispering. He might be the boss, but Grace worked with these people. She did a good job. She brought a little life into the hotel. She deserved their respect. He didn't want to do anything to ruin that.

As the music came to an end he grabbed hold of her hand and pulled her towards the exit. All of a sudden the room felt claustrophobic. There were too many eyes. Too many whispers. He didn't want to share Grace with all these people.

He wanted her to himself.

'Hey, Finlay—what's wrong?'

He leaned into the coat check and grabbed her stole, leaving some cash as a tip. He could hear Grace's feet scurrying behind him as he lengthened his stride to reach the exit as quickly as possible.

They burst outside into the cold night air. He spun around and put the stole around her shoulders. She was breathing heavily; he could see the rise and fall of her chest in the pale yellow light of the lamp post above them. 'What are you doing?' Her voice was high. She sounded stressed.

He took a deep breath. He had no idea what he was doing. But could he really admit that?

He reached out and touched her cheek—just as he had on the roof that night.

'I needed to get out of there.'

He kept his finger against her cheek. It was the slightest touch of her skin. The tiniest piece beneath his fingertip. But it was enough. Enough to set every alarm bell screaming in his brain. Enough to let his senses just explode with overload.

He was past the point of no return.

Grace reached up and captured her hand around his finger, leaving it touching her cheek. 'Why, Finlay? Why did you need to get out of there?'

He could hear the concern in her voice. She didn't have a clue. She thought this might be about something else. She didn't realise that every tiny part of this was about her.

Guilt was racing through his veins in parallel to the adrenaline. Feeling. He was feeling again. And the truth was that scared him.

Guys would never admit that. Not to their friends. Not even to themselves. But most guys hadn't loved someone with every part of their heart, soul and being and had it ripped out of them and every feeling and emotion buried in a brittle, cold grave.

Most guys wouldn't know that they didn't think it could be possible to ever get through that once. Why would they even contemplate making any kind of connection with another person when there was even the smallest possibility they could end up going down the same path?

Once had felt barely survivable. He couldn't connect with someone like that again. How could he risk himself like that again?

Where was his self-preservation? The barriers that he'd

built so tightly around himself to seal his soul off from that kind of hurt again.

Somehow being around Grace had thrown his sense of self-preservation out of the window. All he could think about right now was how much he wanted to touch and taste the beautiful woman in front of him.

She was still watching him with those questioning brown eyes. She was bathed in the muted lamplight—her silver dress sparkling—like an old-fashioned film star caught in the spotlight.

He stopped thinking. 'Because I couldn't wait to do this.'

He pulled her sharply towards him, folding his arm around her waist and pulling her tightly against the length of his body. He stopped for a second, watching her wide eyes, giving her the briefest of pauses to voice any objections. But there were none.

He captured her mouth in his. She tasted of cocktails and chocolate. Sweet. Just the way he'd imagined she would. One hand threaded through her tumbling curls and the other rested on the satin-covered curve of her backside. He'd captured his prize. He wasn't about to let her go.

After two seconds the tension left her body, melding it against his. Her hands wound their way around his neck again, her lips responding to every part of the kiss, matching him in every way.

This was what a connection felt like. He hadn't kissed a woman like this since Anna died. This was what it felt like to kiss a woman you liked and respected. It had been so long he hadn't even contemplated how many emotions that might toss into the cold night air.

Her hand brushed the side of his cheek, running along his jaw line. He could hear the tiny scrape of his emerging stubble against her fingernails. The other hand ran through his hair and then down to his chest again. He liked the feel of her palm there. If only it weren't thwarted by the suit jacket and shirt.

Their kiss deepened. His body responded. He knew. He knew where this could potentially go.

Grace pulled her lips from his. It was a reluctant move, followed by a long sigh. Her forehead rested against his as if she were trying to catch her breath. He could feel her breasts pressed against his chest.

His hand remained tangled in her soft hair and for a few moments they just stood like that, heads pressed together under the street light.

He eventually straightened up. Should he apologise? It didn't feel as if the kiss was unwanted. But they were right in the middle of the street—hardly the most discreet place in the world for a first kiss. He could ask her up to the penthouse but somehow that didn't feel right either—and he was quite sure Grace wouldn't agree to come anyway.

'Thank you for coming tonight,' he said quietly.

Her voice was a little shaky. 'You're welcome.'

He took a step back. 'How about I get one of the chauffeurs to drop you home?'

He had no idea what time it was—but whatever time it was, he didn't want her travelling home alone. He trusted all the chauffeurs from The Armstrong. Grace would be in safe hands.

She gave a little nod. 'That would be nice, thank you.' This time her voice sounded a little odd. A little detached. Had she rethought their kiss and changed her mind?

He put his arm behind her and led her back to the main entrance of the hotel, nodding to one of the doormen. 'Callum, can you get one of the chauffeurs to take Grace home?'

She shivered and pulled the stole a little closer around her shoulders. 'Do you want me to get you another coat?'

She shook her head, not quite meeting his gaze. 'I'll be fine when I get in the car. That'll be warm enough.'

For a couple of minutes they stood in awkward silence. Finlay wasn't quite sure what to do next. He wasn't quite sure *what* he wanted to do next. And he couldn't read Grace at all.

The sleek black car pulled up in front of them and the driver jumped out to open the door. Grace turned to face him with her head held high. 'Thank you for a lovely evening, Finlay,' she said as she climbed into the car.

'You too,' he replied automatically as he closed the door, and watched the car speed off into the distance.

One thing was for sure. Finlay Armstrong wouldn't sleep a wink tonight.

CHAPTER SIX

SHE COULDN'T DESCRIBE the emptiness inside her. It was impossible to put into words.

She stared at the texts on the phone from her friends, teasing her about the party and assuming she'd had the time of her life.

She had—almost.

But last night when she'd opened the door to the cold and empty flat, everything had just overwhelmed her.

Silence echoed around her.

Unbearable silence.

The home that had once been filled with love and happiness shivered around her.

She actually felt it happen.

Even when she flicked the light switch, the house was dark. Emptiness swamped every room. She'd started to cry even before she'd made it to bed, wrapping herself in her gran's shawl, her own duvet and wearing the thickest pair of flannel pyjamas imaginable—but nothing could keep out the cold. Nothing at all.

That feeling of loneliness was enormous. Somewhere, on the other side of the planet, her mother was probably cuddled up to her husband or sitting around a table with her two children. Children she actually spent time with.

It wasn't that she didn't understand. Getting pregnant at sixteen would be difficult for any teenager. But to move away completely and form a new life—without any thought to the old—was hard to take.

It made her more determined. More determined to never feel second best with any man. She'd spent her whole life feeling second best and a cast-off. Although her relationship with her gran had been strong and wonderful, there had still been that underlying feeling of…just not being enough.

For the briefest spell tonight, under that lamp post, she'd felt a tiny bit like that again. All because of that kiss. Oh, the kiss had been wonderful—mesmerising. The attraction was definitely there. But the connection, or the sincerity of the connection? She just couldn't be sure if when Finlay kissed her he was thinking only of her.

She shivered all night. The heating was on in the flat and it didn't matter how high the temperature was —it just couldn't permeate her soul.

The night with Finlay had brought things to a precipice in her head.

Alone. That was how she felt right now.

Completely and utterly alone.

She'd thought being busy at Christmas would help. She'd thought decorating the flat the way it always used to be would help.

But the truth was nothing helped. Nothing filled the aching hole that her grandmother's death had left.

A card had arrived from her mother. The irony killed her. It was a personalised card with a photo of her mum with her new husband, Ken, and their two sons on the front. They were suitably dressed for a Christmas in Florida. It wasn't meant to be a message. But it felt like it.

Her mother had moved on—playing happy families on another continent. She'd found her happy ever after. And it didn't include Grace. It never had.

She received the same store gift card each year. Impersonal. Polite. The sort of gift you sent a colleague you didn't know that well—not the sort of gift you sent your daughter.

As she rode the Tube this morning people seemed to be full of Christmas spirit. It was Christmas Eve. Normally she would be full of Christmas spirit too.

But the sight of happy children bouncing on their parents' knees, couples with arms snaked around each other and stealing kisses, only seemed to magnify the effect of being alone.

Tonight, she'd go home to that dark flat.

Tonight, she'd spend Christmas Eve on her own. There was no way she could speak to any of the girls. They were all too busy wrapped up in their own lives, finding their own dreams, for Grace to bring them down with her depressed state.

The train pulled into the station and she trudged up the stairs to work.

This time last year her stomach had been fluttering with the excitement she normally felt at Christmas. Christmas Eve was such a special day.

It was for love, for families, for sharing, for fun and for laughter. Tomorrow, she would probably spend the whole day without speaking to a single person. Tomorrow, she would cook a dinner for one.

She'd pushed away every single thought about how she might spend Christmas Day. It had been easier not to think about it at all. That way she could try and let herself be swept along with the spirit of Christmas without allowing the dark cloud hanging above her head to press down on her.

But now, it seemed to have rushed up out of nowhere. It was here and the thought of being alone was just too much.

She pulled her phone out of her pocket and dialled. 'Clio? Are there any shifts tomorrow?'

She could almost hear the cogs whirring in Clio's brain at the end of the phone. 'Grace? What's wrong?'

Grace sucked in a deep breath to try and stop her voice from wobbling. She couldn't stop the tears that automatically pooled in her eyes. 'It's just the time of year…it's hard,' she managed.

'Your gran. You're missing her. I get it. But do you really want to spend Christmas Day working?' The compassion in Clio's voice made her feel one hundred times worse.

'Yes.'

There was a shuffle of papers. 'You can work at The Armstrong as normal. There are always lots of shifts at Christmas. I can put you on for that one.'

'Great, thanks.' The words came out easier this time; it was almost as if a security blanket had been flung over her shoulders. 'And, Clio? Congratulations on your engagement. Enjoy your time with Enrique.'

She hung up the phone and sighed. She meant it. She really did. Clio was over the moon with her new relationship and she deserved to be happy.

She changed quickly and started work. The Christmas themed music that she'd chosen was playing quietly in the background *everywhere.*

Other members of staff were smiling and whistling. No one was rushing today. The whole work tempo seemed to have slowed down for the festive season. And Grace noticed a few sideways glances from people who'd attended the staff party.

Her list was long. Lots of people had the day off. But Grace didn't care; it would keep her busy and give her less time to think.

It was surprising the amount of guests who checked in and out around Christmas. Something panged inside her again. People coming to visit families and friends.

Eight hours later her hair was back to its semi-normal

dishevelled state and she really wanted to get changed. One of the staff called her over. 'Can you do one more before you knock off tonight? I'm in a bit of a rush.'

Grace pressed her lips together. She knew Sally had four kids and would want to get home to them early. She held out her hand. 'Of course I will. No problem.'

Sally gave her a hug. 'Thanks, Grace. Have a great Christmas.'

Grace glanced at the list and her stomach did a little flip-flop. She had The Nottingdale Suite to clean—Finlay's place. She glanced towards the office. He'd be in there right now. If she was quick—she could get things done and get back out before he knew she was working.

It was a weird feeling. When he'd held her in his arms last night she'd felt…she'd felt…special. A tiny little fire that had been burning inside her for the last few days had just ignited like a firework—only to sputter out again.

The Nottingdale Suite didn't feel quite so empty as before. One of her Christmas snow globes was sitting on the main table, with a wrapped parcel on the slate kitchen worktop.

Grace couldn't help but pick it up. It was intricately wrapped in silver paper with curled red ribbon and a tag. The writing was copperplate. Grace smiled. She recognised it immediately and set it down with a smile. Mrs Archer had left a present for Finlay. How nice.

She made short work of cleaning the penthouse. The bathroom, kitchen area, bedroom and lounge were spotless in under an hour.

She stared out for a second over the dark London sky. In a few hours Christmas Eve would be over. By the time she got home, she could go straight to bed then get up early for her next shift. She squeezed her eyes closed for a second.

Please just let this Christmas be over.

* * *

'Grace?' She was the last person he expected to see at this time of night. 'What are you doing?'

The words were out before he even noticed the cart next to the doorway.

She jumped and turned around. 'Finlay.' The words just seemed to stop there.

She was wearing her uniform again. But in his head she still had on the silver dress from the last night. That picture seemed to be imprinted on his brain. Seared on it, in fact.

She still hadn't spoken. The atmosphere was awkward.

He wasn't quite sure how to act around Grace.

That kiss last night had killed any ounce of sleep he might have hoped to get.

His brain couldn't process it at all. There was no box to put it in.

It wasn't a fleeting moment with someone unimportant. It hadn't been a mistake. It wasn't a wild fling. It hadn't felt casual. So, what did that leave?

Grace's eyes left his and glanced at the outside view again—exactly where she'd been staring when he came in. He heard a stilted kind of sigh. She moved over towards the cart.

This wasn't going to get any easier. Neither of them seemed able to do the casual and friendly hello.

He had a freak brainwave. This was Christmas Eve. Grace was the woman that loved Christmas. No—she lived and breathed Christmas. What on earth was she doing still working?

Grace picked up some of the cleaning materials and shoved them back in her cart. 'Merry Christmas, Finlay.' The words were stilted. Was this how things would be now?

'Merry Christmas, Grace.' His response was automatic. But something else wasn't.

The feelings that normally washed around a response like that. Normally they were cold. Harsh. Unfeeling and unmeant.

This was the first time in five years he'd actually meant those words as he said them.

He wanted Grace to have a merry Christmas. He wanted her to enjoy herself.

What if...?

The idea came out of nowhere. At least, that was how it seemed. He was flying back to Scotland on Boxing Day to see his family. Chances were, this would be the last time he would see Grace between now and then.

There were a dozen little flashes in his brain. Grace on the roof. Touching the tear that had rolled down her cheek. Drinking hot chocolate with her. The gleam in her eyes when she was cheeky to him. The expression on her face when she'd tried on the pink coat. The wash of emotions when he'd spotted the little girl and bought the rocking horse for her Christmas. Grace's ruffled hair and pushed-up shirt as she'd wound in hundreds of purple bulbs. The way she'd clapped her hands together when he'd first seen the tree.

And the feel of her lips on his. Her warm curves against his. The soft satin of her dress under the palm of his hand.

He'd felt more alive in the last week than he had in the last five years.

And that was all because of Grace.

He reached out to touch her arm. 'It's been nice to meet you. Enjoy Christmas Day.'

The words were nowhere near adequate. They didn't even begin to cover what he wanted to say or what was circulating in his brain.

Grace's dark brown eyes met his. For a second he thought she was going to say the same thing. Then, her bottom lip started to tremble and tears welled in her eyes. 'I'll be working as normal.'

He blinked. What?

Why would the girl who loved Christmas not be spending it with her family and friends?

'What do you mean—you're working? Don't you have plans with those you love?'

As soon as the words were out he realised he'd said exactly the wrong thing. The tears that had pooled in her eyes flooded over and rolled down her cheeks.

He reached out his arms to her. 'What on earth's wrong? Grace? Tell me?'

She was shaking and when the words came out it was the last thing he expected.

'There's no family. My gran…she died…she died a few months ago. And now, there's just no one. I can't face anything.' She looked at him, her gaze almost pleading. 'I thought I could do this. I thought I could. I thought if I kept busy and kept working everything would just fall into place. I wouldn't have time to miss her so much.' She kept shaking her head. 'But it's harder than I could ever imagine. Everywhere I go, everywhere I look, I see people—families together, celebrating Christmas the way I used to. Even Mrs Archer—I love her—but I'm finding it so hard to be around her. She reminds me so much of my gran. The way she speaks, her mannerisms, her expressions.' She looked down as she kept shaking her head. 'I just want this to be over.' Now, she looked outside again into the dark night. In the distance they could see the Christmas red and white lights outlining Battersea Power Station. 'I just want Christmas to be over,' she breathed.

Every hair on his arms stood on end. He got it. He got all of it.

The loneliness. The happy people around about, reminding you of what you'd lost. The overwhelming emotions that took your breath away when you least expected it.

He put his hands on her shoulders. 'Grace, you don't need to be here. You don't need to work at Christmas. It's fine. We can cover your shifts. Take some time off. Get away from this. The last thing you want to do is watch other families eating Christmas dinner together. Stay home. Curl up in bed. Eat chocolate.'

It seemed like the right thing to say. Comfort. Away from people under her nose.

But Grace's eyes widened and she pulled back. 'What? No. You think I want to be alone? You think I want to spend the whole of Christmas without talking to anyone, without seeing another living soul? Do you think anything looks worse on a plate than Christmas dinner for one?'

As she spoke he cringed. What he'd thought might take her away from one type of agony would only lead her to another. He hated this. He hated seeing the pain in her eyes. The hurt. The loneliness. He recognised them all too well. He'd worn the T-shirt himself for five years.

He squeezed her shoulders. 'Then what is it you want for Christmas, Grace? What is it you want to do? What would be your perfect Christmas?'

His agitation was rising. She'd got herself so worked up that her whole body was shaking. He hated that. He hated she was so upset. Why hadn't he realised she was alone? Why hadn't he realised she was suffering a bereavement just as he was?

Grace had always been so upbeat around him, so full of life that he'd missed the signs. He knew better than most that you only revealed the side of you that you wanted people to see.

He'd been struck by Grace's apparent openness. But she'd built the same guard around her heart as he had. It didn't matter that it was different circumstances. This year, she felt just as alone as he had over the last five.

He didn't want that for her. He didn't want that for Grace.

What if...?

The thought came out of nowhere. He didn't know quite what to do with it.

Her eyes flitted between him and the outside view. 'Tell me, Grace. Tell me what your ideal Christmas would be. What do you want for Christmas?' His voice was firm as he repeated his question. The waver in her voice and tears had been too much for him. Grace was a kind and good person. She didn't deserve to be lonely this Christmas. He had enough money to buy just about anything and he was willing to spend it to wipe that look off her face.

Her mouth opened but the words seemed to stall.

'What?' he prompted gently.

'I want a proper Christmas,' she breathed. 'One with real snow, and a log fire, and a huge Christmas turkey that's almost too big to get in the oven.' She took a deep breath. 'I want to be able to smell a real Christmas tree again and I want to spend all day—or all night—decorating it the way I used to with my gran. I want to go into the kitchen and bake Christmas muffins and let the smell drift all around.' She squeezed her eyes closed for a second. 'And I don't want to be alone.'

Finlay was dumbstruck. She hadn't mentioned gifts or 'things'. Grace didn't want perfume or jewels. She hadn't any yearning for materialistic items.

She wanted time. She wanted company. She wanted the Christmas experience.

He glanced out of the window again. He was a little confused. Snow dusted the top of every rooftop in London—just as it had for the last week.

'What do you mean by snow?' he said carefully.

She opened her eyes again as he released his hands from her shoulders. She held out her hands. 'You know—real snow. Snow that's so thick you can hardly walk in it. Snow you can lie down on and do snow angels without feeling the pavement beneath your shoulder blades. Snow that there's actually enough of to build a snowman and make snowballs with. Snow that, when you look out, all you can see is white with little bumps and you wonder what they actually are.' He could hear the wonder in her voice, the excitement. She'd stopped being so sad and was actually imagining what she wished Christmas could be like.

'And then you go inside the house and all you can smell is the Christmas tree, and the muffins, and then listen to the crackle of the real fire as you try and dry off from being outside.' She was smiling now. It seemed that Grace Ellis could tell him exactly what she wanted from this Christmas.

And he knew exactly where she could get it. The snow scene in her head—he'd seen that view a hundred times. The crackling fire—he had that too.

This was Grace. The person who'd shot a little fire into his blood in the last few days. The person who'd made him laugh and smile at times. The girl with the warm heart who had let him realise the future might not be quite as bleak as he'd once imagined.

He could do this. He could give her the Christmas she deserved.

'Pack your bag.'

Her eyes widened and she frowned. 'What?'

He started walking through the penthouse, heading to his cupboards to pull out some clothes. It was cold up north; he'd need to wrap up.

'I'll take you home to grab some things. I can show you real snow. I can light a real fire. We can even get soaked to the skin making snow angels.' He winked at her. 'Once you've done it—you'll regret it.'

Grace was still frowning. 'Finlay, it's after eight o'clock on Christmas Eve. Where on earth are you planning on taking me? Don't you have plans yourself?'

He shook his head as he pushed some clothes in a black bag. 'No. I planned on staying here and going up on Boxing Day to visit my parents and sister. My helicopter is on standby. We can go now.'

She started shaking her head. 'Go where?'

'To Scotland.'

CHAPTER SEVEN

THINGS SEEMED TO happen in a blur after that.

Her cart abandoned, Finlay grabbed her hand and made a quick phone call as they rode down in the elevator. The kitchen was still busy and it only took two minutes for him to corner the head chef.

'I need a hamper.'

The head chef, Alec, was in the middle of creating something spectacular. He shot Finlay a sharp look, clearly annoyed at being interrupted.

'What?'

But enthusiasm had gripped Finlay. 'I need a hamper for Christmas. Enough food for dinner tomorrow and all the trimmings.' He started opening the huge fridges next to Alec. 'What have you got that we can take?'

Grace felt herself shrink back. Alec was clearly contemplating telling Finlay where to go. But after a few seconds he gestured to a young man in the corner. 'Ridley, get one of the hampers from the stock room. See what we've got to put in it. Get a cool box too.'

Finlay had started stockpiling everything he clearly liked the look of on one of the counters where service was ongoing. The staff were dodging around them as they tried to carry on. She moved next to his elbow. 'I think we're getting in the way,' she whispered.

Prosciutto ham, pâté, Stilton and Cheddar cheese, oatcakes, grapes and some specially wrapped chocolates were already on the counter. Finlay looked up. 'Are we?' He seemed genuinely surprised about the chaos they were causing. 'What kind of wine would you like?' he asked. 'Or would you prefer champagne?'

Alec caught sight of her panicked face. He leaned over Finlay. 'Where exactly are you going?'

'Scotland.' It was all she knew.

Alec didn't even bat an eyelid, he just shouted other instructions to some of the kitchen staff. 'Louis, find two large flasks and fill them with the soups.'

Finlay still seemed oblivious as he crunched on a cracker. 'What are the soups?'

Alec didn't even glance in his direction; he was scribbling on a piece of paper. 'Celeriac with fresh thyme and truffle oil, and butternut squash, smoked garlic and bacon.'

A wide smile spread across Finlay's face. 'Fantastic.'

Ridley appeared anxiously with the hamper already half filled and looked at the stack of food on the counter. He started moving things between the hamper and cool box.

'Christmas pudding,' said Finlay. 'We need Christmas pudding.' Ridley glanced over at Alec, who let out a huge sigh and turned and put one hand on his hip and thrust the other towards Finlay.

Finlay frowned as he took the piece of paper. Alec raised his eyebrows. 'It's instructions on how to cook the turkey that's just about to go in your cool box.' He gave Grace a little smile, 'I'd hate it if you gave the lovely lady food poisoning.'

Finlay blinked then stuffed the paper into the pocket of his long black wool coat. 'Great. Thanks.'

Louis appeared with the soup flasks and some wrapped bread.

'We'll grab the wine on the way past. Is there anything else you want, Grace?'

She shook her head. Had she actually agreed to go to Scotland with Finlay? She couldn't quite remember saying those words. But somehow the dark cloud that had settled over her head for the last day seemed to have moved off to the side. Her stomach was churning with excitement. Finlay seemed invigorated.

A Christmas with real snow? It would only be a day—or two. He was sure to want to get back to work straight away. And the thought of a helicopter ride…

'Grace, are we ready?' He had the hamper in one hand and the cool box in the other.

She nodded.

It seemed as though she blinked and the chauffeur-driven car pulled up outside her flat. Her hand hesitated next to the door handle. This part of London was nowhere near as plush as Chelsea. She felt a little embarrassed to show Finlay her humble abode.

But his phone rang and he pulled it from his pocket. She slid out of the car. 'I'll be five minutes.'

He nodded as he answered the call and then put his hand over the phone. 'Grace?'

She leaned back in. 'What?'

He winked. 'Bring layers.'

She was like a whirlwind. Throwing things into a small overnight case, grabbing make-up and toiletries and flicking all the switches off in the house. She flung off her clothes and pulled on a pair of jeans, thin T-shirt, jumper and some thick black boots. The pink coat was a must. He'd bought it for her and it was the warmest thing that she owned.

She grabbed her hat, scarf and gloves and picked up the bag.

Then stopped to catch her breath.

She turned around and looked inside at the dark flat. The place she'd lived happily with her grandmother for years. This morning she'd been crying when she left, dreading coming home tonight. Now, the situation had turned around so quickly she didn't know which way was up.

The air was still in the flat, echoing the emptiness she felt there now. 'Love you, Gran,' she whispered into the dark room. 'Merry Christmas.'

She closed the door behind her. This was about to become the most unusual Christmas ever.

Grace squealed when she saw the helicopter and took so many steps backwards that he thought she might refuse to fly. He put his arm around her waist. 'Come on, it's fine. It's just noisy.'

Her steps were hesitant, but he knew once she got inside she would be fine. The helicopter took off in the dark night, criss-crossing the bright lights of London and heading up towards Scotland.

Once she'd got over the initial fear of being in the helicopter Grace couldn't stop talking. 'How fast does this thing go? Do we need to stop anywhere? How long will it take us to get there?' She wrinkled her nose. 'And where is *there*? My geography isn't great. Whereabouts in Scotland are we going?'

He laughed at the barrage of questions. 'We need to fly around three hundred and eighty miles. Yes, we'll need to stop to refuel somewhere and it'll take a good few hours. So, sit back, relax and enjoy the ride.'

Grace pressed her nose up next to the window for a minute. But she couldn't stop talking. It was clear she was too excited. 'Where are we going to stay? Will your family be there? Can I decorate again, or will they already have all the decorations up?'

Finlay sucked in a breath. His actions in the heat of the moment had consequences he hadn't even considered. His parents weren't expecting him until Boxing Day. He hadn't even called them yet—and now it was after ten at night. Hardly time to call his elderly parents. His sister was staying. He knew there was his old room. But there weren't *two* spare rooms. And his parents would probably jump to an assumption he didn't want them to.

This could be awkward.

He gulped. Not normal behaviour for Finlay. His brain tried to think frantically about the surrounding area. Although he stayed in the country they weren't too far away from the city. There were some nice hotels there. And, if he remembered rightly, there were some nice hotels in the surrounding countryside area.

He pulled out his phone to try and do a search. 'I haven't booked anywhere,' he said quickly as he started to type. 'But I'm sure we can find a fabulous hotel to stay in.'

'A hotel?' It was the tone of her voice.

'Yes.' His fingers were still typing as he met her gaze and froze.

'We're going to *another* hotel?'

It was the way she said it. He stayed part of the year at The Armstrong. The rest of the year he flitted around the globe. He hadn't set foot in his home—the castle—since Anna died.

Disappointment was written all over Grace's face. She gestured towards the hamper. 'Why did we need the food? Won't the hotel have food?' Then she gave a little frown. 'And are you sure you'll be able to find somewhere at this time on Christmas Eve when you don't have a reservation?'

There was an edge of panic to her voice. She hadn't wanted to spend Christmas alone—but she didn't want to spend it at the side of a road either.

She could be right. Lots of the hotels in the surrounding area would be full of families in Scotland for Christmas. 'Give me a second,' he said.

He made a quick call, then leaned forward to confer with the pilot. 'Snow is too heavy around that area,' the pilot said quickly. 'The hotel is too remote. Their helipad is notorious for problems.' He shook his head. 'I'd prefer not to, Mr Armstrong.'

Finlay swallowed. He'd used this pilot for years. If he said he'd prefer not to, he was being polite because Grace was here. He glanced at Grace. 'My parents aren't expecting me until Boxing Day. I don't want to appear early without letting them know.' He pulled a face. 'The hotel I'd thought we could go to has rooms, but—' he nodded to their pilot '—it's remote and our pilot doesn't recommend it.'

Grace's eyes widened. 'So, what do we do, then?'

He sucked in a breath. 'There is somewhere else we could stay.' As he said the words every bit of moisture left his mouth. Part of his brain was in overdrive. Why had he packed the hamper? Had he always known they would end up here?

'Where?' Grace sounded curious.

He hadn't quite met her gaze. He glanced out at the dark night. He had no idea where they were right now. And he had no idea what lay ahead.

Last time he'd been in the castle…

He couldn't even go there. But the practicalities of right now were making him nervous. What would they find at the end of this journey?

After a few years when he'd thought he'd never go back to the castle he'd let his staff go. His mother had made a few casual remarks. He knew that she must have been there. But he also knew that his family respected his wishes.

Grace reached over and touched his arm. Her warm fingers wrapped around his wrist. 'Finlay, where are you taking me? Where will we be staying?'

'My home,' he said before he changed his mind. 'Drumegan Castle.'

Grace pulled her hand back. 'What?' She looked from one side to the other as if she expected the castle to appear out of thin air. 'You own a castle?' Her mouth was practically hanging open.

It had been a while since he'd spoken about the castle. When they'd first bought it, he'd relished the expression on people's faces when he'd told them he owned a castle. But the joy and love for his property had vanished after Anna's diagnosis and then death.

'You own a castle,' Grace repeated.

He nodded. He had to give her an idea of what might lie ahead. 'I haven't been back there in a while.'

'Why?' As soon as she asked the question, realisation dawned on her and she put her hand up to her mouth. 'Sorry,' she whispered. 'Oh.'

'It's all closed up. I don't even know what it will be like when we get there. It will be cold. I hope the heating still works.' He leaned forward and put his head in his hands. 'Please let the electricity be working.' Then he looked upwards, 'Please let the water be working.' This was beginning to feel like a very bad idea. They might actually be better off at the side of the road than in the castle after five years. 'What am I doing?' He was talking to himself but the words came out loud.

Grace's hand came back. 'Finlay, we don't need to go there if you're not comfortable.' She bit her bottom lip. 'But five years is a long time. Maybe it's time to go back.' Her gaze was steady. 'Maybe it's time to think about whether you want to keep the castle or not.' She squeezed his hand again. 'And maybe it won't be quite as bad if you're not there by yourself.'

He could see the sincerity in her eyes. She meant every word. She wanted to help him. She didn't seem worried about the possibility of no water, no electricity or no heating. Just about every other woman in the world that he'd ever known would be freaking out right now. But Grace was calm. The excitement from the helicopter journey had abated now they'd been travelling for a few hours.

Something washed over him. A sense of relief. His stomach had been in knots. A long time ago he'd loved Drumegan Castle. Loved the approach and seeing the grey castle outline against the sky, towering above the landscape on the top of a hill. It used to give him tingles.

Then, for a while, it had given him dread. That had been the point of staying away for so long. He couldn't imagine coming back here himself. He couldn't imagine opening the front door and being swept away by the wave of emotions.

But even though those things were circulating around his brain, he didn't feel the urge at all to break the connection with Grace's steady brown gaze. There was something about being around her. A calmness. A reassurance he hadn't felt in…so long. He placed his hand over hers. 'I think you could be right.' She was trying so hard to help him, but how much had he done for her?

'You should have told me about your gran,' he said quietly.

She shook her head quickly. 'I couldn't. Once you'd told me about Anna… I just felt so guilty. My grief can't compare with yours. They're two entirely different things.'

She was trying so hard to sound convincing, to stop the tiny waver he could still hear in her voice. Her grief was still raw. His?

He kept holding her hand. 'It's not different, Grace. You lost someone that you loved. This is your first Christmas without that person. I get it.' He gave a rueful smile. 'Believe me, I do.'

He pulled her closer and she rested her head on his

shoulder. Next thing he knew the pilot was giving him a shout. 'Five minutes.'

He nudged Grace. 'Wake up, sleepy. We're just about to land.'

She sat up and frowned, rubbing her eyes and looking around. It was still pitch black outside. 'Where on earth are we landing?' she asked.

He smiled. 'At the helipad. The lights are automated.' As he said it they switched on, sending a stream of white light all around them. 'The helipad can be heated to keep it clear. It has its own generator.'

Grace pressed her nose up against the window. 'Is this near the castle? I can't see it.'

She turned and planted one hand on her hip. 'Finlay Armstrong, are you sure you have a castle? It's a caravan, isn't it? You're secretly pranking me and taking me to a forty-year-old caravan with no heating and electricity in the middle of nowhere.'

He raised his eyebrows. 'Don't forget the no water.'

She laughed. 'I couldn't possibly forget that.'

He pulled a face. 'Believe me, once you see the castle, you might prefer a forty-year-old caravan.'

She leaned back with a sigh as they approached the helipad. 'I bet I won't. Stop worrying.'

The helicopter landed smoothly and they jumped out into the biting cold air. 'Whoa!' Grace gave a start. 'I thought London was cold.'

He grabbed her bags. 'I told you to bring layers. Maybe I should have supervised the packing?' He was only half joking. He was curious about where Grace lived and was annoyed he'd been distracted by a business call. It might not have been the most prestigious part of London but he'd have liked to have seen the home she'd shared with her grandmother and had so many good memories of.

He gave a nod to the pilot and walked off to the side

as the helicopter took off again. There was a garage next to the helipad and he pressed a button to open the automated door. There was a squeak. And a creek. And finally it rolled upwards revealing a far too smart four-by-four.

Grace turned to face him. 'This is yours?'

'Last time I checked.' He felt up in the rafters of the garage for the keys, fingers crossed it would start. He knew that his father secretly used the car on occasion to 'keep it in running order'. He was just praying it hadn't been too long since he'd last borrowed it.

He put the bags in the boot and Grace climbed in. He waited until he was ready to get in next to her, then flicked another switch—the external lights of the castle.

She let out a gasp. 'What?'

It was almost as if the castle appeared out of nowhere. The white lights illuminating it instantly around the base, the main entrance, the turrets. At the same time more lights came on, picking out the long driveway between the landing pad and castle.

It might have helped that the whole area was covered in a thick layer of snow, making it look even more magical than normal.

Grace turned to face him, her face astounded. '*This* is your castle?'

'What did you expect?'

She pressed herself back against the leather seat as he started the engine. She was transfixed. She lifted up one hand. 'I don't know. I just didn't expect…that. Look at the snow,' she breathed.

He was fighting back the wave of emotions that was threatening to overtake him. The immense sadness was there. But it wasn't because he was grieving for Anna. It was the sudden realisation that he'd truly been away for too long. As soon as the lights had flashed on he'd been struck by how much he'd missed this sight.

Drumegan Castle had always made him so proud. It was every boy's dream to own a castle. According to Anna it had been every girl's dream too. Drumegan might not have been the pink of some Mediterranean castles, or the beige limestone of many English palaces and large houses. Drumegan Castle was built entirely of grey stone, making it look as if it just rose straight up from the green hill on which it was perched. But to him, just the sight of it gave him immense pride. He'd forgotten that.

It seemed he'd forgotten a lot of things.

He started the car and pulled away. 'What do you think?' It was the oddest sensation, but he wanted her approval. Why? He couldn't quite understand. It was important to him that she liked Drumegan Castle as much as he did.

'How many rooms does it have?' She sounded a bit spaced out.

'Rooms or bedrooms?' His reply was automatic. He'd answered so many questions about his home in the beginning he was practically a walking encyclopaedia on Drumegan Castle.

'Either.' She was still just staring at the structure ahead as they moved along the winding driveway.

'Well, it has wings really. Six bedrooms in each wing. Then two main kitchens. A scullery. A ballroom. Five sitting rooms. Three dining rooms. A few studies. And most bedrooms have separate bathrooms. Some of the top rooms have never been renovated. They're still the original servants' quarters.'

'Ah…so *that's* where you're putting me.' Grace had sparked back into life. 'No bed. No bedsheets. No curtains. And probably…' she pulled her hands around her body '…freezing!' She gave an exaggerated shiver.

He tapped the wheel. 'Hold that thought as you pray the heating is still working properly.'

The car moved up the final part of the drive towards the main entrance of the castle. Normally he would sweep around to the back where there were garages. But there didn't seem much point. He didn't expect anyone else to appear and they were both tired.

He pulled up directly outside the main steps and huge traditional carved double doors.

Grace stepped automatically from the car—she didn't need to be told twice. In the bright outside lights she looked pale. And a little nervous. Even though she was wearing the pink winter coat he could see the slight tremor in her body. He walked around to the back of the car and unloaded the cases, the hamper and the cool box. She came over to help and they walked up the flight of steps to the door.

His hand fumbled slightly as he reached for the lock. 'You'll need to give me a second to turn the main alarm off when we get inside. It should only take a few seconds.'

She nodded.

The lock creaked, then rattled as he twisted and jiggled the key. Finally the key turned around. He breathed a sigh of relief as he opened the iron door handle then shouldered the door completely open.

There was a whoosh. A weird kind of noise. Then an incessant little beep. The alarm.

He dumped the bags and walked to the right. The alarm panel was inside the cupboard at the side of the door. It only took a few seconds to key in the code. The light from outside was flooding in. He'd forgotten to mention the glass dome in the main entrance way. It had been put in by the previous owner—an architect and design engineer who obviously had been born before his time. Together with the lights reflecting from outside and the silver twinkling stars above filling the black sky it was a spectacular sight.

The hamper fell with a clatter from Grace's hand as she

walked forward under the dome. She held out her hands and spun around as her eyes stayed transfixed above. 'I've never seen anything like it,' she said as she turned slowly.

He smiled as he walked over next to her, moving close. 'It's amazing. It was the first thing I noticed when I came to view the castle.' He pointed above. 'At least I know the electricity is working inside as well as out.'

She gave him a curious stare. 'How do you know that?'

He kept looking upwards. 'Sensors. Think about it—the dome should be covered with snow—just like the rest of outside is. But the engineer who designed it knew that the weight of snow could damage it. He designed one of the first thermal sensors to pick up outside temperatures. The glass is heated—just barely—to stop snow gathering there. I had to have a specialist firm out around ten years ago to update the technology and they could hardly believe it.'

She stopped spinning and stared up at him. She didn't seem to notice how close they were—or she didn't seem to mind. She stared up with her chocolate-brown eyes. 'This place looks amazing. I can't wait to see the rest of it.' She touched his arm. 'Are you okay?'

Still thinking about him. Still showing concern. Anna would have loved Grace Ellis.

'I'm fine. Come on.'

They hadn't even closed the door behind them yet and the bitter winds were sweeping in behind them. He slammed the heavy door shut then walked to another small room to flick a few switches. 'Hot water and boiler should be on. But this place takes a long time to heat up. There are separate heating systems in the different wings so I've just put on the main system and the one for the wing we'll be staying in.'

Did that sound pretentious? He didn't mean it to. It was a big place, but it could be morning before they finally felt warm here.

He walked over, opening the door to the main sitting room, flicking on the light switch, then stopped in shock.

Grace walked straight into his shoulder.

The artificial light seemed harsh. What greeted them was even harsher. As soon as his foot hit the floor a white mist puffed upwards.

The five windows were shuttered from the inside. The whole room covered in dust sheets. The dust sheets were covered in dust. The dark wooden floor had its own special coating of dust. One curtain was half hanging from a rail. The things that hadn't managed to be covered in dust sheets were coated from head to foot in a thick layer.

Grace gave a huge sneeze. 'Oh, sorry.'

He spun around, sending up a further cloud. 'No. I'm sorry. I didn't realise it would be quite this bad.' He shook his head. 'I just… I just…' The words wouldn't form in his brain.

She reached up and touched his cheek. 'Finlay, it's fine. It's your home. It needs a bit of work.'

'A bit of work? Grace—how on earth can we stay here?'

She folded her arms and looked around. She flicked the edge of a dustsheet and sneezed again as the air clouded. 'It's like that film—you remember—when the spy comes back to the old Scottish mansion house he was brought up in.'

'Remember what happened to that house?'

She let out a laugh. 'Okay, let's go for another film. I could sing the Mary Poppins song as we cleaned up.'

'You honestly want to clean up?' He couldn't quite believe it.

'Why not?' It was quite ironic. There were no airs and graces around Grace Ellis. She took off her coat and started to roll up her sleeves.

She glanced around. 'Let's check out the kitchen. We have some things to put in the fridge.'

Finlay winced. If this was one of the sitting rooms he had no idea what the kitchen would look like.

But he was in for a surprise. The kitchen wasn't dusty at all. Grace ran her fingers along one of the worktops and looked at him in surprise. Then she started opening cupboards, followed by the larder and fridge.

'This place isn't so bad. Someone has kept it clean. Right enough, there isn't a single piece of food in this house. Just as well we brought the hamper.'

Something clicked in his brain. 'My mum. They did offer to look after the place and I said no.' He was almost ashamed to admit that. He walked around. 'But the main hall wasn't so dusty and in here has certainly been emptied and cleaned.' He gave a slow nod. 'All the other rooms have their doors closed. She hasn't gone into them. But the kitchen is open plan. She's only kept things tidy in here.'

Grace gave a nod. 'The surfaces just need a little wipe down.' She walked through a door off to the side then stuck her head back around. 'And there's enough cleaning products through here to clean this whole place a hundred times over.' She went to lift the hamper.

Finlay moved quickly. 'Slow down. Let me.' He picked up the hamper and then the cool box. She swung the door open on the fridge and started emptying the cool box straight into it. 'Why don't you find a cupboard to put some of the things from the hamper? Then we can get started on the main room.'

She was like a whirlwind. He had no idea what time it currently was but Grace seemed to have endless energy. He shook his head. 'I think we should look at the bedrooms.'

Her hands froze midway into the fridge. She dipped back and stared around the door at him. 'What?'

He shook his head and laughed. 'That didn't come out quite the way I meant it to. You must be tired. I'm tired. Let's put the food away, then go to the wing where I turned the heating on. The beds will all be stripped down. I'll need to find the sheets and bedding and make them up.'

She started restocking the fridge and looked amused. 'Do you have any idea where the bedding will be?'

He nodded. 'It's all vacuum-packed so I think it should be okay. I'm just worried the rooms will be as dusty as the sitting room.' He'd said rooms deliberately. He didn't want to make Grace uncomfortable.

Grace closed the fridge door. 'Okay, then, let's go.'

He flicked the lights on as they walked down the corridors. Some cobwebs hung from the light fittings. 'This place feels like the Haunted House at one of the theme parks.'

Grace shivered. He stopped walking. 'I'm sorry, did I scare you? I didn't mean to.'

She looked surprised. 'No, I'm not scared, silly, I'm cold.'

Of course. She'd taken her coat off and left it in the hall. The whole house was still bitterly cold. He opened the first door and gulped. It was every bit as bad as the sitting room. Grace instantly coughed.

'Let's try another,' he said.

So they did. The next room wasn't quite so bad. It only took him a few moments to realise why. He walked over to the fireplace. 'This room has a chimney—a real fire. There's still a chimney sweep who comes in once a year to clear all the chimneys. Between that—and the fact there's still some air circulating means it's not quite so bad.'

He walked over to a cupboard and pulled out some vacuum-packed bedding. Then paused. There was only one king-sized bed in here. He glanced between Grace and the bed. 'We can find another room.'

She raised her eyebrows. 'How many others in this wing have a fireplace?'

Realisation settled over him. 'Only this one.'

She sighed and held up her hands. 'How much energy do you have?' She stuck her hands on her hips. 'This place is still freezing. No one will be taking any clothes off.'

The way she was so matter-of-fact made him laugh out loud. He'd been a bit wary about saying something. He didn't want her to think he'd deliberately brought her up here with something in mind.

His stomach was flipping over and over. This had been his marital home. This room hadn't been the bedroom that he and Anna had shared—that was in another wing. But Grace was the first woman he'd ever brought to this house since Anna had died. All of a sudden he was in a bedroom, in his castle, with another woman, and he wasn't entirely sure how they'd got there.

Grace seemed unperturbed. She walked over to the curtains and gave them a shake. The little cloud of dust circulated around her like fairy dust from a film. She gave a sneeze and grabbed a chair. 'I'm going to take these down and throw them in the washing machine. If they come out okay, we can rehang them tomorrow.' She pointed to the fireplace. 'Why don't you see if you can light the fire? Once I've put these in the wash I'll make up the bed. If I don't get to sleep soon, I'll sleep standing up.'

She was already unhooking the curtains from their pole.

The uneasy feeling drifted away. She made things so easy. Things seemed to make sense around Grace. It was her manner.

He knelt down and checked the fireplace. It was clean and ready to be stocked. He knew exactly where the supplies were. It would only take a few minutes to collect them.

By the time he returned Grace had a smoky outline on her black jumper and jeans from the curtains. 'They're in the wash,' she said happily. 'But I think I'll need to get cleaned up once I've made the bed.'

She shook out the sheets and made up the bed in record time. It was bigger than the average king-size and Finlay tried not to think about how inviting it looked covered with the thick duvet, blankets and masses of pillows.

Grace put a hand on his shoulder as she wheeled her pull-along case behind her. 'You said the hot water would work?'

He nodded.

'Then I'm going to duck in the shower.'

He stood up quickly, brushing his hands. 'As soon as I light the fire I'll go and check out one of the other rooms.'

She shook her head again. 'Honestly, don't worry. I'm pretty sure we can sleep in the giant bed without either of us feeling compromised.' She gave him a smile, 'You've no idea how many layers I can wear.' She opened the door to the bathroom and dragged her case inside. A few seconds later he heard the shower start to run. She stuck her head back outside as he started trying to light the fire. 'But if you decided to go to the kitchen and make some tea I wouldn't object.' She frowned. 'Tea. We did bring tea, didn't we?'

He nodded as the fire sparked into life. 'Tea, milk and biscuits.' He arched his back, stretching out the knots from the long journey. 'Tea I think I can manage.'

Thank goodness he was tired. Thank goodness he was overwhelmed with stepping back inside the castle. If he hadn't been, he would have spent the whole time wondering how on earth he would manage to keep his distance from Grace while they were the only two people here. He shook his head as he headed to the kitchen. He should have thought about this beforehand. If he hadn't been able to resist kissing her under a lamp post in London, how on earth would he keep thoughts of touching her from his head now? He couldn't even think about that bare skin in the shower. No way.

By the time he came back Grace was sitting on the bed, her hair on top of her head, wrapped up in one of the giant duvets. She looked as if she had old-fashioned fleecy pyjamas on. He was pretty sure he was supposed to find them unappealing and unsexy.

Trouble was—he just didn't. Not when they were on Grace. He set the steaming-hot tea down on the bedside table along with some chocolate biscuits. She nodded towards the bathroom. 'I left the shower running for you. Figured you'd want to wash the dust off.' She leaned forward conspiratorially. 'Just don't tell the owner. I hear he keeps tabs on the water usage.'

He put his tea down next to hers. 'I think I can take him,' he said with a smile on his face.

In the dim light of the room all he could focus on was the warmth from her brown eyes. 'We'll see.' She picked up her tea and took a sip. 'Not bad.' She gave an approving nod. 'And just think, Alec didn't even give you written instructions.'

He laughed as he pulled his bag into the bathroom and closed the door behind him. It only took a few seconds to strip off his dusty clothes and step into the warm shower. Grace had left some shampoo and shower gel—both pink, both smelling of strawberries.

He started using them without thinking, let the water stream over his body along with distinctly female scent. His stomach started to flip-flop again.

She'd made things sound so casual. As if sharing a bed was no big deal.

And it wasn't—to most men.

It wasn't as if he hadn't shared a bed with a woman in the last five years. He had—if only for the briefest of moments.

But that hadn't actually been *sharing* a bed. That had been using a bed. Something else entirely. He hadn't slept next to another woman since Anna had died. He hadn't *woken up* with another woman.

That was what made him jittery. That was what was messing with his head.

He couldn't deny the attraction to Grace. His body thrummed around her. He couldn't pretend that it didn't. When he'd kissed her—he'd felt lost. As if time and space had just suspended all around them. His hands rubbed his head harder than they needed to, sending the shampoo over his face and eyes, assaulting his senses with the scent.

He leaned back against the bathroom tiles, adjusting the water to a cooler temperature. The house was still freezing. But the heat in this bathroom seemed ridiculously high. Steam had misted the mirror. It was kind of clawing at his throat, making it difficult to breathe.

He turned the dial on the shower once more; the water turned instantly icy, cooling every part of his body that had dared to think itself too hot. All breath left his body in shock as he turned the knob off.

He grabbed the already semi-wet towel and started drying himself vigorously. He didn't want to think that this was the same towel Grace had used to dry her silky soft skin. He didn't want to think that at all.

He glanced at his still-closed bag. Oh, no. He wasn't a pyjama kind of guy. Never had been. What on earth could he wear in bed with Grace?

He leaned against the other tiled wall and sighed. Boxers. That was all he usually wore. Maybe he should just stick to that because the room outside was so cold that any part of him that didn't behave might just drop off in the icy temperature. But he wouldn't be comfortable like that around Grace. He had a terrible feeling that in the weird space between almost sleeping and not quite he wouldn't have any control of his thoughts or body reactions. A suit of armour would probably help. Pity the castle didn't have any.

He rummaged through his bag and found a black T-shirt, clean boxers and then, stuck in a zip pocket, a pair of gym shorts. Baggy and mid-thigh-length. He'd obviously planned on visiting the hotel gym on his last trip and not quite managed it. He sent a silent prayer upwards. Thank goodness for being lazy.

He wiped down the mirror with the towel and brushed his teeth as his brain started whirring. What kind of pre-sleep conversation would he have with Grace? What if he snored? What if she snored? He couldn't remember ever feeling this nervous around a woman. It was like being fourteen years old again.

He ran his fingers through his damp hair as he refused to meet his own gaze. He was being ridiculous. He was tired. That was all. That, and being back in the house again, was reviving a whole host of natural memories.

It wasn't quite as hard as he'd thought it would be. Having Grace here certainly helped. Seeing the house so desolate and neglected-looking had been a shock. He'd left it too long. He knew that now.

But now he was here. A thought flicked through his brain. It must be after midnight by now. It must be Christmas Day. At the very least he'd have to wish Grace Merry Christmas and thank her for accompanying him. It was time to stop delaying. Time to realise his duties as a host.

He pulled open the door and was surprised by the warm air that met him. The fire had certainly taken hold. He held his breath.

All he could hear was the comfortable crackle of the fire. And something else.

The noise of deep, soft breaths. Grace was sleeping. Her hair had escaped the knot on top of her head and her dark curls were spread across the white pillowcase. Her pink flannel pyjamas were fastened unevenly, leaving a gap at the base of her pale throat.

She looked exhausted. She looked peaceful. Turned out he didn't need to worry about pre-sleep conversation at all.

He walked over next to her and picked up his cup of now lukewarm tea. She shifted a little as his shadow fell over her and he froze. His fingers itched to reach out and brush a strand of hair away from her face. But he couldn't. He didn't want to do anything to disturb her. Anything to make her feel uncomfortable.

He walked back around to the other side of the bed, sitting down carefully, cringing as the bed creaked. One quick slug of the tea was enough. He shouldn't have spent quite so long in the shower. He slid his legs under the cool duvet, his skin bristling a little. The pillows were soft, the mattress comfortable under his tired muscles. He pulled the duvet a little higher as he turned on his side to face Grace.

The bed was huge. There was plenty of space between them. There would be no reason to end up on the wrong side of the bed, or touch arms or legs accidentally. He leaned his head on his hand and watched the steady rise and fall of her chest for a few minutes.

Even fast asleep Grace was beautiful. Her lips plump and pink, her pale skin flawless. In the space of a few days she'd woken him up. Woken him up to the world he'd been sleepwalking through these past five years.

Part of him was grateful. Part of him was scared. He didn't know what any of this meant. 'Merry Christmas, Grace,' he whispered as he laid his head on the pillow and went to sleep.

CHAPTER EIGHT

GRACE'S EYES FLICKERED OPEN. It took a few seconds for her to remember where she was. The bed was so comfortable. Her fingers and nose were a little chilled but everything else that was under the covers was cosy.

Her body stiffened. She'd fallen asleep last night while Finlay had been in the shower. She'd tried to stay awake, but as soon as she'd finished her tea and the heat from the fire had started permeating across the room her eyelids had grown so heavy that she couldn't keep them open a second longer.

Her eyes flitted around the room. She'd taken the curtains down last night. She'd need to hang them back up and let them dry. Now the pale light of day was filtering through the windows she could see the pale creams and blue of the room. It was much bigger than a normal bedroom, but the size didn't hide the most important aspect.

It was exquisite. Exactly the type of room you'd expect in a castle. The bed, tables and furniture were traditional and elegant. Cornicing on the ceiling and a dado rail around the middle of the room, with a glass chandelier hanging in the middle of the room. The two chairs next to the bed were French-style, Louis XVI, ornate with the thick padded seats covered in pale blue patterned fabric. Was it possible the rest of the castle was this beautiful?

Between the dim light last night and the clouds of dust she couldn't remember the details of the sitting room.

Now, she was conscious of the heavy breathing next to her. She turned her head just a little, scared to shift in the bed in case she woke him.

Finlay Armstrong's muscular shoulders and arms were above the duvet cover. She had a prime view. All of a sudden her mouth felt oddly dry. He was sleeping. For the first time ever, Finlay looked totally relaxed. There were no lines on his face. None at all. All the usual little stress lines around his forehead and eyes had completely vanished.

He almost looked like a different person. Finlay had always been handsome. But there was always some kind of barrier around him, some protective shield that created tension and pressure. This was the most relaxed she'd ever seen him.

His jaw was shadowed with stubble. Her eyes followed the definition of his forearms and biceps, leading up to his shoulders and muscled chest. He shifted and the duvet moved again. Crumpled next to his shoulder looked like a black T-shirt. Did he have anything else on under these covers?

She squirmed under the bedclothes. Her flannel pyjamas were uncomfortably warm. The heating had obviously kicked in overnight. She slid one foot out of bed then realised she hadn't brought any slippers. The carpet was cool. She'd need to find some socks.

How did she get out of bed without waking him?

Her phone beeped. Except it wasn't really a beep. The jangling continued to echo around the room.

Finlay's eyelids flickered open and he stretched his arms out, one hand brushing her hair.

Her heartbeat flickered against her chest as he turned his head towards her and fixed on her with his sleepy blue eyes. 'Morning,' he whispered.

'Morning,' she replied automatically. She felt kind of frozen—even though one of her legs was currently dangling out of the bed.

The edges of his lips turned upwards as the phone tune kept going. 'Or should I say Merry Christmas?'

It was like warm melted chocolate spreading over her heart. She'd had so many images in her head about this Christmas—all of them focusing on the fact she'd be alone.

This was the absolute last thing she'd expected to happen. Waking up in bed next to Finlay Armstrong in a castle in Scotland would never have found a way into her wildest imagination. She almost wanted to pinch herself to check she was actually here.

She couldn't help but smile. 'Merry Christmas, Finlay,' she said in a voice that squeaked more than she wanted it to.

He stretched again and pushed the covers back. If she'd been prepared—and if she'd been polite—she wouldn't have been caught staring at his abs and chest muscles as he jumped up in a pair of shorts and reached over for his T-shirt. He slid it easily over his head. Giving her a smile as she watched every movement. 'I take it the heating's kicked in at least. Not as warm as I might have hoped. The fire in here last night made me too warm. We'll need to try and find a happy medium.'

She swung her leg out of bed and stopped dead. She was facing the window—the one she'd removed the dusty curtains from last night. For as far as the eye could see there was thick white snow. It clung to every bump of the terrain. Every tree. Every fence. Every path. She stood up and moved automatically to the window. 'Oh, wow,' was all that came out.

She felt his presence at her shoulder and tried not to think about the fact there wasn't much between her and those taut muscles. 'You wanted snow,' he said quietly.

She nodded. 'Yes. I did.' She turned her head towards him. 'Just how wet are we going to get?'

He raised his eyebrows. 'How wet do you want to get?'

The air was rich with innuendo. She could play this either way. But she couldn't forget how they'd ended up here. She just wasn't sure where she was with Finlay. All she knew was that the more those deep blue eyes looked at her, the more lost she felt.

'It's snow angels all the way,' she said safely. 'But how about we find the Christmas decorations first?'

He nodded. 'Let's get some breakfast. Then, I think I might have a turkey to stick in the oven before we hit the hills. I know where the Christmas decorations are stored—but I've no idea what state they're in.'

Grace shrugged her shoulders. 'No matter. I'd just like to have Christmas decorations up when we eat dinner tonight. We'll need to clean up the sitting room too.'

He hesitated. 'Are you sure? This isn't a busman's holiday, you know. Just because it's the day job, doesn't mean that I expect you to help clean up around here.' He stuck his hands on his hips as he looked at the white view. 'I should probably get a company in.'

Grace shook her head. 'You can do that after Christmas—for the rest of the house. The kitchen is fine. I can rehang the curtains in here, and I'm sure between us we can sort out the other two rooms. It's just a bit of dust.'

It was more than a bit of dust. They both knew that. But Grace was determined to show Finlay that she wasn't a princess. Last night had been a bit of a dream. Ending up at a castle made her seem like a princess. But emotions ran deep.

This was her first Christmas without her grandmother. It was always going to be tough. But Finlay had already made it a bit easier. The change of scenery. The fact that someone had actually thought about her, and considered her, meant a lot.

Today would be hard. Every Christmas aroma would bring back memories of her gran. She'd worked so hard up until now to try and push the reality of today into a place there wasn't time to think about.

Past Christmases with her gran had also been a panacea for something else. It didn't really matter what age you were—being ignored by your mother would always cut deep.

It didn't matter that she'd reached adulthood intact and totally loved by her grandmother. The big gaping hole was always there. She could never escape the fact her mother had all but abandoned her to make a new life for herself. What kind of person did that?

In a way, it had strengthened the bond between her and her grandmother. Both of them trying to replace what the other had lost. But it also made it hard for her to form new relationships with other people. Grace struggled to make friends easily, because she struggled to trust. The girls from Maids in Chelsea were the closest friends she'd ever made. As for men? It was easy to blame her gran's illness and juggling jobs to explain why she'd never had a truly lasting relationship. She could just say it was down to poor taste in men. But the truth was, she'd always found it hard to trust anyone, to believe that someone would love her enough not to abandon her. It was easier to keep her feelings cocooned. At least then they were safe.

But now? Her biggest problem was that every second she was around Finlay she became a little bit more attached. Saw another side of him that she liked, that she admired, that she might even love a little. But he was her boss. They lived completely different lives. Her heart didn't even know where to start with feelings like these.

So why had they ended up here together?

Finlay's fingers intertwined with hers as they looked at the snow together. The buzz was instant, straight up her arm to her heart. There was so much she could say right now. So many tumbling thoughts.

'Let's get dressed,' said Finlay as he turned and walked away.

Grace folded her arms and smiled out at the untouched snow. This Christmas was shaping up to be completely different from what she'd ever imagined.

Her phone beeped and she pulled it from her bag. Sophie.

Where are you? I dropped by the flat.

Grace pressed buttons quickly, knowing exactly the response she'd get.

With my boss. In Scotland.

She smiled, added a quick, See you all at the Snowflake Ball, and tucked the phone into her bag, knowing it would probably buzz for the rest of the day.

It was like having someone with boundless energy next to you all day. Grace didn't seem to know how to sit down. Five minutes at breakfast was her record. After that, she'd rehung the curtains, then started to power around the dining room.

Meanwhile he'd been in the place he clearly wasn't destined for.

Finlay frowned at the instructions. They must have got a little wet in his pocket. They were a bit smudged. He'd found a suitable tray for the turkey and followed Alec's instructions. But this basting thing looked complicated. Would he even get to leave the kitchen at all today?

Grace appeared with a smudge on her nose, laughing, watching him squint at the instructions. 'How's the turkey?' She smiled with a hand on her hip.

He shook his head. It was too, too tempting. His thumb was up wiping the smudge from her nose instantly, the rest of his hand touching the bottom of her chin.

Whatever she'd opened her mouth to say next had been lost. She just stared at him with those big brown eyes. For a second, he couldn't breathe. He couldn't inhale.

Every thought in his head was about kissing her. Tasting those lips. Running his fingers through her soft hair, tied back with a pink ribbon. She'd changed into a soft pink knit jumper and blue figure-hugging jeans. Her face was make-up-free, but, although she was as beautiful as ever, today she looked different. She looked happy. She was relaxed.

He could almost sense a peaceful aura buzzing around her. His stomach turned over. He'd done the right thing. He'd done the right thing bringing Grace here—both for him, and for her.

It was as if she was caught in the same glow that he was. 'How's your Christmas going?' she whispered.

He couldn't tear his gaze away. 'Better than I could have hoped for.'

She put a hand over his at the side of the turkey tray. 'Then let's get this old girl in the oven. I've found the Christmas decorations, but I couldn't find the tree.'

'Oh.'

Her hand was still on his. 'What do you mean, oh?'

He picked up the tray—this turkey was heavier than it looked—and slid the tray into the oven. He picked up the other items that Alec had given them, onion, stuffing and chipolatas, and pushed them back in the fridge. 'We can put them in later.'

He closed the oven door with a bang and checked the

temperature. Grace folded her arms and leaned against the countertop. Finlay looked around the room for his navy jumper. It only took a moment to find it and pull it on. He glanced at Grace's feet. 'Do you have other boots?'

'Why?'

He walked around her and held the door to the main hall open. 'Because I don't have an artificial tree. I've never used one at Drumegan Castle.' He gestured with his hand. 'I've got a whole wood out there full of pine trees. All we need to do is go and get one.'

Her eyes widened. Even from this far he could see the enthusiasm. 'Really, you're going to cut down a real Christmas tree?'

He nodded. 'Snow angels, anyone?'

Her eyes sparkled. 'I'll race you!'

In the end she hadn't worn the very expensive pink winter coat that Finlay had bought her. He'd found old waterproof jackets in the cupboard and they'd worn them on their hike across the grounds, complete with wheelbarrow and electric saw.

'I'm kind of disappointed,' she teased as he wheeled it towards the wood.

'Why?' He looked surprised.

Her feet were heavy in the snow. It really was deep here. Finlay hadn't been kidding. She gave him a teasing smile. 'I kind of hoped you'd just stomp over here with an axe, cut down the tree then throw it over your shoulder and bring it back to the castle.'

He let out a laugh. 'Really? Just like that?' He stopped wheeling, obviously trying to catch his breath just at the edge of the wood. 'Well, I guess I could do that if you want.' He pointed to a tiny tree just at the front of the wood. It was about two feet tall. 'But this would be our Christmas tree. What do you think?'

She sidled up next to him. It had started to snow again and the snow was collecting on her shoulders with a few flakes on her cheeks. 'Finlay Armstrong, you know how much I love Christmas, don't you?'

She'd tilted her chin towards him. All he had to do was bend down a little.

He couldn't help the smile that automatically appeared. Grace's enthusiasm was infectious. 'Grace Ellis, I might have noticed that about you.'

'You did?' She blinked, snowflakes landing on her thick lashes.

His hand naturally went around her waist, pulling her closer. Her hands slid up the front of his chest. 'I might have. So, I want you to look around the wood and find your perfect Christmas tree. When you find it, it's all yours.'

She was watching him carefully. 'All mine, I like the sound of that.'

He licked his lips. A few weeks ago, if someone had told him he'd be standing in the castle grounds on Christmas Day, waiting to cut down a tree with a beautiful woman in his arms, he would have thought they were crazy.

That would never, ever happen for him again.

And yet…he was here. With Grace. And for the first time in years he actually felt happy. He wasn't imagining this. This was real. There was a real connection between them.

She gave her hand a little thump against his chest and looked upwards. 'Snow's getting heavier.' She winked at him. 'It must have heard I was here. Snow angels waiting. Let's find this tree, Finlay. We have a date in the snow.'

A date in the snow.

He knew exactly what she meant and the words were casual. A date. Hadn't they already had a few dates? Had he been dating without really knowing it?

She walked ahead and gave a shout a few minutes later.

Then she gave a squeal. He darted through the trees. She was jumping up and down, clapping her hands together. 'This is it. This is the tree. It's perfect. Don't you think? It will look gorgeous in the sitting room.'

She was infectious, truly infectious. She was right. She'd picked a perfect tree. Immaculately shaped, even branches and just the right height. 'It's not quite perfect,' he said as he stepped forward.

'It's not?' She leaned back a little, looking up as if she was trying to spot the flaw.

'No,' he said as he reached the tree and stretched his hand through the branches to catch hold of the trunk. 'Too much snow.'

He started shaking the tree as she screamed, covering them both in the tumble of snow from the branches. It fell thick and fast, sliding down his neck and making him shiver.

Grace fell backwards with a shriek, laughing as she fell.

She lay there for a few seconds, trying to catch her breath. He pulled his hand back and stepped over her. 'Okay down there?'

She was lying looking up at the sky. 'No,' she said firmly. 'I've been hoodwinked by a crazy Scots man.' She held her hand up towards him.

He grabbed it, steeling himself to pull her upwards. But Grace was too quick for him. She gave him an almighty wrench, yanking him downwards to her and the heavy snow.

He landed with a splat, face first in the snow next to her, only part of his body on hers.

Her deep, throaty laugh echoed through the wood. Once she started, she couldn't stop.

He sucked in a breath and instead sucked in a mouthful of snow, making him snort and choke. He tried to get up on his knees to clear his mouth, but Grace grabbed hold of his arm. 'Oh, no, you don't.' She was still laughing.

He spluttered again, this time getting rid of snow and starting to laugh himself. She'd got him. She'd got him good.

'You promised me something,' she said.

The laughing had stopped and she sounded deadly serious. He lay down next to her in the snow. 'Okay, then. What did I promise?'

She reached over and touched the side of his cheek. It was the tenderest of touches. 'You promised me snow angels,' she whispered. 'And I plan on collecting.'

He only had to move forward a couple of inches. Maybe she was talking about snow angels. But the heat between them had been rising all day; it was a wonder they hadn't melted all the snow around them.

He captured her sweet lips in his. Her cheeks were cold. The hat she'd pulled from her pocket earlier had landed on the snow, letting her hair fan out in the snow—just as it had on the pillow last night. That memory sparked a rush of blood around his body.

He pulled his hand from his gloves and tangled it through her hair. Her other hand caught around the back of his neck, melding her body next to his. It didn't matter that the ground was freezing and snow was getting in places it just shouldn't. He didn't care about anything other than the connection to this woman.

Somewhere deep inside him a little spark was smouldering. Willing itself to burn brighter and harder.

Grace responded to every movement, every touch, matching him step by step. He didn't have any doubt the feelings were mutual. He was surprised when she slowly pulled back and put one arm against his chest. She was smiling though.

'Parts of me I didn't know could get wet, are wet.' She

sighed. 'I guess this would be the right time to collect on the snow angels.'

He laughed and nodded. Kissing lying in the snow wasn't an ideal arrangement. He knew that. He just didn't care about the wet clothes.

He looked over at the piece of ground a little away from the trees. 'To make snow angels, we need to do it where there are no other marks. Let's go over there.'

He took her arm and pulled her up. They'd only walked a few steps when she stopped dead. 'Look!'

'What?' He looked around near the trees and bush she was pointing to.

'Holly,' breathed Grace. 'It's holly.'

She was right; the jaggy green leaves and red berries were poking out from underneath the snow. She grabbed hold of his arm. 'Can you cut some? Wouldn't it be gorgeous to have some fresh holly in the house?'

There it was again. That infectious enthusiasm. If she could bottle it and sell it she could be a millionaire. He put his arm around her waist. 'Snow angels first, then the tree, then the holly. You could freeze out here.'

She nodded and shivered. 'I think I already am.'

He took her hand and led her across the snow, turning around to face the castle. 'How about here?'

She nodded as she looked at their trail of footprints in the snow.

'Then let's do it.' Finlay grinned as he held out his arms and fell backwards in the snow, landing with a thud. *'Oof!'*

Grace looked a bit shocked, then joined in, turning to face the castle, holding out her arms and falling backwards. Her thud wasn't nearly as loud.

They lay there for a few seconds. The clear blue sky above them, the white-covered world all around them, with the majestic grey castle standing like a master of all it surveyed.

'It's just beautiful here,' breathed Grace.

Finlay wasn't thinking about the cold. His eyes were running over the hundreds of years old building he'd neglected for the last five years. It had stood the test of time, again and again. It had been here before him. And it would still be standing long after he had gone. 'Yes, yes, it is,' he agreed.

Pieces were starting to fall into place for him. The brickwork at one of the turrets looked as if it needed work. There were a few misaligned tiles on one part of the roof—probably the result of one of Scotland's storms. All things that could be easily mended.

The cold was soaking in through his jacket and jeans. All things could be mended. It just depended on whether you were willing to do the repairs.

'Hey? Are you going?'

He smiled again. Grace was the best leveller in the world. 'Yes, let's go.'

They yelled and shouted as they moved their arms up and down in the heavy snow. Grace started singing Christmas songs at the top of her voice.

He hadn't felt this happy in such a long time. He hadn't felt this free in such a long time. He turned his head and watched her singing to the sky with a huge smile on her face—this was all because of Grace. He just couldn't deny it.

When she finally stopped singing they lay in the snow for a few seconds.

'Thanks, Grace.'

She looked surprised. 'For what?'

He held up one damp arm. 'For this. For helping me come back here. For making something that should be hard feel as if I was meant to do it. I was meant to be here.'

She rolled over in the snow onto her stomach, facing

him. 'That's because I think you were, Finlay. Maybe it was just time.'

He nodded in agreement. 'Maybe it was.'

She pushed herself up onto her knees. 'Thank you too.'

'What for?'

She smiled. 'For making a Christmas that I thought I was going to hate, into something else entirely. Snow? A castle? What more could a girl ask for?' She shook some snow off her jacket. 'Except pneumonia, of course.'

He pushed himself up. 'You're right. Let's go. The tree will only take a few minutes to cut down and we can grab some holly along the way.'

From the second they'd got back in the castle and showered and changed, things had seemed different. This time, Grace had put on the only dress she'd brought. It was black with a few sparkles. She'd always liked dressing up on Christmas Day and she was hoping Finlay would appreciate the effort. There hadn't been time to do anything but dry her hair so she left it in waves tied back with the same pink ribbon as earlier. Finlay was in the kitchen, muttering under his breath as he basted the turkey—again.

She nudged him as she watched. 'What do you say we make this easy?'

'How?'

'That tray of roast potatoes, stuffing and chipolatas? Just throw them in next to the turkey.'

'You think that will work?'

She shrugged. 'Why not? Let's put the Christmas pudding on to steam. We might as well. We have a tree to decorate.'

Something flashed behind his eyes. She wasn't sure what, because it disappeared almost as soon as it appeared. He nodded. 'Yes, we do, don't we? Okay, then.' He threw the rest of the food into the turkey tray. 'At least if nothing else works, we still have the soup. It's stored in the fridge. At least it's safe.'

Grace put a pan of water on to boil and arranged the steamer on top with the small muslin-wrapped Christmas puddings. 'All done.'

She'd left the cardboard boxes full of decorations in the sitting room. Finlay had already arranged the Christmas tree on the stand—just waiting to be decorated—and lit the fire to try and warm the room some more.

As they walked through to the room together she could sense something about Finlay. A reluctance. A worry.

The aromas around her were stirring up a whole host of memories. She was so used to making Christmas dinner with her grandmother. While the Christmas pudding was steaming they normally dug out some old board games and played them together.

It was hard not to have her around. It was hard to face the first Christmas without her. Her hand went automatically to her eyes and brushed a tear away. She wanted to enjoy this Christmas. She wanted to know that she could still love her favourite time of year without the person she usually spent it with.

What scared her most was how much she was beginning to feel about the man she was secluded with in this castle. That one kiss had stirred up so many hidden emotions inside her. Apart from a dusty castle, there were no other distractions here.

It was just him. And her.

It was difficult to ignore how he made her feel. It was difficult to fight against a build-up of emotions in an enclosed space.

She rummaged through the box and heard a little tinkle of bells. It reminded her of an old film she'd watched with her grandmother. She looked upwards and smiled. It didn't make her feel sad; instead a little warmth spread through her. 'Love you, Gran,' she murmured.

She pulled a strand of tinsel from one of the boxes, bright pink, and wrapped it around her neck. Then, she flicked the switch on the radio. The words of *Let it Snow* filled the room..

She turned to face him and held up her hands. 'Think they knew where we were?'

'Could be.' His voice seemed a little more serious than before; his eyes were fixed on the cardboard boxes.

She moved over next to him and put her hands on his chest. He'd changed into a long-sleeved black shirt, open at the neck, and well-cut black trousers. It would be easy to spend most of the day staring at his muscular thighs and tight backside. 'We don't have to do this, Finlay.'

He shook his head. 'No, we do. *I* do.' She stood back and let him open the flaps of the first box and start lifting out the decorations.

They were all delicately wrapped in tissue paper. He unwrapped one after the other. She could see the expression on his face. Each one brought back a different memory. She put her hand over his. 'If I was at home right now, I'd be feeling exactly the same way,' she said reassuringly. 'Some of the decorations my gran and I have had for years. Some of them we made together. There were several I just couldn't hang this year. I get it. I do.'

His grateful blue eyes met hers. There was pain in them, but there was something else too. A glimpse of relief.

His hands seemed steady as he handed each one to her to hang. Occasionally he gave a little nod. 'That one was from Germany. This one from New York.'

Her stomach twisted a little. She felt like Scrooge being visited by the ghost of Christmas past. All of these memories were wrapped around Anna. She didn't expect him to forget about his dead wife. But she needed to be sure that when he kissed her, when he touched her, he wasn't thinking of someone else. She wasn't a replacement. She wouldn't ever want to be. Lots of his actions made her think he was ready to move on. But this, this was eating him up. Her stomach flipped over. She'd brought something, lifted something on instinct in the penthouse in London. Maybe it hadn't been such a good idea after all.

She looked in the box and gave him a smile. 'Hey, I haven't found anything purple yet. Isn't there anything that will match our decorations down in London?'

He gave her a smile and shook his head. 'There's nothing in those boxes. But I did think about purple before we left. Give me a second.'

His footsteps echoed down the hall and she looked around. The fire was flickering merrily, giving off a distinctive heat. The smell of the turkey and Christmas pudding was drifting across the main hall towards them. Between that, and the Christmas tree, this place really did have the aroma and feel of Christmas.

Finlay came back holding a string of Christmas lights—the same ones they'd used in the hotel. Grace gasped. 'You brought purple lights?'

He nodded. 'I don't even know. I didn't think I'd planned to come here. But I know the lights we used to have here don't work any more. I liked the purple lights from the hotel so I brought some along.'

He started to wind them around the tree. It was almost finished. The lights should have gone on first, but Finlay managed to wrap them around the tinsel and hanging decorations without any problem. When he'd finished he flicked the switch to light up the room.

It had grown steadily darker outside, now the room was only lit with the orange crackling fire and the purple glowing lights. Together with the smells of Christmas it was almost as if some Christmas spirit had been breathed back into Drumegan Castle.

Grace felt her heart flutter. There was one last thing she had to do. She was doing it for the right reasons. Even if she did have a tiny bit of selfishness there too. She needed to know where Finlay was. She needed to know how ready he was.

'I brought something too. Give me a minute.'

She practically ran along the hall, finding the white tissue paper and bringing the item back. Finlay was standing looking around the room. She couldn't quite read the expression on his face.

So, she took a deep breath and held out the item with a trembling hand.

It was now, or never. Time to find out what the future might hold.

Finlay's breath was caught somewhere in his throat. He didn't need to unwrap the item to know what it was.

Grace's hand was shaking. He could see that. He reached up and put his hand under hers, taking his other hand to pull back the delicate tissue paper.

'You brought this?'

She nodded. It wasn't just her hand that was shaking. Her voice was too. 'I thought it might be important. I thought it might be important for you.'

He pulled back the tissue paper on the white ceramic Christmas angel. This time when he looked at it, he didn't feel despair and angst. He didn't feel anger and regret. He looked into the eyes of the woman that was holding it. It was almost as if she were holding her heart in her hand right now.

He knew exactly how she felt.

Grace had brought this. Even though she'd been feeling lonely and sad this Christmas she'd still thought of him.

He could see how vulnerable she was right now. It was written all over her face. He reached up and touched her cheek. A sense of peace washed over him.

Anna. She was here with him. He could almost feel her smiling down on him. It was as if a little part of him unravelled. Anna had made him promise he'd move on. He'd find love again.

He'd locked that memory away because he'd never imagined it possible.

But he'd never imagined Grace.

Did she know how gorgeous she looked in that black dress that hugged her curves and skimmed out around her hips?

He lifted the white ceramic angel and clasped Grace's hand as they walked over to the tree together. As he lifted the angel to hang it from the top of the tree there was the sound of fireworks outside. Bright, colourful, sparkling fireworks lighting up the dark Christmas night sky.

Everything about this just felt right. He reached up and gave the pink ribbon holding Grace's hair back a little tug. As it came away in his hand he rearranged her hair, letting the loose curls tumble all around her face. 'You always tie it back. I like it best like this,' he said. 'While you're in the snow, and while you're lying in bed.'

Grace's eyes were glistening. This time when she smiled the warmth reached all the way into her brown eyes. Her sadness was gone. Banished. 'We haven't sorted out our sleeping arrangements for tonight,' she said huskily. 'I think we forgot to clean the other bedroom.'

He pulled her closer. 'I think we did. But I've got another idea.'

She tilted her chin up towards him. 'What is it?'

He nodded towards the fire and rug in front of it. 'I was thinking of a picnic. A Christmas picnic with a mishmash of turkey, stuffing, potatoes, chipolatas and Christmas pudding, all in front of our real fire.'

She licked her bottom lip. 'Sounds good to me. In fact, it sounds perfect. Do we have any wine? Or any champagne?'

He lowered his head, his lips brushing against the soft delicate skin at the bottom of her neck. 'I think we might have brought some with us.'

She laughed, her fingers reaching for his chin and bringing it up next to hers. She met his lips with hers. 'How about you grab the food and champagne and I grab us a blanket?'

He didn't want to let her out of his grasp. Not when he could feel all her curves against his. 'How quick can you be?'

She winked. 'Quicker than you. Just grab an oven glove and bring the whole tray and some knives and forks.' She stood on her tiptoes and whispered in his ear. 'Last one back pays a forfeit.'

'What will that be?'

She raised her eyebrows as she walked backwards to the door. 'You'll find out, slowcoach.'

He loved that she was teasing him. He'd already decided she could win. 'Oh, and, Grace?'

She spun around at the door. 'Yes?'

He winked at her as his mind went directly to other places. 'Forget the flannel pyjamas. You won't be needing them.'

CHAPTER NINE

THIS TIME WHEN she woke up in the castle, underneath was hard and uncomfortable. The arms around her were warm and reassuring, as was the feel of Finlay at her back. His soft breathing against her neck and feel of his heartbeat against her shoulder sent waves of heat throughout her body.

She couldn't help the soft little moan that escaped her lips. Neither could Finlay; she smiled as she recognised the instantaneous effect it had on him too.

'How do you feel about a Boxing Day excursion?' he murmured in her ear.

She leaned back further into him, relishing the bare skin against hers. 'What do you mean?'

He cleared his throat. 'I'd told my mum, dad and sister I would visit today, remember? How do feel about coming along?'

She turned onto her back so she could face him. 'You want me to meet your mum and dad?' The tiny hairs on her arms stood on end. Last night had been magical. Last night had felt like a dream. She'd never, ever experienced a connection like that. For Grace, it had felt like coming home to the place she'd always meant to be.

Nothing had ever seemed as right to her. But she was worried about what it meant to Finlay. His inviting her to meet his mum and dad today was sending a million reassuring *go faster* signals through her body.

She snaked her arms around his neck. 'I'd love to meet your mum and dad. And your sister. Do you think they'll be okay about meeting me?'

He gave a gentle laugh. 'Oh, I think my mum will measure you for a pair of family slippers.' He dropped a kiss on her lips. 'Don't worry, my family will love you.'

It was easy to respond to his kisses. Even though her brain was focusing on the family-loving-her part. Everything about this Christmas was turning out to be perfect.

The expression on his mother's face when she opened the door was priceless. She flung her arms around his neck while the whole time she stared at Grace.

'This is Grace,' he said quickly as he slid his hand into hers for reassurance. 'We met at work and she came up for Christmas at the castle with me.'

His mother's chin bounced off the floor. 'Fraser!' she shouted at the top of her voice. 'Aileen!' He imagined his father pushing himself out of his chair at the pitch of his mum's voice. 'You spent yesterday at the castle? Why? You could have come here.'

He glanced at Grace and gave her a smile. Yesterday had been better than he could ever have imagined. Nothing could have matched that. He edged around his mother, who was still standing in the doorway in shock. 'You knew I was coming today. That seemed enough.'

His father walked through from the living room and only took a few seconds to hide his shock. He greeted Finlay, then Grace with a huge bear hug. He wasn't even discreet about the whisper in Grace's ear. 'Watch out for Aileen, she's pregnant, cranky and will ask a million questions.'

For Grace it was a wonderful day. The love between the family members was clear. It reminded her of the relationship she'd shared with her grandmother. Aileen didn't hide in the least the fact she was quizzing Grace. But it was all good-natured.

The family shot occasional glances between each other. But all of them were of warmth, of relief. It was obvious they were delighted that Finlay had brought someone to meet them. They obviously wanted him to be happy. Anna was mentioned on occasion. But it wasn't like a trip down memory lane. It was only ever in passing, in an occasional sentence. And she was glad; she didn't want them to tiptoe around her. Not if there was any chance that this relationship could go somewhere.

The board games were fiercely competitive. She paired up with Finlay's dad and managed to trounce him on more than one occasion. When it got late, Finlay's mum, Fran, gave her a little nod, gesturing her through to the kitchen where she was making a pot of tea. 'I've made up Finlay's room for you both. No need to go back to the castle. We usually drink tea, then move on to wine or port and some Christmas cake.'

Grace smiled. She liked the way Fran said it. It was like a warm welcome blanket. Letting her know she was welcome to stay, as well as introducing their family traditions. She picked up the tray with the teapot and cups. 'Thanks, Fran, will I just take these through?'

Fran picked up the port bottle and tray with Christmas and Madeira cake and gave Grace a nudge. 'Let's go.'

Finlay met her at the door; he opened his mouth to speak but his mother cut him off.

'I was just letting Grace know the sleeping arrangements. Now, we're going to have a drink.' She raised her eyebrows at Finlay. 'I believe there was some cheating going on at that last game. I mean to get my revenge.'

Finlay slung his arm around Grace's shoulder. 'Are you okay with this?'

She knocked him with her hip as she smiled back. 'Oh, I'm fine. I mean to defend my winner's crown by all means necessary.' She leaned forward and laughed. 'Brace yourself, Mr Armstrong. You haven't even seen my winning streak yet.'

Firsts. These last few days had been full of them.

It woke him in the middle of the night.

First time since Anna had died that he'd allowed the hotel to be decorated. First time he'd brought someone else to the castle. First time he'd kissed another woman and actually *felt* something. First time he'd introduced his family to someone. First time in five years he'd actually enjoyed a Christmas instead of working straight through.

First time he'd woken up in his mother's house with someone who wasn't his wife.

What was completely obvious was how much his family had relished having Grace there. He could almost see the relief flooding from his mum and dad that he might actually have met someone, and he might actually be ready to move on.

He could hear her steady breathing next to him. But instead of feeling soothed, instead of wanting to embrace the idea of listening to this time after time, he felt an undeniable wave of panic.

They headed back to London today. Reality was hitting. How on earth would things be when they got back to the real world?

He worked goodness knew how many hours a week. He spent most months ping-ponging around the world between various hotels. There was no way he had time for a relationship.

It was as if a cold breeze swept over his skin.

Guilt was creeping in around the edges of his brain. He'd brought another woman to Drumegan Castle and slept with her there. He'd let Grace decorate, feel at home, help clean up and make snow angels in the ground. Most of the time he'd spent with Grace at Drumegan he'd enjoyed. He'd only thought of Anna in fleeting moments. And Grace had been the biggest instigator of that when she'd brought out the ceramic angel. His last physical link to Anna.

The woman that he should have been thinking of. Not Grace.

He shivered as her warm eyes flickered open next to him. 'Morning.' Her sexy smile sent pulses through his body and he pushed the duvet back and stood up quickly.

'Morning. I've got some work to do. Some business calls to make. I might be a few hours. I'm sure my mum will fix you some breakfast.' He was slipping on his jeans and pulling a T-shirt over his head as he spoke. Grace sat upright in the bed, her mussed-up hair all around her face. She looked confused—and a little hurt. 'Oh, okay. No problem. I'm sure I can sort myself out.'

There was no excuse. None. But he couldn't help it. His head was so mixed up he just needed some space.

And that was easy. Under the fake guise of work his mum, dad and sister were delighted to entertain Grace for the next few hours. Right up until they were ready to head back to the helipad at the castle.

His mother's bear hug nearly crushed him. 'It's been so good to see you, honey. She's fabulous. I love her. Bring her back soon.'

His hand gripped the steering wheel the whole way back to Drumegan Castle's helipad. All of a sudden he didn't feel ready for this. It seemed rushed. It had come out of nowhere. Could he really trust his feelings right now, when he'd spent the last five years shut off?

He couldn't help the way he was withdrawing. It seemed like the right thing to do.

'I think I should be honest, Grace. The past few days

have been wonderful. But up here—in Scotland, staying in the castle—this isn't the real world. I'm sorry. I think I made a mistake asking you up here. I knew how you were feeling about Christmas, and I was dreading coming up here again, and I think I might have given you the wrong idea. I'm just not ready for another relationship. Not yet, anyway. I'm not going to be able to give you what you want, Grace, or what you deserve. You should have a partner who loves only you, who wants to settle down and can commit time and energy to your family. I'm sorry, but I'm just not that person.'

She'd stopped noticing the whirring of the helicopter blades. All she could hear right now was the quiet voice next to her. It was almost as if he was speaking in hushed tones so she'd have to lean closer to hear. But the truth was, these were words she'd never wanted to hear.

This morning had been awkward. This afternoon had been worse. She'd almost been relieved when they'd said their goodbyes to Finlay's lovely family and driven back to the helipad at the castle.

She hadn't been able to ask Finlay why he was on edge. And now that made her angry. She'd been close enough to get naked and make love to him, but she didn't feel secure enough to ask what was wrong. Now, after giving her a Christmas she could only have dreamed of, he was unceremoniously dumping her. And he wasn't even doing it that well. He might have waited until they'd landed at The Armstrong. At least then she could have walked straight down the stairs and into the bar.

She tried to push all the angry thoughts aside. Finlay looked terrible. He was pale and his hands were constantly twitching on his lap. He wasn't the cool, remote man she'd first met. But he wasn't the dashing businessman either. Who was it she'd actually fallen in love with?

Her heart stuttered. That was it. That was why those few words felt as if they were wrenching her stomach inside out. Slowly but surely over the last few days Finlay Armstrong had stolen piece after piece of her heart. From that first moment on the roof of The Armstrong, from that tiny stroke of her cheek. From the shopping trip for the decorations, the drinks at the staff party and that first kiss under the lamppost.

He'd recognised her aching and lonely soul and embraced it. She'd given him space. She'd understood visiting Drumegan Castle was hard. But she'd felt as if they'd stood shoulder to shoulder the whole way. When they'd made love on Christmas Day, and he'd taken her to meet his family on Boxing Day, everything had just seemed to be surrounded in pink clouds.

But the storm had swept in. Why? What on earth had she done wrong?

She nervously licked her lips. The last few days had given her something else. A confidence she'd never felt before. She'd had a glimmer of a job that she might love. She'd found something she enjoyed and could be good at. It was a path she wanted to explore.

But she'd wanted Finlay to walk that path alongside her.

She lifted her chin and looked at him. Losing her gran had taught her one thing: love was worth reaching for and holding onto. She deserved love. She deserved to find happiness. She couldn't accept anything less.

It was so hard not to reach for his hand. She took a deep breath. 'I understand this Christmas has been hard, Finlay—I do. I understand that visiting the castle took courage. And it must have whipped up a whole host of memories that maybe you'd forgotten. But I have to ask you this.' She met his gaze, even though it killed her to do so. 'It's been five years, Finlay. Five years that you've turned your back on love. How much longer will it take? Do you think you'll ever be ready to love someone again?'

He could barely meet her gaze. 'It's been an amazing few days, Grace, but no, I'm not looking for love again. I don't think I'll ever be ready.'

She breathed in slowly through her nose. She wanted to shout. She wanted to cry. She wanted to punch him right in the chest. Hadn't he looked at Drumegan Castle and said he'd left things far too long? Hadn't he said that in a few different ways to her?

She'd obviously misunderstood—and that was her own foolish fault. When he'd talked about the neglected castle she'd assumed there was some parallel to himself and his life.

But that was clearly all in her head.

Finlay Armstrong might be the most handsome man she'd ever met. He might be the only man she'd ever felt a connection like this with. He might be the only man who'd stamped all over her fragile heart.

She could almost hear her gran's voice in her ears. She straightened her shoulders and looked him straight in the eye. He'd been right. She deserved so much better than he could offer. She loved him completely, with her whole entire heart. The one that was currently shattered all around them. She had too much pride for this. She wasn't going to hang around waiting for any scrap of his attention when she was worthy of so much more.

She bit her lips as tears threatened to pool in her eyes.

No. She wouldn't let them. He wouldn't see her cry. He wouldn't know just how much this hurt.

She kept her voice steady. 'Then thank you for a nice Christmas, Finlay. But now we're on our way home—it's clearly best that we both resume our own lives.'

CHAPTER TEN

HE FELT WRETCHED. It was as if a huge cloud of misery had descended over his head in an air of permanence.

He'd been miserable before. He could buy the T-shirt and wear it. But this was different.

He hadn't lost his wife. That was an understandable misery.

This time, he'd lost Grace. The strong, proud woman he still saw walking about his hotel on a daily basis. She didn't look in his direction—not once. She didn't try and engage in conversation. His few 'good mornings' had been resolutely ignored.

But that wasn't the thing that made him feel wretched.

It was the fact that when she thought no one was watching, her shoulders would slump, her head would bow and she'd pull a tissue from her apron.

Grace. The girl with the sparkling eyes, gorgeous smile and biggest heart in the world.

He'd done this.

This morning he'd woken up and turned over in bed. The empty space beside him hadn't just felt empty—it had felt like a massive void.

He'd never considered himself a coward. But why had he retreated so quickly? Was he actually scared? He hated feeling like this. And he hated the way he'd made Grace feel.

The sunlight sparkled off something in the corner of

the room. Silver paper. The gift that Mrs Archer had left him. He'd forgotten to open it.

He stood up and walked over. It took a few minutes to unfurl the curling silver ribbons and unwrap the silver paper. Inside was a black box. He flipped it open. An engraved silver heart gleamed at him.

Memories are special in every single way,
But new memories can be made every single day.

A long red ribbon was attached at the top. It was a Christmas decoration. Ready to be hung on a tree.

Right alongside his ceramic angel.

There was noise outside her flat as she approached. Grace froze. The last thing she needed was trouble. All she wanted to do was get inside, pull on her pyjamas and make some toast.

As she took another step forward she recognised the voices. She straightened up and walked around the corner. 'Emma, Sophie, Ashleigh—what are you doing here?'

'Grace!' Their shouts were probably heard all up and down the stairwells of the flats. She found herself enveloped in a group hug. Tears prickled at her eyes.

'You missed Christmas with us.' Emma held up a bag that clinked.

Ashleigh held up another, her engagement ring gleaming in the dim hall lights. 'Let us in, we want to hear all your news.'

Sophie was clutching a huge trifle in a glass bowl. 'What happened with your boss?'

She couldn't hold it together a second longer. She'd tried so hard all day. Seeing Finlay at the hotel was torture. Because now she knew what they could share together, she was having trouble being anything but angry.

She dissolved into tears of frustration.

'Grace? Grace? What's wrong?'

The keys were fumbled from her hands, her door opened and she was ushered into the flat. Within two minutes glasses appeared, wine was poured and her jacket was pulled from her shoulders. She sank down onto the sofa as Ashleigh opened the biggest box of chocolates in the world and dumped them on her lap.

It just made her cry all the more. Right now she valued her friends more than anything.

One hour later they were all gobsmacked. Emma slid her arm around her shoulders. 'Why didn't you tell us how you were feeling? You could have spent Christmas Day with any one of us.'

Grace shook her head. 'I didn't want to put a dampener on anyone else's Christmas.'

Sophie narrowed her eyes. 'But what about your Christmas? Finlay's certainly put a dampener on that.'

Grace sighed. 'It's not his fault I fell hook, line and sinker. I knew right from the start that he was a widower. I should have known better than to fall in love.'

Ashleigh leaned forward and slipped her hand into Grace's. 'But we can't always control where our heart will take us. Finlay took you to the staff party, he kissed you, he took you to Scotland, he slept with you. Then he took you to meet his family.' She shook her head and leaned back on her heels. 'It doesn't matter what way I look at this, Grace. He led you on. He didn't guard your heart the way he should have.'

'People don't always love you back,' Grace replied flatly.

Sophie slammed her hand on the table. 'Then the man's a fool.' She lifted her glass towards Grace. 'Whatever happens next, we're here for you, Grace. All of us. We're your family now.'

The words made her heart swell. She looked around at her friends with love and appreciation. 'Thank you, girls. That means so much. But I know what I need to do. I know how to take things forward for me.' She gave her head a shake. 'I don't need a man to determine what to do with my life. I have plans. I need someone who can stand by my side and support my choices in life. If Finlay can't do that—then he isn't the right man for me.' She lifted her glass to raise a toast then paused. Something sparked in her brain. She turned towards Sophie. 'Ashleigh said you went for drinks with some gorgeous Italian. I haven't heard about it yet. Spill.'

Anything to distract her from the way she was feeling right now.

Because one thing was for sure. The next steps would be the hardest.

He couldn't take it. He couldn't take it for a second longer. Four days were already four days too many.

He'd only needed one glimpse of Grace to know that this situation couldn't continue.

She was standing at the lifts with her cart, waiting to go upstairs. He walked over purposely and caught her by the elbow. 'Come with me for a second.'

'What?' She looked shocked. He'd caught her off guard.

He steered her towards one of the nearby empty rooms. 'We need to talk.'

She lifted her chin determinedly and folded her arms across her chest. 'Do we? I thought everything had been said.'

He ran his fingers through his hair and tried to find the right words. 'I hate seeing you like this.'

'Like what?'

'I hate seeing you so miserable—especially when I know it's all my fault.'

'I'm glad there's something we can agree on.' The words had obviously been on the tip of her tongue. She gave a little shake of her head. 'I'm a grown-up, Finlay. And so are you.'

He stepped closer. Her perfume drifted around him, giving him agonising flashbacks to the Christmas party and to Christmas night. 'Maybe we should have a rethink? Maybe, now that we're back, we could see each other when I'm back in London? I mean, I'm away a lot on business. But we could have drinks. Dinner.' He was rambling. Words were spilling out.

Her face paled. 'Tell me that you're joking?'

Not quite the effect he was looking for. 'Why?'

He could see the bottom edge of her jaw line tremble. It was something he'd never seen before in Grace Ellis. Rage.

'Why?' She shouted so loudly he winced. Guests in the bar next door would have heard.

She marched straight up under his chin, her eyes flashing madly. 'I'll tell you exactly why, Finlay Armstrong.' She pushed her finger into his chest. 'I am so much better than this.' She shook her head fiercely. 'I am not having a three-way relationship with a ghost. You can't move on because you won't let yourself. I don't want to spend my life living in the shadow of another woman. I don't deserve it and I don't need this. Don't come in here and offer me a tiny piece of yourself, Finlay. I don't want that. It's not enough. It will never be enough.' The fury started to dissipate from her voice. She took a step backwards. Her hand was shaking.

He saw her suck in a breath and pull herself back up. The expression in her brown eyes just about ripped out his soul. He'd tried to conjure up some remedy, some patchwork arrangement that might work. But his misplaced idea had backfired spectacularly.

'I want a change of shifts. I don't want to be around

when you're here. I'm going to speak to Clio about a transfer. We work in the Corminster across town. I'll ask if I can do my shifts there instead.'

'What?' Panic gripped him like a hand around his throat.

Her eyes focused on the door. She started walking straight towards it. Her shoulders seemed straighter, her head lift stronger. 'You'll have my resignation in the morning. I'll make it official and keep everything above board.'

For the briefest of pauses her footsteps faltered. There was so much circulating in his head. This was exactly what he didn't want. This was the absolute opposite of what he wanted.

Grace's voice softened for a second. 'Goodbye, Finlay,' she said as she opened the door and left.

CHAPTER ELEVEN

HE'D BEEN ON the roof most of the night. It was Frank who finally found him.

'Mr Armstrong? What are you doing? Why—you're freezing.' Frank whipped off his jacket and put it around his shoulders.

He hadn't meant to stay up here so long. But the frustration in him had built so much that he'd punched a wall in the penthouse and knew he had to get outside and away from anyone. The roof had been the ideal solution. Too bad he hadn't thought to bring a coat.

One hand held the ceramic angel. He'd pushed it into his pocket when he'd closed up the house. The other hand held the silver heart from Mrs Archer. One symbolised a lost love, the other a new.

Looking out over the darkness of London, lit only by Christmas lights, had been haunting. Watching the sun start to rise behind Battersea Park and the Albert Bridge had been a whole new experience. It made him realise that the lights at Battersea Park should be purple instead of white and red. Purple seemed a much more festive colour.

Frank's fierce grip pulled him to his feet and over to the stairs. The heat hit him as soon as he stepped inside again. He hadn't realised he was quite so cold.

Frank walked him down to the penthouse and made a quick phone call. 'I've ordered you some breakfast and some coffee.' He paused. 'No, scrub that. Give me a second.' He picked up the phone again and spoke quietly before replacing it. 'I've ordered something more appropriate.' He walked over to the room thermostat and turned it up. He looked around the room, then left and scouted in the bathroom, coming back with a fleecy dressing gown that Finlay rarely wore. 'Here, put that on too. I'm going to deal with something else. But I'll be back up in ten minutes to check on you.'

Heat was slowly but surely starting to permeate his body. His fingers were entirely white with almost a tinge of blue. They were starting to tingle as they warmed up.

He was still staring at the Christmas decorations. He'd made so many mistakes. He just didn't know where to start to try and put them right.

He closed his eyes for a second, trying to wish away some of the things that he'd said. When Anna had died, he'd truly believed the biggest part of him had died too. It wasn't true. Of course it wasn't true. He just hadn't been able to face up to his grief.

Concentrating on business and only business had been his shield. His saviour. It had also been his vice.

He'd let relationships with friends deteriorate. He'd shunned any pity or sympathy. It was so much easier to shut himself off from the world. A wave of embarrassment swept over him as he realised he'd also shut out his mum, dad and sister.

His sister had got married two years ago. He hadn't participated at all. He'd hardly even been able to bear attending. The occasion when he should have been happy for his sister, and dancing her around the marquee floor, he'd spent nursing a whiskey at the bar.

Now, she was pregnant with her first child and clearly nervous. Had he even told her how delighted he was to be an uncle? How much he was looking forward to seeing her with her child in her arms?

What kind of a person had he become?

There was a ping at the door. Room service. The trolley was wheeled in. He lifted the silver platter. Pancakes, eggs and bacon. Unusual choice. He looked in the lower part of the trolley for the coffee.

But there was no coffee. Instead, there was a hot chocolate, piled high with cream and marshmallows and dusted with chocolate.

He sagged back into his chair. Frank. How did he know?

The first sip was all it took. Two minutes later he was tearing into the pancakes, eggs and bacon. He flipped open his computer and did a quick search, made a few calls.

Then he made another.

'Mum? Hi. Yeah… Yeah… I'm fine. Well, I'm not fine. But let me handle that. I wanted to ask a favour. How would you feel about supervising the staff from a cleaning and restoration company for me? They can be there on the sixth of January.'

It was amazing. Just one simple but major act made him feel as though a huge dark cloud had been pushed off into the distance.

She spoke for a long, long time. Finlay knew better than to interrupt. He just gave the occasional, 'Yes…yes…yes…thanks…'

Her final words brought tears to a grown man's eyes. He put the phone back down as Frank came into the room.

The room seemed brighter, the early-morning sun sending a yellow streak across the room. Frank looked approvingly at the empty plate. 'Good, you've eaten. You're looking a bit more like yourself.' He bit his lip.

Finlay stood up. He wanted to shower and get changed. The more his head cleared, the stronger his heart pounded.

For the first time in five years he had personal clarity. His business acumen had never been affected, but his own life?

It was time to finally get started.

Frank was still standing.

'What's wrong?'

'You have a guest. She wanted to leave something in your office. But I told her to come upstairs.'

Finlay caught his breath. Frank's face was serious. 'I'll take this,' he said briskly as he stepped forward for the empty tray. His face was impartial but his muttered words weren't. 'Don't you dare upset her. Just don't.'

Somehow he got the feeling that if he were the last man on a sinking ship right now, Frank wouldn't let him in the lifeboat. Frank's green coat disappeared.

There could only be one person that would cause this type of fatherly protection in Frank.

The heart that had already been pounding started to race to a sprint. 'Grace?'

He stuck his head out of the door. Grace was standing rigid, a white envelope clutched in one hand.

'Grace?'

Her steely gaze met his. He'd never seen her look quite so determined. His heart gave a little surge.

She straightened her shoulders. She was wearing a classy black wool coat, with an unusual cut. It emphasised her small waist. There were red skirts sticking out from the bottom of the coat and he could see the red collar at her neck.

But there was something else—a real assuredness about her. His heart swelled a little. Grace just got more spectacular every time he saw her.

She marched forward and thrust the envelope towards him. 'I just wanted to leave this for you, but Frank insisted I spoke to you. My resignation.'

It was as if all his best dreams and worst nightmares had decided to cram themselves into one hour of his life.

Grace's hair was styled a little differently and her lips were outlined in red.

She looked vaguely familiar and it took a few seconds to realise why. 'You look like Alice Archer,' he said quietly. His hand reached up to touch her hair but Grace flinched backwards. He swallowed. 'The only thing different is your hair colour. You look amazing, Grace.'

Her eyebrows shot up. 'Really?'

As he realised what he'd just said he gave a nervous laugh. 'I mean it, though. I do.'

She was still holding out the envelope towards him. She had her black leather gloves on that he'd bought her. He shook his head. 'I'm not taking it.'

Her brow furrowed. 'You have to. You can't stop me resigning.' His reaction seemed to spur her on. 'There's no way you can stop me. I've made plans. I'm transferring my shifts. I've enrolled at college to do interior design and Clio will give me shifts that suit. I'm moving on, Finlay. I'm not going to stay here and watch you walk about in a fog for the rest of your life.'

There were rosy spots on her cheeks. There was an edge of determination to her. He loved it. He loved everything about it.

He walked over and put his hands on her shoulders. 'Grace, that's the best thing I've heard this year. You will be a fantastic interior designer. You *are* a fantastic interior designer. I can't think of anything more perfect for you. But you don't need to leave here to do that.'

There was an almost startled expression on her face. 'Yes. Yes, I do. I can't be around you, Finlay. I *won't* be around you.'

His heart twisted inside his chest. 'Not even if I tell you that I love you? Not even if I tell you I've been a complete fool?' He stopped to draw breath. 'Grace, for the first time in years you've made me wake up and look around. I wasn't paying attention to life—oh, I thought I was, but not really, not the way I should have.' He ran his fingers through his hair. He wished he'd showered. He wished he'd changed out of the clothes he'd spent all night wearing on the roof. He put his hands on his hips. 'It wasn't just Drumegan Castle that I neglected. It was everything else too.'

'What does that mean?'

He reached out for her hands. 'It means everything, Grace. I think I have been ready to move on. The only person that hadn't acknowledged that was me.'

She shook her head as he clutched her hands even tighter.

'I'm sorry. I don't know how to do this any more. I've forgotten every rule of dating that I ever knew.' He pressed one hand against his heart. 'All I know is that ever since I met you, I've felt alive again. I've woken up and had something to look forward to. I'll never forget Anna, but, for a few days there, I felt guilty because I'd hardly thought about her at all. My mind was just filled with you, Grace. Every time you smiled, every time you winked at me, every time you looked sad. The way you loved Christmas. When you shared with me about your grandmother. But I looked at you, and your capacity to love, and wondered if I could ever meet that. Ever fulfil that for you.'

Grace blinked and licked her red lips. Her gaze was steady. 'What are you doing, Finlay? Where has this come from?'

He laughed and pointed to his head. 'In here.' Then his heart. 'And in here. I spent most of last night sitting on the roof trying to get my head in order. You know, after a while, you start to think the Battersea Power Station lights should be purple.'

The edges of her lips curled upwards for a few seconds. 'But I still want everything. I don't want half a relationship. Anna's gone, Finlay. But I'm not. I'm here. I won't share. Not with anyone dead or alive.'

She was deadly serious. It was written all over her face and it just made his heart ache all the more for the pain he'd caused her. 'I love you, Grace Ellis. How long does it officially take people to fall in love? Can it happen in a few hours, a few days, a few weeks? Because that's what it feels like to me. I'm sorry for what I said in the helicopter. I'm sorry for what I suggested yesterday. I don't want just to see you now and then. I want to see you every single day.' He reached over and touched her cheek. 'Every single day for the rest of my life.'

Her eyes were wet. He could see her struggle to swallow. 'I don't know, Finlay. I just don't know. You hurt me.'

His hands were shaking by now. 'I know. I'm sorry. I can't promise that I'm good at all this. But what I can promise is that every day, for the rest of my life, I'll try and show you how much I love you. How much you mean to me. Will you let me, Grace? Will you let me try?'

He pulled his hands back. He had to give her space. He had to respect her wishes. He'd already trampled all over her heart once.

She turned and looked out of the window, across the snow-dusted rooftops of London.

'How long were you up on that roof?'

'What?'

'How long were you up on that roof?'

He shook his head. 'I'm not sure. I went up to try and clear my head. It must have been the early hours. I was there until Frank found me this morning.'

'And you didn't freeze to death?'

He could see her watching his reflection in the glass. 'Not yet. There wasn't enough snow. And I didn't have anyone to make snow angels with. It didn't seem like the right place, or the right time.'

'How do I know any of this is true?'

He nodded and walked over to the kitchen counter. 'When I phoned my mother this morning about cleaning up the castle, she threatened me with grievous bodily harm if I came back to visit without you.'

She spun around. 'So, your mother wants you to date me?'

He smiled. 'No, my mother wants me to marry you. But I have to beg for forgiveness first.'

She sucked in a breath and pulled her hands around herself. She rocked back and forth a little. 'You're going to clean up the castle?'

He nodded. 'Starting January the sixth. Once it's clean, I will probably need to hire an interior designer to help me redecorate.' He raised his eyebrows. 'Can you think of anyone I might ask?'

She took a step closer to the counter. 'I might do. You should think about the person who thought purple was such a Christmas colour. She decorated one of the most exclusive hotels in London.' He nodded and smiled as she added, 'But I've heard she's expensive.'

He picked up the decorations from the counter top. 'There's one last thing I need to do. To make this official. To make this right.' He held out his hand towards her. 'Will you come with me?'

She looked at his hand for a second before finally reaching out and sliding her hand into his. He walked them over to the private elevator, pressing buttons to take them to the ground floor.

It was New Year's Eve. The hotel was busy with guests staying for the New Year's celebrations. Finlay ignored them all. He strode across the foyer with Grace's hand in his, only slowing down when they reached the main Christmas tree.

He took a deep breath. 'A few weeks ago you found

something and set it on my pillow.' He pulled the ceramic angel from his pocket and lifted it, hanging it on the tree. 'You also remembered to bring it to Scotland with us.' He lifted his hand towards it. 'It's a memory. One that I will treasure and respect.' He pulled something else from his pocket. 'But I have another gift.' He nodded his head and smiled. 'This one was left in my office. It's from a mutual friend. Discreet. Knowledgeable. With more finesse in her little finger than I can ever hope to achieve in my life.' He lifted up the silver heart and hung it on the tree in front of them. 'Alice gave me this before we'd ever met. She knew before I did, before *we* did, the potential that was in the air.'

He spun the silver heart around so Grace could see the engraving.

She read it out slowly. *'"Memories are special in every single way, But new memories can be made every single day."'* She gasped and put her hand to her mouth. 'Alice gave you that?'

He nodded as he turned Grace around and slid his arms around her waist.

'How do you feel about making some new memories, for The Armstrong, and for Drumegan Castle?'

She smiled and wound her arms around his neck. 'I think I might have to be persuaded.'

He caught the twinkle in her eye. 'And how might I do that?'

She laughed. 'I can think of a few ways.' Then stood on her tiptoes to whisper in his ear.

He picked her up and swung her around. 'Grace Ellis, we're in public!' He put her feet back on the floor. 'But we've got to start somewhere.'

And so he kissed her—again and again and again.

* * * * *

WINTER WEDDING FOR THE PRINCE

BARBARA WALLACE

For Second Lieutenant Andrew Wallace, who commissioned five days after I typed "The End."
Merry Christmas!

CHAPTER ONE

"THEN, AFTER THE children finish their sing-along, Babbo Natale will arrive to distribute presents. We were lucky enough this year to get each child something from their wish lists, even the girl who asked for a dragon and one thousand chocolate cookies. The internet is a wonderful thing." Rosa Lamberti looked up from her paperwork. "Are you even listening?" she asked the man in front of her.

Armando Santoro, crown prince of Corinthia, paused midstep to give her a narrow-eyed look. "Of course I did. Babbo Natale. Dragons. Cookies. Why do you ask?"

"I don't know, maybe because you have been wearing a path in the carpet for the past thirty minutes." Pacing like a caged panther was more like it. He had been crossing the hand-woven Oushak with long, heavy-footed strides that took advantage of his extra-tall frame. Between that and the scowl plastered on his face, she half expected him to start growling. "I have a feeling I could have announced a coup and you wouldn't have heard me."

"I'm sorry," he said, running a hand through his dark curls. "I'm a bit distracted this morning."

Clearly. Setting her paperwork aside, Rosa helped herself to a fresh cup of coffee. On good days, being the prince's personal assistant was a three-cup job. When he was distracted, the number increased to four or five.

"Don't tell me you're upset about your sister," she said. Only that morning, Princess Arianna had announced her engagement to an American businessman named Max Brown whom she had met in New York City. The details of the courtship were sketchy. According to Armando, the princess had taken off for America without a word why. A few days after her return, Max Brown forced his way into the castle demanding to see her. The pair had been inseparable ever since.

"No," he said. It was more a sigh than reply. "If Arianna is happy, then I am happy for her."

Happy was too mild a term. Rosa would go with delirious or ecstatic. The princess had lit up like Corinthia City on San Paolo Day when Max burst through the door.

Rosa suppressed a sigh of her own. Wild, passionate declarations of love and sudden engagements. It was all quite romantic. She couldn't remember the last time a man declared anything to her, unless you counted her ex-husband and his many declarations of disinterest.

Fredo had been very good at telling her she wasn't worth his time.

She returned to the question at hand. "If it is not your sister, then what is it?" she asked over the rim of her coffee cup. “And don’t say nothing, because I know you.” One didn’t spend seven years of life attached to someone—four as a sister-in-law—without learning a person’s tics.

An olive-skinned hand reached over her shoulder and took the cup before her lips had a chance to make contact. “Hey!”

Turning, she saw Armando already drinking. “You forgot the sugar,” he said with a frown.

“I forgot nothing.” What little was left of the warm liquid splashed against the rim as she snatched the cup free. “I’m on a diet.”

“You’re always on a diet. A teaspoon or two of sugar will not kill you.”

Said the god of athleticism. He wasn’t in danger of finishing out the year a dress size larger. Even sitting perfectly straight, she swore she could feel the button on her waistband threatening to pop.

Sucking in her belly, she said, “Stop trying to change the subject. I asked you a question.”

“Did you just demand I answer you? I’m sorry, I was under the impression that you worked for me.”

“Yes, but I’m family. That gives me special privileges.”

“Like bossiness?”

“I’m not the one ruining a one-hundred-and-fifty-year-old rug.” Reaching for the coffeepot, she poured him a fresh coffee of his own, making sure to add the two sugars before refilling her cup. “Seriously, Armando. What’s wrong?”

This sigh was the loudest of the three. Taking the coffee, he came around to the front of the love seat and sat down beside her. Rosa did her best to squeeze into the corner to accommodate him. She didn't know if her brother-in-law kept forgetting she wasn't as petite as his late wife or what, but he always insisted on invading her personal space rather than taking a seat across the way. As a result, they sat wedged together, their thighs pressed tight. Rosa gave a silent thank-you for long jackets. It provided another layer between their bodies.

Oblivious, as usual, to the close quarters, Armando stared at the coffee she'd handed him. "Arianna's pregnant," he said in a dull voice.

No wonder they were rushing the engagement. "But that's a good thing, isn't it?" she asked. "Your father finally has another heir to the throne." It was no secret the king was eager to establish a third generation of Santoros to protect his family's legacy.

"It would be," Armando replied, "if Max Brown were the father."

"What?" Rosa's hand froze mid-sip. She would ask if he was joking, except this wasn't something to joke about. "Who…?" It didn't matter. "Does Max know?"

"Yes, and he doesn't care."

"He must love your sister very much." Took a special kind of love to marry a woman carrying another man's child. Certainly not the kind of love people like Rosa got to witness. People like her got a leftover kind of love. As Fredo had been so fond of telling her, she was flavorless and bland.

"Max's devotion is wonderful for Arianna, but..."

But it didn't erase the problems this pregnancy caused. "He or she can't be the heir."

Corinthian law stated that only the biological offspring of both parents could inherit the throne. Should anything happen to Armando and Arianna, then the title would skip to someone else, such as Arianna and Max's child or one of the distant cousins. Either way opened a host of complications.

"Not to mention that if the truth were to come out, that child would spend the rest of his or her life hounded by gossip and innuendo. Max and Arianna, too. The whole house of Santoro, for that matter."

"Unless Arianna and Max lie." Armando scowled at her suggestion. "What?" she asked. "You don't think that's happened before?" Not even the house of Santoro was that lily pure. In fact, someone trying to slip an illegitimate heir into the mix was probably the reason for the inane law to begin with.

"Whether it's been done before or not isn't the point," he replied. "Other generations didn't have tabloids or your wonderful internet."

Good point. Today, secrets couldn't last forever. Eventually the truth would come out, and when it did, there would be challenges. Corinthia would be plunged into a protracted legal battle that benefited no one.

"I take it you've already thought of trying to change the law," she said.

"Of course, but again, this isn't the old days, when

the king could change the laws on a whim. The ministers would want to know the reason for the change."

"All hail increased democracy," Rosa muttered. There wasn't much more that could be done, barring Armando remarrying and having children of his own, and a monk dated more than he did. The Melancholy Prince, the papers called him. The title fit. While Armando had always been serious, Christina's death had added an extra layer. It was as though he was suspended in permanent mourning. He never attended anything that wasn't an official event, and those he attended alone. Other than his sister, Rosa was the only woman in his life.

The prince had returned his attention to his coffee, studying the untouched contents from beneath thick lashes as if they contained the answer. Rosa couldn't help but indulge in a moment of appreciation. If he decided to date again, Armando's return to the dating world would be a welcome one. Even if he wasn't the future king of Corinthia, he was a man worthy of desire. Granted, he wasn't the most beautiful man in the country; his Roman features were a little too pronounced, although not so much that they looked out of proportion. Besides, she always thought a strong man should have strong features. Fredo, for all his self-importance, had had a weak chin.

The muscles in Armando's chin twitched with tension.

"You know King El Halwani," he started.

"That's a silly question." Of course she knew the

man. The sultan of Yelgiers was a frequent visitor. Corinthia and the tiny principality had a long history of economic and political relations. "What does he have to do with anything?"

"His daughter, Mona, is of marrying age."

"Is that so? I didn't know." Rosa's insides ran cold. Surely, he wasn't…

"A union between our two countries will be a tremendous alliance."

Did he say will? The chill spread down her spine, ending in a shiver.

Apology darkened his eyes to near black. "I called him this morning and suggested we discuss an arrangement."

"You—you did." Rosa set down her cup. The coffee she'd been drinking threatened to rise back up her throat.

Armando, remarrying.

She shouldn't have been surprised. Royalty lived a different kind of life than commoners like her. Marriages were arranged for all kinds of reasons: trade relations, military alliances. Why not to secure an heir?

The news still made her queasy. It was too quick. Armando wasn't the type to make rash decisions. For crying out loud, he'd waited a year before proposing to her sister, and they'd fallen in love at first sight. For him to wake up and decide he was going to marry a virtual stranger was completely out of character, looming scandal or no looming scandal. At the very least, he would have asked her what she thought.

But he hadn't. He hadn't sought her opinion at all. So much for being his right hand. Apparently the familiarity she thought they had developed over the past three years had been in her head.

She forced a smile. Pretended she was excited for his news. "I'm sure the people of Corinthia will be thrilled. As will your father."

"I'm not doing this for my father," he replied.

"I know. You're doing it to protect your sister."

"No, I'm doing it for Corinthia." His voice was sharp, the way it always was when his will was questioned. "I'm first in line. It is my responsibility to do whatever I can to ensure Corinthia has a long and peaceful future."

"Of course. I'm sorry." If there was anything Armando took seriously, it was his duty to his country.

Leaving Armando, she stood and walked toward the windows. The crown prince's suite overlooked the south lawn. The famed topiary menagerie remained green, but the grass had gone brown from the winter, and the flowerbeds were empty. Across the street, a pair of business owners were filling their outside window boxes with fresh evergreen—a Corinthian Christmas tradition. When they finished, a single white candle would be placed in the center, another tradition. Greens for life, light for the blessings of the future.

Apparently, Armando's future involved a bride.

What did that mean for her future then? For three years, it had been the two of them, prince and assistant, tied together as they both began lives without their spouses. Being there to help Armando had given her strength and purpose. She'd been able to rebuild the layers of self-esteem Fredo had destroyed.

What now? A new queen would mean new staff, new routines. Would she even have a place in Armando's life anymore? The grip on her chest squeezed tighter.

She watched as a *merli* poked at the barren grass looking for seeds. Poor little creature wasn't having much luck. She could identify. She felt a little like she'd been left wanting, too.

The thing was, she had always known there was the chance Armando would move on with his life. The news shouldn't be this disconcerting.

Then again, he should have told her. They were supposed to be friends. Family. They'd held hands at her sister's bedside and cried together. She let him drink her coffee, for God's sake. Why hadn't he told her?

"When are you making the announcement?" she asked. It would have to be soon if Armando wanted to draw attention from his sister. Depending upon how far along in her pregnancy Arianna had been when she met Max last month, there was a good chance the princess would start to show soon.

Behind her, she heard the soft clap of a cup against the coffee table, but she didn't turn around.

"We're making the formal announcement on New Year's Day."

What? When she thought soon, she didn't mean that soon. No wonder she couldn't breathe. In three and a half weeks, everything she'd come to know and rely on was going to change forever.

"Is everything all right?" she heard him ask.

"Of course," she lied. "Why wouldn't it be?"

"It truly is the best solution."

"I know." He had no reason to defend himself any more than she had the right to be upset.

Clearly, that didn't stop either of them from doing so anyway.

She was upset with him. Armando could tell because when she spoke, every third or fourth word had an upward inflection. Not that he was surprised. From the moment he made his decision, he'd worried she might see his remarrying as betraying her sister.

Staring at her back, he wished he knew what she was thinking. But then, she was good at hiding behind things. Her poker face was among the best.

"You know that if there was any other way..." he said.

"I know."

Did she? Did she know he'd been up half the night weighing options, or that, given his druthers, he would never remarry? He'd had his chance at love. Four wonderful years with the girl of his dreams. If the price for those years was spending the rest of his life in solitude, he'd been prepared. He didn't mind. After all, if he needed a companion, he had Rosa. She was better company than any consort might be.

Unfortunately, for men like him, what he wanted

didn't always matter. The mantle of responsibility outweighed personal desire every time.

Leaving his coffee behind, he joined her at the window. "Corinthia's almost ready for the holiday," he said, noting the men arranging greenery outside. "They'll be lighting the candles tonight."

Rosa didn't answer. She stood with her hands clasped tightly behind her back, stiff and formal, like a proper royal servant, a pose she usually only struck in public. Armando didn't like it. He preferred the relaxed, irreverent Rosa who kept him on his toes and saved him from drowning in his grief.

After Christina died, he'd wanted to die, too. What good was living if his heart lay six feet underground? Rosa had been the only one who had been able to break through the darkness that filled his soul. She needed him, she'd claimed, to help her rebuild following her divorce. It was a lie, of course—Rosa was one of the strongest women he knew—but he let her think he believed the excuse. Helping her find a lawyer and place to live gave him a reason to drag himself out of bed that first day. Then, when she became his assistant, there were meetings and charitable initiatives and other projects she insisted needed his attention, and so he continued dragging himself out of bed. Until the day came when getting up was no longer a trial.

She'd kept him tied to the land of the living, Rosa did. Without her, he would still be lost in his grief. Or rather, lost even deeper.

Which was why he needed her support now.

"You never met my grandfather, did you?"

"King Damian? No." She wasn't so annoyed that she couldn't give him a side-eyed look. Of course she hadn't met the man. Illness forced him off the throne before Armando was born.

"He came upstairs to my room one night, a few weeks before he died, and got me out of bed so I could see what it looked like with candles lit in every window. I must have been seven or eight at the time. Corinthia City wasn't as developed as it is now. Anyway, he told me how all those candles represented Corinthians hoping for the future. 'One day you will be responsible for those candles,' he told me. 'It will be up to you to keep them burning bright.' I never forgot." The words were the weight pressing on his shoulders every time he saw a candle flickering.

He turned to look at his sister-in-law. "Father's aging, Rosa. I could see it this past month when Arianna disappeared. He's never truly gotten over Mama's death..." He paused to let the irony of his words settle between them. The curse of the Santoro men: to live a lifetime of grieving. "And I think he would like to step down, but he's afraid for the future. It's important he know that as his successor, I am willing to do whatever it takes to keep those lights burning."

"Including political marriage."

He shrugged. "Ours won't be the first royal marriage based on obligation rather than love." If anything, a man in his position was lucky to have spent four years with a wife he did love. “It would be nice, however, to know I have my best friend’s support. Do I?”

The clock on the nearby mantel ticked off the seconds while he waited for her response. Unfortunately, her eyes were cast downward. They were the one feature that couldn’t mask her feelings. In that way, she was like her sister. Christina had also had expressive brown eyes. Beyond their eyes, however, the two were dramatically different. Christina had been all passion and energy, with a beauty that commanded attention. Rosa was softer. Whereas Christina was bright like a star, her sister was more the glow of a candle.

Finally, her shoulders relaxed. “Of course you have my blessing,” she said. “You know I can never say no to you.”

Armando’s shoulders relaxed in turn. “I know. It’s my charm.”

“No, it’s because you’re going to be king. I say no and you might have me thrown in the dungeon.”

“As one does.” He relaxed a little more. Rosa making jokes was always a good sign. “I’m serious, Rosa. Your support is important to me.” Just thinking he might not have it had left a tight knot in the center of his chest.

A hand brushed his arm. Initiating contact with a member of the royal family was considered a violation of protocol, but he and Rosa had been together too long for either of them to care about rules. There were times, in fact, when he found her touch comforting. Like now, the way her fingertips seemed to brush the tension from his muscles. "You have it. Seriously. I just wish…"

"What?"

She shook her head. "Nothing. I'm being silly. You have my support, 'Mando."

"Good." Although he wondered what she had started to say. That she wished there didn't have to be a wedding? If so, Armando agreed.

But there was going to be a wedding, and he was glad to have his best friend's support.

Hopefully, she wouldn't change her mind when she heard his next request.

CHAPTER TWO

"I CANNOT BELIEVE you want me to attend a meeting with you and your future father-in-law. How is that possibly in good form?"

She had been complaining since yesterday. When he'd said he'd called King Omar, Armando left off that the sultan was in Corinthia and that they were going to meet for lunch the next day.

"And how is it no one was told of his visit?" she asked as they rode the elevator down to the first floor. "He's a visiting head of state. There are protocols to be followed."

"Since when do you follow protocol?"

"I always follow protocol when other royalty is involved. Exactly how long has he been in Corinthia?"

"Since Wednesday. You might as well get used to it," he added when she opened her mouth to speak. "Omar has decided to personally oversee the resort development." Such was the major difference between the two small countries. The Yelgierian royal family insisted on maintaining control of everything, while

Armando and his father preferred giving their subjects more freedom. "Between that and the upcoming…arrangement…" He couldn't bring himself to say the word *wedding*. Not yet. "I suspect Omar will be going back and forth quite a bit."

An odd looking shadow crossed her face. "With his daughter?"

"I—I don't know." Armando hadn't given his bride-to-be much thought. "I imagine she will, considering all the preparations that need to take place."

"Unless the wedding is in Yelgiers," Rosa replied. She was studying her shoes as she spoke, so he almost didn't hear her.

"True." He hadn't given much thought to logistics. Those kinds of details were usually up to the bride. "But it doesn't matter to me where the wedding takes place." Only that it did, and Corinthia's future was secure.

The elevator opened, and they stepped out into the guarded enclave near the driveway. Rosa's sedan had been brought around and sat running by the curb.

"I still don't understand why you need me for this meeting," she said as a guard stepped out to open the passenger door. "Surely, you can finalize your—" she glanced at the guard "—agreement without me."

"I told you, this meeting isn't about my 'agreement,'" Armando replied. "I'm meeting with him to discuss the development project." And perhaps finalize a few details regarding yesterday's telephone conversation. Sometimes she was a little too astute for his liking.

"You know I like to have you with me when I discuss business."

He waited until the guard shut her door and they once again had privacy. "Not to mention you are my favorite driver." The way Rosa handled a car made him feel comfortable. For a long time, just the thought of being on the road filled him with dread. He would hear the sound of an engine, and images of twisted steel filled his brain. But, just like she coaxed him back to the land of the living, Rosa had eased him onto the road.

Sometimes he wondered what his life would be like without her.

"So now I'm your driver," she replied. "If that's the case, maybe I should get a cap to wear."

"And have me listen to you complain about the hat ruining your hair? No, thank you. What you're wearing will suffice."

For a meeting she didn't want to attend, she was dressed rather nicely. As usual, her brown hair was pulled up in one of those twisty, formal styles she seemed to prefer, but unlike her usual skirt and blouse, she had on a brocade dress with matching jacket. A long one that seemed designed to hide a woman's shape. She wore those a lot—long, bulky jackets, that was. He wasn't a fan. It was as though she was trying to discourage attention.

"When's the last time you had a date?" he asked her.

For the first time he could remember, she stripped

the car gears. Turning her head, she squinted at him. "Excuse me?"

The question did sound like it came out of nowhere. It was just that looking at her, and thinking about how she continually hid her assets, had him curious. "I was wondering when was the last time you had been on a date."

"Why do you want to know?"

"No particular reason. Only that it dawned on me that I can't remember the last time you mentioned one."

This time she downshifted smoothly. "My being silent doesn't have to mean I'm not dating. How do you know I'm not simply being discreet?"

"Are you? Being discreet, that is." The thought that she might be seeing someone and had not said anything irritated him. At the same time, he found it hard to believe a woman as attractive as Rosa didn't have offers.

"Isn't that a bit personal?" she asked him. "It's called a private life for a reason."

"Yes, but you can tell me—we're friends."

His comment earned him a sharp laugh. "You mean like you told me about your plans to get married?"

"I did tell you."

"After the fact."

What was she talking about? "You were the first person I told."

The car slowed as she looked at him again. "I was?"

"Of course." He thought she knew that. "I told you how much your support meant to me."

"I know, but I didn't think..." Was that pink creeping into her cheeks? It was hard to tell, the driver's side being in shadow. "I'm sorry I snapped."

"I am sorry for prying. It was rude of me." He still would like to know, however. It was protectiveness as much as curiosity. To make sure she chose better this time around. While he didn't know much about her marriage, beyond the fact it had ended badly, he did know her ex enough to dislike him. Back when Christina was alive, Fredo and Rosa had attended a handful of state dinners. Armando found the man to be a narcissistic bore. He'd decided the man had to be a closet romantic or something, because how else could he have won a woman as soft and gentle as Rosa?

Then again, maybe Armando's first impression was right, since she'd divorced him. That Rosa, for her part, refused to talk about the man said as much.

"The answer is no," Rosa said, shaking him from his thoughts. "I'm not dating."

"At all?" He wasn't sure why he felt relieved at her answer. Perhaps because he feared a serious relationship might cause her to leave her job. "Surely you've had offers, though."

Again, she gave a strange laugh, although this one had less bite than the other. "Not as many as you would think. In case you didn't realize, my job eats up most of my time."

Was that truly the reason? The undercurrent in her laugh made him wonder. "Is that your way of hinting you need time off?" he asked. If so, it would be the first. Usually she had no trouble speaking up.

Another reason to question the excuse.

Rosa shook her head. "Not at all. At least not right now."

They'd reached the point in the highway where they had to choose whether to take the mountain pass or the longer, more circuitous route. Armando gave a slight smile as she turned onto the longer route. By mutual agreement, they hadn't driven the mountain road in three years. Feeling a warmth spreading across his chest, he reached over and gave her hand a grateful squeeze. Her eyes widened a little, but she smiled nonetheless.

"The truth is," she said, after he'd lifted his hand, "I haven't had a lot of interest in dating. I'm still working on getting to know myself again."

What an odd thing to say. Then again, maybe it wasn't so odd. Certainly he wasn't the same man following Christina's death, the hole caused by her absence impossible to repair. No doubt, Rosa's divorce left a similar wound.

She'd also lost a sibling. Sometimes, in his selfishness, he forgot that Rosa had suffered as much loss as he had. The idea that she might have been hurting as bad as he made his conscience sting that much more.

"Aren't we a pair," he mused out loud. "Three years removed, and we're still struggling to move forward without our spouses. What do you think that says about us?"

"Well, in your case, I'd say it's because you have a singular heart."

"I would think the same could be said for you."

"Hardly," she replied with a bark. "Do not insult my sister by even mentioning our marriages in the same breath. Fredo isn't fit to carry Christina's water."

On that they agreed, but to hear her say so with such forcefulness surprised him nevertheless. Usually when the topic of her former husband came up, she pretended the man didn't exist.

"What did he do to you? Fredo," he asked. Had he been unfaithful? Armando couldn't believe anyone married to Rosa would want to stray, but Fredo was a boor.

She shot him a look before changing lanes. "Who says Fredo did anything?"

The defensiveness in her tone. "Did he?"

"Water under the bridge," was her only reply. "My marriage is over, and I'm better off for it. Let's just leave things at that."

"Fine." Today wasn't the day to press for details and start an argument. That didn't mean he wasn't still curious, however, or that he wouldn't try again another time.

Rosa kept one eye on the rearview mirror as she moved from lane to lane. What had she been thinking bringing Fredo's name into the mix in the first place? Her marriage—or rather, her role in it—was her greatest shame; she would rather pretend it never happened than admit her own pathetic behavior. Especially to

Armando, whose pain and loss far outweighed hers. To hear him now, trying to equate the two…

At least he'd agreed to change the subject. Hopefully telling him she was working on herself satisfied enough of his curiosity. After all, it wasn't as though she was lying. She *was* rediscovering herself. Learning, little by little, that there was a capable woman inside her chubby shell. As her therapist one reminded, her value went beyond being her husband's verbal whipping post. And, while she was still a work in progress, she had begun to like herself again.

There were days, of course, when Fredo's insults haunted her, but his voice, once so prominent in her ear, was growing softer. If she learned anything from Christina's death, it was that life was too short to settle for anything, or anyone. She'd stupidly let herself believe she had no choice when Fredo proposed. Never again. She realized now that she deserved nothing less than unconditional love. Next time, if there was a next time, she wouldn't settle for anything less. There would be no settling the next time around. She wanted someone who loved her body and soul. Who made her heart flutter whenever she heard his voice, and whose heart fluttered in return.

She wanted what Armando had with Christina.

What he would eventually have with his bride-to-be. Sure, Armando's marriage might begin for political reasons, but time had a way of warming a person's heart, especially if the person deserved to be loved. Rosa had done some internet searching last night, and discovered Mona El Halwani was a caramel-skinned beauty whose statuesque body weighed at least forty pounds less than Rosa's. She was exquisite. A walking, talking advertisement for perfection.

How could Armando's heart not warm to perfection?

They left the city behind. The landscape around them began to change revealing more and more of Corinthia's old-world. Stone farmhouses lined the streets, their window boxes stuffed with fresh greens.

Seeing the candles in the windows, Rosa couldn't help but think of what Armando had said about being responsible for every light in every window. Such a heavy weight to grow up bearing—the future of your country on your shoulders. She suddenly wanted to pull over, wrap him in a hug and let him know he didn't have to bear the burden alone.

As if those words coming from her would mean anything. Providing solace was his future wife's job. Not hers. She might as well get used to the new hierarchy right now and just do her job.

An hour later, they arrived at the Cerulean Towers, the luxury high-rise that housed Yelgiers's development concern. It was as unheralded an arrival as King Omar's, with only the doorman to greet them.

The sultan was waiting for them in his penthouse suite. Tall and exceptionally handsome, he greeted Armando with the very type of embrace Rosa had considered earlier. "I have been awaiting this moment since yesterday's phone conversation," he said, clapping Armando on the back. "That our families will be forever joined warms my heart."

Rosa stifled a giggle as she watched Armando, clearly caught off guard by the effusiveness, awkwardly pat the man in return. His cheeks were crimson. "You honor me, Omar."

"On the contrary, it is you who honor my family by taking Mona as your bride. Your union marks the beginning of a long and fruitful alliance between our countries."

"Your enthusiasm humbles me," Armando replied as he disentangled himself. "My father sends his regards, by the way, and his welcome."

"Please send my regards in return. Tell him I look forward to the day he and I toast the birth of our grandson."

Rosa choked on the cough rising in her throat. All the effusiveness was making her insides cringe.

Armando arched his brow at the sound. "You remember my assistant, Rosa Lamberti," he said, motioning to her.

She started to bow only to have her hands swept up in the sultan's large bronze grasp. Apparently, his enthusiasm didn't only apply to Armando. "Of course. A man would never forget a beautiful woman. Especially one whose face makes the flowers weep." As the sultan pressed a kiss to her knuckles, Rosa heard Armando give a cough of his own. She waited until King Omar turned and flashed him a smirk.

He led them inside and to the penthouse dining

room. The table, Rosa noticed, had been set with a combination of Yelgierian and Corinthian colors, including a large centerpiece of greens, jasmine and dianthus, the official Yelgierian and Corinthian flowers. Meant to be a tribute to their merging families, the red and gold looked unexpectedly festive as well. There was wine chilling and a trio of uniformed waiters standing at the ready next to the sideboard.

"A working lunch," King Omar explained. "I thought it would be more efficient."

That depended upon your definition of efficient, Rosa thought, counting the silverware. Chances were she would be eating salads for the next week to make up for the excess.

"I am sorry Mona couldn't be here to join us," the king said as the waiters wheeled out the first course, a rich, spicy-smelling soup that had Rosa amending her plans to two weeks of salad. "I called and requested that she fly here this morning, but sadly, she told me she wasn't feeling up to traveling."

"She's not well?" Concern marked Armando's face. Rosa knew what he was thinking. If she was sickly, Mona might not have the stamina to meet the demands that came with being queen.

"The flu," King Omar replied. "Caught during one of her visits to our local children's hospital."

"One of?" Rosa asked.

"She spends a great deal of time there. Children's charities are among her passions. In fact, she recently completed her degree in children's psychology."

"Impressive," Armando replied.

"Public service is a duty our family takes quite seriously. We understand the responsibility that comes with power. Although of all my children, I have to say that Mona takes her responsibility the most seriously."

Smart, charitable and, guessing from King Omar's looks, beautiful. Rosa reached for her water to cool the heartburn stuck behind her breastbone. Call her a cynic, but Rosa thought the woman sounded too good to be true. If the glint in Armando's eyes was any indication, however, he was impressed.

"That is good to hear," he said, "as our family is extremely interested in social reform. Sadly, as beautiful as Corinthia is, the country is not without its blemishes. We are as susceptible to the problems of the world as every country. Disease. Drugs. Violence. We're currently working quite hard to stem the problems of domestic abuse."

"Interesting," King Omar replied. "How so?"

"Being an island country can be detrimental," Armando replied. "If women in trouble cannot afford airfare for themselves and their children, they often feel trapped. It's hard to start over when you're looking over your shoulder."

Omar replied, "Are there not laws in place to protect them?"

"Yes, but laws on the books aren't always enough," Rosa said. She could tell from the widening of the king's eyes he hadn't expected her to speak up over

Armando, but as always happened when the subject came up, she couldn't contain herself.

"Many of our villages are small and contain generations of connected families," Armando explained. "Women often fear going to the authorities because of their husbands' connections."

"I see," Omar replied. "You said you are working to change this? How?" Rosa wondered if he was thinking about his own small country with its tribal population.

"We've created a number of programs over the past couple years, but the one we're most proud of is called Christina's Home, which gives women who don't have the resources a place where they can escape."

King Omar frowned. "Are you saying you built a safe house?"

"Yes, although we prefer the term *transitional home.* We provide education, legal services and such to help them start over. Right now, we have one home, but our hope is to eventually have a network of two or three Christina's Homes that can address a variety of transitional needs."

During his explanation, the waiters replaced the soup with a plate of flaky fried pastries and salad of greens and roasted peppers that had Rosa extending her salad fast until after the new year. The sultan picked up one of the pastries and took a healthy bite. "Interesting name, Christina's Homes," he said when he finished chewing. "Named after your late wife?"

Some of the light faded from Armando's eyes. "Yes. One of the qualities that made her so special was the way she cared for the welfare of our people. By naming the shelter program after her, we're honoring her memory twofold. In name and in deed. It was Rosa's idea," he added. "She shares her sister's passion for helping people."

She had heard Armando make the same compliment dozens of times without reaction. Today, however, her stomach fluttered. She felt awkward and exposed.

"My sister always believed in taking action," Rosa said. Whereas she'd needed her sister's death before she found the courage to do anything. Reaching for her glass, Rosa hid her shame behind a long drink of water.

On the other side of the table, she could feel the sultan studying her. "This sounds exactly like the type of work my daughter would want to be involved with. How many families have you helped?" he asked.

"Too many to count," Armando replied. "Some only stay for a night or two while they make arrangements in another part of Europe, while others stay longer. This time of year is among our busiest, as we like to make sure circumstances don't prevent the children from enjoying the magic of the holidays. Every year we host a Christmas party for current and past residents, complete with traditional foods and presents."

"It's also when we host our largest fund-raiser," Rosa added. "The Concert for Christina's Home is broadcast nationwide and is fast becoming a tradition." Even though she felt ashamed about her own behavior, she was spectacularly proud of how her sister's legacy had taken hold. All those late nights she and Armando worked, neither of them willing to go home and face their sad empty lives. That the program thrived proved amazing things could come out of even the most profound sadness. It was almost as much of a legacy to their triumph over grief as it was a tribute to Christina.

"The program sounds exactly like the kind of work Mona would want to see continued." Rosa jerked from her thoughts just in time to hear King Omar mention his daughter's involvement. "I have no doubt she would be honored if you allowed her to help expand the work being done in your first wife's name."

Armando would never allow it, she thought as possessiveness took hold. Christina's Home was too sacred to let a stranger—even one he planned to marry—become involved. She looked across the table, expecting to find him giving her a reassuring look. Instead, she found him taking an unusually long drink of water.

"The people of Corinthia would appreciate that," he said finally. He looked to her, eyes filled with silent apology.

Rosa lost her appetite.

"He backed me into a corner," Armando said when they were on the elevator and heading back downstairs. "It would have been insulting to say anything other than yes."

Rosa didn't reply. Mainly because she didn't want to admit Armando was right. The king had practically forced his daughter's involvement on Armando. That didn't make it sting any less.

Christina's Home had been her idea as a way of honoring her sister. She'd been the one poring over the budget with Armando and massaging corporate donors. What made King Omar think his daughter could waltz in and become Armando's partner?

Because Mona was to be his wife, that's what. Next year at this time, it would be Mona helping Armando. Mona going over party plans in his dimly lit office while he shed his jacket and tie. Letting him drink her coffee when he grew punchy. For a man who could dominate a room of leaders, Armando managed to look like a sleepy cat when tired. So adorably rumpled. She'd bet Mona wouldn't be able to resist running a hand through his curls when she saw him.

Oh, for crying out loud, you'd think she was jealous, worrying what Mona did with Armando's hair. What mattered was maintaining control over a charity she'd helped create.

"Clearly, he thought playing up his daughter's generous nature would impress me," Armando replied. Busy adjusting his jacket, he thankfully missed Rosa's scowl. The man certainly had been eager to paint his daughter in a good light.

"Did it work?" she asked.

"Did what work? Singing his daughter's praises?" He gave his cuff a tug. "I suppose. It's good to know the future queen has a keen understanding of her responsibilities. Although right now King Omar is going out of his way to paint her in the most positive light possible. He's quite a salesman in that regard."

"You think he's exaggerating?" She was ashamed at the thrill she felt over the possibility of a problem.

The shake of Armando's head quickly squelched the notion. "Oh, no, the El Halwani dedication to social causes has been well documented. They are considered among the most progressive ruling families in the region."

Of course they were. No doubt the mythical Mona would be extremely dedicated to bettering Corinthian society, including helping Christina's Home. Next year, she would be the one working by Armando's side. While he left Rosa behind.

She pressed a fist to her midsection. Lunch truly wasn't agreeing with her. What started as a burning sensation had grown to a full-blown knot that stretched from her breast to her throat.

"Do you feel all right?" Armando asked. "You've been pale since lunch."

"Too much spicy food. My stomach wasn't expecting such an exotic lunch."

"Are you sure that's all?" he asked, turning in her direction.

Rosa hated when he studied her like that, like he could read her mind. She could almost feel his blue eyes reaching through her outer layers and into her thoughts. "I—"

The elevator doors opened, saving her from trying to tap-dance in close quarters. Quickly, she stepped out into the lobby. "Why would there be something else?"

she asked once she was safely a step or two ahead. "Can't a woman have a problem digesting spices?"

"Of course. She can also be hurt."

How was she supposed to respond to that? What could she say that didn't sound jealous and possessive? "I don't know what you're talking about," she said.

"I think you do." His fingers caught her wrist, stopping her from going farther.

In the center of the lobby stood an indoor fountain, ruled over by a small marble cherub. Maintaining his grasp, Armando tugged her toward the fountain edge, where he took a seat on the marble wall. "I think we should talk," he said, pulling her down next to him. "I know why you're upset, and I understand."

"You do?" Rosa doubted his did. How could he, when she wasn't 100 percent sure why she was reacting so strongly herself.

What she did notice was how the marble beneath them made her more aware of their close position than usual. She could feel Armando's body warmth radiating against her leg, even though the only parts of them touching were his wrist on her hand. And, she realized, looking down, that was no longer true.

Looking up again, she came eye to eye with Armando's gentle expression.

"Christina's Home," he said. "You're worried what will happen if Mona gets involved with the program."

Perhaps he understood after all. "It's just that you and I worked so hard to build something together…"

"Which is why I want you to know that I understand, and I promise—" Rosa gasped as he reached up to cradle her face between his hands "—I will never let anything, or anybody, take away your sister's legacy."

Christina, of course. What had she been thinking? She gave him a smile anyway, since his reassurance was well intentioned.

When he smiled back, an odd squiggling sensation passed through her.

"Good," he said. "I'm glad, because you know how much I would hate for you to be upset."

Smile softening even more, he fanned his thumbs across her cheekbones. "I would be lost without you, you know."

He held her cheeks a beat longer before getting to his feet. "Now that we've settled that, do you feel up to driving?" he asked.

"Absolutely," she replied.

As soon as Armando started toward the front door, however, she pressed her hand to her stomach to quell the odd quivering sensation that had sprung up.

CHAPTER THREE

WHEN ROSA AND ARMANDO first conceived of Christina's Home, they wanted to build a place that the late princess would have built herself. Therefore, the home was a sprawling stone villa set at the end of a gated access road. State-of-the-art security assured residents the privacy and safety they needed to rebuild their lives, while acres of grass and gardens gave their children the chance to be children.

For this year's Christmas party, thanks to local businesses and designers eager to earn a royal blessing, the central dining room had been transformed into a winter wonderland. In addition to the traditional Corinthian red and green window boxes, there were "snow"-covered evergreens lining the walls and animated snowmen with motion detectors that brought them to life. There was even an indoor jungle gym modeled after the ice castle from a famous children's movie. All afternoon long, kids had been laughing as they hurled themselves down the indoor "ice" slide into a pile of fake snow.

Rosa stood at the back of the room, near the partition that blocked the corridor and kept the chaos contained to the single room. Near to her, a giant window looked out on snow-covered mountains, including Mount Cornier, whose winding roads had been Christina's final destination. During his dedication speech, Armando said that the view guaranteed the princess would be forever looking down on her legacy.

Rosa wondered what Christina would think if she knew her older sister had spent the last several days fighting a disturbing awareness when it came to Armando. All of a sudden, it seemed, someone had flipped a switch and she was noticing things about him she'd never noticed before, such as how elegant his fingers looked when gripping a pen or the how the bow in his upper lip made a perfect V. What's worse, each detail came with an intense collection of flutters deep inside her, the source of which was a place long dormant. Why, after all this time, she would suddenly and inexplicably be attracted to the man, she didn't know, but there it was. Nature's way of ensuring her self-esteem didn't get too strong, probably. No worries there. Not with Fredo's voice renting space.

"Next year, we are hiring an actor." The object of her thoughts poked his head around the barricade. Rosa tried not to notice he was clad only in a white T-shirt. "I am making it a royal decree."

"You realize you said the same thing last year," she replied.

"Yes, but this year I mean it."

"You said that last year as well." Along with the year before that, when the official shelter was still being built and they housed families at the Corinthian Arms hotel. "You love playing Babbo Natale and you know it." Interacting with the children under the Christmas tree was one of the few times she saw him truly relax. Not to mention it kept them both from feeling maudlin on a day that was supposed to be joyful.

Armando mumbled something unintelligible.

"What?" she whispered.

"I said, then at least get me a better beard next year. This one makes my skin itch."

"Yes, Your Highness."

"Be careful. Mock me and Babbo will put you on the naughty list."

"Oh, goody. Naughty girls get all the good gifts."

"How would you know? Is there something you're not telling me, Signora Rosa?"

"I'll never tell." Rosa immediately clamped her jaw shut. She didn't know what horrified her more, the flutters that took flight at his question or her flirty response. To cover, she made a point of studying her watch dial. "Are you almost ready? I think the natives are getting restless."

"I thought Arianna and Max had them under control." The party was serving as the couple's first official appearance. Currently, the princess was playing carols on the shelter piano while her fiancé led the crowd in a sing-along. He was already proving a people's favorite with his movie-idol looks and exuberant off-key singing.

"They are," she told Armando, "but you know children's attention spans. Especially children who have been gorging on cake and gelato."

"The Christmas cake was delicious, was it not?"

"Mouthwatering," she replied, hoping he didn't notice the catch in her voice. Truth was, she had been more transfixed by the way Armando licked the frosting from his fork.

Their conversation was interrupted by the arrival of the future Prince Max. "I have been asked when Santa might be arriving," he said. "We're running out of Christmas songs. If he doesn't arrive soon, I may have to break out the 1940s standards."

"Please no, not that," Rosa replied. She leaned back to look behind the screen only to find herself inches away from Armando's bearded face.

"Never fear, Babbo Natale is here." He grinned. "Ready to see who has been naughty or nice. Should I start with you, Signora Rosa, since you seem to think the naughty list is the place to be?"

Too bad she wasn't wearing a beard, if only to hide her warm cheeks. She had to settle for looking down and adjusting the hem of her white sweater. "I'm sure there's much more interesting people on that list than me," she said. "Besides, you don't want to keep the children waiting for their presents much longer or we could have a riot on our hands."

Proving her point, one of the youngsters spotted

his red hat poking out from behind the screen. "It's Babbo!" he yelled out. "He's here!" Half a second later, the rest of the children started cheering his arrival as well. The mothers had to corral their children to keep them from rushing the cloth screen.

"Looks like I'm on," Armando whispered. He stepped out, and in the blink of an eye, every trace of reluctance disappeared as the prince threw himself into his performance. "Ho, ho, ho!" he called out. "*Buon Natale!* One of my helpers told me I might find some good boys and girls here. Is that true?"

"Yes," the kids screeched at the top of their lungs.

"Wonderful. Because I happen to have a sack full of toys that I brought especially for them."

Someone dragged over a folding chair from one of the tables, and he perched on it as regally as if it were an actual throne, despite the fact his athletic frame dwarfed the chair. "Let me see," he said, reaching into the velvet sack he had brought with him, "who is going to be first?"

At the chorus of "Me!" that rang through the room, Armando let out a deep rumbling laugh worthy of the Babbo himself.

Rosa's heart warmed at the sight. She had known from the very beginning that playing Santa would be a balm for Armando's grief, but it never ceased to amaze her how good he was at the job. He made sure every child got special one-on-one time with Babbo, he treated them as miniature adults, going along with the pretense for the children's sake. He was going to make a wonderful father.

When he had children with Mona. Beautiful, royal children. A wave of envy, fierce and cold, sent her spirits plummeting.

Max, who she didn't realize had disappeared, returned carrying a pair of paper coffee cups. "All this time I've been thinking Babbo Natale was some old-world European tradition and it turns out he's a more athletic version of Santa Claus," he said, tilting his head to where Armando was teasing a young girl with a stuffed rabbit. "I feel cheated."

"If it makes you feel better, there are Corinthians who embrace Befana."

"What's that?"

"An Italian witch who arrives on Epiphany."

The American's lips turned downward. "A witch on Christmas?"

"More like a crone. She brings treats."

"In that case, yes, I do feel better." He handed her one of the paper cups. "Turns out marrying the princess comes with some benefits. I mentioned wanting an espresso and the caterer made me two. You look like you could use a cup."

"Thank you." Caffeine sounded like just what she needed to perk her sagging mood. "Speaking of Arianna, where is she?"

"Putting up her feet in the back room," he replied. "Sitting on the piano stool for so long was hard on her back."

"She should have said something."

"Are you kidding? You know what Arianna's like when it comes to pianos. She was having way too much fun." From the center of the room, a child let out a high-pitched squeal. "Sounds like they're having fun, too," he noted.

"Who? The children or Prince Armando?"

"Both. I think this is the first time I've actually seen Arianna's brother smile. Granted, I've only known him about a week, so I might be misjudging…"

"No, you're not," Rosa replied, thinking of the media's nickname. "Prince Armando isn't known for his jovial side in public. This is definitely one of the few events where he truly lets himself relax and enjoy the moment."

"Hard not to enjoy yourself when you're around children," she added, as out on the floor Armando scooped up another toddler. "Although some people can't shake their mean streaks no matter what. If they could, we wouldn't need a place like Christina's Home." Wives wouldn't be made to feel like second-class citizens simply because they weren't perfect or, heaven forbid, carried a few extra pounds.

"Tell me about it," Max said. The bitterness in his voice surprised her. "Only thing that made my old man happy was a bottle. Or smacking my mom."

Rosa winced. "Some people need to mistreat their loved ones to feel better about themselves."

"That sounds like personal knowledge."

"A little."

He paused to look at her over his cup. "Your father was an A-hole, too? Pardon the language."

"No, my ex-husband." Normally, she avoided talking about Fredo, especially here at the shelter where there were women who had suffered far worse than she, but it was hard to brush off a kindred spirit. "And the word you used is a very apt description."

"I'm sorry."

Rosa stared at her untouched espresso, grateful he didn't press for more. But then, one of things about a kindred spirit was they didn't want to share either, so not asking worked to their benefit. "Me, too," she replied. "But at least when I finally worked up the courage to leave, I had people to turn to. I'm not sure what I would have done otherwise." Most likely, she would be with Fredo still, fifty pounds heavier and with her self-esteem completely eroded.

"So Christina's Home is more than a memorial to your sister then," Max said.

"My sister would have been the first person to say we need places like Christina's Home," she replied. She also would have been horrified to learn about the truth of Rosa's marriage. "But yes. If someone like me, with connections to the king, of all people, had trouble working up the courage to leave, I can't imagine what it is like for a woman who has no one."

Max's tight smile said he knew but wasn't going to talk about it. "At least you left eventually. More power to you."

Much to Rosa's relief, he tossed his crumpled paper cup into a nearby trash bin, indicating the conversation was over. "I better go check on Arianna and make sure she's truly resting. She's only just over the morning sickness stuff, and I don't want her pushing herself more than she needs to."

"If she's anything like her brother, she will," Rosa replied. "When the Santoros make a commitment, they do so one hundred and ten percent. It's ingrained in their DNA."

"No kidding. I almost lost Arianna because of it," Max replied. "Wish me luck getting her to put her feet up."

"Good luck," She waited until he'd moved away before letting her smile fade. Talking about Fredo had taken the edge off her holiday cheer.

"Is it true?" a familiar voice asked.

Armando stood behind her, still in costume. His eyes were like bright blue glass amid all his fake white hair. "What you told Max about Fredo, is it true?"

Dammit. How much had he heard? Rosa wanted to look anywhere but at him and those eyes filled with questions and…and pity. Exactly what she didn't want to see. God, looking her reflection in the eye was hard enough. How was she supposed to look at him every day if he saw her as some kind of…of…victim?

"I'm going to get some more cake," she announced. She didn't want to talk about Fredo right now, and cake never asked questions.

"Rosa, wait." He chased after her, catching her hand just as she got to the serving table.

"Armando," she whispered harshly, "the children."

Armando looked around, saw several of the youngest ones watching their interaction, and released her hand. "Why didn't you tell me?" he asked.

"Because…" She didn't finish. The anguish in her eyes answered for her, and it nearly kicked the legs out from under him. "It's in the past. What does it matter now?"

It mattered to him. If he had known, he might have done something. Stopped it somehow.

All those nights discussing the shelter… He'd thought Rosa's passion lay in memorializing her sister, but he'd been wrong. While he had been waxing sympathetic about the women they were helping, Rosa never said a word. How long had she suffered? Why hadn't he or Christina noticed? Were they so caught up in their own worlds they missed the signs? Or had Rosa been skilled at hiding them? His stomach ached for wondering. The strength it must have taken for her to walk away, the courage.

He took a good long look at the woman he'd been calling his right hand these last three years. She looked the same as always, and yet it was as though he was seeing her for the first time. What else didn't he know about her?

Suddenly he wanted to be free of the party so the two of them could talk. He had so many questions.

Before he realized, he was taking her hand again. The anguish flashed in her eyes again. "Armando…" she pleaded.

Fine. He wouldn't push her right now. That didn't mean the conversation was over. He had too many questions—was too angry and ashamed of himself—to let the subject drop. "Just tell me one thing," he asked. "Did Christina know?"

She shook her head. "No."

In a weird way, he found himself relieved. He wasn't sure how he would feel if he'd discovered Christina had known, but apparently Rosa had suffered in silence. If only he'd known…

Someone tugged on his hem of his jacket. "Babbo, Babbo, Babbo!"

Damn this costume. Biting back a sigh, he instead turned to see what his visitor found so urgent.

A pair of blond pigtails and giant brown eyes looked up at him. Armando recognized the girl from earlier, a five-year-old named Daniela who had gotten a circus play set. In fact, she held one of the set's plastic elephants in her hand. Quickly he cleared his voice. Wasn't the child's fault she'd interrupted an important moment. "Ho, ho, ho, Daniela. You're not trying to get another early present out of me, are you?" he asked, hoping his voice sounded lighthearted.

The little girl shook her head. "You're standing under the mistletoe."

What? He looked up and saw the familiar sprig of

white berries dangling from a ceiling panel. "And you want a kiss from Babbo, is that it?"

Again, Daniela shook her head. "You have to kiss her," she said pointing behind him. Slowly, he turned to Rosa, whose hand he still held. Which was the only reason she was still standing there, if the look on her face was any indication.

His eyes dropped to her lips, causing his pulse to skip. He hadn't kissed a woman since Christina's death.

Meanwhile, some of the older children who had been standing near the refreshment table figured out what was happening and began chanting in a singsong chorus, "Babbo's under the mistletoe. Babbo's under the mistletoe." The little devils. The lot of them were old enough to know his true identity, too. Probably thought it would be funny to make the prince kiss someone. He looked back at Daniela.

"Aren't I supposed to kiss the person who caught me under the mistletoe?" he asked. A quick peck on the little girl's cheek to quiet everyone.

"No. It has to be her. She was the one standing with you."

"Kiss her. Kiss her," the other children started chanting. Didn't they have parents to teach them how to behave?

"Babbo has to leave to go back to his workshop," Rosa said. In the short time since he'd turned toward her, her expression had transformed from wanting to flee to sheer terror. Armando's ego winced. Surely the idea of kissing him couldn't be that terrible?

"Daniela is right, signora," he said. "Tradition is tradition. You wouldn't want to break tradition, would you?"

"I—I suppose not." Her gaze dropped to her feet. She had very long lashes, he realized. Reminded him of tiny black fans.

"Good." It was only one small kiss. The two of them could argue about its awkwardness tomorrow morning.

Still holding her hand, he slipped his other arm around her waist and pulled her close. It was, he realized, the first time he'd ever put his arms around her, and he discovered her body was as pleasantly soft and curvy as it looked. The swell of her behind rested just beneath his splayed fingers, and it seemed to dare him to slip his hand lower. Instead, he focused on her lips, which were apparently as dry as his mouth had suddenly become, because she was running her tongue across the lower one. Her lips looked pleasantly soft and full, too.

"Kiss her. Kiss her," the children chanted.

He dipped his head.

The kiss lasted five seconds. When he stepped away, Rosa's cheeks were bright pink, and he…

His lips were tingling.

He didn't know what to say. "I—"

"Gelato," Rosa cut in. "I—I mean, we need to check the gelato." She turned and hurried toward the kitchen.

"Rosa, wait," he called after her, but she disappeared behind closed doors without turning around. Apparently the moment hadn't erased her desire to flee their discussion.

"Are you all right, Babbo?" Daniela asked. The little girl's eyes were wide with concern.

"That's a good question, Daniela." Looking back to the kitchen door, Armando ran his tongue across his lip, which tasted faintly of espresso. Was he?

CHAPTER FOUR

BY TIMING HER comings and goings around Armando's schedule, Rosa was able to avoid the man for much of the next week. She was being a coward, yes, but she needed the space considering the way she'd reacted to Armando's kiss.

Hardly a kiss. A peck under the mistletoe. Yet here she was, reliving every detail from the way his lips tasted—like breath mints—to the sensation of his artificial beard against her skin. He was right—it scratched.

She was running her finger across her lips again. *Stop it, stop it, stop it.* Balling her fingers, she tried hammering her fist against the chair arm in time with her silent chant, only the rhythm was too similar to *Kiss her, kiss her, kiss her.* Before she could help herself, the chants had switched.

Apparently her increased awareness wasn't going away any time soon.

It was all so awkward and weird, this sudden realization that Armando was a man. She could only assume his getting married caused her subconscious to wake up as far as dating was concerned. Why else would her chest be filled with a hollow, jealous ache whenever she thought about it? She wanted what Armando would have. Or so she was telling herself. She didn't want to contemplate the other reason for her reactions.

As for Armando…the kiss obviously hadn't fazed him. He'd left a note the other morning saying that Mona would be attending the Christina's Home concert on Friday night. Escorting the woman to his late wife's memorial concert would certainly let Corinthia know he was ready to move on.

Hammering her fist on the chair arm again, she sat back and took another look at the morning's paper. In the upper left-hand corner ran Mona's photo with a headline that read Our New Princess? A small story on the inside page reported on Armando's growing closeness with the Yelgierian royal family as of late, and implied there would be a marriage announcement soon.

"We missed you last evening." Princess Arianna strolled into the office without notice, knocking not being a royal requirement. She was dressed casually—for her, anyway—in a simple black skirt and flowing pink silk blouse. In deference to her pregnancy, the hem hung untucked. "At the tree lighting," she added. "You didn't attend."

The tree lighting, when King Carlos lit the tree in the palace's grand archway, marked the official start of Corinthia's holiday season. Until last night, Rosa had attended almost every one. Next to the shelter festival, it was one of her favorite Christmas traditions.

"I'm sorry," she said. "I simply had too much work to do to get away."

"Funny, Armando didn't mention you were working. In fact, he didn't seem to know where you were."

But he hadn't been looking for her, either. "I worked at home," she replied. "Armando…that is, he didn't know I was behind."

"Is that so?" Rosa tried not to react when the princess looked down at her pristinely organized desk. People with neat desks could be busy, too.

"Maybe he should get you some help. It's not fair that you have so much work that you have to miss a Corinthian tradition."

"That's not necessary, Your Highness. I'm caught up now." That was all she needed, to look like she couldn't handle her workload.

"Glad to hear it," Arianna replied, "because I would kill Armando if you were too busy to celebrate with us next week. Which reminds me, you are coming to the dinner, are you not?"

"I— Are you sure you want me there?" The dinner was a private affair for family and dignitaries the night before the ceremony.

"Of course I do," Arianna replied. "You're family, aren't you?"

"Technically, no."

"Close enough. You're an important part of Armando's life, and therefore you're important to all of us."

"How can I say no after that?" Rosa replied, surprised to feel a lump in her throat. It had been a long time since someone had said she was anything other than a stupid waste of time. And while the idea of spending an evening watching Armando and Mona get acquainted left a sour taste in her mouth, the princess was smiling such a sweet, sincere smile, Rosa didn't have the heart to decline.

Besides, she would have to face Armando—and Mona—eventually. Maybe seeing them together would kill the weird feelings she was having.

Meanwhile, Arianna's smile grew broader upon Rosa's acceptance. "I'm so glad. Max's best friend from New York is coming, too, and I can't wait for the two of you to meet. Not for romantic reasons," she added when Rosa started to say something. "I just think he needs a dinner partner who will keep him on his toes."

"Oh. Thank you, I guess." She couldn't imagine keeping anyone other than Armando on his toes, but if Arianna thought so, she would try.

"It's a compliment, I assure you." Perching on the edge of Rosa's desk, Arianna turned the newspaper around. "Future princess, huh? Wonder where they came up with that idea?"

"I read the article. It's mostly speculation."

Arianna arched her brow. "I'm going to blame your naïveté on not having enough coffee. Armando hasn't dated since Christina passed away, and out of the blue the press start speculating on the exact woman he plans to marry? Impossible. Someone whispered in a reporter's ear. The only question is who is doing the whispering—Armando or King Omar. My guess is on Armando."

Rosa didn't understand. Princess Arianna's explanation about a leak made perfect sense, but she would think King Omar the more likely source, not her brother. "Why would His Highness leak information about his private life?"

"Because I know how my big brother's mind works. I'm starting to show. It's obvious to anyone who can add that I've been pregnant longer than I've known Max." A soft smile curled her lips as her hand patted her abdomen. She glanced back at the photograph. "This is Armando's way of diverting attention away from my growing bump."

Made sense. After all, he'd arranged a marriage to prevent scandal. Why not arrange for a little well-timed tabloid gossip, too? "He's trying to be a good king," she said.

"That's Armando. Corinthia and family first."

Responsible for every light in every window. "He takes fulfilling his duty very seriously," she replied.

"Always has," Arianna said. "Although he's gotten worse the last couple years. Sometimes I think he's decided that if he can't be happy anymore, he'll make sure everyone else in Corinthia is."

Rosa's heart twisted at the thought. She didn't know what bothered her more, Armando falling for his wife or him going through the motions for the rest of his life.

"Speaking of my brother, what do you think?"

It took a moment for Rosa to realize the princess was talking about Mona herself. Took a lot of discipline, but she managed to swallow the sour taste in her mouth before replying. "I wouldn't know, Your Highness."

"Please," the princess replied. She added an eye roll for good measure. "Don't go into acting, Rosa. You're terrible."

"But I really wouldn't know," Rosa replied honestly. "I haven't met her. She's very beautiful, though. And her father certainly speaks highly of her."

"Fathers usually do," Arianna replied. "According to mine, I am the purest creature to ever walk the earth." Her grin was nothing short of cheeky as she pointed to her midsection. "I think I'll wait until I've met the woman to see if she lives up to her advance praise. Armando says she's attending the concert tonight?"

"Yes. She is supposed to arrive late this afternoon." Rosa had been trying to figure out an excuse to avoid her arrival all week.

"You don't look happy about the idea."

"Excuse me?" So much for keeping her thoughts private. She really was a terrible actress.

"No worries," Arianna replied. "I understand. This is a concert for your sister, and here's Armando infringing upon her memory by introducing his future wife."

"No, that's not the reason." Everyone was so quick to blame her loyalty to Christina. Armando thought the same thing regarding the shelter party. The simple, shameful truth, however, had nothing to do with Christina.

"What is the reason then?"

Rosa opened, then shut her mouth. What did she say? She couldn't very well tell Armando's sister the truth—that she was dreading a night of simultaneous jealousy and embarrassment.

Fortunately the telephone saved her. When she heard the voice on the other end, her eyes widened.

"That was King Omar's secretary," she said when she hung up. "Apparently his daughter hasn't completely recovered from the flu and is feeling too ill to fly."

"Meaning she's not coming tonight?"

"I'm afraid not." Rosa's stomach took a happy little bounce at the news, even though she knew it shouldn't.

From Arianna's expression, she didn't do a good job of hiding her reaction, either. "Armando will be disappointed," she noted.

Immediately Rosa was ashamed of herself. "Yes," she said, "I imagine he will be." He no doubt meant for this appearance to be Mona's introduction to the Corinthian people.

"Where is my dear brother, anyway?" Arianna asked. "I came by because I wanted to talk to him about a rumored cut to the arts endowment budget."

"According to the note he left on my desk, he is at the swimming pool doing laps."

"Really? Max is swimming laps right now as well." With surprising spryness for a pregnant woman, the princess hopped off the desk. "I was planning to go visit him after I spoke to Armando. Why don't the two of us go together and you can tell Armando about Mona's cancellation?"

See Armando. At the pool. That happy little bounce turned into a shiver as she pictured a muscular and wet Armando emerging from the water like a men's fragrance advertisement come to life. "I thought I would send him a text…" she started.

"Don't be silly. I don't feel like waiting for him to check his messages before talking to him about it. Come down with me, and we will tell him in person."

This was the downside of working for royalty. It was impossible to refuse when they decided a plan of action. Suppressing a sigh, Rosa pushed to her feet. "After you, Your Highness."

Maybe she'd get lucky, and Armando would stay in the water while they talked.

The pool was an Olympic-size addition built in what had been an unused greenhouse on the edge of the palace gardens in the mid–twentieth century. When his children were younger, King Carlos had the aging facility refurbished, transforming what had been a bland indoor pool into a paradise filled with flowers and soothing flowing water. The bamboo and hibiscus served as more than decoration—they created a foliage privacy wall so that the royal family could relax in peace. For as long as Rosa had known Armando, the room had been one of his favorite places. Since moving into the palace, Max, had taken to visiting the pool as well.

A block of hot humid air hit Rosa when she opened the door to the building. It'd been a while since she'd visited Armando in his sanctuary, and so she had forgotten how much of a contrast there was between here and the garden path that connected the two buildings, especially during the winter. She could feel her shirt starting to stick against her skin in the dampness, destroying every bit of flowing camouflage. Wasn't worth pulling the garment free, either, since it would only cling right back.

A shout called her attention toward the pool where Armando and Max were splashing their way from one end to the other.

"Looks like they are racing," Rosa remarked.

"Of course they are. They're men," Princess Arianna replied. She did peel her shirt away from her skin. "This is the first time I've ever watched Max swim. I didn't know he was such a good swimmer."

He was definitely the faster of the two—his pale body was a good length ahead—but Armando had better style. His bronze shoulders rose up and down in the water, like a well-tuned piston. Rosa envied how he could be graceful both on land and in the water.

Unsurprisingly, Max reached the wall first. When he realized Arianna and Rosa were standing there, he pulled himself out of the water.

"Well, isn't this a pleasant surprise?" he said, leaning forward to give Arianna a kiss. From the way he twisted his body, he was doing everything he could not to let his wet body come in contact with hers.

Rosa couldn't help but look him up and down. The man was definitely as well built as his movie-star looks implied. Princess Arianna was a lucky woman.

Armando's voice sounded behind her. "Next time, we do more. We'll see if you're so fast when you have to make a turn, eh? Can someone hand me a towel?"

Someone being her, of course. Rosa should have known he wouldn't stay in the water. There was a large white one draped over the back of a nearby chair. Steeling herself for what she was about to see, Rosa grabbed it and turned around.

Oh, my.

Forget fragrance ad come to life. Try sea god.

Anyone who met the man could tell Armando was well built simply from the way his clothes draped his body. What the clothes didn't show was how virile he was. He made Max Brown look like a young boy. Awareness spread from her core as she took in the muscular, wet body, its contours glistening under the lights. Droplets clung to his chest hair, like tiny crystal ornaments. Wordlessly, she watched as he wiped them away with the towel, her breath catching a little on each stroke across his skin.

If she couldn't stop thinking about a peck on the lips…

"Rosa?"

She jerked her attention back to his face to find him

looking at her with unusual intensity. "Is everything all right?" he asked. "You looked flushed."

Because you're beautiful. "It's the heat," she replied. "It's like a sauna in here."

"Well, the room was designed for people in bathing suits." He wrapped the towel around his waist, and Rosa let out a breath. Never did she think wearing a towel would be modest. "I said I was surprised to see you. You've been avoiding me."

He'd noticed? Of course he had. She hadn't exactly been subtle about staying away. "No, I haven't," she lied anyway. "There is a lot going on, is all. I have been very busy coordinating the various year-end events."

"Right. Coordinating. I understand," he said in a voice that said he didn't believe her in the slightest. "Why are you here now, then? Did something happen?"

His eyes had not just dropped to her lips and back. He was a man about to marry an amazing beauty. The last thing he would waste time on was their mistletoe kiss, unless he was remembering her foolish bolt through the kitchen door.

"I—" Rosa began. This would have been so much easier if Arianna had let her send a text. Thanks to his half-dressed state, the moment felt far more intimate than it was. What was more, the princess wasn't even talking to Armando. She and Max had taken themselves to one of the many lounge chairs, leaving her and Armando alone.

"King Omar's office called. Mona is still feeling ill and won't be able to attend the concert tonight."

"Oh."

That was an…odd reaction. Detached and almost relieved sounding. Surely that couldn't be the case. "I thought I should let you know as soon as possible in case this affects your plans for the evening."

"You could have texted."

"Arianna wanted me to tell you in person."

"Oh." That answer did come with a reaction. A conspiratorial smile that said he understood exactly what had happened. They usually shared dozens of such smiles during the course of a normal week. Seeing this one made her feel all melty inside. She'd missed his company, dammit.

"Anyway…" She cleared her throat. "If you would like to cancel…"

"Cancel? Why on earth would I cancel?"

"I only thought that with Mona not attending…" Seeing his frown, she left her answer hanging. "Never mind."

"Never mind is right. I can't believe you even suggested I wouldn't attend." He headed toward a bench by one of the bamboo trees where a robe and additional towels lay. As he brushed past her, his bare shoulder made contact with hers, and Rosa's insides turned to jitters at the feeling of dampness through her blouse. It was as close to skin against skin as she'd felt in a long time.

"You're right," she replied, rubbing the goose bumps from her arms. "I don't know what I was thinking. This morning's newspaper article speculating on your marriage must have skewed my reasoning."

He was flipping a towel around his neck when she asked. Gripping both ends, he cocked his head. "What does that mean?"

"It means, I know it was to be an important public appearance for the two of you." The first step in establishing the seriousness of their relationship."

An odd look crossed his features. "Right. I forgot about the gossip column. It would have been nice to have Mona make an appearance, but seeing as how the marriage is all but a fait accompli, it's not completely necessary.

"Besides," he added as he reached for his robe, "it's not as if the people aren't used to seeing me attend events alone.

"You're still attending, right?" he asked, shrugging into the robe.

"Of course. It's my sister's memorial concert. I wouldn't miss it for the world." Not even Mona's presence would have stopped her. "I can't believe you asked."

"What are you talking about? You asked me the same question two minutes ago. And, considering I haven't seen you all week, I didn't want to assume."

There was a bite to his comment that took her aback. She thought they had addressed this. "I told you, I have had a lot to take care of this week."

"Coordinating. So you said." He tugged on his terrycloth belt before looking her in the eye. Rosa tried not to squirm, but the intensity of his stare was too unnerving. He was trying to see inside her again. "Look, I know why you have been avoiding me," he said.

"You do?" Heaven help her, could they go back to talking about Mona? Please? Not only was her embarrassing reaction to their mistletoe kiss the last thing she wanted to talk about, this was the last place where she wanted to not talk about it—in a steamy pool house with him wearing nothing but a bathrobe.

"I owe you an apology."

"You do?" she repeated. For what?

"It was…rude…of me to confront you the way I did. Regarding Fredo. I put you on the spot, and I shouldn't have."

"I see." She had forgotten their argument about Fredo, her mind focused on their kiss. Apparently, circumstances were the other way around for Armando. He wasn't thinking about the kiss at all. Which was a good thing, right? Meant she didn't have to avoid him anymore.

There was no reason for her insides to feel deflated. "Th-thank you," she replied. "I appreciate that."

On the other side of the pool, Arianna and Max lay side by side in one of the lounge chairs. Max had slipped on his bathrobe, and the two of them looked to be in deep conversation. Whatever problem Arianna had with the budget seemed to have taken a backseat to her fiancé. They looked so happy and engrossed with each other. Maybe it was talking about Fredo, but looking at them left Rosa aching with envy. What she wouldn't give for a man who listened to what she had to say with interest instead of patronizing her or putting her down. Someone who respected her and didn't continually remind her of her many, many flaws. *You're fat. You sound like an idiot.*

A girl could dream, couldn't she? Even if the odds of a woman like her finding someone like Max Brown were slim to none. Heck, the only person she knew who fit her bill was… Max.

She turned back in time to discover Armando was studying her again. Only this time, instead of feeling like he was looking inside her, she broke out in a tingling, achy sensation that cut through her stomach to deep below her waist.

"Get dressed," she said abruptly. "I mean, you need to get dressed and I… I should get back to the office. I'll see you when you return."

Spinning on her toe of her shoe, she turned and headed toward the pool house door. Arianna was right about her acting skills. At least this time, her excuse sounded better than having to double-check gelato quantities.

"Rosa, wait."

Armando chuckled when Rosa turned around. She looked like an animal trapped in the headlights of an automobile. Wide-eyed and hesitant. And damn if he didn't find it appealing.

"Are you bringing a guest to the concert?" he asked.

He could tell she didn't know what to make of his question. "You mean, do I have a date?"

"Exactly. I was curious if, after our conversation the other day, you weren't inspired to…improve…your social life."

Was that a blush creeping into her cheeks or simply a flush from the warm air? "You're curious about a lot of things lately."

About her, he was. It disturbed him to realize he didn't know her as well as he thought. Like the proverbial onion, there were layers he'd yet to peel back, and dammit if he didn't want to see what lay beneath. "Are you?" he asked.

"No," she replied after a pause. "I haven't had the opportunity to…improve…anything. I've been busy."

"Why don't we sit together, then?"

Rosa nearly choked. "Together? As in sit with you in the front row of the royal box?"

"Why not? Now that Mona isn't attending, the seat next to me will be empty."

"Yes, but I always sit behind you at royal events."

A rule of her own making. Armando couldn't care less about seating arrangements. In fact, it sometimes aggravated him the way Rosa would stick herself in the background, as though she were afraid to take up space. "Well, tonight I'd like you to sit in the front row with me."

"I—"

"As you said, this concert is as important to you as it is me. Tonight will be the last concert I will host before I get married. This is our opportunity to pay homage to Christina together one last time."

A shadow darkened her features. Using Christina was a low blow, but her sister's memory was the one thing Rosa couldn't resist. "I suppose," she said in a soft voice.

"Good, it's settled. We'll attend together. I will pick you up at your apartment at seven."

"Fine. Seven o'clock," she replied. "Is there anything else?"

Yes, she could try to sound a little excited. "Feel free to take the afternoon off. I know how you women like to primp for these things."

"Thank you," she replied. Armando wondered if she was grateful for the extra preparation time or the chance to avoid him a little longer. Just because she seemed to accept his apology didn't mean she wasn't still upset with him, as her reluctance to attend the concert together showed.

He watched as she turned and continued to the door. Damn, but he hated those long blazers of hers. This one was charcoal gray and went to the hem of her skirt. If there was one thing he'd noticed over the years it was that Rosa had an unparalleled walk, as good as any of the runway models in Milan. Whenever she moved, she led with her pelvis, causing her hips to swivel from side to side. And, because unlike a runway model, she carried some actual meat on her bones, her bottom half undulated with a fluidity that was amazingly sensual. Reminded him of wine swirling in a glass.

Except when she wore those blasted blazers. If she tried to wear one tonight, he would burn it.

"Was that Rosa leaving?" Arianna asked when the door clicked shut.

"I gave her the afternoon off," he replied. "She's attending the concert with me—that is, we're going to cohost the event." The other way made it sound like a date, which this wasn't. No matter how his body had reacted when she said yes.

"What a nice idea," his sister said.

"I thought we should since Mona is unable to come." And it would be their last opportunity.

Did his relief upon hearing Mona had canceled make him a horrible person? One would think he would want to spend time with his prospective bride. Wasn't that why he'd invited her to the concert in the first place? So they could get to know each other?

And then he could start fantasizing about her rather than about the kiss he'd shared with Rosa.

He shoved that last thought to the back of his mind where it belonged. He was not fantasizing about Rosa. Not really. She was his sister-in-law, for crying out loud. His sex drive had reawakened, that was all. A man could only live as a monk for so long, and Rosa happened to be the woman who was there when his inner male returned.

As for tonight, it was only fitting they cohost the event. To honor Christina.

And if he wanted to make sure she had a proper time? Well, that was simply because she deserved an enjoyable evening and had nothing to do with wanting to make her feel special.

Nothing at all.

CHAPTER FIVE

WHAT HAD SHE been thinking? Rosa smoothed her hands along her hips. When she tried it on, the saleswoman flattered her to Rome and back with a pitch about how this dress's straight cut accentuated her figure rather than making her look large and hippy. Flush from the ego boost, Rosa had let herself be talked into going against her normal style. It wasn't just the silhouette that was out of character; it was the bright red color and slightly bare shoulders, too. *Live a little*, she'd thought at the time. *No one's going to care what you wear.*

That was before she knew she would be sitting in the front row.

Next to Armando.

As his date.

Not a date. Calling tonight a date made the evening sound like it was something special rather than two friends attending an event together. Which the two of them had done dozens of times before. The only thing different about tonight was the seating arrangement.

And the fact he was picking her up.

And that the concert would be broadcast across all of Corinthia. With her seated by Armando's side, which would make her look like his date.

Had he known that when he asked her?

Her palms started to sweat. Moving to rub them on her skirt, she caught herself in time.

Squaring her shoulders, she turned left, then right, looking for any unshapely bumps or bulges. The saleswoman had been right about one thing—the dress certainly emphasized her shape. Daily walking had made her legs firm and toned, while good old control-top undergarments had firmed up the rest. She looked, dare she say it, not that bad. If only the dress weren't bright. So attention seeking.

What makes you think anyone is going to be looking at you?

Three years and Fredo's voice was as loud as ever in her head, taking her confidence and crushing it into bits.

You're a cow. You're an embarrassment.

The last thing she wanted was to embarrass Armando.

Maybe she had time to change. The black dress from last Christmas, he had liked that one, hadn't he? Or the navy blue one she wore two years ago with the sequined bodice. Could she still fit into it?

She never stressed like this over dresses before.

Then again, she'd never been Armando's date before. Not a date, she quickly amended.

Just then her living room clock chimed seven. Barely

had the last clang sounded when the doorbell rang. Rosa jumped. What the— Three years of having to hustle him out the door, and the one night he had to get ready without her, he was on time?

She opened the door to find him with one shoulder propped against the door frame. Naturally, he looked amazing, the stiff white collar gleaming against his darker skin. In a flash, Rosa's mind peeled off the clothing to picture the man she saw swimming this morning. All six feet three inches of carved muscle.

"Hi." The greeting came out a breathy whisper, far too intimate sounding for the circumstances. She cringed inwardly.

Armando eyes widened. "You look..."

She knew it. The dress was too bright.

"Gorgeous," he finished. "I mean it, that dress is..."

"Thank you. The woman at the boutique talked me into trying something different."

"Good for her. You should wear red more often. The color suits you."

Rosa hoped so, because now her cheeks were the same color as her dress, a combination of modesty and embarrassment over her reaction. This wasn't the first time Armando had ever paid her a compliment, yet awareness ghosted across her skin like it was. Made her feel more feminine and beautiful than she had in years. "You look nice, too," she told him, looking up through her lashes. "Very...regal."

"Damn. I was going for dashing."

Mission definitely accomplished. Almost. "One little

thing," she said. His tie was crooked. "You never can get your tie proper," she said, reaching up.

"That's because you weren't there to help me," he replied, lifting his chin. "Arianna had to tie it for me."

"Well, that explains why it's better than usual."

Rosa felt his warm breath on the top of her head as she adjusted the tie. Despite having done this dozens of times, she'd never noticed the distinctness of his aftershave until now. Reminded her of a wood after summer rain, earthy and cool. The kind of scent that made a person want to run barefoot through the moss.

Or comb their fingers through their hair.

"There." Smoothing his collar, she stepped back before her thoughts could embarrass her again. "Much better."

He gave her a smile. "Whatever would I do without you?"

"Spend eternity with a crooked tie, for one thing." Once again, her body reacted as though he weren't making a comment he'd made before. This was ridiculous. Tonight was really no different from any other night. Why, then, was she acting as though it was? Surely she wasn't so desperate for male validation that her subconscious needed to assign deeper meaning to everything Armando said and did. "I just need to get my wrap and I'll be ready to go."

"You're not..."

"What?" She'd not gotten more than a few feet before he spoke. Turning around, she caught the hint of a blush crawling down his cheekbones.

"You're not going to put on some jacket and wear it all night, are you?"

"No. Just a velvet wrap for when we're outside. Why?"

"No reason," he replied quickly. "It's…well, I'm not as big a fan of jackets as you are."

"I wouldn't be either, if I had your rock-hard abdomen." Rosa squeezed her eyes shut. Please say she didn't speak those words aloud.

Armando chuckled as he sauntered toward her. "You were looking at my abdomen, were you?"

"Not on purpose. It's difficult to ignore a man's torso when he's standing in a bathing suit."

"I see. Well, I'm glad you found my torso to your satisfaction."

"That's not what I meant."

"Oh?" He reached around her to lift her wrap from where it lay draped on the back of her chair. "What did you mean, then?"

"Simply that your midsection doesn't need camouflaging."

"Neither does yours," he replied, laying the velvet across her shoulders. "You worry too much about your weight. Curves are to be celebrated. There's a reason Botticelli didn't paint stick figures, you know," he added, low in her ear.

Rosa's knees nearly buckled at the way his breath tickled her skin. "I'll try to remember that."

"Please do. There's nothing worse than listening to a beautiful woman denigrate herself."

"Nothing?" Rosa asked, trying to react to the word *beautiful*. He'd handed her more compliments in the past five minutes than she'd had in the last decade.

His returning smile was devastating. "Well, maybe not as bad as reviewing the revised energy regulations or listening to Arianna complain about the arts endowment, but definitely bad." He held out an arm. "Shall we?"

No matter how many times Rosa told herself that technically this evening was no different than any other, Armando and the evening kept proving her wrong. To begin with, there was a lot of difference between sitting in the rear of the royal box and sitting with the crown prince. In the past she would take her seat several minutes before the performance and patiently wait along with everyone else for Armando to take his seat. Tonight, she was the one hanging back while the audience assembled, the one receiving the applause as she entered the box at the Royal Opera House. Really it was Armando receiving the applause, but standing by his side, she couldn't help but feel special, too.

Armando himself was contributing to the feeling as well. She couldn't put her finger on how, but there was something about his behavior tonight. He was solicitous, charming. Flirtatious, even, peppering his conversation with subtle touches and low, lilting commentary. The skin behind her ear still tingled from their conversation in her apartment. *Curves are to be celebrated.*

She squeezed her knees together.

"Everything all right?" Armando asked, mistaking her shifting as discomfort.

"Just sitting up straight," she replied. "I don't want to get caught on camera slouching."

"Fortunately, most of the time they stay focused on the orchestra, or so I've been told. I was afraid you might not be having a good time."

"Why would you think that?" she asked, doing her best not to frown as she turned toward him.

"I don't know, perhaps because you've been avoiding me all week. I wasn't sure if you were still angry with me."

"I was never angry with you. I had a lot to do, is all."

"Then you weren't annoyed that I asked about Fredo?"

He was kidding, right? What was it that drove him to introduce awkward conversations at the most inopportune times?

"I know," he added when she opened her mouth, "you don't want to talk about him right now."

No, she did not, but now that the door was open, she figured she should at least give him a quick explanation. "Nothing personal. In my experience, anything to do with Fredo will only spoil a good time." As far as she was concerned, her ex was an ugly cloud she'd rather forget.

She started as a hand settled atop her forearm. Looking up, she noticed Armando wore a pleased expression. "Does that mean you're having a good time?"

"Very."

"Good." His hand squeezed her arm and then remained. "I'm glad. You deserve the best evening possible," he added in a low voice. His whispered breath caressed her jaw, reminding her of gentle fingertips. Thankfully, the house lights had started to dim, hiding how her skin flushed from the inside out.

Onstage, the conductor emerged from behind a curtain, drawing another round of applause. After bowing to Armando, the man stepped on his dais and tapped his baton. Like a well-trained army, the musicians raised their instruments. A moment later, the room filled with the delicate hum of violins.

"Don't tell my family," Armando whispered in her ear. Between the dark and the hand on her arm, the innocent comment sent a trail of goose bumps down her spine. "But I do not like classical music."

"Since when?" Considering the way his sister and late mother had revered music, the confession wasn't just shocking, it was almost treasonous.

"Since ever," he replied. "Why do you think Arianna is the only one who still plays the piano? As soon as I could, I stopped lessons and haven't touched a keyboard since."

"I didn't realize." Both that he disliked classical music and that he played piano. Keeping her eyes forward, she leaned her shoulder closer to his. There was something naughty about whispering together in the dark. "How long did you have to take lessons?"

"Twelve very long years."

That long? "Why didn't you stop sooner?"

"Because it was expected I would become a master."

Expected. Sadly his answer didn't surprise her. So much of what he did stemmed from expectations or tradition. Even this concert, in a way. Made her wonder how long it had been since he did anything purely for fun.

She settled back against her seat as the music crescendoed over them. "Does this mean I'll need to poke you in the ribs to keep you from nodding off?" she whispered.

"Don't be silly. I never fall asleep."

"Never?"

"Okay, not since I was twelve. I have a secret trick."

"What's that?" she asked.

Behind them, Vittorio Mastella, the head of security, gave a sharp cough, and Rosa bit her lip. Because it was the crown prince doing the whispering, no one was going to say anything directly, but apparently the security chief had no problem delivering a subtle hint. Armando smiled and winked. "I'll tell you after the concert," he whispered.

They spent the rest of the concert in silence. Unlike Armando, Rosa did enjoy classical music, although purely as an amateur. She hadn't had many opportunities to enjoy it when she was married, since Fredo would only attend a concert if there was business involved. The few times they did attend, however, were some of the best memories of her marriage. She would sit in the dark and let the music send her to a world far away, to a place where she was beautiful and happy. Like the Rosa she used to be.

As the music washed over her tonight, she realized she already felt beautiful and happy. Whether it was the dress or Armando's appreciative words or the two combined, she was content with herself for the first time in a long time. More than content—it was as though she'd woken up from a long sleep and remembered she was a woman. Her body was suddenly aware of even the lightest of touches. Armando shifted in his seat, and the brush of his pant leg against her ankle left her insides aching. It did not help that he shifted in his seat a lot. Nor the fact that his hand lingered on her forearm till midway through the concert, his long fingers absently tapping a melody against the lace. The more he tapped, the more she couldn't stop remembering how he looked climbing out of the pool. Did he know what he was doing to her? The thoughts he was putting into her head? She had no business thinking of Armando this way, like a strong, desirable man. He was… Armando. Her boss. Her brother-in-law. Her future king.

And yet, his fingers kept toying with her lace sleeve, and she kept feeling beautiful, and the fantasies played in her head until the concert ended.

Until the lights in the hall brightened and she looked down at the orchestra seats only to find herself looking into the eyes of the one man capable of washing all her confidence away.

Fredo.

* * *

Armando noticed the moment the smile disappeared from Rosa's face. It was inevitable, seeing how he couldn't stop stealing glances at her all night long. He'd always considered her attractive, but tonight was different. With her hair clipped loosely at her neck, and that dress… She had to stop wearing those damn blazers and sweater sets. A body like hers, all soft curves made for a man to run his hands down, should never be hidden. Of course, he'd always known she had a good figure. What surprised him was that he was thinking about hands and curves. Apparently he wasn't as sexually dead as he thought.

Now he followed her line of sight, zooming in on Fredo Marriota immediately. Rosa's former husband was looking up at her with an expression of surprise and disbelief. Armando watched as, despite having a date of his own, the man openly assessed Rosa's appearance. It was clear seeing Rosa in the royal box irritated him. His stare was callous and sharp and made Armando's jaw clench.

At first, Rosa appeared to shrink under her ex's scrutiny, reminding Armando of the conversation he'd overheard at the shelter. Her display of weakness lasted only for a moment, because the next thing he knew, she'd reached inside herself and found a backbone. Her shoulders straightened, and she met Fredo stare for haughty stare.

Shooting Fredo a side glance of his own, Armando made a point of slipping his hand around Rosa's waist and pulling her tight to his side. "Well played," he whispered. From Fredo's vantage point, it must have looked like he was nuzzling her neck, since the man immediately blanched. "I had no idea he would be here."

"Me neither. But then again, this is a large networking event, so I shouldn't be surprised."

"He doesn't look very happy to see the two of us together."

"It has more to do with seeing me in a capable position," Rosa replied. "What are you doing?"

He'd leaned close again, so he could talk in her ear. "Playing with him." The man could use a reminder of what he'd lost. "Every time I lean close, his eyes bulge like a frog's, or haven't you noticed?"

"I noticed. So has everyone else in the theater, for that matter. How will you explain to Mona if your picture ends up in tomorrow's paper?"

Mona, whom he hadn't thought about once since Rosa opened her front door. "She will understand," he replied.

"Are you sure? I don't want to cause trouble between you."

And Armando wanted to put Fredo in his place. She moved to break free; he held her tight.

"I am positive," he said. "I hardly think Mona's the jealous type." One of the reasons he'd selected her was her decidedly implacable nature. "Your ex-husband, however, looks as though someone stole his favorite toy." Reaching up, he pretended to brush a stray hair from her cheek. To make Fredo seethe, he said to himself. Still, he felt an unfamiliar tightening at how her skin turned pink where his fingers touched.

"Insulted, more likely. I'm sure in his mind, I attended with you on purpose just so I could make him look foolish."

"But that's..."

"Ridiculous? Not to him. Do you mind if we leave now? The car is probably waiting out front." She turned in his grip so that her back faced the orchestra, essentially dismissing the man they'd been talking about. Trying to dismiss the topic altogether, Armando suspected.

"Of course." Casting one final look over her shoulder, he guided her from the box to the door where Vittorio and other members of the royal contingent waited patiently.

"Will His Majesty be heading anywhere else this evening?" Vittorio asked as they passed.

"Just home," Rosa answered for them, forgetting she wasn't his assistant tonight. "I mean, my apartment building first, and then His Highness will be heading home."

"Actually..." Armando took another look behind him before looking back at Rosa. Despite her proud stance, the standoff with Fredo had taken a toll. The glow she'd maintained all evening had faded. He hated seeing her evening end on such a sour note. "We will both be returning the palace."

"We will? Why?"

He smiled. Was it a trick of the light or were Rosa's

eyes always this soft and brown? What would they look like lit by hundreds of Christmas lights? Would they sparkle like chocolate diamonds?

He would find out soon enough.

"Royal decree," he teased in answer to her question.

Her eyes narrowed. "What does that mean?"

"It means it is a surprise."

Normally, Armando wasn't one for surprises. It had been years since he did anything remotely spontaneous, and while in the scope of things, this surprise wasn't anything dramatic, he still found himself energized by the idea. He couldn't remember the last time he'd been excited. Bouncing on the balls of his feet, rapid pulse excited. Yet here he was, wrapped in a haze of exhilaration.

All over what was really something very silly. Didn't matter. He still looked forward to his plan.

Because he wanted to be sure Rosa's evening ended on a positive note.

It had nothing to do with wanting to see her eyes under Christmas lights.

"Have I told you that I do not like surprises?" Rosa remarked when the car pulled into the underground entrance behind the palace.

"Since when?" he replied. "I seem to recall you and your sister planning all sorts of surprises together before she and I got married."

"Correction, Christina planned surprises. I was there solely for support and labor. My life was unpredictable enough. The last thing I needed was more unpredictability."

He didn't answer until the driver had opened the door and they stepped onto the pavement. "Unpredictable. You mean Fredo." Her comments from earlier had stayed with him. They, along with the comments she'd made to Max at the shelter, were forming a very ugly picture.

Her steps stuttered. "I don't want to talk about Fredo right now," she said, looking to her shoes.

She never did, Armando wanted to say. That she continued to shut down the conversation when he asked hurt. Childish, he knew, but he needed her to open up to him. Why wouldn't she? They were family, were they not?

Except the appreciation running through him as he watched her walk ahead of him didn't feel very familial. All women should move so fluidly.

Good Lord, but his thoughts were all over the map this evening.

At least he wasn't the only one having appreciative thoughts, he said to himself as he caught the overnight guard stealing a glance in Rosa's direction. Yet again, his mind went back to Fredo, and he wondered what was wrong with the man that he could find fault with a woman as likable and attractive as Rosa.

Looking at her now, standing by the elevator with a bag clutched to her chest, her gaze contemplative and distant, something inside him lurched. She really was beautiful.

"I'm sorry if I upset you," he said. Thus far, the excursion wasn't going as planned.

"No, I'm the one who should apologize. Here you are trying to do something nice, and I'm being difficult."

Unlike at the concert hall when he'd pretended in front of Fredo, this time there was real hair clinging to her cheek. Armando brushed it free with the back of his hand. "You couldn't be difficult if you tried."

"I hope you don't expect me to say neither are you," she replied, ducking her head.

"Why not? It wouldn't kill you to lie, would it?"

"Possibly."

Normally, the banter diffused any tension that was between them, but this time, the air remained thick as they stepped on the elevator. Armando wasn't completely surprised. A strange atmosphere had been swirling around them all evening.

At nearly four hundred years old, the grand palace of Corinthia could be broken into two major sections—the original front section, which was open to the public, and the royal residence and offices, which resided in the more modern rear section. When the elevator doors opened, Rosa instinctively headed toward the offices. Chuckling, he grabbed her hand and tugged her toward the original castle.

"Okay, I admit I'm curious now," she said. "Isn't this section of the building closed this time of night?"

"To the public. It is never closed to me. Come along."

In the center, a quartet of stairways came together in a large open area known as the grand archway. Armando literally felt a thrill as he led her toward one of the staircases. Below them, the floor below the archway was pitched in blackness.

"Now," he said, pausing, "I need you to wait here and close your eyes."

"And then what? You will push me down the stairs?"

"I might, if you don't do what I say."

He waited until she obliged, then hurried down the darkened stairwell. Thankfully, years of childhood explorations left him with indelible memories of every nook and cranny. He located everything in a matter of minutes. When he finished, he positioned himself at the bottom of the stairs.

"All right," he called up. "Open your eyes."

Rosa's gasp might have been the most beautiful noise he had heard in a very long time.

CHAPTER SIX

HE'D LIT THE Corinthian Christmas tree.

Rosa had seen the official tree many times in her life, but this was the first time she'd ever seen the archway illuminated solely by Christmas lights. She gazed in marvel at the towering Italian spruce. The theme this year was red and gold, and somehow the decorator had managed to find golden Christmas lights. As a result, the entire archway was bathed in the softest yellow.

From his spot at the bottom of the stairs, Armando smiled at her. "What do you think? Do you still not like surprises?" he asked.

Rosa's answer caught in her throat. Standing there in the golden glow of the trees, he looked a tuxedoed Christmas god, beautiful and breathtaking.

"Amazing," she whispered. She didn't mean the lights.

"You missed the ceremony the other night, so I thought I would treat you to a private one. I realize as surprises go, it's a little underwhelming..."

"No." She hurried down to join him. "It's perfect."

He'd lit more than the tree. The phalanx of smaller trees that stood guard around the main one sparkled with lights, too, as did the garlands hanging from the balustrade.

"I had to skip the window candles," he told her. "They're too hard to light without a step stool."

"I'll forgive you."

Unbelievable. She sank down on the bottom step to better study the room. This was the first time she'd seen this space so quiet. Because it was the palace hub, the archway was a continual stream of noise and people. Sitting here now, in the solitude, felt more like she was in an enchanted forest filled with thousands of golden stars. There was a feeling of timelessness in the air. Watching the shadows on the stone walls, it was easy to imagine the spirits of Armando's ancestors floating back and forth among the trees. Generations of Santoros connected by tradition for eternity.

And he'd created the moment for *her*. As if she were someone important. The notion left her breathless.

"Why…" she started.

"I didn't want your encounter with Fredo to be how you ended your evening. So now, it can end with Christmas trees instead."

Rosa's insides were suddenly too full for her body. She was being overly romantic, getting emotional over a simple kindness.

But then, there'd been so many simple kindnesses tonight, hadn't there.

Armando wedged himself between her and the banister and stretched his legs out in front of him. "When my sister and I were children, we would sneak in here after everyone went to bed and light the trees," he said. "When it came to Christmas, Arianna was out of control. She couldn't get enough of the Christmas lights."

"Neither could you, it sounds like."

He shook his head. "You know Arianna. She acts first and thinks later. I had to go along if only to keep her from getting into trouble. Did you know she used to insist on sneaking into our parents' salon to try and catch Babbo Natale every year? I spent every Christmas worried she was going to knock over the tree on herself or something."

Rosa smiled. "Taking responsibility even then."

His sigh was tinged with resignation. "Someone had to."

The Melancholy Prince, thought Rosa. Told as a child he carried the responsibility for a nation. When, she wondered, was the last time he had done something purely because doing so made him happy? She already knew the answer: he'd married her sister. While Christina was alive, he had at least shown glimpses of a brighter, lighter self. Now that side of him only appeared when Rosa arm-twisted him into situations that required it. Like playing Babbo.

Until tonight. Even though at his age lighting the palace couldn't be called mischievous, his face had a brightness she hadn't seen in years. You could barely see the shadows in his blue eyes. The look especially suited him. If she could, Rosa would encourage him to play every night.

Again, he had done this *for her*.

"Thank you." She put her hand on his knee and hoped he could feel the depth of her appreciation in her touch.

"You're welcome." Maybe he did know, because he covered her hand with his.

"Christina and I used to wait up for Babbo, too," she said, looking up at the twinkling treetop. "Her idea, of course. I was always afraid he would be mad and switch us to the naughty list. I don't know why, since Christina would have talked our way out of it." No one could resist her sister, not even Santa Claus.

"True." He nudged her shoulder. "Your arm-twisting skills aren't half-bad, either. I bet you could have done some sweet talking, too."

"No, I would have stuttered and fumbled my words. I would have been the one who fell down the stairs, too. I might still, if I'm not careful. Grace is not my middle name."

Armando drew back with a frown. "Are you kidding? You're one of the most graceful women I've ever met."

"I—I am?"

"You should watch yourself walk out of a room sometime."

"You do know, now that you've said something, I'll never walk unconsciously again?"

"Sorry."

"No, I am. Putting myself down is a bad habit. I'm getting better, but conditioning takes time to overcome. Hear something enough times, and it becomes a part of you."

"Yes, it does," he replied. Like Armando and responsibility.

Together, they sat in silence. Rosa could feel the firmness of Armando's thigh against hers. Taking its cue from the hand resting atop hers, the contact marked her insides with warmth that was simultaneously thrilling and soothing. She selfishly wished Fredo would appear again so that she might feel Armando pull her tight in his arms, the way he had at the concert hall, and indulge in even more contact.

Instead, he did her one better.

"Fredo is an ass," he muttered, and she stiffened, afraid he'd read her thoughts. "I know," he said. "You don't want to talk about him, but I have to say it. The guy is a class-A jerk."

She could end the discussion right there by not saying a word, but the indignation in his voice on her behalf deserved some type of comment. "Yes, he is, although he can be charming when he needs to be."

"They always are. Isn't that what they told us at the shelter? It's why a lot of very intelligent women who should know better find themselves trapped."

A woman who should know better. That certainly described her. Rosa could feel Armando holding back his curiosity. Trying so hard to honor her request in spite of the questions running through his head.

From the very start of their friendship, he'd treated her with kindness and respect. More than any man she'd known. Most people—her parents, even—thought she was crazy to leave a wealthy, successful man like Fredo; they couldn't understand why she wouldn't be happy. But Armando had never judged her. Never asked what she thought she was doing. He trusted that she had a reason.

Perhaps it was time she offered him a little trust in return.

"I never told anyone. About Fredo," she said softly.

"Not even Christina?"

She shook her head. "Although I think she knew I was unhappy. Thing is, for a long time I thought the problem was with me. That if I wasn't such a fat, stupid fool, my marriage would be better."

"What are you talking about? You're none of those things."

"Not according to Fredo. He never missed an opportunity to tell me I was second-rate." Looking to her lap, she studied the patterns playing out in the lace. Tiny red squares that formed larger red squares, which then formed ever larger squares. She traced one of the holes with her index finger. "Didn't help that Christina was everything that I wasn't. I loved my sister, but she was so beautiful…"

"So are you."

Armando's answer made her breath catch. "You are," he repeated when she looked at him. "Your face, your eyes, your figure. The way you walk…"

"Regardless," she said, looking back to her lap. She wasn't trying to fish for compliments, even if his comments did leave her insides warm and full enough to squeeze tears.

"The point is for a long time I believed him. Same way I believed him when he reminded me how fortunate I was that he was willing to take me off my father's hands."

"I'm going to shoot the bastard," Armando muttered.

It was an extreme but flattering response. Rosa found herself fighting back a smile. "There's no need. Your performance tonight wounded him more than enough."

Armando shook his head. "He deserves worse. If I'd known—"

"Don't," she said, grasping his hands in hers. This time he wasn't talking about her not sharing, but about his not stepping in to defend her. She wouldn't have him feeling guilty because her shame kept her from speaking up. "I told you, I didn't want anyone to know."

"But why not? I could have helped you."

"You and Christina were in the middle of this great romance—I didn't want to ruin the mood with my problems. And then, after Christina died, you were grieving. It wasn't the time. Besides…" Here was the true answer. "I was ashamed."

"You had nothing to be ashamed about."

Didn't she? "Do you know how hard it is to admit you spent nearly a decade allowing someone to strip you of your self-respect because you thought you deserved it?" Even now, the regret choked her like bile when she thought of the power Fredo had held over her. Power she'd given him. A tear slipped from the corner of her eye. She moved to swipe the moisture away only to have Armando's thumb pass across her skin first. When he was finished, his hand remained, his palm cupping her cheek. "No one ever deserves to be abused," he said.

"I told you, Fredo never struck me."

"You know as well as I do abuse doesn't always come from a fist."

So her counselor always told her. Words could cut deep, too.

Armando's touch was warm and comforting, calling to her to lean in and absorb its promised strength. "Took me a long time to learn that," she said. "I figured as long as I wasn't sporting a black eye, I didn't have a right to complain. Besides, when it was happening…" Her voice caught. How she hated talking about those years out loud. Admitting she thought she deserved everything Fredo did and said.

Armando's fingers slid from her cheek to her jaw, lifting her face so their eyes would stay connected. The smile he gave her was gentle and understanding. It told her that he wouldn't ask for details.

Knowing she had a choice gave her the strength to say more.

"It catches you by surprise, you know? At first, it's subtle. Constructive criticism. An outburst over something you did that doesn't seem worth fighting about, because, well, maybe you didn't communicate well enough. Meanwhile, your parents are telling you how lucky you are that such a successful, handsome man wanted to be with you, and you start to think, *he's so charming and agreeable with everyone else—it has to be my fault.* That you are the one letting him down by being inferior."

Armando squeezed her knee. "You are not—"

"I am also not Christina," she said, anticipating his protest.

The feel of his touch against her skin was too enticing, so she turned her face away. As his hand dropped, a chill rushed in to fill its absence. She stared at the Christmas lights. "Life is not always easy when your baby sister is a great beauty," she told him. "Soon as she walked in the room, I ceased to exist."

"That is not true."

"Isn't it?" She had to smile, weak as it was, at Armando's protest. He, the man who fell in love with Christina the moment he laid eyes on her. "The day you met her, at the reception, did you know I was standing with her?"

He stiffened. "That was different."

No, it wasn't. "You were not the first person to lose their heart at first sight, 'Mando. Just the first one whose feelings she reciprocated."

They fell silent again. Out of the corner of her eye, she saw Armando studying his hands, a scowl marring his profile. "Do not feel bad. It was just the way things were. Christina was extraordinary." Whereas Rosa was merely average, a fact she was only now starting to realize was a perfectly fine thing to be. Not everyone could be Christina. To hold a grudge against her sister for being special would have been a waste of energy.

For some reason, talk of her sister's superiority made her think of Mona, another winner in the beauty and character lotto. Someone else with whom Rosa couldn't compete. Not that there was a competition.

Next to her, Armando shifted his weight on the stone step. "You really believed Fredo was the best you could do?"

"Silly, I know." Shameful was more like it. That a bully like Fredo was able to chip away at her self-esteem the way he did. "But Fredo had me convinced I would be a lonely nothing without him. Not only was he doing me a favor by being my husband, but I had no other options. Everything I had—money, a home—were because of him. If I left, I would have nothing."

"What made you change your mind?"

"Strange as it sounds, it was Christina's accident," she told him. "I was sitting at her bedside, holding her hand, thinking how unfair it was that someone like her, whose life was wonderful, should die when there were so many like me who could go in her place, and suddenly, I heard her voice in my head. You know that voice she used when she got exasperated."

Armando gave a soft chuckle. "I certainly do."

"Well, that voice told me life was too short and unpredictable to waste time being miserable, so take back control. So I divorced Fredo as soon as I could."

His hand found hers again. "I'm glad," he whispered.

"Me, too." Who knew where she would be if she had not? Certainly not sitting on the steps in a lace ball gown surrounded by an enchanted palace wonderland. Armando would be but a distant part of her life. Her insides started to ache. The idea of a life without Armando was…was…

Right around the corner. The thought struck her, hard. Mona would be taking him away forever.

Before she realized, there was moisture rimming her eyes. "I'm sorry," she said, sniffing the tears back. "Here you are trying to end the evening on a happy note, and I go and spoil it by acting maudlin."

"You didn't spoil anything. I'm honored you trusted me enough to finally tell me."

"Trust was never the issue, Armando. I told you, I was ashamed. And afraid," she added in a small voice.

"Afraid? Of me?"

She closed to her eyes. "Of seeing pity in your eyes." That last thing she wanted was Armando looking at her like a victim. She couldn't bear it.

"Never in a million years," she heard him say. A wonderful promise, but… She squeezed her eyes tighter.

"Rosa, look at me." Rosa couldn't. She didn't want to know what she might see.

But Armando was persistent. Capturing her face in his hands, he forced her out of hiding. "Rosa, look at me," he urged. "Look me in the eye. Do you see pity?"

Slowly, she lifted her lids. Armando was gazing at

her with eyes blue and nonjudgmental. "I would sooner cut them out than look at you with anything less than admiration."

"Little dramatic, don't you think?"

"Not in this case. What you did took courage, Rosa. Courage and strength. If anyone needs to fear judging, it's me for not being worthy of your friendship."

"You'll always be worthy," she whispered. This time, it was she who reached across the space to touch his face. His cheeks were rough with the start of an early beard. For some reason, the sensation aroused her, as if the whiskers were scratching inside her and not her skin. She wondered if her touch had shifted something inside him as well, because the blue began to take on different shades. What had been light was slowly growing dark and hooded.

"You're wrong."

Focused on the shifting of his eyes, Rosa nearly missed his words. "Wrong?"

"Thinking you're not special. You couldn't be more wrong. You're smart, strong. Beautiful." It'd been too long since someone had said such lovely words to her, and the way Armando said them was so sincere that Rosa melted with pleasure.

"I wasn't looking for compliments," she said.

"Not compliments. Truth."

Rosa nearly sighed aloud at his answer. The moment must going to her head, she decided. Why else would she think Armando's gaze had dropped to her mouth? Or long for him to move closer?

"We—" She started to say that they should say goodnight, but her mind was distracted by the way Armando's lips curled into a smile. He whispered something. It sounded like Fredo was an idiot, but she couldn't be sure. Next thing she knew, those beautiful curved lips were pressed against hers.

Rosa's breath caught.

Her heart stopped.

Her eyes fluttered shut, and her hand slid to the curls at the back of his head. Sweet and lingering, it was a kiss worthy of a fairy tale. Only it was Armando whose lips were gently coaxing a response. Armando whose fingers trailed down her neck to caress the base of her throat.

A moment later, he pulled away, leaving her dazed and confused. *What...?*

"Mistletoe," he said, pointing upward. "Be a shame to ignore tradition."

Dazed and mute, Rosa simply nodded. Looking up, she saw nothing. If the mistletoe was there, it was hidden in shadows.

Armando lifted her hair off her shoulder, tucking it neatly to the base of her neck. His smile was enigmatic. There was emotion playing in the depths of his gaze, but what it was, Rosa couldn't tell. She wasn't used to seeing anything but sadness in his eyes, so perhaps it too was the shadows playing tricks.

In a way, she felt like the whole evening had been one giant illusion from the moment Armando knocked on her door. Everything had been too romantic, too close to perfect to be anything else. For five wonderful hours, he'd made her feel desirable and special. Like a princess. There was no way those feelings could last. As soon as she said good-night, reality would return.

The question was, would their relationship return to normal as well? Or would this newfound awareness continue to simmer inside her?

"It's getting late," Armando said. "We should get you home."

And there it was—reality. Armando was already standing, a hand out to help her to her feet. Although she tried to fight it, desire pooled in the pit of Rosa's stomach the moment his fingers closed around hers, answering her question.

"Are you all right?"

Naturally, he would notice and show concern. Her fantasy evening wouldn't be complete otherwise.

"Everything's perfect," she replied. Except for one tiny problem, that was.

She'd just realized she was falling for him.

Armando called for the car to be brought around, then accompanied Rosa downstairs. Back in the bright light, he saw that the front of her hair had worked loose from its clip, the result of their kiss. The strands begged to be brushed away from her skin, and he had to clench his fists rather than give in to the temptation.

The driver was waiting when they stepped outside. Upon seeing them, he opened the door and snapped to attention. "Your Highness." He sounded surprised.

"Just walking Rosa out," Armando replied. For a second, he had the crazy idea of joining her on the ride, but steeled himself against that temptation as well. There was no telling what he might do pressed against her in the darkened backseat.

As it was, he had to go upstairs and make sure there really was mistletoe.

"I'll see you Monday?" he asked instead.

"Of course."

"And no more avoiding each other?"

You couldn't blame him for asking. The last time, just mentioning her marriage had her dodging him for days. Who was to say what this last conversation might cause. Especially considering her expression—part dazed and part shadowed.

Mirrored how he felt inside.

They exchanged good-nights, then the driver closed the door. As Armando watched the rear lights disappear into the darkness, he kicked himself for not stealing another kiss.

What excuse would he give, though? There was definitely no mistletoe hanging above them this time, and "I want to be close to you" sounded too much like a line, even if it was true.

The kiss upstairs had been born from admiration. When they were establishing the shelter, he'd heard story after story of women who found the strength to walk away despite being told by their abusive husbands that they would never survive on their own. To leave and start over took real courage. But then, he'd always known Rosa was strong. Hell, he'd been drawing on her strength for three years.

She was wrong, too. Years of verbal debasement were abuse; she might not have had bruises, but she'd been hurt nonetheless. Fredo's rising financial career had just ground to a halt. No way would Armando reward the man after what he did. Telling Rosa she was an embarrassment? Killing her self-esteem? If only he could throw people in the dungeon.

"Pardon me, Your Highness. Is something wrong? It's just that you've been standing in the middle of the driveway for a while now," his security guard added when Armando turned to look at him, "and I was—"

"Lost in thought," Armando replied. First Daniela, now the guard. What was it about his kissing Rosa that required people to ask if he was all right?

On the other hand, both times had left him off balance. It felt like something was shifting inside him—something deeper than sexual attraction. There was a yearning inside him that hadn't been there before, and, incredible as it sounded, Rosa was the trigger. If he didn't know better, he would think he was developing feelings for her.

Impossible. He'd already had the love of his life. His heart was buried with her. He hadn't felt anything for three years. Tonight was simply a product of traumatic confessions and Christmas lights. Nothing more. Turning on his heel, he headed back inside.

There had better be mistletoe hanging in that archway.

CHAPTER SEVEN

THE NEXT MORNING, instead of Christmas shopping like she planned, Rosa left her local coffee shop and headed for the palace. She needed a bit of grounding. After Armando had walked her to the car, she'd spent the entire ride home, not to mention most of the early hours, trying not to relive their kiss. No matter how hard she focused on other things, the memory of Armando's lips pressed to hers kept forcing its way to the front. For crying out loud, she even tasted him in her dreams.

Wasn't it just her luck? Three years of longing for someone to awaken the woman inside her, and it was Armando, the one man in Corinthia miles beyond her reach. If she didn't have interest in dating before, how would she ever now, having experienced the gold standard of kisses?

Which was why she needed a second shot of reality, to hammer home the fact that last night was nothing but a fantasy.

Despite the early hour, the lights in the grand archway were already lit in preparation for the day's tours.

Or maybe Armando never turned them off. Either way, the arrival of day had washed away last night's magic. Whatever spirits had been dancing along the walls were back in hiding as well, giving Armando and the rest of the royal family a rest from their presence.

The sight of plain gray walls put Rosa on firmer mental ground. Gripping the balustrade, she peered upward to find a sprig of green and berries hanging from the chandelier.

Did she really think there wouldn't be?

"Rosa?"

So much for grounded. One word from the familiar voice and her stomach erupted in a swarm of butterflies. Looking over her shoulder, she saw Armando walking toward her. Seemed impossible, but he looked more handsome than he did last night. His faded jeans and black turtleneck sweater were a far cry from the tuxedo, but he wore them as with the same elegance. Casual was a look he did well. Pity his subjects didn't get to see him like this—women would be storming the gate.

The closer he got, the faster the butterflies flapped. "What are you doing here?" he asked. "I thought you took the weekend off to finish your Christmas shopping."

"I left my list in my office," she lied. "Can't very well shop without one. Well, I could, but I might forget someone. Or something. What about you?" she asked, quickly changing subjects before her babbling got out of control. "What has you wandering the halls this early in the morning?"

"Oh, you know," he said with a shrug. "Paperwork, royal proclamations. Not to mention Arianna and her wedding planners have taken over the royal residence."

"In other words, you are hiding out."

"Precisely. If I stay, I'm liable to be asked my opinion on embossed napkins. My future brother-in-law can deal with that stress on his own.

"It's not the same during the day, is it?" he said, helping himself to the coffee cup in her hand. "The tree loses something when the lights are on."

Right. The tree. For a moment, she'd been distracted by the way his lips curled around the foam. If he kissed her now, she would taste the coffee on them. "Definitely. But then, most things aren't." She wondered if the rule applied to kisses, too. If Armando were to lean in right now, would she feel the same swirl of desire? Considering the way her insides buckled over watching him drink coffee, she was pretty sure the answer was yes.

Armando's lips glistened with liquid. "I'll tell you what's not the same," he said with a frown. "Coffee without sugar. I thought you were going to stop this diet nonsense."

"There's nothing wrong with watching your weight."

"Drinking bad coffee is not weight watching, it's torture. I forbid you from doing it anymore."

"I've got a better idea. Drink your own coffee," she

said, snatching back her cup. The banter felt good. She'd been afraid last night might taint their friendship.

At least it felt good until she went to take a sip and realized her lips were touching the same spot as his. Instantly, the butterflies returned.

"By the way, I—I had a great time last night," she said.

"So you said last night."

She knew that, but talking seemed a far better alternative to her other impulse, which was running her tongue along the cup rim.

"I just wanted to make sure you know how much," she said.

"I had a good time, too." To her surprise, pink inched along his cheekbones. "I was afraid you might regret opening old wounds..."

"No, not at all. In a weird way, telling you was liberating. I never realized how much the secret was weighing on me." Or rather, the shame of it. "Thank you, by the way, for not thinking me a complete failure."

"You're not a failure, period. Your taste in men could be a little better... I mean, I could have told you Fredo was a poor choice. For starters, the man eats far too much garlic."

"Yes, he does," Rosa laughed. "And too much dairy. What was I thinking?" Her smile faded. "Sometimes I could kick myself for being so stupid," she said.

"Not stupid. Naive, maybe, but never stupid." When he said it, she believed him. Maybe last night's magic hadn't completely dissipated after all.

The sounds of footsteps floated up from below. Beneath them, security guards were readying the archway for the public. Armando leaned his forearms on the stone railing. Rosa joined him, cradling her coffee and watching the activity on the first floor.

"Clearly there is only one solution," he said after a moment.

"Solution?"

"Regarding your terrible taste. From now on, you'll have to run all your potential dates by me, and I will decide if they are worthy of you."

"Is that so?" He was joking, but Rosa's spirits sagged slightly nonetheless. A tiny part of her had been hoping last night's kiss…

"Absolutely," he continued. "You're going to need my discerning eye. We don't want you falling for any old line. Just the ones I like." The sparkle in his eyes belied his seriousness. "I have to warn you, though. I have exceedingly high standards. In fact…" He pressed his shoulder against hers, and the wave of warmth that passed through her almost made her drop her coffee. "There is a very good chance I won't find anyone suitable at all."

"Is that so?"

"No. Very few men will measure up, as far as I'm concerned."

"None at all?" she asked.

His gaze aligned with hers. Between the shadows and his pupils, Rosa could barely make out the blue. "Maybe one or two," he replied.

She suddenly had trouble swallowing, the air from her lungs having stopped midway in her throat. "One would be enough," she managed to say. Had his pupils gotten even larger? The blue had been completely obliterated.

"One, then," he replied. "One very qualified candidate."

"Very qualified?"

"The best." Rosa didn't know a few inches could be so far away until Armando leaned in toward her. They were in their own private space. "We're standing underneath the mistletoe again," he whispered. "You know what that means..."

Most definitely. What's more, this time, there was no crowd or midnight confession to spur the moment forward. Just them. She parted her lips.

Armando's phone rang.

"You should answer," Rosa replied when he groaned. "It could be your father."

"If it is, he has horrible timing."

Still, no one in Corinthia ignored a phone call from the king, not even his son, so he reached into his breast pocket. One look at his expression told Rosa the caller wasn't King Carlos.

"It's Mona," Armando replied. There wasn't enough room in his eyes to hold their apology. "I'm sorry."

Rosa wasn't. As far as she was concerned, Mona's timing couldn't be more perfect. It saved her from making a very foolish mistake. So foolish, she almost laughed out loud.

With the walls of the archway closing in, she turned and hurried down the stairs. Once outside, she kept hurrying, through the front gate and down the block, stopping only when she reached the same coffee shop where she began.

Collapsing against the brick facade, she closed her eyes and told herself her heart was racing from exertion and not from the feelings swirling around inside her.

We're standing underneath the mistletoe again...

Heaven help her, she wanted to go back. Didn't matter if it was foolish or if Armando was making a joke, she wanted to go back, stand beneath that mistletoe and wait for Armando to take her in his arms.

She wanted him.

How? When did everything change? When did he stop being Armando, the man who married her sister, and become simply Armando the man? Last night amid the Christmas lights? Or earlier? Thinking back, Armando had always been one of two measures by which she rated others—Fredo at the low end and Armando at the top—and she'd told herself that when she decided she was ready to date, she would shoot for someone in the middle. After all, while she might not be the lump of clay Fredo thought her to be, she knew better than to put herself at Armando's level, either. So what did she do? Fall for Armando anyway. Could she be a bigger idiot?

Banging her head against the brick, she let out a loud sigh. Armando had just said she had terrible taste in men.

If only he knew.

* * *

Armando tried his best to focus on the voice talking on the other end of the line and not on the red-coated figure heading down the stairs.

"I wanted to apologize for missing the concert," Mona was saying. "I thought I would be well enough to travel, but I still have a fever. The doctor is afraid I might be contagious."

"Then it was definitely a good idea to stay home," Armando replied.

"Perhaps, but I am still sorry. I know how important this event is to you."

"There is no need to apologize. You can't control what your body is going to do." Sometimes your body wanted you to kiss a woman senseless. Confessions and Christmas lights, huh? What was his excuse this morning? Because he wanted to kiss her as badly as ever.

More than kiss her. He wanted to wrap her in his arms and not let go.

Below him, he saw Rosa crossing the tile, and his body clutched in frustration. He wanted to call for her to stop, but Mona was still talking.

"I swear I am normally very healthy. The doctor says this is one of the worst strains of flu he's ever seen," Mona was saying. "But I am definitely on the upswing, and will be one hundred percent as soon as possible. You have my word."

You have my word. Mona's statement was the perfect antidote to the spell that had gripped him as well as a reminder that Armando had made a promise of his own. "I'm looking forward to it," he replied, gripping the phone a little tighter. Rosa, meanwhile, had disappeared through the exit, leaving the archway cold and quiet. Just as well. "I also should be the one apologizing." For many things. "I didn't realize you were as sick as you are."

"I downplayed the situation when we spoke. I had the idea that if I told myself I was healthy, I would get healthy. Unfortunately..." She paused to cough. When she spoke again, her voice was raspy. "Unfortunately, I was wrong."

She certainly sounded terrible, Armando thought guiltily. "Why don't I fly in and visit? I promise to stay out of germ range. It would give us a chance to spend time together." Not to mention putting some distance between him and Rosa. Hypocritical, considering he'd admonished Rosa about avoiding him not five minutes ago.

His suggestion was met with a pause. "That is very nice of you, but I am afraid I would not be very good company. I wouldn't be able to show you around. Plus I look a sight."

"People with the flu often do," Armando noted.

"I know, but I would spend the entire visit feeling self-conscious. I hate whenever anyone sees me not looking my best."

Dear God, they were going to be man and wife. Did she think a fever and messy hair might send him running?

Armando thought of all the states he and Rosa had seen each other in, including one very embarrassing incident right after she started work when she vomited in his office waste receptacle. She'd been mortified. Spent the entire time apologizing and choking back feverish tears. Now that he remembered, she'd said she didn't want him seeing her in such a state, too. He'd ignored her. Instead, he sat by her side, rubbed circles on her back, passed her tissues and told her he was right where he belonged. "We're a team," he'd told her. "What's a little flu bug between partners?" Then he'd bundled her down the hall to one of the guest rooms, and they'd watched a movie until she fell asleep. Oddly enough, it was one of his fondest memories of their friendship.

He tried to picture rubbing Mona's back only to imagine being told to stay away.

"I would hate to think my company was causing you stress," he said, partly to the image in his head.

On the other end of the line, he heard a relieved sigh. "Thank you for understanding. We will enjoy our visit much better when I'm back to myself. Perhaps next week?"

"At the wedding?"

"That would be nice. I will let you know in a few days if I think I'll be feeling well enough so we can make arrangements."

"Sounds good." It struck him how formal and businesslike their conversation sounded. This was what he wanted, though, wasn't it? A business arrangement? A week ago he couldn't imagine thinking about anything more. His heart wasn't looking for more.

His eyes looked up at the mistletoe.

He squeezed them shut. Even if his heart was looking for more, he couldn't. He'd made a promise, and Corinthia's reputation rested on his honoring it.

He talked to Mona for a few more minutes, about the concert and what few details he knew about Arianna's wedding, then agreed to talk later in the week. He had just disconnected when he spied his father strolling the corridor. "There you are," Carlos said. "Your sister ordered me to find you."

"Funny," he replied. "I thought you were the one in charge."

"Of Corinthia, maybe. Of the bride..." He paused. "Is any father of the bride ever in charge?"

"In other words, my sister has you wrapped around her little finger." No surprise there.

"What can I say? She is my baby girl. I want her to be happy."

It might be early, but King Carlos was dressed as dapperly as always. He'd once told Armando a king needed to be on any time he stepped outside his private quarters. "The people expect their king to act like a king," he'd said. As his father drew closer, Armando noticed the older man's jacket hung looser than it used to. Seemed as if every week, he grew a little older. The weight of pending responsibility that rested perpetually on Armando's shoulders grew a little heavier.

"Surely you didn't think you could escape unscathed," his father remarked.

"I'd hoped."

"You might as well get used to it. This is only a small ceremony. Yours and Mona's will be far more elaborate."

"Must it? We are talking about my second marriage."

"Regardless, you are the crown prince," his father replied. "The people will want to celebrate."

Right, the people. Those thousands of candles relying on him to stay lit. The universe was certainly intent on reminding him of his duties today, wasn't it?

His father clapped him on the shoulder, breaking his thoughts. "I know what you are thinking, son."

"You do?" How, when he wasn't sure himself? A week ago yes, but now? Not so much.

"But of course," the king replied. "I know better than anyone how difficult it is to move forward when what you really want is to bring back the past. I know how much you loved Christina." Armando felt a stab of guilt. He hadn't been thinking of Christina last night—or this morning. Only of Rosa.

"When your mother died, it was all I could do to hold myself together, I missed her that much."

"I know," Armando replied. All too well he remembered the sight of his father with his face buried in his hands.

"I still miss her. Every day." He gave a soft laugh. "We Santoros love hard."

"So I've been told." At least his father did. Armando didn't know what he was doing anymore.

"What I'm trying to say is that I know what you are doing is difficult. You're putting your sister's happiness—not to mention the welfare of this country—ahead of your own needs." His hand still lay on Armando's shoulder, and so he gave a squeeze. "I hope you know how grateful I am. Grateful and proud. When I step down, Corinthia will be in wonderful hands."

For an aging man, he had an amazing grip. The pressure brought moisture to Armando's eyes. "Thank you."

"No, son, thank you. Now…" Lifting his hand, his father slapped him between the shoulder blades. "Let us go see what duties your sister has assigned to us, shall we?"

"I'll be right there. I just have to make a quick phone call."

"Don't dally too long. I don't want to go looking for you again."

Armando chuckled. "Five minutes."

"I will hold you to that," his father replied, waggling a finger. "I love my daughter, but I refuse to deal with her bridal preparations by myself."

"Coward."

"Absolutely. One day you will have a daughter, and you will understand."

He was probably right. "Don't worry, you have my word." And Armando always kept his promises.

His eyes flickered to the mistletoe. Unfortunately.

* * *

Instead of going shopping like she said, Rosa ended up spending the weekend at Christina's Home, helping the residents with their Christmas baking. Working with the other women helped ground her, reminded her there were worse things in life than unrequited feelings. Seriously, what did it matter if Armando didn't return her attraction? It wasn't as if it was a surprise. She was a chubby, average personal assistant. And that wasn't her insecurity talking. Those were simply the facts. She also had a job and a place to call home, which made her better off than a lot of people. To quote Fredo, which she hated doing even when he was right, she had it pretty damn good.

She'd get over her crush or whatever it was.

By the time she returned to work on Monday, she was in a much better place. In fact, she thought as she stepped into the elevator, she'd even go so far as to say her feelings were shifting back to normal. Why not? They crept up on her overnight—who's to say they couldn't disappear just as quickly? Right?

Right?

Armando was sitting at her desk when she walked in. Wearing one of his dark suits, his tie and pocket square a perfect Corinthian red, he was busy reading her computer screen and didn't see her. Rosa's insides turned end over end anyway. "Isn't that desk a little small for you?" she asked. She was not trying to sound flirtatious; his long, lean figure dwarfed the writing table.

Nor did the way his eyes brightened when Armando looked mean anything. “I was looking for the notes on last week’s meeting with the American ambassador. He’s coming by this afternoon, and I deleted the copy you sent me.”

“You do that a lot.”

“What can I say? I don’t like a crowded inbox.”

“Thank goodness you have me, then.” She turned to hang up her coat on the coatrack in the corner.

“I know.”

Rosa paused. It was the same banter they’d exchanged dozens of times, only this time, the words sounded different. There was a note of melancholy attached to the gratitude that unnerved her. Slowly she draped her coat onto its brass hook. “It’s snowing outside,” she said. “I heard one of the guards say we might even see accumulation on the ground. Might be the first time in years Corinthia could have a white Christmas.”

Armando was looking at her now, not the computer. She could tell because her spine felt his attention and had begun to prickle. Still afraid to turn around, she made a show out of brushing the droplets of water from the blue wool. “Is something wrong?” she asked.

“I wanted…”

Hearing his exasperated sigh, Rosa stopped fussing with her coat and turned around. It wasn’t like Armando to sound this uncertain. It made her uneasy.

The contrite look on his face didn’t help. “I wanted to apologize…”

Oh, Lord, he was going to tell her he was sorry for kissing her. "It's all right," she cut in. "There is no need to apologize. It's a silly holiday tradition."

"Maybe, but my behavior the other morning crossed the line. I was inappropriate, and I apologize."

In other words, he was sorry he'd made the suggestion. "That's what happens during the holidays," she said, forcing a smile. "All the celebrating makes people say things they don't mean. Don't worry, I didn't take offense."

"It's not that I didn't mean it, I just…"

Just what? Rosa knew she should ask, but she was too stuck on the first part of his sentence to say the words. Was he saying he wanted to kiss her again?

Pushing himself to his feet, he moved around to the front of the desk. "You're a beautiful woman, Rosa. What man wouldn't want to kiss you?"

"You would be surprised," she murmured.

"That is Fredo talking. Believe me, any man with half a brain would kiss you in a heartbeat."

She would have smiled at his calling Fredo stupid if he weren't filling her personal space. Rejection would be so much easier with a desk between them. Or breathing room. Anything besides the scent of his skin teasing her nostrils. "There's no need to oversell your point," she told him.

"I mean every word."

She risked looking him in the eye. "But?" There had to be a *but*. After all, for all his sweet words, he was apologizing, not taking her in his arms.

Shaking his head, Armando stepped away. "I'm not dead," he said. "I see a beautiful woman, I am going to feel desire. It's only natural."

He started pacing, a sign that he was thinking out loud. Trying hard to move past his finding her desirable, Rosa leaned back and waited for him to work out the rest of the explanation. The part that would pour cold water over the rest of his words.

"It wouldn't be fair," he said. "To kiss you. Not when I don't… That is…"

"I understand." There was no need for her to hear the words after all. She'd heard them often enough. His heart was buried with Christina. He was emotionally dead.

He might as well marry a stranger and help Corinthia, because he would never love again.

That's what he meant by it not being fair. He might want her, but his feelings didn't—couldn't—go deeper.

Then there was Mona. Even if he could care, there was Mona.

At least he cared enough to worry about leading her on. She should take solace in that. Then, his sense of honor was one of the qualities that made him so special.

The least she could do was let him off the hook. Inserting a lightheartedness she didn't feel into her voice, she asked, "Aren't you being a bit egotistical?"

Armando stopped his pacing. "I beg your pardon?"

"We were flirting under the mistletoe. You might

be a good kisser, but that is still a big leap to go from a kiss to breaking my heart."

"So, you didn't feel—"

"I'm not dead," she said, throwing his answer back at him. "You're a wonderful kisser. But even I'm smart enough to know that one kiss does not a relationship make."

"That's good to know," he said, nodding. The note in his voice was embarrassed relief, Rosa told herself. It just sounded like disappointment.

"Now," she said, walking around and taking her seat, "if we are finished making needless apologies, would you like me to print out the notes for your meeting with Ambassador Wilson?"

His smile was also tinged with embarrassed relief. "Please. I'll be in my office. And, Rosa?" She looked up from her computer screen to find his eyes filled with silent communication. "Thank you."

"You're welcome." She dropped her gaze back to her screen before he could see her moist-eyed response. It had been for the best, this conversation. Better to be reminded of reality than to make a fool of herself pining for something that couldn't be.

Like she told herself when she got on the elevator, there were worse things than unrequited feelings. She couldn't think of any right now, but there were.

Didn't he feel like the proper fool? Blast his decision to keep the office door open, since right now Armando wanted to slap the back of his desk chair with all his might. Dragging a hand through his curls, he glared at the snow falling outside his window. Egotistical was right. Here he'd been worrying about whether he had been leading Rosa on and all this time she hadn't been the least concerned. From the sounds of it, she hadn't given their moments under the mistletoe a second thought.

Why the hell hadn't she? Surely she had felt the same frightening intimacy he'd felt on the stairs? Why then weren't her thoughts swirling with the same confusion and desire?

Don't look a gift horse in the mouth, 'Mando. Regardless of what Rosa did or did not feel, the arguments for his apology still applied. Rosa's lack of interest merely made closure that much easier. He should be relieved.

Check that. He was relieved, and now that matter was settled, his and Rosa's relationship could go back to the way it had always been.

"Here are your notes."

Or maybe not. Just like it had when she entered the outer office, his insides clutched the second he looked at her. So sweet and soft, he literally ached to pull her close. Desire, it appeared, needed a little more than an apology to disappear.

He gripped the back of his chair instead. "Thank you," he said as she dropped the papers on his desk.

Her eyes barely lifted in acknowledgment. "You're welcome."

With his fingers gouging divots into the chair leather, he watched her walk to the door. “Making things easier,” he repeated with each sway of her shapeless jacket.

Still, why the hell wasn’t she as affected as he was?

CHAPTER EIGHT

AMAZING HOW QUICKLY time went when you weren't looking forward to something. If Rosa had been excited for Arianna's rehearsal dinner, the days before the ceremony would have dragged on, but since she was dreading the event—as well as the wedding itself—time sped by in a flurry of activity.

Before she realized, it was the night before Christmas Eve and she was standing by herself in the east dining room. While the wedding was small, it was by no means unelaborate. They would be dining tomorrow off three-hundred-year-old royal china bearing the Santoro crest. Tonight they were using the more modern state china with its fourteen-karat edging and matching tableware. The gold gleamed bright amid the red and white table linen. Arianna counted the forks. Six courses. Her cream-colored gown tightened at the thought.

She made a point of arriving early, while the rest of the party was in the chapel. If anyone asked, her purpose was to help Arianna's assistant. The real reason was because she couldn't face any kind of wedding reference with Armando in the room. Actually, she was trying to avoid thinking of Armando in terms of weddings, period. New Year's Day was only a week away. Each passing day left a tighter knot in the pit of her stomach. Nine days and Armando would be lost to her forever.

Not that she'd ever had him, as he had stumblingly reminded her on Monday. No one other than Christina would ever have him. But the day he announced his engagement? That spelled the absolute end. The minute sliver of hope to which her heart continued to cling would cease to exist. One would think its demise would be a relief—that it would be better to have no hope than an improbable sliver—but in typical Rosa fashion, it wasn't.

And so, rather than sit in the chapel and face reminders of Armando's pending engagement, she decided to spend a few moments alone in the dining room preparing herself.

She was standing by the fireplace warming her toes when she heard the sound of approaching footsteps. A moment later, Armando entered at the far end of the room. Upon seeing her, he stopped short. "I wondered where you might be," he said. "I noticed you weren't in the chapel during the rehearsal."

Did that mean he had been looking for her? Rosa's pulse skipped in spite of herself. She needed to stop trying to read things into his comments. "I thought Louise might need help. She's had her hands full this week, what with the gifts and the preparations."

"You would think the wedding was ten times the size considering the number of people who have sent their regards. My sister will never want for silver ice tongs again."

"Nor soup tureens," Rosa replied. "At last count, she'd received three."

"I know, I saw the display in the other room." As per tradition, the gifts were lined up for guests to see. "I shudder to think what it would have looked like if the wedding was a major affair."

He'd know soon enough. His upcoming engagement hung between them, unmentioned. The conversation was reminiscent of others they'd had this week. Friendly, but with unspoken tension beneath the surface. Even their silences, normally comfortable, had an awkwardness about them.

Watching him watch the fire, she noted the black tie hanging loose around his neck. "Do you need assistance?" she asked. "With the tie?"

He glanced down. "Please," he said. "Damn thing keeps coming out crooked when I try." Rosa had to smile. "Arianna said she would help after rehearsal, but I have a feeling she will be distracted, and since you are here…"

"It's not as though I haven't done it a couple dozen times before," Rosa replied. Stepping close, she took hold of the ends and tugged them into place. The cloth was cold from being outside. His skin, however, emanated warmth. The heat buffeted her fingers, making them feel clumsy. "One of these days you're going to have to learn to do this yourself," she murmured.

"Why, when I have you to do it for me?"

"Who says I'm always going to be around?" In the middle of looping one end over another, she heard the portent in her words and fumbled. "I would think your bride would prefer she do this for you."

She felt his muscles tense. "Perhaps," he answered, rather distractedly. "But will she be as good as you?"

"Oh, I think most people are. It isn't as hard as you think."

"Or as easy," he replied.

"I'm not sure what you mean."

"Nothing." His Adam's apple bobbed up and down as he swallowed. "I imagine you'll be glad to be free of the duty. Taking care of me must get tiring after a while."

That was an odd choice of words. Rosa pulled the bow tight. "I've never minded doing things for you," she told him. In fact, it was one of the best parts of her job. She'd found a certain kind of symbiosis in taking care of him while he grieved. The more she did, the more she remembered how strong and capable she could be. Taking care of Armando had brought back part of the woman Fredo nearly erased.

She pulled the ends of the tie, then smoothed the front of his jacket. The planes of his chest were firm and broad beneath her fingers. "There," she said. "Perfect as always."

"So are you," he replied with a smile. "You look beautiful."

"My dress is too tight.

"Stop channeling Fredo. You look perfect. You always look perfect."

The sliver of hope throbbed inside her heart. He needed to stop making her feel special.

"Armando…"

"Rosa…"

They spoke at the same time, Armando reaching for her hand as she attempted to back away.

"I—" Whatever he was going to say was halted by a pair of deep voices. She managed to slip from his grip just as Max and another man strolled in.

"And you're telling me this is only one of the dining rooms?" the stranger was asking.

"One of three," Max replied.

"Damn. This place makes the Fox Club look like a fast food joint. Hello, who's this?" He smiled at Rosa. "You weren't at the rehearsal, were you? I would have remembered."

"Dial it back, cowboy. I don't need a scandal." Max clasped the man on the shoulder. "Rosa Lamberti, may I present to you my best friend, Darius Abbott. He just arrived from New York."

"Pleasure to meet you," Rosa replied, recognizing the name. "You're Max's best man, right?"

The African-American was slightly shorter than Max, but had a muscular build, the kind you might expect from a rugby player. The shoulders of his rented tux pulled tight as he lifted her hand to his lips. "They don't make them better," he replied, winking over her fingers. Rosa giggled at his outrageousness. Max's friend was a first-class flirt.

"Rosa is Prince Armando's assistant," Max told him. "She's been a huge help this week, too. Without her and Louisa, I'm pretty sure Arianna would have lost it."

"I didn't do that much," Rosa replied. "A little organizing is all."

"As usual, Rosa is underselling herself," Armando chimed in.

"Didn't I warn you, dude?" said Darius. Eyes sparkling, he leaned in toward her as though to divulge a dark secret. "I told him something about weddings make women crazy. Even good ones like Arianna."

"My sister didn't go crazy," Armando replied.

"Much," Rosa said. "Her nerves got to her at the end. But overall, she was pretty good," she added, looking over to Armando.

"Probably because she got such good help," Darius said. "I know I'm feeling calmer."

"What can I say, I have a gift."

"You certainly do."

Good Lord, but he was over-the-top. Rosa couldn't remember the last time a man—other than Armando—complimented her so audaciously. She would be lying if she didn't say she found his behavior immensely flattering.

Out of the corner of her eye, she could see Armando watching them with narrowed, disapproving eyes. Immediately she dialed back her behavior so he wouldn't be upset.

What was she doing? Max's friend was a charming, handsome man. If she wanted to flirt with him, that was her business. A little ego stroking was exactly what she could use right now.

It was definitely better than pining for Armando, who didn't—couldn't—want her.

Feeling audacious, she offered up her best charming smile. "Have you found where you're sitting yet, Darius?" she asked. "If you'd like, I can help you find your place setting. We don't assign places the same way as they do for American head tables."

"That'd be great." Darius's perfect teeth gleamed white as he grinned back. "Maybe I'll get lucky and you'll be sitting near me."

"You know what? I think that could be arranged." Hooking her hand through his crook in his elbow, she proceeded to lead him away from the group, patting herself on the back every step of the way. She didn't once turn back and look in Armando's direction. Even if he was boring holes in the back of her head.

Armando hated the American. Why did Max have to insist on his being the best man? So what if they were childhood friends? He could have been a peripheral guest; he didn't need to be front and center, grinning his perfect white teeth at everything Rosa said. And kissing her hand hello. Americans didn't kiss hands. He kept waiting for Rosa to shoot him a look over the man's outlandish behavior. Instead, she giggled and offered to find the man's seat. He was pretty certain they'd swapped placards as well, because there she was, four seats down next to him rather than by Armando's elbow, where she belonged.

"Do you plan to eat your soup or simply stir it all night?" his father asked.

Armando set his spoon down. "My apologies, Father. I'm afraid I don't have much of an appetite this evening." How could he with such completely inappropriate behavior going on?

"I'm just saying, it's weird to segregate one little fork. Put it on the left with all the others," he heard Darius remark.

Why was Rosa laughing? It wasn't that funny. Head tipped back, notes like the trill of a thrush…he thought that was the laugh she reserved for him.

"It is a shame Mona was unable to attend this evening," Father was saying.

"Yes, it is. I don't think she expected the weather to be as bad as it is in Yelgiers." On the inside, he was far less disappointed. Despite the fact the days were ticking closer to New Year's, he found himself fighting to stir interest in his future bride. He figured it was because they hadn't spent time together. After much persuasion, he had convinced her to chat by video the other evening. A perfectly nice talk during which she supported many—no, all—of his views and left him feeling strangely flat.

"She will be here in time for the ceremony tomorrow," he said.

"I look forward to seeing her as well as her father," King Carlos said. Down at the far end of the table, the sultan was happily engrossed in conversation with Armando's second cousin, who also happened to be the deputy defense minister. "I imagine you're eager to begin your formal courtship as well."

"Definitely," Armando replied. Perhaps when they met in person, there would be more of a spark.

Although if there wasn't one, he could hardly blame Mona, could he? Not when the reason for an arranged marriage was his inability to become emotionally involved. Funny that he should be worried about a spark all of sudden.

Soup became salad. He opted for wine. On the other side of Father, Arianna and Max were ignoring their guests in favor of gazing into each other's eyes. They'd been like that since Max stormed into the palace and declared his feelings. Eyes only for each other. His heart twisted with envy. He remembered what it was like to be that deeply in love, so everything around you faded when you were with that other person. To never feel lonely because you knew there was someone in this world who understood you, who recognized your flaws and cared anyway, about whom you felt the same.

Dammit, Rosa was laughing again. What was it about the American she found so amusing? Armando kissed her, and she told him he was reacting egotistically. This… Darius made a silly comment about oyster forks and she laughed as though it were the wittiest thing she ever heard.

"Poor tomato."

Arianna's maid of honor, Lady Tessa Greenwich, pointed to the salad. "I don't know what the vegetable did to upset you, but I'm glad you're mad at it and not me."

He looked down at the cherry tomato skewered on his fork. "That's what it gets for being the easiest to spear," he said.

"Here I thought you were angry with it."

"Angry? No," he replied. Just extremely irritated with people's lack of decorum. "Would you excuse me a moment?" He left the napkin next to his plate and stood up. "I'll be back a moment."

"Everything all right?" Lady Greenwich asked.

"It will be." Soon as he had a word with his assistant. As he walked by Rosa and Darius, he leaned in to her ear. "May I see you in the corridor?" he whispered. "Now?"

Naturally, she was smiling when he spoke. She turned the smile in his direction, which only fed his agitation. "Is there a problem?" she asked.

Rather than answer, he continued walking, knowing she would follow. Once in the corridor, he led her past two additional entrances. They ended up in the gallery next to the grand arch.

"What do you think you're doing?" he asked once he was certain they couldn't be overheard.

Her eyes widened, then narrowed. "What are you talking about?"

Dear God, but she looked beautiful tonight. Her silk gown looked like cream poured over her body. Even as irritated as he was, he wanted to run his hands along every curve and sensual swell.

"I'm talking about you and Max's friend," he replied. "The way you're laughing at everything he says."

"Because he's funny. Since when is that a crime?"

Since she wasn't laughing with Armando, that's when.

"Except that you're my assistant. You were supposed to be by my side in case I need anything." Not laughing it up with handsome foreigners.

"Come on, you're not that needy, are you? Are you serious? I'm four seats away, not on the other side of the country. An extra twenty feet will hardly make a difference. Besides," she added, folding her arms across her chest, "technically I'm not working. I'm here as a guest. That means I get to sit where I want."

"That doesn't mean you get to flirt with every man in the room."

"Flirt with…?" It was the first time he had ever seen her flare her nostrils. Unfolding her arms, she held her hands stiffly by her side and leaned in. "It's called enjoying myself."

"It's called flirting," Armando charged back. "Tossing your hair over your shoulder, laughing. Like a peacock showing her plumage," he muttered to the paintings on the wall. With Darius strutting in kind. Was it any wonder he'd lost his appetite?

"So what if I am?" Rosa asked, stepping up to his shoulder. "It's been a long time since a man has found me attractive."

Armando whipped his head around. "What are you talking about? I tell you that you're attractive all the time."

"I mean someone who isn't… It's nice, is all," she said. Their shoulders knocked as she pushed past him toward the archway.

Armando stalked after her. She stood with her back to him, staring up at the Christmas tree. For a moment, his annoyance faded as he lost himself in the skin exposed by the drape of her dress.

Until the way his fingers itched to trace her spine reignited it again. "It's inappropriate," he snapped. "You're making a spectacle of yourself."

"Says who?" she asked, turning.

Said him. It killed Armando to watch her encouraging Darius's attention when she had so easily brushed off his. "You're my personal assistant," he replied. "I expect you to behave with more decorum."

Again, she folded her arms. "What would you have me do, Armando? This is your sister's wedding rehearsal. Should I just ignore the man? Stop talking to him?"

That had been exactly what he wanted. Hearing the words aloud, however, he realized how unrealistic they sounded. "Just stop throwing yourself at him," he said.

Rosa inhaled deeply through her nose. Though they sparkled, her eyes had none of the warmth they'd had the other night.

"No," she said.

One word, spoken sharply like a slap. In fact, Armando's reflexes stiffened as if it was one. "I beg your pardon?" This was where she usually turned passive-aggressive, agreeing while showing her displeasure with a sarcastic *yes, Your Highness.*

"I said no," she repeated. The first time in three years that she had defied him.

It was the most arousing sight Armando had ever seen.

Taking another breath, she started walking toward him with careful, measured steps. "I'm not going to let people tell me what to do anymore. Not Fredo. Not you..."

"I am not Fredo," Armando shot out. "Do not compare me to that bottom dweller."

"Then stop acting like him!" she snapped back. "So long as I don't hurt anyone, who I find attractive and who I don't is none of your business. Now if you'll excuse me."

Armando grabbed her wrist. He regretted it as soon as she stiffened, but the agitation in his stomach had reached epic proportions. All he could picture was Darius's handsome face and his big hands curling over those creamy shoulders. "Are you planning to kiss him?" he asked.

"That's none of your—"

But he wouldn't be deterred. Some perverse part of him needed to know. "You just said you found him attractive. Does that mean you're planning to kiss him?"

"Maybe I am," she replied, yanking her arm free. "And so what? Unlike you, I can care again. Just because you've declared yourself dead doesn't mean I have to."

"Then you are planning to kiss him."

"Whether I do or don't is none of your business."

Armando wasn't sure if it was the assertiveness or the imaginings assaulting his brain, but he couldn't let her go. Grabbing her wrist a second time, he pulled her close. Caught off guard, her body fell into his, enabling him to slip his free arm around her waist.

"Let me go," she said.

The gentleman inside him was about to when he looked into her eyes. Beautiful, fiery eyes demanding answers. And all of a sudden, he had them. The emotions that had been swirling inside him since the concert came together with astonishing clarity. Before he could stop himself, he leaned in to kiss her.

She jerked her head back. "What do you think you're doing?"

"I—" He was acting on instinct. "I'm sorry."

Breaking their embrace, he walked over to the stairway and sat down, the irony of the location not lost on him. With his eyes focused on the floor, he listened to the sounds of Rosa straightening her dress. "I want you," he said simply.

She let out a noise that sounded like a snort. "Seriously?" she said. "Five days ago you stood in your office and apologized for wanting me, said you weren't being fair to me. And now all of a sudden you're doing everything you apologized about?"

"I know. My actions don't make much sense."

"They don't make any sense, Armando."

Seeing her standing there so gloriously indignant, Armando's stomach lurched. How could he have been so blind? "I only realized myself," he said.

"Realized what?"

"How much I care."

The color drained from her cheeks. "Care?" Her voice cracked with emotion as she repeated the word. The sound forced Armando to his feet, but when he reached out, she held up her hand. "For three years, I've listened to how your heart was buried with Christina."

"I thought it was." In fact, if someone had asked him eight hours ago, he would have given that very answer. "Then tonight, when I saw you and Darius…"

"That's your possessiveness talking," she said. "I've seen it before. Darius paid attention to me, so suddenly you decide you don't want to share. Then, soon as his interest wanes…" She shrugged.

"No." Damn Fredo. No doubt her ex was responsible for that kind of thinking. "I mean, yes," he continued. "I won't lie. I wanted to break Darius's finger every time he touched you. But my jealousy was only the final piece of the puzzle. What I'm feeling inside…"

She was facing away from him. Seemed that was her favorite position tonight, giving him the cold shoulder.

Curling his hands around those shoulders, he buried his nose in her hair for a moment before struggling to find the right words.

"Have you ever looked through an unfocused telescope, only to turn the knob and make everything sharp and clear?" he asked.

Rosa nodded.

"That is what it was like for me, a few minutes ago. One moment I had all these sensations I couldn't explain swirling inside me, then the next everything made sense. The way your kisses haunted me, the fact I wanted to deport Darius for kissing your hand—they weren't isolated sensations at all. They were my soul coming back to life."

"Just like that?" She still sounded skeptical, but she had continued leaning against him. Armando took that as progress.

"Like a bolt of lightning," he said, kissing her neck again.

She pulled away, leaving him standing in the middle of the archway by himself. "You don't believe me."

"I…"

"Or…" A second thought came to him. About how easily she brushed off his apology as his ego. "Is it that you don't care?"

So excited had he been about his revelation that he didn't stop to think that she might not share his feelings. He was ashamed of himself, although not nearly as ashamed as he was disappointed. Having come back to life, he desperately wanted her to feel the same intensity of desire and need that he felt.

Still, if she didn't, he had no choice but to respect her wishes. "I'm sorry if I've made you feel uncomfortable," he told her. "I let my enthusiasm cloud my judgment."

"No, you didn't," she said, turning. "Make me feel uncomfortable, that is. I do care. I'm not quite sure when things changed, but I care a lot."

"But?" There was no mistaking the hesitancy in her voice. As much as her proclamation made his spirits want to soar, Armando held them in check and prayed what came next wasn't rejection.

Rosa shrugged, palms up. "I don't know what to think," she said.

"Then don't think," he replied. "Just go with your heart."

"I—I don't know," Rosa replied.

He made it sound easy. *Just go with your heart.* But what if your heart was frightened and confused? She had come to terms with her feelings being one-sided, only to hear him say they weren't. How could she be sure this sudden realization wasn't a reaction to another man coveting his possession? After all, Armando was used to having her undivided attention. Who was to say that once he claimed her attention again he wouldn't lose interest? Chubby, divorced, insecure. Wasn't as if she had a bucket load of qualities to offer.

Nor had he said he loved her. He cared for her, needed her, wanted her. All wonderful words, but none of them implied he was offering his heart. For all his talk of coming to life, he was essentially in the same place as before, unable or unwilling to give her a true emotional commitment. He was simply done trying to be fair. Flattering to think his desire for her was great enough to override his sense of honor.

On the other hand, her feelings wanted to override her common sense, so maybe they were even. As she watched him close the gap between them, she felt her heartbeat quicken to match her breath.

"You do know that we're under the mistletoe yet again, don't you?"

Damn sprig of berries had quite a knack for timing, didn't it? Anticipation ran down her spine breaking what little hold common sense still had. Armando was going kiss her, and she was going to let him. She wanted to lose herself in his arms. Believe for a moment that his heart felt more than simple desire.

This time when he wrapped his arm around her waist, she slid against him willingly, aligning her hips against his with a smile.

"Appears to be our fate," she whispered. "Mistletoe, that is."

"You'll get no complaints from me." She could hear her heart beating in her ears as his head dipped toward hers. "Merry Christmas, Rosa."

"Mer—" His kiss swallowed the rest of her wish. Rosa didn't care if she spoke another word again. She'd waited her whole life to be kissed like this. Fully and deeply, with a need she felt all the way down to her toes.

They were both breathless when the moment ended. With their foreheads resting against each other, she felt Armando smile against her lips. “Merry Christmas,” he whispered again.

Rosa felt like a princess.

Behind them, a throat cleared. “I beg your pardon, Your Highness.”

The voice belonged to Vittorio Mastella, head of security. He stood in the doorway as statue-like as ever, dare she say even overly so, the way his hands were glued tight against his thighs. “I’ve been asked to deliver a message to you.”

Armando tightened his hold on her waist, clearly afraid she might flee. “If it’s Father, tell him I’m not feeling well, and I will see him in the morning,” he said, smiling at Rosa. “I’m in the middle of a very important discussion.”

“I’m afraid it’s not from your father.” The way his eyes flickered between the two of him made Rosa uneasy. Whatever the message, it sounded like unwanted news.

She couldn’t have been more right.

“Princess El Halwani has arrived,” Vittorio announced. “She’s on her way to the dining room as we speak.”

CHAPTER NINE

ENTER THE BIGGEST stumbling block of all. How on earth could Rosa have forgotten about Mona, the ultimate reason for holding back her heart? At the sound of her name, she broke free of Armando's embrace. Easy enough since his grip had gone lax.

"Thank you, Vittorio," Armando replied.

From his shell-shocked expression, it appeared he had forgotten about Mona as well. Small consolation, but Rosa took it nonetheless.

Vittorio bowed in response. "Again, I'm sorry for the interruption, Your Highness."

"No need to apologize, Vittorio. Your timing was fine."

Fortuitous even, Rosa would say. This was the second time she and Armando had been stopped from kissing. Maybe the universe knew the troubles that lay ahead and had stepped in to protect them. Certainly it had saved her from heartache tonight.

Partly, anyway.

The two of them stood listening to Vittorio's receding footsteps. Armando looked as dazed as she felt. His eyes were flat and distant.

She broke the silence first. "We'd best be heading back to the dining room as well. You don't want the princess wondering where you went."

"Yes, we should," he replied in a voice as far away as the rest of him. Then he coughed. The action seemed to shake him back to life, because when he looked at her, his eyes were sharper. Apologetic. "We should talk later."

"There isn't that much to talk about," she replied. Whatever they'd been about to discover was a missed opportunity.

They were met at the dining room entrance by both King Carlos and King Omar. While Armando's father wore a concerned frown, the sultan looked ready to burst with excitement. "There you are, my friend! I wondered where you had gone to for so long."

"I was feeling under the weather," Armando replied, "and went out for some fresh air."

"With your assistant?" King Carlos asked.

"I asked Rosa if she would get me something for my stomach. Vittorio told me Mona has arrived."

"Yes!" replied Omar. "The weather finally cleared, and our pilot was able to get clearance. She is freshening up after her flight and will be back momentarily. You do look pale," the sultan noted, cocking his head. "I hope it is nothing serious. This arrangement has been plagued enough by illness. Ah, here is my daughter now."

It was like a scene in a movie. At the sound of King Omar's pronouncement, all heads turned to the far end of the room to see Princess Mona walk in.

Not walk, float. She moved like she was moving on air with the amethyst color of her gossamer gown trailing behind her. "My deepest apologies, King Carlos," she said after executing a perfect curtsy, "for arriving so late. I hope I am not disrupting your daughter's special evening."

"You can blame me," Omar said. "Mona was going to go to a hotel, but I insisted she make an appearance. She and your son were long overdue to spend time together."

"You are most right, Omar," King Carlos replied before kissing Mona's fingers. "Your presence is welcome no matter how late. I've already instructed the staff to add a setting next to Armando."

"You're too kind, Your Highness." She cast her eyes down in appropriate demureness, her eyelashes fluttering like butterfly wings.

For a woman who wasn't planning to attend, she looked breathtaking. Her dark hair was pulled back tight to give accent to her almond-shaped eyes and high cheekbones. And her skin…her complexion looked like someone had airbrushed her.

The woman turned her curtsy to Armando. "Prince Armando, I'm so pleased to see you again."

Armando nodded. "I'm glad to see you are fully recovered. You…" He cleared his throat. "You look as lovely as I remember."

"I'm a fright from rushing to get here, but thank you for the compliment. I'm looking forward to our getting to know each other better over this next week."

"The same here." He coughed again. "Sorry. I think might need a glass of water."

"As good a cue as any to take our seats before your sister notices we are gone," King Carlos said. "Although I would say the odds are in our favor."

"They do appear very much enamored with one another," Omar noted.

"Indeed," said the king. "If we were to all go to bed right now, I am not sure they would care. In fact, we may have to tell them when dinner has ended."

Speaking of not being noticed… Rosa lagged behind as the royal quartet walked away. There was a brief moment when Armando looked back, but she purposely didn't catch his eye. Looking at him would only cause her to replay their conversation in the archway, and she felt cold and alone enough as it was.

"Hey, beautiful, I'd wondered where you'd gone. They're just about to serve the main course. Or so the forks tell me." Leaping to his feet, Darius pushed in her chair. "Everything okay with the boss man?"

She looked across the table to where Armando was introducing the princess to the rest of the guests. They made a good-looking couple, the two of them. They would make good-looking heirs as well.

"Why wouldn't it be?" she asked.

"The two of you were gone for a while. I was afraid something might have happened. Some kind of royal attack or something. We're not under attack, are we?" he whispered teasingly.

Rosa forced a smile. It wasn't Darius's fault she'd left her affinity for flirting back in the archway. "No attack. Yet," she replied. "His Highness had a problem he was trying to work out."

"Did he?"

"Turns out he forgot an important piece of information. But," she said as Mona laughed, making it her time to feel sick to her stomach, "now that he has it, I'm sure he knows what he has to do."

It was the longest meal of Armando's life. Bad enough before, when he was listening to Darius attempting to charm Rosa. But once Mona came, he was forced to be charming himself while listening to Darius. All the while wishing he was standing under the mistletoe with Rosa.

Rosa, who refused to catch his eye.

Just as well. It had been wrong of him to declare his feelings when he was obligated to Mona. Selfish and wrong. His only defense was that he'd been doing exactly what he'd advised Rosa to do: not think.

Now, as punishment for his greediness, he could spend the rest of the evening tasting Rosa's kiss. The sensation of her mouth moving under his overrode his taste buds, turning everything that passed his lips bland and lifeless. By the time dessert arrived, he wanted to toss his napkin on the table and tell everyone he was through.

He didn't, of course. One abrupt departure was enough. Besides, between his behavior and Mona's late arrival, he'd stolen the spotlight enough.

Well, he had wanted to give people something to gossip about besides Arianna's pregnancy. Sitting to his left, Mona dabbed her lips with her napkin. "Father was right," she said. "Your sister and her fiancé are very devoted to one another. No wonder your father is willing to be so…accepting…of the circumstances."

"What do you mean?"

"Please don't get me wrong," she said. "I only meant that Corinthia has a reputation for being almost as traditional and conservative as my country. That your father doesn't seem fazed by your sister doing things out of order, if you will, says something."

"The order doesn't matter. Max's devotion to Arianna is indisputable."

"She is very lucky. As you and I both know, love matches in royal marriages are rare."

Yes, they were. Yet again, he tried to catch Rosa's attention, but her profile was firmly turned toward Darius.

Armando flexed his fingers to keep from forming a fist. A lock of hair had fallen over her eye, loosened no doubt, when they'd kissed. He wanted to comb it away from her face simply so he could run his fingers through her hair.

He wanted to do a lot of things. Apparently being

haunted by her kiss wasn't enough—all his other buried urges returned as well.

Coming back to life was killing him.

"Over time..."

Mona was talking to him again. He jerked his attention back. "I'm sorry. I missed what you said."

"I was talking about royal marriages," she said. "That the absence of love in the beginning doesn't mean the marriage won't be successful. After all, if two people are compatible, there is no reason why they won't develop feelings for one another over time. Love doesn't always happen at first sight."

"No, it doesn't," Armando murmured. Sometimes love crept up on you over a period of years, disguising itself as friendship until your heart was ready.

"Especially when there are children and mutual interests involved," Mona continued. "When two people are committed to the same goals."

"Working as a team," Armando said.

"Precisely."

That's what he and Rosa were. A perfectly matched team.

You didn't break up a perfect team.

He would tell Mona tonight that their arrangement was off. There would be a scandal, which would divert attention away from Arianna and her child's illegitimacy. That had been the point of accelerating his marriage plans in the first place. Meanwhile he would court Rosa properly.

Fingertips grazed the back of his hand, causing him

to stiffen. Mona smiled apologetically. "You looked a million miles away," she said.

"I'm sorry. I was thinking about the future." One that looked bright for the first time in years.

"I'm glad to hear it," she replied, "because I have, too."

Sadly, they weren't thinking of the same future, and for that, he felt terrible. It wasn't Mona's fault love had a bad sense of timing. "Perhaps we should talk after dinner," he said.

"I would like that," Mona replied. She looked down at their hands, which were still connected, she having left hers atop his. "I hope you don't think me too forward, but I believe you and I could do a lot of good together."

The muscles along the back of Armando's neck began to tense. "Good?" he repeated.

"Yes. The flu I caught the other week. Father told you I caught it volunteering at the hospital? He lied. What he didn't tell you was that the people of Yelgiers are suffering from a terrible health care crisis. A lot of our citizens, mostly women and children, are without decent medical attention. The fact that women are still treated as second-class citizens in many parts of the country, and are therefore seen as undeserving of care, only exacerbates the problem. So many women suffer in silence."

"Too many," Armando noted, thinking of the women at Christina's Home.

"I've been reading up on how much your government

has done these past years to improve conditions for women and children. I'm hoping that when our countries are united," she said, squeezing his hand, "our countries' combined assets will help all our people."

Our people. Armando stared at his untouched dessert, the weight of Mona's speech pressing down upon his shoulders. With a few eloquent sentences, Mona had reminded him how much was at stake. Their engagement wasn't just about them. It wasn't even about protecting his family from scandal. It was about doing what was best for his people. Corinthia was counting on him to lead them to a prosperous future. To keep them safe and healthy. And now, thanks to his agreement with Omar, so were the people of Yelgiers.

Every single candle in every single window…

If he broke off the engagement, it would mean far more than some headlines and bad blood. While they might not realize it, there were people who needed his marriage to Mona to make their lives better.

How could he walk away knowing he was failing people? His people. Mona's people. As much as he loved Rosa—and, oh, God, he did love her, more than he thought possible—he could never live with himself.

Better to settle for kisses under the mistletoe and be able to look at himself in the mirror.

He'd been right earlier. Love really did have terrible timing.

For the first time in her life, Rosa couldn't find comfort in a chocolate dessert.

"Don't tell me you're pregnant, too," Darius joked. "You've got that same green-around-the-gills look the princess used to get when she first showed up in New York."

No such luck, she thought, putting a hand to her stomach. If she were pregnant with Armando's child, she would be doing cartwheels of joy. The only thing making her green was a bad case of jealousy. Brought on by seeing Mona holding Armando's hand.

"Just indigestion," she replied.

"I hear ya," Darius replied. "That was a lot of food. Makes me wonder what we're going to get at the wedding tomorrow."

Oh, Lord, the wedding. Maybe she could claim illness and stay home. That way she wouldn't have to face another eight hours of seeing Armando and Mona together.

The American leaned back in his chair with a satisfied sigh. "Thank goodness I've got till tomorrow night to digest everything. Otherwise, I might need some emergency tailoring on my tuxedo. Max would kill me. You sure it's indigestion?" he asked at her half-hearted laugh.

"It is." Rosa was still staring at the joined hands across the way. Whatever Mona was talking about had to be serious. Armando was frowning at his untouched plate.

"I don't know," Darius replied. "That prince of yours looks pretty green, too."

"He's not my prince," Rosa answered reflexively. Never was, but for five minutes under the mistletoe.

Now that Darius mentioned it, though, Armando did look pale. Good. Petty as it was, she wanted him to feel as terrible as she did. She also wanted Mona to trip over her floaty train and fall on her face.

No, she didn't. It wasn't the Yelgierian's fault she was beautiful and graceful and probably brilliant.

She wasn't even angry with Armando. Not much, anyway. It had been her choice to kiss him. He'd said to stop thinking, and she did. A smarter woman would have heeded her own warnings. Then again, a smarter woman wouldn't have fallen for Armando in the first place.

To think, she'd started dinner feeling empowered. The joke was on her. She was a bigger fool than even Fredo thought she was.

The wedding of Princess Arianna Santoro and Maxwell Brown, the newly named Conte de Corinth, went flawlessly. Not only did security keep the press away, but the bride's former boyfriend departed that morning on a lengthy trip to the continent. With all potential drama eliminated, the result was an intimate and beautifully romantic ceremony that even the people of Corinthia seemed content to let stay private.

Armando and his father had to be pleased. A week from now, Armando would announce his engagement, the country would be plunged into wedding fervor yet again and no one would ever remember the princess's pregnancy started before she met Max in New York.. Plus by this time next year, Mona would probably be pregnant—because she was no doubt amazingly fertile along with all her other qualities. Success all around. Long live the royal family of Corinthia.

Because it was Christmas Eve, the reception did double duty as a holiday celebration, only instead of trees, there were towers of poinsettias, each near ten feet high. People could be seen exchanging gifts by them when they weren't dancing and enjoying the wedding festivities. Seated at a table by one of the ballroom windows, Rosa triple-checked whether the decorations included mistletoe. Given her and Armando's recent track record with the plant, one could never be too careful.

There wasn't any. Meaning there was no excuse for even the most casual of kisses.

She cursed the way her heart fell.

"You should be careful. I hear there's a law in this country against outshining the bride." Darius handed her a glass of wine before helping himself to the seat next to her.

"Little chance of that, I'm afraid. Did you see Arianna?" She nodded to where the princess and her husband were posing for a photograph. Given the circumstances, Arianna had forgone a traditional gown in favor of simple pink satin, but her happy glow made her easily the most beautiful woman in the room.

"She looks good, but you're definitely a close second."

Rosa rolled her eyes. “Sounds like someone’s been helping himself to the champagne.”

“Sounds like someone needs to help herself to a little more.” To prove his point, his added the remaining contents of his glass to hers. “Here, drink up,” he said, sliding the glass toward her. “It’ll make watching them a little easier.”

“I don’t know what you’re talking about.” Surely she wasn’t that transparent.

Apparently she was, because the man immediately gave her a look. “Sweetheart, I’m a New York bartender. I know how to read people. In your case, it’s not that hard. You’ve been watching the guy since last night’s main course.”

No sense pretending she didn’t know what he meant. Directly across the dance floor, Armando and Mona were talking to her father, Omar. Mona was the one dangerously close to upstaging the bride. Her strapless gown looked sewn onto her body.

She paled compared to Armando, though. Both he and his father were in full regalia for the wedding, navy blue uniforms complete with sash and sword. He looked like he belonged on a white charger.

“For crying out loud, you’re staring at him right now,” Darius said. “Damn good thing I don’t have self-esteem issues.”

“I’m sorry. I don’t mean to be rude. I…”

“Got a thing for the guy?”

Rosa felt her cheeks burn. Quickly, she grabbed her wine and swallowed. “I’m afraid it’s complicated.”

"I know. I met her last night. What's her deal, anyway?"

Rosa told him.

"Fiancée, huh? Then why were you two sneaking off last night? I told you, I'm observant," he added when she gasped.

Because Armando got jealous and said he wanted her. He kissed her like she'd never been kissed before, and probably never would be again. He let her pretend for a moment that a woman like her could be a princess, and now she was sitting at a wedding angry at her own foolishness.

"I told you," she said. "It's complicated."

"I bet. Complicated is why I'm glad I'm single. Come on." He stood up and held out his hand. "Let's fox-trot."

Rosa shook her head. "I don't think..."

"You really want to sit here looking like a sad chipmunk all night, or do you want him to see you enjoying yourself next time he looks in your direction?"

Rosa looked over to see Mona place a proprietary hand on Armando's arm. The woman certainly didn't waste time marking her territory. "There's a good chance I'll step on your toes."

"Good, that makes two of us."

Darius, it turned out, was a worse dancer than she was. By the second song, they were both laughing over how much they were tripping up the other. Rosa had to admit, it felt good to make mistakes and laugh about them. Made her forget her heartache for a little while.

That was, until a familiar hand tapped Darius on the shoulder. “May I?” Armando asked. His eyes, as well as his request, were directed at her.

Rosa could feel Darius tightening his grip in an effort to protect her. “It’s all right,” she told him. Actually, it was probably a mistake, but the chance to be in Armando’s arms was too great a temptation to pass up.

“You two seem to be enjoying yourselves,” Armando said when she stepped into his arms. “I’m sorry I had to interrupt.” Rosa bristled at his barely disguised jealousy. What made him think he had any right?

“Isn’t that the point of a wedding? To enjoy yourself?”

“I didn’t mean that the way it sounded,” he replied. He twirled their bodies toward a far end of the dance floor. “That’s a lie. I meant it exactly as it sounded. It killed me to see you in his arms.”

“Really? Because watching you with Mona is a picnic.”

Her jab hit its mark, because he immediately winced. “You’re right. I have no business saying anything, and I’m sorry.”

“So am I,” she replied. If these were to be the only moments Armando held her, she didn’t want to waste them fighting. It was because the position reminded her too much of last night, and the memories were too raw to handle politely. She ached for him to close the distance between their bodies. A few inches, that was all. Enough for her to rest her head on his shoulder and pretend the rest of the world didn’t exist.

Instead, the song ended. She started to step away, but Armando tightened his grip on her waist. "One more dance," he said. "There's something I need to say."

"Armando…" He was going to talk about Mona and obligations and all the other topics she wanted to forget.

"Please, Rosa."

Whatever made her think she had a chance? Letting out a breath, she relaxed into his touch. "You know I can never say no to you."

"I know," he replied.

While he spoke, his gaze traced a line along her cheek, performing the caress he couldn't do by hand. Rosa's insides cried for the touch.

They danced in silence for what felt like forever. Finally, just when she was ready to say something, Armando spoke. "Do you know what I did last night?" he asked.

She shook her head.

"I couldn't sleep, so I counted the lights I could see from my bedroom window. Seven hundred fourteen. In that one patch of space. Do you know how many there are in the entire country? One point two million."

"Oh, 'Mando." She knew where this was going.

"Never have I resented so many lights," he said, gazing past her.

"That's not true. You don't resent them," she replied. "You love them."

Still looking past her shoulder, Armando sighed.

"You're right. I wish I did hate them, though. I wish I didn't care what happened to any of them."

He pulled his gaze back to her, and she saw that the perpetual melancholy that clouded his eyes was twice as thick. "I do, though. Dammit, I do."

"I'm glad." Yes, a selfish part of her wanted him not to care, but it was Armando's love for his people that made him who he was.

"She wants to improve medical care. Mona. That's what she wants to do when we're married. Improve medical care in both countries. There will be thousands more candles to look after."

She could feel the responsibility pushing down upon him. Suddenly Rosa understood. He was backed into a corner. Choose duty and save lives. Choose for himself and fail two countries. Whatever anger she might still have began to fade. "You're doing the right thing," she told him. Like he always did. The responsible young boy who looked out for his sister on a bigger scale. "Corinthia—and Yelgiers—are lucky to have a leader who cares so much."

"Perhaps." He didn't look convinced. He looked… sad. "I had no right to kiss you, Rosa. It was wrong."

"Don't say that."

"But it's true. I knew I had obligations, and yet, like a selfish bastard, I went after what I wanted anyway. Who knows what would have happened if Vittorio hadn't interrupted us?"

They both knew what would have happened.

"How does that make me any different than Fredo?" he asked.

His self-loathing had gone too far. Halting her steps, she touched her fingers to his lips to silence him. "You are nothing like Fredo."

He smiled and kissed her fingertips. "Aren't I, though? You deserve better."

Except there wasn't anyone better. If the feelings in her heart were to be believed, there never would be. "In case you didn't notice, there were two people kissing," she told him. "We both ignored our common sense."

Armando shook his head. "Dear, sweet Rosa. You still won't admit you are a victim."

"Because I'm not a victim." Not this time. "Last night, you made me feel more special in five minutes than I had ever felt in my entire life. I would trade all the common sense in the world for that."

"If I could, I would make you feel special every day. You deserve nothing less."

"Neither do you."

He smiled sadly. "But apparently I do."

The song ended, but they had stopped dancing long ago in favor of standing in each other's arms. Rosa's first assessment was right—it was much too similar to last night's embrace. When Armando's eyes dropped to her mouth, common sense was again poised to disappear.

"I love you, Rosa. I'm sorry I didn't come to my senses sooner."

He pulled away, leaving her to shudder from the

withdrawal. She was still in a daze. Did he say he loved her? *Loved?*

The sound of a spoon against crystal rang across the ballroom. King Carlos had stepped up to the front of the room.

“Ladies and gentlemen, might I have your attention?” Instantly, the ballroom went silent.

“Arianna asked me to refrain from formal toasts and speeches during last evening’s dinner, and as you all know, while I rule Corinthia, she rules me.” Low laughter rippled through the crowd. Rosa sneaked a look at Armando and saw he hadn’t cracked a smile. “However, I cannot let this evening end without saying a few words, not as your king, but as a father.”

The king’s smile softened. “This family has seen its share of loss over the past few years. My wife. Princess Christina.” At the sound of her sister’s name, Rosa looked to the floor.

“But now, as I look at the faces around the room and I see the smile on my daughter’s beautiful face, my heart is filled with so much hope. Hope for new beginnings. Hope for the next generation, and the generations of Santoros to come. I’ve never been prouder of my children. Just as I am proud of my newest son, Maxwell. I hope also to add a new daughter soon as well.” Everyone but she and Armando looked in Mona’s direction. Armando kept his attention on his father, while Rosa lifted her eyes to watch Armando.

“I am getting older,” the king continued. “Older and

tired. There may come a day in the future when I decide to step down."

A gasp could be heard in the crowd. King Carlos held up a hand. "No need to be upset. I'm not worried. Because I see the people who will be taking my place, and I couldn't be more pleased."

The rest of his toast was a flurry of well wishes for Arianna and Max. At least that was what she assumed. Armando had turned to her, and she found herself transfixed by his blue stare. *I'm sorry*, his eyes were saying. *I have no choice.*

All Rosa could hear were the words she'd convinced herself he wasn't going to say. *I love you.* A lifetime and she wouldn't hear three more beautiful words.

She loved him, too.

What was she going to do come Monday? And the Monday after that? What about when Armando announced his engagement? Knowing he loved her might sound wonderful today, but how was she going to face him day in and day out when he belonged to someone else?

Simple answer was, she couldn't. Not without the self-esteem she'd worked so hard to rebuild crumbling into pieces again.

There was only one answer.

CHAPTER TEN

"ALL ARE ONE..." The last words of the Corinthian national anthem rose from the crowd gathered below the balcony. Arianna and Max had been officially presented as a royal couple.

Leaving Father and the happy couple to greet their well wishers, Armando stepped back inside. There was only so much joy a man could take, and he had met his limit.

He was happy for his sister, truly he was, but if he had to watch her and Max gaze into each other's eyes a second longer, he would scream.

A few moments alone in the empty gallery would clear his head. Then he would be ready to tackle the rest of Christmas Day. Mona and her father were joining the celebration. Another day being reminded of the hole he'd dug himself into. At least he'd apologized to Rosa, taking that guilt off his shoulders. Somewhat. He doubted he would ever be completely guilt-free.

Because part of him would never regret kissing her.

To his surprise, Rosa was in the gallery when he

entered, studying one of the china cabinets. One look and his energy returned, even if she was wearing one of those ridiculous long blazers he hated. He hadn't expected to see her for a few days. He'd wanted to—oh, Lord, had he wanted to—but common sense had made a rare appearance and suggested otherwise. If he went to her apartment, he would be tempted to pull her into his arms. Much like he was tempted right now.

When she saw him, she smiled. "Merry Christmas," she greeted.

Something wasn't right. He could tell by the sound of her voice. "The crowd sounds thrilled with their princess's new husband" she said.

"So it would seem. If I were a gambling man, I would bet Max embraces his royal role very quickly."

"That would be good for Corinthia."

"Yes." That was what mattered, wasn't it? The best for Corinthia? "What are you doing here?" he asked. The question came out more accusatory than he meant. "I thought you were helping out at the shelter this afternoon."

"I wanted to come by and give you your Christmas present." She pointed to a wrapped box on the seat of a nearby chair.

Armando walked over and fingered the cheerful silver bow. He didn't know what to say.

"Don't worry, it's not booby-trapped, I promise," she said. A halfhearted attempt to shake off the awkward atmosphere.

It wasn't booby trapping that had him off balance—it was wondering whether he deserved the kindness.

"My gift for you is under the tree upstairs," he said. A gold charm bracelet marking moments from their friendship.

"You can give it to me later. I can't stay long, and I want to see you open yours. Go ahead," she urged.

He peeled back the gift wrap. It was an antique wood statue of Babbo Natale. The colors were fading, but the carving itself was flawless.

"I found it in a shop outside the city. The owner thought he was handmade around the turn of the century. Silly, I know, but what else do you get the guy who has everything? You've already got plenty of ties," she added with a self-conscious laugh.

"Don't apologize," Armando told her. "It's beautiful. Truly handcrafted pieces are hard to find."

"When I saw him, I thought he looked a little like you do when you're wearing the costume. Around the eyes."

He turned the statue over in his hands. "I'll take your word for it." It didn't matter if the statue resembled him or the queen of England. She could have given him a paper doll and he would have treasured the piece. Because it came from her.

He longed to pull her into a hug. "Thank you. I love it." *And you.*

"I..." All of a sudden, she stopped talking and pivoted abruptly so she stood with her back turned to him. Something was definitely wrong, he thought, his shoulders stiffening. "I thought it would make a good memory to share with your child," she continued. "About those times you played Santa Claus at the shelter."

"You talk as if I won't be there anymore." That was never going to happen. The shelter and its mission were too important to him. More so now that he knew her story.

"Not you," Rosa replied, her back still turned. "Me."

Her? Armando's stomach dropped. "What are you talking about?"

When she didn't reply right away, he reached for her shoulder. To hell with not touching her. "What do you mean, you?"

"I-I'm leaving."

No. She couldn't be. Armando's hand fell away short of its goal. "You're not going to be my assistant anymore?"

"I can't." Finally, she turned around. When he saw her face, Armando almost wished he hadn't. Her eyes were damp and shining. "I can't come to work every day and see you. It's too dangerous."

"I don't understand." His mind was too stuck on her resignation to make sense of anything else. "Dangerous for whom?"

"Me," she replied.

She started to pace. Rosa being the one to mark paths on the carpeting for a change would be amusing if the circumstances were different. "I thought about what you said last night, about my deserving better," she said.

"You do. You deserve—"

She cut him off. "I know. Surprisingly. Fredo convinced me I would never deserve better than dirt, and for a long time I believed it."

He watched as a tear dripped down her cheek. "Then you said you loved me. Loved. And I started thinking, if a man like you thinks he loves me…"

"I do love you," he said, rushing toward her.

"Don't." With her hands in front of her chest, she shook her head. "This is why I have to quit."

"You don't want to be near me."

"Don't you understand? I want to be near you too much. You're marrying someone else, 'Mando.

"And I get it," she said when he opened his mouth to tell her she was—she would always be—his first choice. "I understand the responsibility you feel toward your country, and why you need to keep your word. I love your sense of honor.

"But if I stay, I'll be tempted to be with you no matter what the circumstances, and I can't be the woman you love on the side. I worked too hard on being myself again."

She was shaking by the time she finished. With tears staining her cheeks. It killed him to stand there when every fiber of his being wanted to steal her away to a place where they could be together. It killed him, but he knew it was what Rosa wanted. Just as he knew he couldn't fight her leaving.

"What will I do without you?" he asked instead.

"You survived without me for years, 'Mando. I'm

sure you'll survive again." Armando hated to think the last smile he'd see on her face would be this sad facsimile that didn't reach her eyes.

"Where will you go? What will you do?"

"I don't know yet. Right now, I'm going to focus on celebrating Christmas. I'll figure out the rest tomorrow."

"You survived once, you'll survive again," he repeated softly.

"Exactly." Her fingers were shaking as she wiped her cheeks. "Merry Christmas, Your Highness. Happy New Year, too."

Not without her in it.

With Babbo Natale cradled in his arms, he stood alone in the gallery and listened to the sound of the elevator doors closing. "Don't go," he whispered.

But like her sister had three years before, Rosa left anyway.

"Was that Rosa I saw getting on the elevator?" Arianna asked. She strolled in with Max and Father trailing behind. Her face pink from the cold, she shrugged off her coat and draped it over the arm of a chair. "I wish I'd known she was coming by. I have a Christmas present for her. Is that what Rosa gave you?" she asked, noting the wood carving. "It's lovely."

"What's lovely?" Max asked.

"The carving Rosa gave Max," Arianna replied.

"I'm not surprised," Father said. "She's always had impeccable taste." He went on to tell Max a story about an ornament Armando's mother bought the year Arianna was born. Armando continued to watch the doorway in case Rosa decided to return.

"She was determined to find the perfect ornament to mark Arianna's first Christmas. We must have gone to every shop, craftsman and artist in Corinthia, and nothing was good enough. If I'd thought I could learn fast enough, I would have taken up glassblowing myself so she could design her own. It has to be perfect for our baby, she kept saying."

Armando had already heard the ending. How his mother finally found the ornament in a gift shop in Florence, and it turned out to have been made by a Corinthian expatriate who insisted on giving the ornament as a gift for the new princess. The reverence in his father's voice as he spoke was at near worship proportions. His words practically dripped with love.

Armando's head started to hurt.

"I know she would be thrilled to look down and see the ornament on your tree, for your child."

"I'm only sorry she isn't here," he heard Arianna say with a sniff.

"We can only hope she is watching right now, happy and proud of both of you."

Would she be proud, Armando wondered. Would she be happy to know her eldest son had let the woman he loved walk away?

He worked up the courage to turn around, only to find a portrait of marital bliss. Max stood behind Arianna, arms wrapped around her to rest his hands on her bump. His father stood a few feet away, beaming with paternal approval. He tried to imagine himself in the picture, his arms around a pregnant Mona. Imagine himself content.

All he could see was Rosa's back as she walked away.

It wasn't fair. Father had said last night, their family had seen its share of dark days. Armando had buried his wife, for God's sake. He turned off a machine and watched her take her last breath! Did that moment truly mean he would never have love again? If that was the case, then why wake his heart up? Why torment him by having him fall in love with Rosa after he'd agreed to marry King Omar's daughter? Wouldn't it be better to keep his heart buried? Or was loving and losing another woman his punishment for some kind of cosmic crime?

"Armando!" Arianna was staring at him with wide eyes. "What is wrong with you?"

"You're choking Santa Claus," Max added.

He looked down and saw he had a white-knuckle grip on the statue. A more delicate piece would have snapped in two.

"I..." He dropped the figurine on the closest table like it was on fire. Babbo landed off balance and fell over, his wooden sack of toys hitting the table first with a soft thud.

Arianna appeared by his side, reaching past him to set the statue upright. "Are you all right?" she asked him. "You've been acting odd since late last night. Did something happen between you and Rosa?"

"Why would you ask that?"

"Because you and she are usually joined at the hip, and the past few days..."

"I have a headache is all," he snapped. The air in the gallery was feeling close. He needed space. "I've got to get some air."

Of course he would end up sitting in the archway, under the mistletoe. Trying to put your head on straight always worked best in a room full of memories. Sinking down on the next to last step, he scrubbed his face with his hands, looking to erase the night of the concert from his brain. Instead, he saw Rosa, her face bathed in golden light.

What was he going to do? Leaning back, he stared up at the mistletoe sprig. "You have been nothing but trouble, do you know that?"

If the berries had a retort, they kept it to themselves. Bastards.

A flash of gold and green caught his eye. A few feet to his left, he noticed an angel perched near the top of the tree. Unlike the other ornaments, which were ornate almost to the point of ostentation, the angel was simple and made of felt with a mound of golden hair surrounding her face. He really must be losing his mind; the way the angel was hung, it looked like she was watching him. "What do you think I should do, angel? Do I do the honorable thing and keep my promise to Mona? Or do I go against everything I've ever been taught to run after Rosa?"

Nothing.

That's what he thought. As if a Christmas ornament would know any more than a branch of mistletoe.

Why then did he feel as though the answer was right there, waiting for him to see it? "Why did Christina have to die in the first place?" he asked the angel. "Life would be so much easier if she had just taken the curve a little slower. I wouldn't have needed to enter an agreement with King Omar because I wouldn't need a wife."

And Rosa would still be with Fredo. Unacceptable. As much as he had loved Christina, he would never bring her back if it meant leaving Rosa married and fearful. Christina wouldn't want to come back under those circumstances.

But she would tell you to follow your heart. That life is too short to waste time feeling angry and unhappy. Not when happiness is within your reach. All you have to do is to be brave enough to take a chance. To sneak out after dark and turn on the Christmas lights.

To leave the abusive husband. If Rosa could be brave enough to walk away from Fredo, if the other women could walk away from worse, then surely he could summon up enough bravery to be happy.

"Armando! Are you here?"

Looked like he would be tested sooner than he thought. "In the archway, Father."

"I should have known." King Carlos appeared at the top of the opposite stairs. "I swear you are as bad as your sister regarding these lights," he said as he navigated the steps.

"It's too cold to go outside," Armando told him. "This is the next best thing."

"You are aware you are sitting under the mistletoe?"

"Believe me, I know. Damn plant is following me."

His father chuckled. "You, my son, might be the first person I have ever heard complain about kissing traditions. Or is it a more specific problem?" he asked, settling himself on the step as well. "Your sister is right. You've been out of sorts for a few days now. Did something happen?"

"You could say that," Armando replied. He stared at his palms. Maybe one of the lines had the words he needed to explain. "Did you mean what you said last night? About being proud of Arianna and me?"

Whatever his father had been expecting, that wasn't it. He leaned back a little so he could see Armando's face. "Of course I did. You make me immensely proud."

Would he still feel that way once Armando finished—that was the question. "Even if I dishonored Corinthia?"

"Considering your sister married a man who is not the father of her child, it would be hypocritical of me, don't you think? Besides, I doubt there's anything you could do that would dishonor Corinthia too much."

"Don't be so sure."

His father paused as what Armando said sank in. "What have you done?"

"More like what I can't do," Armando replied and looked up from his hand. He didn't need a love or life line to tell him what needed to be said. "I can't marry Mona."

"I see." There was another pause. "And why can't you?"

"Because I'm in love with someone else." He laid out the entire story, from why he contacted King Omar in the first place to his goodbye to Rosa a short time earlier. When he finished, he went back to studying his palms. "I know we're responsible for every light in Corinthia. I know that backing out of this arrangement means dishonoring our reputation and making an enemy out an important economic ally, but I just can't.

"It's selfish, but I'm tired of being unhappy, Father," he said, staring at the shadows flickering along the wall. "It's been three years of not being among the living. I need to live again."

By this point, he'd been expecting his father's silence, so it was a surprise when his father responded immediately. "Every light in Corinthia? Sounds like someone spent time with his grandfather."

He reached over and patted Armando's knee, something he hadn't done in Armando's childhood. "My father was a good man, but some of his advice could be heavy-handed. If I had known he was putting such notions in your head when you were young… Apparently I've failed you as well."

"No, you didn't," Armando said, shifting his weight to face him. "You have been an exemplary king…"

"And a mediocre father," he replied. "I wallowed in my grief and, as a result, taught you by example. Of course you should be happy, Armando. You can't lead a country if you're angry and bitter. If Rosa is the woman who will make you happy, embrace her."

Armando planned to. He took a deep breath. Perhaps his father had a point. Having made his decision, he no longer felt the pressing weight on his shoulders. Like on the night of the rehearsal dinner, the bits and pieces kicking around his head had solidified, making his thoughts clear. He could breathe.

"Omar is going to be furious," he said. Mona, too. And deservedly so.

"Omar is also pragmatic. His main concern is helping his people. If we offer economic aid, I think he and Mona will be willing to swallow their hurt pride. Although I wouldn't expect an invitation to stay at the Yelgierian palace any time soon."

If that was the only fallout, Armando would live. "I would like to start an initiative as well to encourage Corinthian and other EU doctors to set up practice in Yelgiers. From what Mona says, a dearth of doctors is one of their most pressing concerns."

"We'll make it a priority," his father replied. "Now, what are you doing sitting under a mistletoe with me? Don't you have a future princess to collect?"

Yes, he did. With his cheek muscles aching from the grin on his face, Armando jumped to his feet.

"Armando!" his father called when he reached the door. "Merry Christmas."

Impossibly, Armando's grin grew even wider. "Merry Christmas, Father."

* * *

Rosa was trying. She was serving food and reminding herself that her life could be a lot worse. She had her brain. She was strong and capable. Moreover, while she might be alone, Armando loved her. Wanted, needed and loved. She should take solace in the fact she was special enough to win the heart of the crown prince.

"I'd rather have Armando."

"Are you talking to your imaginary friend, Miss Rosa?"

Daniela, she who started everything by spotting the first mistletoe, yanked on her blazer. "I have an imaginary friend, too," she said. "His name is Boco. He's a talking elephant. Is your friend an elephant, too?"

"No," said Rosa, embarrassed to be asked about her imaginary friend. "She's an angel named Christina."

"Like the name of this place?"

"That's right. She's been helping me make sense of a very confusing problem."

"Is it helping?" Daniela asked.

"Not yet," Rosa replied. "But we'll keep trying." Broken hearts were never solved in one day. And when the person you loved had also been the center of your life…she suspected she'd be trying to sort things out for a very long time.

"Maybe cake would help," Daniela said. "When my mama needs to think, she always eats cake. And ice cream."

"Your mother is a very smart woman." Though in

this case, cake would only make matters worse. She'd already eaten her weight in Christmas cookies.

Sending the little girl back to play with the other children, Rosa stole a couple more cookies and made her way to the rear picture window. In the distance, Mount Cornier's snow-covered peak had been swallowed by clouds. She bit a cookie and imagined her sister's spirit sitting on a fluffy white cushion, watching over her legacy.

Holidays and heartache made her overly poetic.

If Christina was watching, the least she could do was tell her what to do next, since Rosa didn't know. In some ways, she was worse off than when she left Fredo. Then, she'd had Armando. This time she would have to lean on herself. Maybe she would go to the continent and find a job there. Or America. She didn't care so long as she could start fresh.

And someday forget Armando.

Maybe.

If she didn't—couldn't—forget him, she knew she would still survive. She wasn't the same woman who had scurried away from Fredo thinking she was a fat, ugly lump of clay. Oh, she still had days…but there were also days when she felt good about herself. The fact she made the choice to walk away from Armando said she was stronger.

In time, she would be all right. Sad. Lonely. But all right.

"If only you could make my heart stop feeling like it was tearing in two," she whispered to the glass.

"Ho, ho, ho! *Buon Natale!*"

The entire shelter burst into high-pitched squeals. "Babbo!"

It couldn't be. They must have hired a professional impersonator for the day, as a surprise for the kids.

The director hadn't mentioned anything to her, though.

"Is everyone having a good Christmas?"

Uncanny. They even sounded alike. She looked in the glass hoping to catch a reflection, but it was too bright out. All she could see was a darkened silhouette in costume.

"Babbo needs your help, boys and girls."

This was silly. Armando was not at the shelter playing Babbo. As soon as she turned around she would see that the person…

Was Armando.

Why? He was dressed in costume and surrounded by children. "There's a very special person whose present Babbo forgot to deliver," he was telling them in his boisterous Babbo voice, "and I'm afraid she thinks I decided to give her present to another girl. It's really important I find her, boys and girls, so I can tell her that I would never pick someone else. That she's the most important person in the world to Babbo. In fact, Babbo cares about her so much that he wants her to come back to the North Pole with him."

Throughout his speech, Rosa moved closer. Spotting her, he dropped his voice back to normal. "Her name's Rosa," he said. "Do you know where I can find her?"

"Right there!" the children screamed, two dozen index fingers pointing in her direction.

Rosa was too stunned to breathe. "What are you doing?" she whispered.

"What do you think I am doing?" Armando said. "I've come to bring you back home where you belong." He reached through the throng to catch her fingertips. "I love you, Rosa."

Beautiful as those words were to hear, they were still only words. "I told you, Ar—Babbo. I can't stay at the North Pole." Out of the corner of her eye, she saw the children watching intently and lowered her voice to a whisper. "It hurts too much."

"But you don't understand," he whispered back. "Mona's gone. Come with me." Grabbing her hand, he led her to the shelter's lobby and closed the community room door. "I told Mona I couldn't marry her."

She had to have heard wrong. "What about your agreement with King Omar? You gave him your word."

"It's a long story. What matters is I love you and I don't want to be with anyone else."

Rosa couldn't believe what she was hearing. It was too unreal. "Are you saying that you damaged relations with one of your closest allies for me?"

"When you put it that way...yes." He pulled off his hat and beard, leaving only his disheveled self. His beautiful, disheveled self. "I would do it again, too. Are you crying?"

"Like a newborn baby." All those years married to Fredo, believing she wasn't anyone special. How wrong she had been. Armando made her feel beyond special. Not because he'd nearly created an international incident on her behalf, or tracked her down dressed like Santa Claus, although both were amazingly romantic.

No, the reason he made her feel special was in his eyes. They were shining as clear and bright as a summer's day without a trace of melancholy to be found. He was happy being with her, and that was all she needed.

"I love you," she told him.

Her reward was an even brighter shine. "Does that mean you'll come back with me to the North Pole?"

"Absolutely, Babbo. Right after you kiss me under the mistletoe."

"Forget the mistletoe," he said, tossing the beard over his shoulder. Rosa gasped as he pulled her into his arms and dipped her low. "All I need is you."

New Year's Eve

"Five minutes left in the year. Will you be sad to see it end?"

Rosa took one of the glasses of champagne Armando was carrying. "Yes," she said. "And no. I'll be sorry to see December end. For all the ups and downs, it turned out to be a pretty wonderful month."

"The last week certainly was." Armando gave her a champagne-flavored kiss that quickly deepened. "Have I mentioned how glad I am that we decided to skip a formal courtship?" he asked, lips continuing to tease hers.

"Well, it did seem a little silly, considering…"

"Mmm, considering," he said, kissing her again. What they were discovering was the intimacy that came from being friends before becoming lovers. There was a level of trust that made everything they shared feel deeper. Of course, the fact Armando was an amazingly enthusiastic lover didn't hurt, either.

"You know what else I'll miss," Rosa said, turning in his arms. "Once Epiphany passes, this will become a plain old archway again."

They were in their archway now, preferring to ring in the new year alone rather than in a ballroom full of dignitaries.

Armando kissed her temple. "If you'd like, I can insist the trees stay up by royal decree."

"Is this the same royal decree where you're going to ban the use of fake Babbo beards?"

"The fibers give me a rash."

"My poor baby. Too sensitive for synthetic fibers." She snuggled closer. "As much as I'll miss the decorations, they need to go. How else will they stay special?" Christmas decorations weren't like the man with his arms around her—Armando woke up being special.

While she woke up feeling like the luckiest woman in the world.

"Besides," she told him, "we still have tonight."

"Which switches to tomorrow in less than two minutes," he replied.

A brand-new year. Given how wonderfully this year was ending, Rosa couldn't imagine what the next year had in store. As far as she was concerned, she had everything she could want sitting next to her with his arms wrapped around her waist. She loved Armando, and he loved her. What could be better?

"Do you realize," she said, pausing to take a drink, "that if we hadn't gotten our act together, you would be announcing your engagement to Mona at this very moment?"

"You're right—I did plan to be engaged by New Year's, didn't I?"

"That was before." Armando's breaking the engagement to date his assistant turned out to be scandal enough to push Arianna's pregnancy out of the papers completely. Fortunately, Mona and King Omar, while hurt, didn't hold too big a grudge. Hard to be angry at a country that was funding doctors' relocation efforts.

"There is still the matter of my producing an heir, though," Armando said, shifting his weight.

"That can be arranged," Rosa said with a smile.

"Very amusing. If you don't mind, I would like to establish my family in the proper order. Marriage, then heirs. What do you think?"

"I think that's a very logical..." Armando had moved to his knee. In his hand was the most beautiful diamond Rosa had ever seen. "Are you—" She couldn't finish the sentence; her heart was stuck in her throat.

"I am," he whispered with a nod. "Rosa Lamberti, would you do me the honor of becoming my wife?"

She never did say the word *yes*. Instead, Rosa threw her arms around his neck and kissed him until there was no doubt as to her answer. “I would be honored,” she told him.

Down the hall, the crowd began chanting a count-down to midnight. Rosa and Armando didn’t care. Their time was already here.

* * * * *

MERRY CHRISTMAS, BABY MAVERICK!

BRENDA HARLEN

For loyal readers of all the Montana Mavericks series,
from Whitehorn to Thunder Canyon and
Rust Creek Falls.

This book is also dedicated to Robin Harlen
(May 8, 1943–December 20, 2014)— a wonderful
father-in-law to me and granddad to my children.
He would be pleased to know that I finished this
book on schedule.

Prologue

Fourth of July

Trey Strickland did a double take when he first spotted Kayla Dalton at the wedding of local rancher Braden Traub to Jennifer MacCallum of Whitehorn.

Although Trey was only visiting from Thunder Canyon, his family had lived in Rust Creek Falls for a number of years while he was growing up. His best friend during that time was Derek Dalton, who had two older brothers, Eli and Jonah, and two younger sisters, twins Kristen and Kayla.

Trey remembered Kayla as a pretty girl with a quiet demeanor and a shy smile, but she'd grown up—and then some. She was no longer a pretty girl, but a beautiful woman with long, silky brown hair, sparkling blue eyes and distinctly feminine curves. Looking at her now, he couldn't help but notice the lean, shapely legs showcased by the short hem of her blue sundress, the tiny waist encircled by a narrow belt, the sweetly rounded breasts hugged by the bodice…and his mouth actually went dry.

She was stunning, sexy and incredibly tempting. Unfortunately, she was still his friend's little sister, which meant that she was off-limits to him.

But apparently, Kayla was unaware of that fact, because after hovering on the other side of the wooden dance floor that had been erected in the park for the occasion, she set down her cup of punch and made her way around the perimeter of the crowd.

She had a purposeful stride—and surprisingly long legs for such a little thing—and he enjoyed watching her move. He was pleased when she came to a stop beside him, looking up at him with determination and just a little bit of trepidation glinting in her beautiful blue eyes.

"Hello, Trey."

He inclined his head in acknowledgment of her greeting. "Kayla."

For some reason, his use of her name seemed to take her aback. "How did you know it was me?"

"I haven't been gone from Rust Creek Falls *that* long," he chided gently.

Soft pink color filled her cheeks. "I meant—how did you know I was Kayla and not Kristen?"

"I'm not sure," he admitted. But the truth was, he'd never had any trouble telling his friend's twin sisters apart. Although identical in appearance, their personalities were completely different, and he'd always had a soft spot for the shyer twin.

Thankfully, she didn't press for more of an explanation, turning her attention back to the dance floor instead. "They look good together, don't they?"

He followed her gaze to the bride and groom, nodded.

They chatted a little bit more about the wedding and

various other things. A couple of older women circulated through the crowd, carrying cups of wedding punch to distribute to the guests. The beverage was refreshingly cold, so he lifted a couple of cups from the tray and handed one to Kayla.

When they finished their drinks and set the empty cups aside, he turned to her and asked, "Would you like to dance?"

She seemed surprised by the question and hesitated for a moment before nodding. "Yes, I would."

Of course, that was the moment the tempo of the music changed from a quick, boot-stomping tune to a soft, seductive melody. Then Kayla stepped into his arms, and the intoxicating effect of her soft curves against him shot through his veins like the most potent whiskey.

A strand of her hair had come loose from the fancy twist at the back of her head and it fluttered in the breeze, tickling his throat. The scent of her skin teased his nostrils, stirring his blood and clouding his brain. He tried to think logically about the situation—just because she was an attractive woman and he was attracted didn't mean he had to act on the feeling. But damn, it was hard to remember all the reasons why he needed to resist when she fit so perfectly against him.

As the song began to wind down, he guided her to the edge of the dance floor, then through the crowd of people mingling, until they were in the shadows of the pavilion.

"I thought, for a moment, you were going to drag me all the way to your room at the boarding house," Kayla teased.

The idea was more than a little tempting. "I might have," he said. "If I thought you would let me."

She held his gaze for a long minute then nodded slowly. "I would let you."

The promise in her eyes echoed her words. Still, he

hesitated, because this was Kayla—*Derek's sister*—and she was off-limits. But she was so tempting and pretty, and with her chin tipped up, he could see the reflection of the stars in her eyes. Dazzling. Seductive. Irresistible.

He gave in to the desire churning through him and lowered his head to kiss her.

And she kissed him back.

As her lips moved beneath his, she swayed into him. The soft press of her sweet body set his own on fire. He wrapped his arms around her, pulling her closer as he deepened the kiss. She met the searching thrust of his tongue with her own, not just responding to his demands but making her own. Apparently, sweet, shy Kayla Dalton wasn't as sweet and shy as he'd always believed—a stunning realization that further fanned the flames of his desire.

He wanted her—desperately and immediately. And the way she was molded to him, he would bet the ranch that she wanted him, too. A suspicion that was further confirmed when he started to ease his mouth away and she whimpered a soft protest, pressing closer.

"Maybe we should continue this somewhere a little more private," he suggested.

"More private sounds good," she agreed without hesitation.

He took her hand, linking their fingers together, and led her away.

Chapter One

Kayla walked out of the specialty bath shop with another bag to add to the half dozen she already carried and a feeling of satisfaction. It was only the first of December, and she was almost finished with her Christmas shopping. She'd definitely earned a hot chocolate.

Making her way toward the center court of the mall, she passed a long line of children and toddlers impatiently tugging on the hands of parents and grandparents, along with babies sleeping in carriers or snuggled in loving arms. At the end of the line was their destination: Santa.

She paused to watch as a new mom and dad approached the jolly man in the red suit, sitting on opposite sides of him after gently setting their sleeping baby girl—probably not more than a few months old—in his arms. Then the baby opened her eyes, took one look at the stranger and let out an earsplitting scream of disapproval.

While the parents fussed, trying to calm their infant daughter so the impatient photographer could snap a "First

Christmas with Santa" picture, Kayla was suddenly struck by the realization that she might be doing the same thing next Christmas.

Except that there wouldn't be a daddy in her picture, an extra set of hands to help console their unhappy baby. Kayla was on her own. Unmarried. Alone. A soon-to-be single mother who was absolutely terrified about that fact.

She'd always been logical and levelheaded, not the type of woman who acted impulsively or recklessly. Not until the Fourth of July, when she'd accepted Trey's invitation to go back to his room. One cup of wedding punch had helped rekindle her schoolgirl fantasies about the man who had been her brother's best friend. Then one dance had led to one kiss—and one impulsive decision to one unplanned pregnancy.

She owed it to Trey to tell him that their night together had resulted in a baby, but she didn't know how to break the news when he apparently didn't even remember that they'd been together. Even now, five months later, that humiliation made her cheeks burn.

She wasn't at all promiscuous. In fact, Trey was the first man she'd had sex with in three years and only the second in all of her twenty-five years. But Trey had also been drinking the wedding punch that was later rumored to have been spiked with something, and his memory of events after they got back to his room at the boarding house was a little hazy. Kayla had been relieved—and just a little insulted—when he left Rust Creek Falls to return to Thunder Canyon a few weeks later without another word to her about what had happened between them.

But she knew that he would be back again. Trey no longer lived in Rust Creek Falls but his grandparents—Gene and Melba Strickland—still did, and he returned two or three times every year to visit them. It was inevitable that their paths would cross when he came back, and she'd have to tell him about their baby when he did.

Until then, she was grateful that she'd managed to keep her pregnancy a secret from almost everyone else. Even now, only her sister, Kristen, knew the truth. Thankfully, she'd only just started to show, and the cold Montana weather gave her the perfect excuse to don big flannel shirts or bulky sweaters that easily covered the slight curve of her belly.

Regardless of the circumstances of conception, she was happy about the baby and excited about impending motherhood. It was only the "single" part that scared her. And although her family would likely disapprove of the situation, she was confident they would ultimately support her and love her child as much as she did.

The tiny life stirred inside her, making her smile. She loved her baby so much already, so much more than she would have imagined possible, but she had no illusions that Trey would be as happy about the situation. Especially considering that he didn't even remember getting naked and tangling up the sheets with her.

She pushed those worries aside for another day and entered the line in the café. After perusing the menu for several minutes, she decided on a peppermint hot chocolate with extra whipped cream, chocolate drizzle and candy-cane sprinkles. She'd been careful not to overindulge, conscious of having to disguise every pound she put on, but she couldn't hide her pregnancy forever—probably not even for much longer.

Which, of course, introduced another dilemma—how could she tell anyone else about the baby when she hadn't even told the baby's father? And what if he denied that it was his?

The sweet beverage she'd sipped suddenly left a bad taste in her mouth as she considered the possibility.

A denial from Trey would devastate her, but she knew that she had to be prepared for it. If he didn't remember sleeping with her, why would he believe he was the father of her child?

"It really is a small world, isn't it?"

Kayla started at the question that interrupted her thoughts, her face flaming as she glanced up to see Trey's grandmother standing beside her table with a steaming cup of coffee in her hands. Not that Melba Strickland could possibly know what she'd been thinking, but Kayla couldn't help but feel unnerved by the other woman's unexpected presence.

She forced a smile. "Yes, it is," she agreed.

"Do you mind if I join you?"

"Of course not." There weren't many empty chairs in the café, and it seemed silly for each of them to sit alone as if they were strangers. Especially considering that Kayla had known the Stricklands for as long as she could remember.

Melba and Gene were good people, if a little old-fashioned. Or maybe it was just that they were old—probably in their late seventies or early eighties, she guessed, because no one seemed to know for sure. Regardless, their boarding house was a popular place for people looking for long-term accommodations in Rust Creek Falls—so long as they didn't mind abiding by Melba's strict rules, which included a ban on overnight visitors. An explicit prohibition that Kayla and Trey had ignored on the Fourth of July.

"Goodness, this place is bustling." Melba pulled back the empty chair and settled into it. "The whole mall, I mean. It's only the first of December, and the stores are packed. It's as if everyone in Kalispell has decided to go shopping today."

"Everyone in Kalispell and half of Rust Creek Falls," Kayla agreed.

The older woman chuckled. "Looks like you got an early start," she noted, glancing at the shopping bags beneath the table.

"Very early," Kayla agreed, scooping up some whipped cream and licking it off the spoon.

"I love everything about Christmas," Melba confided. "The shopping and wrapping, decorating and baking. But mostly I love the time we spend with family and friends."

"Are you going to have a full house over the holidays this year?" Kayla asked.

"I hope so," the older woman said. "We've had Claire, Levi and Bekka with us since August, and Claire's sisters have hinted that they might head this way for Christmas, which would be great. I so love having the kids around."

Kayla smiled because she knew the *kids* referred to—Bekka excluded—were all adults.

They chatted some more about holiday traditions and family plans, then Melba glanced at the clock on the wall. "Goodness—" her eyes grew wide "—is that the time? I've only got three hours until I'm meeting Gene for dinner, and all I've bought is a cup of coffee."

"Mr. Strickland came into the city with you?"

The older woman nodded. "We've got tickets to see *A Christmas Carol* tonight."

"I'm sure you'll enjoy it," Kayla said. "The whole cast—especially Belle—is fabulous."

Melba smiled at her mention of the character played on the stage by Kayla's sister. "Not that you're biased at all," she said with a wink.

"Well, maybe a little." Her sister had always loved the

theater, but she'd been away from it for a lot of years before deciding to audition for the holiday production in Kalispell. The part of Scrooge's former fiancée wasn't a major role, but it was an opportunity for Kristen to get back on stage, and she was loving every minute of it.

In support of her sister, Kayla had signed on to help behind the scenes. She'd been surprised to discover how much she enjoyed the work—and grateful that keeping busy allowed her to pretend her whole life wasn't about to change.

"Lissa and Gage saw it last week and said the costumes were spectacular."

"I had fun working on them," she acknowledged.

"But you have no desire to wear them onstage?"

"None at all."

"You know, Kristen's ease at playing different roles has some people wondering if she might be the Rust Creek Rambler."

Kayla frowned. "You're kidding."

"Of course, I wouldn't expect you to betray your sister if she is the author of the gossip column."

"She's not," Kayla said firmly.

"I'm sure you would know—they say twins have no secrets from one another," Melba said. "Besides, she's been so busy with the play—and now with her new fiancé—when would she have time to write it?"

"I'm a little surprised there's been so much recent interest in uncovering the identity of the anonymous author, when the column has been around for almost three years now."

"Three and a half," Melba corrected, proving Kayla's point. "I suspect interest has piqued because some people think the Rambler is responsible for spiking the punch at the wedding."

Kayla gasped. "Why would they think that?"

"The events of that night have certainly provided a lot of fodder for the column over the past few months," the older woman pointed out. "It almost makes sense that whoever is writing it might want to help generate some juicy stories."

"That's a scary thought."

"Isn't it?" Melba finished her coffee and set her cup down. "The Rambler also noted that you were up close and personal with my grandson, Trey, on the dance floor at Braden and Jennifer's wedding."

Kayla had long ago accepted that in order to ensure no one ever suspected she was the Rambler, it was necessary to drop her own name into the column every once in a while. Since her turn on the dance floor with Trey hadn't gone unnoticed, the Rambler would be expected to comment on it. As for *up close and personal*—that hadn't come until later, and she had no intention of confiding *that* truth to Trey's grandmother.

Instead, she lifted her cup to her lips—only to discover that it was empty. She set it down again. "We danced," she admitted.

"That's all?" Melba sounded almost disappointed.

"That's all," Kayla echoed, her cheeks flushing. She'd never been a very good liar, and lying to Trey's grandmother—her own baby's great-grandmother—wasn't easy, even if it was necessary.

The older woman sighed. "I've been hoping for a long time that Trey would find a special someone to settle down with. If I had my choice, that special someone would live in Rust Creek Falls, so that he'd want to come back home here—or at least visit more often."

"Maybe he already has someone special in Thunder Canyon," she suggested, aiming for a casual tone.

"I'm sure he would have told me if he did," Melba said. "I know he sees girls, but he's never been serious about any of them. No one except Lana."

"Lana?" she echoed.

Melba's brow furrowed. "Maybe you don't know about Lana. I guess Jerry and Barbara had already moved away from Rust Creek Falls before Trey met her."

Kayla hadn't considered that the father of her baby might be involved with someone else—or that he might even have been in a relationship when he was visiting in the summer. Thinking about the possibility now made her feel sick. She honestly didn't think Trey was that kind of guy—but the reality was that neither of them had been thinking very clearly the night of the wedding.

"Anyway, he met Lana at some small local rodeo, where she won the division championship for barrel racing," the other woman continued. "I think it was actually her horse that caught his eye before she did, but it wasn't too long after that they were inseparable.

"They were together for almost two years, and apparently Trey had even started looking at engagement rings. And then—" Melba shook her head "—Lana was out on her horse, just enjoying a leisurely trail ride, when the animal got spooked by something and threw her."

Kayla winced, already anticipating how the story would end.

"She sustained some pretty serious injuries, and died five days later. She was only twenty-three years old."

"Trey must have been devastated," Kayla said softly, her heart aching for his loss.

"He was," Melba agreed. "We were all saddened by her death—and so worried about him. But then, when I heard that he was dancing with you at the wedding, well,

I have to admit, I let myself hope it was a sign that his heart was healed."

"It was just a dance," she said again.

"Maybe it was," Melba acknowledged, as she pushed her chair away from the table. "And maybe there will be something more when you see him again."

"Did you leave any presents in the mall for anyone else to buy?" Kristen teased, as she helped her sister cart her parcels and packages into the sprawling log house they'd grown up in.

The Circle D Ranch, located on the north side of town, was still home to Kayla, but her twin had moved out a few weeks earlier, into a century-old Victorian home that their brother Jonah had bought after the flood for the purposes of rehabbing and reselling. Since Kristen had started working at the theater in Kalispell, this house, on the south edge of town and close to the highway, had significantly cut down her commuting time—and given her a taste of the independence she'd been craving.

"Only a few," Kayla warned her, dumping her armload of packages onto her bed.

"That one looks interesting," her sister said, reaching for the bag from the bath shop.

Kayla slapped her hand away. "No snooping."

"Then it *is* for me," Kristen deduced.

"You'll find out at Christmas—unless you try to peek again, in which case it's going back to the store."

"I won't peek," her sister promised. "But speaking of shopping, I was thinking that you should plan a trip to Thunder Canyon to check out the stores there."

Kayla gestured to the assortment of bags. "Does it look like I need to check out any more stores?"

Kristen rolled her eyes. "You and I know that your

shopping is done—or very nearly, but no one else needs to know that. And shopping is only a cover story, anyway—your *real* purpose would be to see Trey and *finally* tell him about the secret you've been keeping for far too long."

Just the idea of seeing Trey again made Kayla's tummy tighten in knots of apprehension and her heart pound with anticipation. Thoughts of Trey had always had that effect on her; his actual presence was even more potent.

She *really* liked him—in fact, she'd had a major crush on him for a lot of years when she was younger. Then his family had moved away, and her infatuated heart had moved on. Until the next time he came back to Rust Creek Falls, and all it would take was a smile or a wave and she would be swooning again.

But still, her infatuation had been nothing more than a harmless fantasy—until the night of the wedding. Being with Trey had stirred all those old feelings up again and even now there was, admittedly, a part of her that hoped he'd be thrilled by the news of a baby, sweep her into his arms, declare that he'd always loved her and wanted to marry her so they could raise their child together.

Unfortunately, the reality was that five months had passed since the night they'd spent together, and she hadn't heard a single word from him after he'd gone back to Thunder Canyon.

She'd been pathetically smitten and easily seduced, and he'd been so drunk he didn't even remember being with her. Of course, another and even more damning possibility was that he *did* remember but was only pretending not to because he was ashamed by what had happened—a possibility that did not bode well for the conversation they needed to have.

"I know I have to talk to Trey," she acknowledged to

her sister now. "But I can't just show up in Thunder Canyon to tell him that I'm having his baby."

"Why not?" Kristen demanded.

"Because."

"You've been making excuses for months," her sister pointed out. "And you don't have many more left—excuses *or* months."

"Do you think I don't realize that?"

Kristen threw her hands up. "I don't know what you realize. I never thought you'd keep your pregnancy a secret for so long—not from me or the rest of your family, and especially not from the baby's father.

"I've tried to be understanding and supportive," her sister continued. "But if you don't tell him, *I* will."

Kayla knew it wasn't an idle threat. "But how can I tell Trey that he's going to be a father when he doesn't even remember having sex with me?"

Kristen frowned. "What are you talking about?"

"When I saw Trey—later the next day—he said that his memory of the night before was hazy."

"A lot of people had blank patches after drinking that spiked punch."

She nodded. "But Trey's mind had apparently blanked out the whole part about getting naked with me."

"Okay, that might make the conversation a little awkward," Kristen acknowledged.

"You think?"

Her sister ignored her sarcasm. "But awkward or not, you have to get it over with. I'd say sooner rather than later, but it's already later."

"I know," Kayla agreed.

"So…shopping trip to Thunder Canyon?" Kristen prompted.

"Three hundred miles is a long way to go to pick up

a few gifts—don't you think Mom and Dad will be suspicious?"

"I think Mom and Dad should be the least of your worries right now."

Kristen was right, of course. Her sister always had a way of cutting to the heart of the matter. "Will you go with me?"

"If I had two consecutive days off from the theater, I would, but it's just not possible right now."

She nodded.

"And no," Kristen spoke up before Kayla could say anything more. "That does not give you an excuse to wait until after the holidays to make the trip."

"I know," she grumbled, because she had, of course, been thinking exactly that—and her sister knew her well enough to know it.

"So when are you going?" Kristen demanded.

"I'll keep you posted. I have to get to the paper."

RUST CREEK RAMBLINGS: THE LA LAWYER TAKES A BRIDE

Yes, folks, it's official: attorney to the stars Ryan Roarke is off the market after being firmly lassoed by a local cowgirl! So what's the next order of business for the California lawyer? Filing for a change of venue in order to keep his boots firmly planted on Montana soil and close to his beautiful bride-to-be, Kristen Dalton. No details are available yet on a date for the impending nuptials, but the good people of Rust Creek Falls can rest assured that they will know as soon as the Rambler does…

Chapter Two

Trey Strickland had been happily living near and working at the Thunder Canyon Resort for several years now, but he never passed up an opportunity to visit his grandparents in Rust Creek Falls. His family had lived in the small town for nearly a decade while he was growing up, and he still had good friends there and always enjoyed catching up with them again.

Now it was December and he hadn't been back since the summer. And whenever he thought of that visit, he thought of Kayla Dalton. Truth be told, he thought of Kayla at other times, too—and that was one of the reasons he'd forced himself to stay away for so long.

He'd slept with his best friend's little sister.

And he didn't regret it.

Unfortunately, he wasn't sure he could say the same about Kayla based on her demeanor toward him the next day. She'd pretended nothing had happened between them, so he'd followed her lead.

He suspected that they'd both acted out of character as a result of being under the influence of the wedding punch. According to his grandmother, the police now believed the fruity concoction had been spiked and were trying to determine who had done so and why.

Trey's initial reaction to the news had been shock, followed quickly by relief that there was a credible explanation for his own reckless behavior that night. But whatever had been in the punch, the remnants of it had long since been purged from his system, yet thoughts and memories of Kayla continued to tease his mind.

As he navigated the familiar route from Thunder Canyon to Rust Creek Falls, his mind wandered. He was looking forward to spending the holidays with his grandparents, but he was mostly focused on the anticipation of seeing Kayla again, and the closer he got to his destination, the more prominent she figured in his thoughts.

He'd had a great time with her at the wedding. Prior to that night, they hadn't exchanged more than a few dozen words over the past several years, so he'd been surprised to discover that she was smart and witty and fun. She was the kind of woman he enjoyed spending time with, and he hoped he would get to spend more time with her when he was in town.

But first he owed her an apology, which he would have delivered the very next morning except that his brain had still been enveloped in some kind of fog that had prevented him from remembering exactly what had happened after the wedding.

He didn't usually drink to excess. Sure, he enjoyed hanging out with his buddies and having a few beers, but he'd long outgrown the desire to get drunk and suffer the consequences the next morning. But whatever had been in that wedding punch, it hadn't given any hint of its incredible potency…

It was morning.

The bright sunlight slipping past the edges of the curtains told him that much. The only other fact that registered in his brain was that he was dying. Or at least he felt as if he was. The pain in his head was so absolutely excruciating, he was certain it was going to fall right off his body—and there was a part of him that wished it would.

In a desperate attempt to numb the torturous agony, he downed a handful of aspirin with a half gallon of water then managed to sit upright without wincing.

The quiet knock on his door echoed like a thunderclap in his head before his grandmother entered. She clucked her tongue in disapproval when she came into his room and threw the curtains wide, the sunlight stabbing through his eyeballs like hot knives.

"Get up and out of bed," she told him. "It's laundry day and I need your sheets."

He pulled the covers up over his head. "My sheets are busy right now."

"You should be, too. Your grandfather could use a hand cleaning out the shed."

He tried to nod, but even that was painful. "Give me half an hour."

He showered and dressed then turned his attention to the bed because, as his grandmother was fond of reminding him, it wasn't a hotel and she wasn't his maid. So he untucked one corner and pulled them off the bed. There was a quiet clunk as something fell free of the sheet and onto the floor.

An earring?

He slowly bent down to retrieve the sparkly teardrop, his mind immediately flashing back to the night before, when he'd stood beside Kayla Dalton on the edge of the dance floor and noticed the pretty earrings that hung from her ears.

Kayla Dalton?

He curled his fingers around the delicate bauble and sank onto the edge of the mattress as other images flashed through his mind, like snapshots with no real connection to any particular time and place. He rubbed his fingers against his temples as he tried to recall what had happened, but his brain refused to cooperate. He'd danced with Kayla—he was sure he remembered dancing with her. And then...

He frowned as he struggled to put the disjointed pieces together. She'd looked so beautiful in the moonlight, and she'd smelled really good. And her lips had looked so temptingly soft. He'd wanted to kiss her, but he didn't think he would have made that kind of move. Because as beautiful and tempting as she was, she was still Derek's sister.

But when he closed his eyes, he could almost feel the yielding of her sweet mouth beneath his, the softness of her feminine curves against his body. Since he'd never had a very good imagination, he could only conclude that the kiss had really happened.

And in order for her earring to end up in his bed—well, he had to assume that Kayla had been there, too.

And what did it say about him that he didn't even remember? Of course, it was entirely possible that they'd gotten into bed together and both passed out. Not something to be particularly proud of but, under the circumstances, probably the best possible scenario.

He tucked the earring in his pocket and finished stripping the bed, shaking out the sheets and pillowcases to ensure there weren't any other hidden treasures inside. Thankfully, there were not. Then he saw the cor-

ner of something peeking out from beneath the bed—and scooped up an empty condom wrapper.

He closed his eyes and swore.

The idea that he'd slept with Kayla Dalton had barely sunk into his brain when he saw her later that day.

She'd been polite and friendly, if a little reserved, and she'd given absolutely no indication that anything had happened between them, making him doubt all of his own conclusions about the night before.

It had taken a long time for his memories of that night to come into focus, for him to remember.

And now that those memories were clear, he was determined to talk to Kayla about what happened that night—and where they would go from here.

Kayla was on her way to the newspaper office when she spotted Trey's truck parked outside the community center.

She'd heard that he was coming back to Rust Creek Falls for the holidays, but she wasn't ready to face him. Not yet. There were still three weeks until Christmas. Why was he here already? She needed more time to plan and prepare, to figure out what to say, how to share the news that she knew would turn his whole world upside down.

The back of his truck was filled with boxes and the doors to the building were open. She'd heard that last year's gift drive for the troops was being affiliated with Thunder Canyon's Presents for Patriots this year, and she suspected that the boxes were linked to that effort.

"Kayla—hi."

She didn't need to look up to know it was Trey who was speaking. It wasn't just that she'd recognized his voice, it was that her heart was racing the way it always did whenever she was near him.

But she glanced up, her gaze skimming at least six feet

from his well-worn cowboy boots to his deep green eyes, and managed a smile. “Hi, Trey.”

“This is a pleasant surprise,” he said, flashing an easy grin that suggested he was genuinely happy to see her.

Which didn’t really make any sense. She not only hadn’t seen the guy in four months, she hadn’t spoken a single word to him in that time, either. There had been no exchange of emails or text messages or any communication at all. Not that she’d expected any, but her infatuated heart had dared to hope—and been sorely wounded as a result of that silly hope.

“How have you been?” he asked.

Pregnant.

The word was on the tip of her tongue because, of course, that reality had been at the forefront of her mind since she’d seen the little plus sign in the window of the test. But she didn’t dare say it aloud, because she knew he couldn’t understand the relevance of the information when he didn’t even remember sleeping with her.

“Fine,” she said instead. “And you?”

“Fine,” he echoed.

She nodded.

An awkward silence followed, which they both tried to break at the same time.

“Well, I should—”

“Maybe I could—”

Then they both stopped talking again.

“What were you going to say?” Trey asked her.

“Just that I should be going—I’m on my way to the newspaper office.”

“Do you work there?”

She nodded. “I’m a copy editor.”

“Oh.”

And that seemed to exhaust that topic of conversation.

"It was good to see you, Trey."

"You, too."

She started past him, relieved that this first and undeniably awkward encounter was over. Her heart was pounding and her stomach was a mass of knots, but she'd managed to exchange a few words with him without bursting into tears or otherwise falling to pieces. A good first step, she decided.

"Kayla—wait."

And with those two words, her opportunity to flee with her dignity intact was threatened.

Since she hadn't moved far enough away to be able to pretend that she hadn't heard him, she reluctantly turned back.

He took a step closer.

"I wanted to call you," he said, dropping his voice to ensure that his words wouldn't be overheard by any passersby. "There were so many times I thought about picking up the phone, just because I was thinking about you."

Her heart, already racing, accelerated even more. "You were thinking about me?"

"I haven't stopped thinking about you since we danced at the wedding."

Since we danced?

That was what he remembered about that night?

She didn't know whether to laugh or cry. Under other circumstances, it might have been flattering to think that a few minutes in his arms had made such a lasting impression. Under her current circumstances, the lack of any impression of what had come afterward was hurtful and humiliating.

"I really do have to go. My boss is expecting me."

"What are you doing later?"

She frowned. "Tonight?"

"Sure."

"I'm going to the movies with Natalie Crawford."

"Oh."

He sounded so sincerely disappointed, she wanted to cancel her plans and agree to anything he wanted. Except that kind of thinking was responsible for her current predicament.

"Well, I guess I'll see you around," she said.

He held her gaze for another minute before he nodded. "Count on it."

She walked away, knowing that she already did and cursing the traitorous yearning of her heart.

Trey helped finish unloading the truck, then headed over to the boarding house. He arrived just as his grandmother was slicing into an enormous roast, and the tantalizing aroma made his mouth water.

"Mmm, something smells good."

Melba set down her utensils and wiped her hands on a towel before she crossed the room to envelop him in a warm hug. "I was hoping you'd be here in time for dinner."

"I'd tell you that I ignored the speed limit to make sure of it, but my grandmother would probably disapprove," he teased.

"She certainly would," Melba agreed sternly.

"In time for dinner but not in time to mash the potatoes," Claire said, as she finished her assigned task.

His grandmother let him go and turned him over to his cousin, who hugged him tight.

He tipped her chin up to look into her brown eyes. "Everything good?"

"Everything's great," she assured him, her radiant smile confirming the words.

"Levi?" he prompted, referring to the husband she'd briefly separated from in the summer.

"In the front parlor, playing with Bekka."

"It's so much fun to have a child in the house again," their grandmother said. "I can't wait for there to be a dozen more."

"Don't count on me to add another dozen," Claire warned. "I have my hands full with one."

"At least you've given me one," Melba noted, with a pointed glance in Trey's direction.

He moved to the sink and washed his hands. "What can I do to help with dinner?" he asked, desperate to change the topic of conversation.

"You can get down the pitcher for the gravy." Melba gestured to a cupboard far over her head. "Then round up the rest of the family."

Trey retrieved the pitcher, then gratefully escaped from the kitchen. Of course, he should have expected the conversation would circle back to the topic of marriage and babies during the meal.

"So what's been going on in town since I've been gone?" he asked, scooping up a forkful of the potatoes Claire had mashed.

"Goodness, I don't know where to begin," his grandmother said. "Oh—the Santa Claus parade was last weekend and the Dalton girl got engaged."

The potatoes he'd just swallowed dropped to the bottom of his stomach like a ball of lead. "Kayla?"

His grandmother shook her head. "Her sister, Kristen."

Trey exhaled slowly.

He didn't know why he'd immediately assumed Kayla, maybe because he'd seen her so recently and had been thinking about her for so long, but the thought of her with another man—*engaged* to another man—had hit him like a physical jab.

He'd been away from Rust Creek Falls for months—it wasn't just possible but likely that Kayla had gone out with other guys during that time. And why shouldn't she? They'd spent one night together—they didn't have a relationship.

And even if they did, he wasn't looking to fall in love and get married. So why did the idea of her being with another man make him a little bit crazy?

"Who'd she get engaged to?" he asked, picking up the thread of the conversation again.

"Maggie Roarke's brother, Ryan," Claire said.

Trey didn't know Ryan Roarke, but he worked with his brother, Shane, at the Thunder Canyon Resort. And he knew that their sister had moved to Rust Creek Falls the previous year. "Maggie's the new lawyer in town—the one married to Jesse Crawford?"

His grandmother nodded. "She gave up her fancy office in LA to make a life here with Jesse, because they were in love."

"I thought it was because he knocked her up," Gene interjected.

Melba wagged her fork at her husband. "They were in love," she insisted.

"And five months after they got married, they had a baby," Gene told him.

His wife sniffed—likely as much in disapproval of the fact as her husband's recitation of gossip. "What matters is that they're together now and a family with their little girl."

"Speaking of little girls," Trey said, looking at his cousin's daughter seated across from him in her high chair. "I can't get over how much this one has grown in the past few months."

"Like a weed," Levi confirmed, ruffling the soft hair on the top of his daughter's head.

Bekka looked up at him, her big blue eyes wide and adoring.

"No doubt that one's a daddy's girl," Claire noted.

Her husband just grinned.

"Speaking of Kayla Dalton," his grandmother said.

"Who was speaking of Kayla Dalton?" Gene asked.

"Trey was," Melba said.

"We were talking about Bekka."

"Earlier," Melba clarified. "When I mentioned the Dalton girl got engaged, he asked if it was Kayla."

"Hers was just the first name that came to mind," Trey hastened to explain.

"And I wonder why that was," his grandmother mused.

"Probably because he was up close and personal with her at Braden and Jennifer's wedding," Claire teased.

"Anyway," Melba interjected. "I was wondering if you were going to see Kayla while you're in town."

"I already did," he admitted. "She walked by the community center when we were unloading the truck."

His grandmother shook her head as she began to stack the empty plates. "I meant, are you going to go out with her?"

"Melba," her husband said warningly.

"What? Is there something wrong with wanting my grandson to spend time with a nice girl?"

Claire pushed away from the table to help clear it.

"Kayla is a nice girl," Trey confirmed. "But if you've got matchmaking on your mind, you're going to be disappointed—I'm not looking to settle down yet, not with anybody."

"And even if he was, Kayla is hardly his type," Claire noted.

Levi's brows lifted. "Trey has a type?"

"Well, if he did, it wouldn't be the shy wallflower type," his wife said.

"Still waters run deep," their grandmother noted.

"What's that supposed to mean?" Trey asked warily.

"It means that there's a lot more to that girl than most people realize," Melba said, setting an enormous apple pie on the table.

Claire brought in the dessert plates and forks.

"And ice cream," her grandmother said. "Bekka's going to want some ice cream."

"I think Bekka wants her bath and bed more than she wants ice cream," Claire said, noting her daughter's drooping eyelids.

"Goodness, she's falling asleep in her chair."

"My fault," Levi said, pushing his chair away from the table and lifting his daughter from hers. "She missed her nap today when I took her to story time at the library."

"Didn't I tell you to put her down as soon as you got back?" Claire asked.

"You did," he confirmed. "But every time I put her in her crib, she started to fuss."

"Why don't you give in to me whenever I fuss?" his wife wanted to know.

He kissed her softly. "Are you saying I don't?"

"Not *all* the time," she said, a small smile on her lips as they headed out of the dining room.

"I guess they've worked things out," Trey mused, stabbing his fork into the generous slab of pie his grandmother set in front of him.

"I really think they have," Melba confirmed. "There will still be bumps in the road—no relationship is ever without them—but over the past few months, they've proven that they are committed to one another and their family."

"If the kid doesn't want ice cream, no one else gets ice cream?" Gene grumbled, frowning at his naked pie.

"You don't need ice cream," his wife told him.

"You didn't need those new gloves you came home with when you were out Christmas shopping last week, but you bought them anyway."

Trey fought against a smile as he got up to get the ice cream. His grandparents' bickering was as familiar to him as the boarding house. They were both strong-willed and stubborn but, even after almost sixty years of marriage, there was an obvious affection between them that warmed his heart.

After they'd finished dessert, his grandmother asked, "So what are your plans for the evening?"

"Do they still show movies at the high school on Fridays?" Trey had spent more than a few evenings in the gymnasium, hanging with his friends or snuggling up to a pretty girl beneath banners that declared, "Go Grizzlies!" and had some fond memories of movie nights at the high school.

"Friday *and* Saturday nights now," she told him.

"Two movie nights a week?" he teased. "And people say there's nothing to do in Rust Creek Falls."

His grandmother narrowed her gaze. "We might not have all the fancy shops and services like Thunder Canyon, but we've got everything we need."

"You're right," he said. "I shouldn't have implied that this town was lacking in any way—especially when two of my favorite people in the world live here."

She swatted him away with her tea towel. "Go on with you now. Take a shower, put on a nice shirt and get out of here."

Trey did as he was told, not only to please his grandmother but because it occurred to him that the high school was likely where Kayla and Natalie were headed.

Chapter Three

Kayla gazed critically at her reflection in the mirror and sighed as she tugged her favorite Henley-style shirt over her head again and relegated it to the too-tight pile. The nine pounds she'd gained were wreaking havoc with her wardrobe.

Of course, it didn't help that most of the styles were slim-fitting and she was no longer slim. Not that she was fat or even visibly pregnant, but it was apparent that she'd put on some weight, and covering her body in oversize garments at least let her disguise the fact that the weight was all in her belly.

She picked up the Henley again, pulled it on, then put on a burgundy-and-navy plaid shirt over the top. Deciding that would work, she fixed her ponytail, dabbed on some lip gloss and grabbed her keys.

"Where are you going tonight?" her mother asked when Kayla came down the stairs.

She'd mentioned her plans at dinner—when she'd asked her dad if she could take his truck into town—but her mother obviously hadn't been paying attention. Ever since Ryan put a ring on Kristen's finger, her mother had been daydreaming about the wedding.

"I'm meeting Natalie at the high school," she said again. "We're going to see *A Christmas Story* tonight."

"Is it just the two of you going?" her mother pressed.

"No, I'm sure there will be lots of other people there."

"Really, Kayla, I don't know why you can't just give a simple answer to a simple question," Rita chided.

"Sorry," she said automatically. "And yes—it's just me and Natalie tonight. We're not sneaking out to meet boys behind the school."

"Your turn will come."

"My turn for what?" She was baffled by the uncharacteristically gentle tone as much as the words.

"To meet somebody."

"I'm not worried about meeting somebody or not meeting somebody," she assured her mother.

"I had sisters, too," Rita said. "I know it's hard when exciting things are happening in their lives and not your own."

"I'm happy for Kristen, Mom. Genuinely and sincerely."

"Well, of course you are," she agreed. "But that doesn't mean you can't be a little envious, too." A career wife and mother, Rita couldn't imagine her daughters wanting anything else.

She'd been appalled by Kristen's desire to study theater—worried about her daughter associating with unsavory movie people. She'd been so relieved when her youngest child graduated and moved back home to teach drama. Unfortunately, Kristen had faced numerous roadblocks in her efforts to get a high school production off the ground, causing her to turn her attention to the community theater in Kalispell.

Kayla was actually surprised their mother had approved of Kristen's engagement to a Hollywood lawyer. But Ryan had fallen in love with Montana as well as Kristen and was planning to give up his LA practice—as his sister, Maggie, had done just last year when she moved to Rust Creek Falls to marry Jesse Crawford.

But, of course, now that Kristen and Ryan were engaged, it was only natural—to Rita's way of thinking—that Kayla would want the same thing. Her mother would be shocked to learn that her other daughter's life was already winding down a very different path.

"Getting out tonight will be good for you," Rita said to Kayla now. "Who knows? You might even meet someone at the movies."

Meet someone? Ha! She already knew everyone in Rust Creek Falls, and even if she did meet someone new and interesting who actually asked her to go out on a date with him, there was no way she could say yes. Because there was no way she could start a romance with another man while she was carrying Trey's baby.

And no way could she be interested in anyone else when she was still hopelessly infatuated with the father of her child.

"I'm meeting Natalie," she said again. Then, before her mother could say anything else to continue the excruciating conversation, Kayla kissed her cheek. "Don't wait up."

When Kayla arrived, Natalie was standing outside the main doors, her hands stuffed into the pockets of her coat, her feet—tucked into a sleek pair of high-heeled boots that looked more fashionable than warm—kicking the soft snow.

"Am I late?" Kayla asked.

"No, I was probably early," Natalie admitted. "I needed to get out of the house and away from all the talk about weddings."

She nodded her understanding as she reached for the door handle. Natalie's brother had also recently gotten engaged. "When are Brad and Margot getting married?"

"That was one of the topics of discussion. Of course, Brad was married before, so he just wants whatever Margot wants. But Margot lost her mother almost three years ago, and her father's been AWOL since the infamous poker game, so as much as she's excited about starting a life with my brother, I think it's hard for her to be excited about the wedding, and I don't think my mother's being very sensitive about that."

"Believe me, I understand about insensitive mothers," Kayla told her friend.

They paid their admission at the table set up in the foyer for that purpose then made their way toward the gymnasium.

"I always get such a creepy feeling of déjà vu when I'm in here," her friend admitted.

"I know what you mean," Kayla agreed. "It doesn't help that Mrs. Newman—" their freshman physical education teacher "—works at the concession stand."

Natalie nodded her agreement. "Even when I count out the exact change for her, she gives me that perpetual look of disapproval, like I've just told her I forgot my gym clothes."

Kayla laughed. She was glad she'd let her friend drag her out tonight. Not that much dragging was required. Kayla had been feeling in a bit of a funk and had happily accepted Natalie's invitation. Of course, it didn't hurt that

A Christmas Story was one of her all-time favorite holiday movies.

"Oh, look," she said, pointing to the poster advertising a different feature for Saturday night. "We could come back tomorrow for *The Santa Clause*."

"Well, I'm free," Natalie admitted. "Which tells a pretty sad tale about my life."

"Actually, I'm not," Kayla realized.

"Hot date?"

"Ha. I'm helping out at the theater in Kalispell tomorrow night."

"Well, even working in the city has to be more exciting than a night off in this town," Natalie said. Then she stopped dead in her tracks. "Oh. My. God."

"What?" Kayla demanded, as alarmed by her friend's whispered exclamation as the way Natalie's fingers dug into her arm.

"Trey Strickland is here."

Her heart leaped and crashed against her ribs as she turned in the direction her friend was looking.

Yep, it was him.

Not that she really believed Natalie might have been mistaken, but she'd hoped. After a four-month absence, she'd now run into him twice within hours of his return to town. Whether his appearance here was a coincidence or bad luck, it was an obvious sign to Kayla that she wouldn't be able to avoid him while he was in Rust Creek Falls.

Natalie waved a hand in front of her face, fanning herself as she kept her attention fixed on the ginger-haired, broad-shouldered cowboy. "That man is *so* incredibly yummy."

Kayla had always thought so, too—even before she'd experienced the joy of being held in his arms, kissed by his lips, pleasured by his body. But she had no intention of sharing any of that with her friend, who she hadn't realized harbored her own crush on the same man. "Should we get popcorn?" she asked instead.

"I'd rather have man candy," Natalie said dreamily.

Kayla pulled a ten-dollar bill out of the pocket of her too-tight jeans and tried to ignore the reason her favorite denim—and all of her other clothes—were fitting so snugly in recent days. "I'm going for popcorn."

"Can you grab me a soda, too?" Natalie asked, her gaze still riveted on the sexy cowboy as he made his way toward the gym doors.

"Sure."

"I'll go find seats," her friend said, following Trey.

Kayla just sighed and joined the line for concessions. She couldn't blame her friend for being interested, especially when she'd never told Natalie what had happened with Trey on the Fourth of July, but that didn't mean she wanted to be around while the other woman made a play for him.

When she entered the gymnasium with the drinks and popcorn, she found Natalie in conversation with Trey. Though her instinct was to turn in the opposite direction, she forced her feet to move toward them.

Trey's gaze shifted to her and his lips curved. "Hi, again."

"Hi," she echoed his greeting, glancing around. "Are you here with someone?"

Please, let him be here with someone.

But the universe ignored her plea, and Trey shook his head.

"Why don't you join us?" Natalie invited, patting the empty chair on her left.

"I think I will," he said, just as an elderly couple moved toward the two vacant seats beside Natalie.

Trey stepped back, relinquishing the spot she had offered to him. Kayla didn't even have time to exhale a sigh of relief before he moved to the empty seat on the other side of *her.*

She was secretly relieved that her friend's obvious maneuverings had been thwarted, but she didn't know how she would manage to focus on the screen and forget that he was sitting right beside her for the next ninety-four minutes.

In fact, she didn't even make it through four minutes, because she couldn't take a breath without inhaling his clean, masculine scent. She couldn't shift in her seat without brushing against him. And she couldn't stop thinking about the fact that her naked body had been entwined with his.

She forced her attention back to the screen, to the crowd gathered around the window of Higbee's Department Store to marvel at the display of mechanized electronic joy and, of course, Ralphie, wide-eyed and slack-jawed as he fixated on "the holy grail of Christmas gifts—the Red Ryder two hundred shot range model air rifle."

"Are you going to share that popcorn?" Trey whispered close to her ear.

"I am sharing it," she said. "With Natalie."

But deeply ingrained good manners had her shifting the bag to offer it to him.

"Thanks." He dipped his hand inside.

She tried to keep her attention on the movie, but it was no use. Even Ralphie's entertaining antics weren't capable of distracting her from Trey's presence. It was as if every nerve ending in her body was attuned to his nearness.

It probably didn't help that they were in the high school—the setting of so many of her youthful fantasies. So many times she'd stood at her locker and watched him walk past with a group of friends, her heart racing as she waited for him to turn and look at her. So many times she'd witnessed him snuggled up to a cheerleader on the bleachers, and she'd imagined that she was that cheerleader.

Back then, she would have given almost anything to be in the circle of his arms. She would have given almost anything to have him just smile at her. She'd been so seriously and pathetically infatuated that just an acknowledgment of her presence would have fueled her fantasies for days, weeks, months.

When his family had moved away from Rust Creek Falls, she'd cried her heart out. But even then, she'd continued to daydream, imagining that he would come back one day, unable to live without her. She might have been shy and quiet, but deep inside, she was capable of all the usual teenage melodrama—and more.

Sitting beside him now, in the darkened gym, was a schoolgirl fantasy come to life. But he wasn't just sitting in the chair beside her, he was so close that his thigh was pressed against hers. And when he reached into the bag of popcorn she was holding, his fingertips trailed deliberately over the back of her hand.

At least she assumed it was deliberate, because he didn't pull his hand away, even when her breath made an audible catch in her throat.

Natalie glanced at her questioningly.

She cleared her throat, as if there was something stuck in it, and picked up her soda.

She felt a flutter in her tummy that she dismissed as butterflies—a far too usual occurrence when she was around Trey. Then she realized it was their baby—the baby he didn't know about—and her eyes inexplicably filled with tears.

You have to tell him.

The words echoed in the back of her mind, an unending reel of admonishment, the voice of her own conscience in tandem with her sister's.

He has a right to know.

You-have-to-tell-him-he-has-a-right-to-know-you-have-to-tell-him-he-has-a-right-to-know-you-have-to—

"Excuse me," she whispered, thrusting the bag of popcorn at Trey and slipping out of her seat to escape from the gymnasium.

The bright lights of the hallway blinded her for a moment, so that she didn't know which way to turn. She'd spent four years in these halls, but suddenly she couldn't remember the way to the girls' bathroom.

She leaned back against the wall for a minute to get her bearings, then made her way across the hall. Thankfully, the facility was empty, and she slipped into the nearest stall, locked the door, sat down on the closed toilet seat and let the tears fall.

In recent weeks, her emotions had been out of control. She'd been tearing up over the silliest things—a quick glimpse of an elderly couple holding hands, the sight of a mother pushing her child in a stroller, even coffee commercials on TV could start the waterworks. Crying in public bathrooms hadn't exactly become a habit, but this wasn't the first time for her, either.

No, the first time had been three months earlier. After purchasing a pregnancy test from an out-of-the-way pharmacy in Kalispell, she'd driven to the shopping center and taken her package into the bathroom. Because no way could she risk taking the test home, into her parents' house, and then disposing of it—regardless of the result—with the rest of the family's trash.

She remembered every minute of that day clearly. The way her fingers had trembled as she tore open the box, how the words had blurred in front of her eyes as she read and re-read the instructions to make sure she did everything correctly.

After she'd managed to perform the test as indicated, she'd put the stick aside—on the back of the toilet—and counted down the seconds on her watch. When the time was up, she picked up the stick again and looked in the little window, the tears no longer blurring her eyes but sliding freely down her cheeks.

She hadn't bothered to brush them away. She couldn't have stopped them if she'd tried. Never, in all of her twenty-five years, had she imagined being in this situation. Pregnant. Unmarried.

Alone.

She was stunned and scared and completely overwhelmed.

And she was angry. At both herself and Trey for being careless. She didn't know what he'd been thinking, but she'd been so caught up in the moment that she'd forgotten all about protection until he was inside of her. Realization seemed to have dawned on him at the same time, because he'd immediately pulled out of her, apologizing to her, promising that he didn't have unprotected sex—ever.

Then he'd found a condom and covered himself with it before he joined their bodies together again. She didn't know if it was that brief moment of unprotected penetration that had resulted in her pregnancy, or if it was just a statistical reality—if she was one of the two percent of women who was going to be a mommy because condoms were only ninety-eight percent effective in preventing pregnancy.

Of course, the reason didn't matter as much as the reality: she was pregnant. She didn't tell anyone because she didn't know what to say. She didn't know how she felt about the situation—because it was easier to think about her pregnancy as a situation than a baby.

She found an obstetrician in Kalispell—because there was no way she could risk seeing a local doctor—and then, eighteen weeks into her pregnancy, she had an ultrasound.

Everything changed for her then. Looking at the monitor, seeing the image of her unborn child inside of her, made the existence of that child suddenly and undeniably real. That was when she finally accepted that she wasn't just pregnant—the unexpected consequence of an impulsive night in Trey's bed—she was going to have a baby.

Trey's baby.

And in that moment, when she first saw the tiny heart beating, she fell in love with their child.

But he still didn't have a clue about the consequences of the night they'd spent together—or possibly even that they had spent the night together— and she'd resolved to tell him as soon as possible. He had a right to know about their baby. She didn't know how he would respond to the news, but she knew that he needed to hear it.

Of course, at the time of her ultrasound, he'd been in Thunder Canyon, three hundred miles away. So she'd decided to wait until he came back to Rust Creek Falls. And another three-and-a-half weeks had passed. Now he was here—not just in town but in the same building. And she had no more excuses.

She had to tell him about their baby.

She pulled a handful of toilet paper from the roll and wiped at the wet streaks on her cheeks. The tiny life inside her stirred again. She laid a hand on the slight curve of her tummy.

I've always tried to do what I think is best for you, even when I don't know what that is. And I'm scared, because I don't know how your daddy's going to react to the news that he's going to be a daddy. I will *tell him. I promise, I will. But I'm not going to walk into the high school gym in the middle of movie night and make a public announcement, so you're going to have to be patient a little longer.*

Of course, there was no way the baby could hear the words of reassurance that were audible only inside of her head, but the flutters inside her belly settled.

"Everything okay?" Natalie whispered, when Kayla had returned to her seat inside the darkened gym.

She nodded. "My phone was vibrating, so I went outside to take the call."

Lying didn't come easily to her, but it was easier with her gaze riveted on the movie screen. Thankfully, Natalie accepted her explanation without any further questions.

When the credits finally rolled, people began to stand up and stack their chairs. Trey solicitously took both Kayla's and Natalie's along with his own.

"I'm sorry," Kayla said to her friend, taking advantage of his absence to apologize—although she wasn't really sorry.

"For what?"

"Because I know you wanted to sit next to him."

Natalie waved away the apology. "*I* should be sorry," she said. "When I invited him to join us, I completely forgot that you two were together at the wedding—"

"We weren't together," Kayla was quick to interject.

"Even the Rust Creek Rambler saw the two of you on the dance floor."

"One dance doesn't equal together."

"Well, even if that's true—" and her friend's tone warned Kayla that she wasn't convinced it was "—I'm getting the impression that Trey is hoping for something more."

She shook her head. "You're imagining things."

"I am *not* imagining the way he's looking at you," Natalie said, her gaze shifting beyond her friend.

Kayla didn't know what to say to that. She didn't know how—or even if—Trey was looking at her because she was deliberately avoiding looking at him, afraid that any kind of eye contact would somehow give away all of her secrets to him.

"Which means I have to find myself a different cowboy," Natalie decided.

"Do you have anyone specific in mind?" Kayla asked, happy to shift the conversation away from Trey—and especially talk of the two of them being together at the wedding.

"I'm willing to consider all possibilities," Natalie said. "And since it's still pretty early, why don't we go to the Ace in the Hole to grab a drink?"

She shuddered at the thought. "Because that place on a Friday night is a bad idea."

The local bar and grill was more than a little rough around the edges at the best of times—and a Friday night was never the best of times as the cowboys who worked so hard during the week on the local ranches believed in partying just as hard on the weekends. As a result, it wasn't unusual for tempers to flare and fists to fly, and Kayla had no interest in that kind of drama tonight.

Natalie sighed. "You're right—how about a hot chocolate instead?"

That offer was definitely more tempting. Though Kayla hadn't experienced many cravings, and thankfully nothing too unusual, the baby had definitely shown signs in recent weeks of having a sweet tooth, and she knew that hot chocolate would satisfy that craving. But, "I thought you had to open up the store in the morning."

Natalie waved a hand dismissively. "Morning is a long time away."

"Hot chocolate sounds good," she admitted.

"It tastes even better," Trey said from behind her.

Kayla thought he'd left the gym after helping to stack the chairs, but apparently that had been wishful thinking on her part.

"But where can you get hot chocolate in town at this time of night?" he asked.

"Daisy's," Natalie told him. "It's open late now, with an expanded beverage menu and pastries to encourage people to stay in town rather than heading to the city."

"I always did like their hot chocolate," Trey said. "Do you mind if I join you?"

"Of course not," Natalie said, buttoning up her coat as they exited the gym.

They said "hello" to various townspeople as they passed them in the halls, stopping on the way to chat with some other friends from high school. A few guys invited Trey to go for a beer at the Ace in the Hole, but he told them that he already had plans. When they finally made their escape, Natalie pulled her phone out of her pocket and frowned at the time displayed on the screen. "I didn't realize it was getting to be so late."

Kayla narrowed her gaze on her friend, wondering how it had gone from "still pretty early" to "so late" in the space of ten minutes.

"I think I should skip the hot chocolate tonight," Natalie decided. "I have to be up early to open the store in the morning."

"You were the one who suggested it," Kayla pointed out.

"I know," her friend agreed. "And I hate to bail, but there's no reason that you and Trey can't go without me."

Kayla glanced at Trey. "Wouldn't you rather go to the Ace in the Hole with your friends than to Daisy's with me?"

"Let me see—reminiscing about high school football with a bunch of washed-up jocks or making conversation with a pretty girl?" He winked at her. "It seems like a no-brainer to me."

"Great," Natalie said, a little too enthusiastically.

Then she leaned in to give Kayla a quick hug and whisper in her ear. "I'll call you tomorrow to hear all of the juicy details, so make sure there *are* some juicy details."

Chapter Four

"She's not very subtle, is she?" Trey asked Kayla, after her friend had gone.

"Not at all," she agreed. "And if you want to skip the hot chocolate—"

"I don't want to skip the hot chocolate," he told her.

"Okay."

It was one little word—barely two syllables—which made it hard for him to read her tone to know what she was thinking. But her spine was stiff and her hands stuffed deep in the pockets of her jacket, clear indications that she was neither behind her friend's machinations nor pleased by them.

"Do *you* want to skip the hot chocolate?" he asked her.

Her hesitation was so brief it was barely noticeable before she replied, "I never say no to hot chocolate."

Despite her words, he suspected that she wanted to but couldn't think of a way to graciously extricate herself from the situation that had been set up by her friend.

Was she avoiding him? Was she uneasy because of what had happened between them in the summer? He couldn't blame her if she was, especially since they hadn't ever talked about that night. Not since that first day, anyway, before he'd had a chance to really remember what happened.

He didn't want her to feel uncomfortable around him. Aside from the fact that her brother was one of his best friends, Rust Creek Falls was a small town, and it was inevitable that they would bump into one another. For that reason alone, they needed to clear the air between them.

"I'd offer to drive, but I walked over," he told her.

His grandparents' boarding house being centrally located, there wasn't anything in the town that wasn't within walking distance. Which included Daisy's Donuts, only a block over from the high school.

"We'll go in my truck," she said, because driving was preferable to walking even that short distance in the frigid temperatures that prevailed in Montana in December.

She unlocked the doors with the electronic key fob, and he followed her to the driver's side and opened the door to help her in. It was a big truck, and she had to step up onto the running board first. He cupped her elbow, to ensure she didn't lose her balance, and she murmured a quiet "Thanks."

By the time he'd buckled himself into the passenger side, she had the truck in gear. Either she was really craving hot chocolate or she didn't want to be alone with him for a minute longer than necessary. He suspected it was the latter.

He wasn't sure if she was sending mixed signals or if he was just having trouble deciphering them. When he'd stepped out of the community center earlier that afternoon and saw her walking past, he'd been sincerely pleased to see her. His blood had immediately heated and his heart had pounded hard and fast inside his chest. And he'd thought that she was happy to see him, too.

In that first moment, when their eyes had met, he was sure there had been a spark in her blue gaze and a smile on her lips. Then her smile had faltered, as if she wasn't sure that she should be happy to see him. Which confirmed to him that they needed to talk about the Fourth of July.

As she parked in front of Daisy's Donuts, he realized this probably wasn't the place to do so. Not unless they wanted to announce their secret to all of Rust Creek Falls, which he was fairly certain neither of them did.

"Why don't you grab a table while I get our drinks?" he suggested.

"Okay," she agreed.

"Any special requests?" He glanced at the board. "Dark chocolate? White chocolate? Peppermint? Caramel?"

"Regular," she said. "With extra whipped cream."

"You got it."

He decided to have the same and added a couple of gingerbread cookies to the order, too.

"I thought you might be hungry," he told her, setting the plate of cookies between them. "Considering that I ate all of your popcorn."

"I'm not hungry," she said, accepting the mug he slid across the table to her. "But I love gingerbread cookies. My mother used to make a ton of them at Christmastime, but there were never any left when company came over because Kristen and I used to sneak down to the kitchen and eat all of them."

"You said she used to make them," he noted. "She doesn't anymore?"

"She makes us do it now. She decided that since we eat most of them anyway, we should know how to make them."

He nudged the plate toward her, silently urging her to take a cookie. She broke the leg off one, popped it into her mouth.

"Good?"

She nodded.

"My grandmother used to make gingerbread houses—one for each of the grandkids to decorate. When I think back, she must have spent a fortune on candy, and we ate more than we put on the buildings." He broke a piece off the other cookie, sampled it. "I wonder if she'd make one for me this year, if I asked."

"I'm sure she'd make anything you wanted," Kayla said.

"What makes you say that?" he asked curiously.

"Three words." She broke off the gingerbread boy's other leg. "Vanilla almond fudge."

He smiled, thinking of the plate he'd found on his bedside table—neatly wrapped in plastic and tied with a bow. "She does spoil me," he admitted.

Kayla smiled back, and their eyes held for a brief second before she quickly dropped her gaze away.

The group of teenagers who had been sitting nearby got up from their table, put on their coats, hats and gloves and headed out the door. There were still other customers around, but no one close enough that he needed to worry about their conversation being overheard.

"Did I do something wrong?"

She looked up again. "What are you talking about?"

"I'm not sure," he admitted. "But I get the feeling that you're not very happy to see me back in town."

She sipped her cocoa and shrugged. "Your coming back doesn't have anything to do with me."

"Maybe it does," he said. "Because I haven't stopped thinking about you since I left Rust Creek Falls in the summer."

She blinked. "You haven't?"

"I haven't," he confirmed, holding her gaze.

"Oh."

He waited a beat, but she didn't say anything more. "It would be nice to hear that you've thought about me, too...if you have."

She glanced away, color filling her cheeks. "I have."

"And the night of the wedding?" he prompted.

He watched, intrigued, as the pink in her cheeks deepened.

"You mean the night we were both drinking the spiked punch?" she asked.

"Is that the only reason you started talking to me that night?"

"Probably," she admitted. "I mean—I would have wanted to talk to you, but I wouldn't have had the nerve to start a conversation."

"And the kiss? Was that because of the punch, too?"

"*You* kissed *me*," she said indignantly.

"You kissed back pretty good," he told her.

She remained silent, probably because she couldn't deny it.

"And then you went back to my room with me," he prompted further.

She nodded slowly, almost reluctantly.

"Are you sorry that you did?"

She kept her gaze averted from his, but she shook her head.

"I'm not sorry, either," he told her. "The only thing I regret is that it took me so long to remember what happened."

"Lots of people had memory lapses after that night—because of the punch," she said.

"Do you really think that what happened between us only happened because of the punch?"

"Don't you?"

He frowned at her question. "I don't know how drunk *you* were, but I can assure you, there isn't enough alcohol in the world to make me get naked with a woman I'm not attracted to."

Her perfectly arched brows drew together. "You were attracted…to me?"

"Why do you find that so hard to believe?"

"I'm the quiet one. Kristen's the pretty one."

"You're identical twins."

She lifted a shoulder. "You seem to be able to tell us apart."

"There are some subtle differences," he acknowledged. "Your eyes are a little bit darker, your bottom lip is just a little bit fuller and you have a mole on the top of your left earlobe."

"I never would have guessed you were so observant," she said, blushing a little.

"I didn't realize how much I observed you," he admitted. "Are you worried now that I'm a stalker?"

She shook her head. "No, I'm not worried you're a stalker."

"Then you should trust me when I say that you're a beautiful woman, Kayla. Beautiful, sweet, smart and sexy."

"Sexy?"

"*Incredibly* sexy," he assured her.

She folded her arms over her chest. "Is *that* what this is about?"

"What?" he asked warily.

"You figure that since I fell into your bed so easily that

night, I'd be eager to do so again. Is that the real reason you wanted to see me?"

He held up his hands as his head spun with the effort of following her convoluted logic. "Whoa! Wait a minute."

"*You* wait a minute," she said. "I'm not so pathetic that I'm willing to go home with any guy who says a few kind words to me."

His jaw dropped. "*What* are you talking about?"

"I'm talking about your apparent effort to lure me back into your bed."

"*I* didn't lure you the first time," he reminded her. "*You* were the one who approached me at the wedding. *You* were the one who rubbed your body against mine on the dance floor. And *you* were the one who said you'd go back to my room with me."

She dropped her face into her hands. "Ohmygod—I did do all of that, didn't I? It was all my fault."

Her reaction seemed a little extreme to him, but she sounded so distraught, he couldn't help wanting to console her. "I'm not sure there's any need to assign blame," he said. "Especially considering that I didn't object to any of it."

"I really am pathetic."

He reached across the table and pulled her hands away from her face. "No, you're not."

"I am," she insisted. "I had such a crush on you in high school."

"You did?"

"And you didn't even know I existed."

"I knew you existed," he said. "But you were Derek's little sister."

She nodded. "And I guess…when you asked me to dance… I got caught up in the high school fantasy again."

"You had fantasies about me?" He was intrigued by the possibility.

"You played the starring role in all of my romantic dreams."

"I'm flattered," he told her sincerely. "But why are you telling me this now?"

Why was *she telling him this*? Kayla asked herself the same question.

Because she was nervous, and she always babbled when she was nervous. Of course, now that she'd confided in him about her schoolgirl crush, she could add *mortified* to the list of emotions that were clouding her brain.

"I'm trying to explain…and apologize."

"I don't want an apology."

"But I threw myself at you," she said miserably.

And, as a result of her actions, she was now pregnant with his baby. Which was what she was trying to work up to telling him, but she was sure that when she did, he would hate her—and she really didn't want him to hate her.

"It wasn't like that at all," he assured her. "And even if it was, I was happy to catch you."

"I don't usually…do what I did that night."

Trey was quiet for a minute before he finally said, "It seems obvious that you think that night was a mistake, and your brother would undoubtedly agree—after he pounded on me for taking advantage of you. And while I'm sorry you feel that way, I have no intention of telling anyone about what happened between us, if that's what you're worried about. As far as I'm concerned, it will be our little secret, okay?"

His speech left her speechless. The words that Kayla had been struggling to put together into a coherent sentence faded from her mind. Tears clogged her throat, burned her eyes, as she shook her head.

"I'm not sure that's possible," she admitted.

"You told somebody about that night?" he guessed.

She nodded. "My sister."

"Oh." He considered for a minute, then let out a weary sigh. "Well, I'm sure you can trust your sister to keep your secrets. Unless…"

"Unless what?"

"I've heard some speculation that she's the Rust Creek Rambler," he admitted.

"She's not."

"You're sure?"

"I'm sure," she confirmed. "If she was the Rambler, I would know."

"Then our secret is safe," he said again.

She thought about the baby she carried, the tiny life that was even now fluttering in her belly. She'd managed to keep her pregnancy a secret from everyone—even her own family—for months. But she'd put on nine pounds already, and the bulky sweaters she'd been wearing wouldn't hide the baby bump for much longer.

You have to tell Trey.

She opened her mouth to do so when her cousin, Caleb, came in with his wife, Mallory. They waved a greeting across the room before stepping up to the counter to order their drinks.

When they took their beverages to the table behind Kayla and Trey, she knew that the opportunity to tell him about her pregnancy had slipped away.

RUST CREEK RAMBLINGS: LIGHTS! CAMERAS! ACTIVIST!

Lily Dalton, the town's littlest matchmaker (though

certainly not the only one!) has turned her talents toward a new vocation: acting. But when the sign-up sheet was posted for auditions for the elementary school's production of *The Nutcracker*, the precocious third-grader refused to succumb to gender stereotypes. Uninterested in the traditional female parts, she insisted on auditioning for the title role—and won! The revised tale will undoubtedly be the highlight of this year's holiday pageant...

"I can't believe I had to hear about your date with Trey Strickland from Natalie Crawford," Kristen grumbled. "Why didn't you tell me?"

"It wasn't a date," Kayla pointed out. "And I didn't have a chance to tell you, because this is the first time you've been home since Friday night."

"You could have called or texted."

She could have, of course, but she hadn't been ready to talk to her sister about it. The shock of seeing Trey so unexpectedly had churned up all kinds of emotions, and she needed some time to sift through them before she could talk about them. Unfortunately, the thirty-six hours that had passed since then still hadn't been nearly enough.

"It wasn't that big a deal," she hedged.

Kristen's brows lifted. "The father of your baby is back in town—I think that's a pretty big deal."

Kayla pushed her bedroom door closed. "Can you please keep your voice down?"

"Everyone is downstairs having breakfast."

"Which is where we should be, too," Kayla said. "And if we don't go down, Mom's going to come up here looking for us."

"We'll go down in a minute," Kristen said. "I want

to know how many times you've seen Trey since he got back."

"Once."

Her sister's gaze narrowed.

"Okay, twice," she acknowledged. "But they were both the same day."

"Did you tell him?"

"No."

"Why not?"

"Because I didn't know how."

"It's only two words—I'm pregnant."

Kristen made it sound so easy, as if Kayla was making it harder than it needed to be. And maybe she was. But she was the one who had to find the right time and place to say those two words, and she didn't appreciate being bullied by her sister.

She blinked back the tears that threatened. "And on that note, I'm going down for breakfast."

Kristen reached out and touched her arm, halting her departure.

"I'm sorry," she said softly, sincerely. "It's just that I can see how this is tearing you up inside, and it's going to continue tearing you up until you find a way to tell Trey—and that's not good for you or the baby."

"I know," she admitted.

"Besides, I saw an adorable little bib the other day that read, 'If you think I'm cute, you should see my aunt,' and I want to be able to buy things like that and bring them home for your baby."

Kayla managed a smile. "You're going to spoil this kid rotten before it's even born, aren't you?"

"I'm going to try," Kristen confirmed.

They left the room together, Kayla feeling confident

that whatever happened with Trey, her baby was going to be surrounded by the love and support of her family.

Trey decided that he wanted to see Kayla again more than he wanted to play it cool. Besides, what was the point in waiting a few days to call when it only wasted a few days of the short time that he was in town?

She answered the phone with a tentative hello—obviously not recognizing his number. But even hearing her voice say that one word was enough to make him smile.

"I was hoping to take you out for dinner tonight."

She paused. "Trey?"

"Yeah, it's me," he confirmed. "Are you free?"

"Oh. Um. Actually, I'm not," she said. "I'm on my way to Kalispell with my sister."

"What's in Kalispell?"

"*A Christmas Carol*."

"Another movie?"

"No, the play. Kristen is Ebenezer Scrooge's fiancée, Belle."

"I didn't know Scrooge was married."

"He wasn't. She ended their relationship when she realized he loved money more than he loved her."

"I don't remember that part of the story," he admitted.

"Maybe you should buy a ticket to see it onstage, to refresh your memory."

"Would you go with me?"

"I've seen it a dozen times already from the wings."

"Is that a yes?"

She laughed softly. "No."

"Okay—what are you doing tomorrow?"

"I don't have any specific plans," she admitted.

"Can I take you out for lunch?"

She hesitated, and he wondered if she was searching for

another excuse to say no. And if she did, then he should finally take the hint and stop asking. He wasn't in the habit of chasing women, and he wasn't going to sacrifice his pride—and his relationship with Derek—to chase after his friend's little sister.

But when she finally responded, it was to say, "That would be nice."

"I'll pick you up at noon."

"I'll meet you," she said quickly.

"You don't want me coming to the ranch?" he guessed.

"I just don't think there's any reason for you to drive all the way out here just to turn around and drive back into town again," she said. "Especially when I have to stop by the newspaper office in the afternoon, anyway."

"Okay," he relented. "Where do you want to meet?"

"How about Daisy's again?"

He made a face that, of course, she couldn't see. But when he mentioned lunch, he was thinking a thick juicy burger or a rack of ribs from the Ace in the Hole. Sure, the donut shop did hot beverages and pastries, but he wanted a real meal. "Do they have much of a lunch menu?"

"I'm sure you'll find something that appeals to you."

He suspected she was right, though he wasn't thinking about the diner's menu.

"Okay, I'll see you at noon tomorrow."

He was smiling when he hung up the phone—then he turned and found his grandmother in his doorway.

"Who are you seeing at noon tomorrow?"

He could hardly take her to task for eavesdropping when he hadn't bothered to close his door. "A friend."

"A female friend, I'd guess, based on the smile on your face."

He focused his attention on the plate in her hands. "Is that sandwich for me?"

"You didn't come down to make anything for yourself, and I didn't want you messing up my kitchen after I'd cleaned it up."

He kissed her cheek. "Thank you."

"Do you have beverages?" Melba asked, glancing toward the mini-fridge in the corner of his room.

"I do," he confirmed. "And chips in the cabinet."

"Don't be getting crumbs all over," she admonished.

"I won't." And he knew where the broom was kept if he did.

She nodded. "Was that the Dalton girl you were talking to?"

"You don't give up, do you?"

"I should give up hoping that my grandson finds a nice girl to spend his life with?"

He held up his hands. "You're getting way ahead of me here," he told her. "I'm talking about lunch, not a lifetime commitment."

"Every relationship has to start somewhere," she said philosophically.

He knew she was right. He also knew it was far too soon to be thinking about anything long-term with Kayla Dalton. They hadn't even been on a real date, and he wasn't sure that their lunch plans even counted as such.

He really liked Kayla. He wasn't sure what it was about her that set her apart from so many other girls that he'd met and dated in recent years. He only knew that he wanted to spend time with her while he was in town and get to know her better.

And yes, he wanted to make love with her again when his brain wasn't clouded by alcohol. He wanted to know if her lips would taste as delicious as he remembered, if her skin would feel as soft beneath his hands, if her body would respond to his as it did in his dreams.

But he was prepared to take things slow this time, to enjoy every step of the journey without racing to the finish. And he was looking forward to lunch being that first step.

Chapter Five

Kayla was waiting for Trey outside the diner when he arrived. She'd dressed appropriately for the weather and looked cute all bundled up in a navy hip-length ski jacket with a knitted pink scarf wrapped around her throat and a matching hat on her head. Her legs were clad in dark denim, her feet tucked into dark brown cowboy boots.

"Busy place," he noted, opening the door for her so they could join the lineup of customers waiting to order at the counter.

"As I'm sure you're aware, dining options are pretty limited around here."

He was aware—and reassured to see a few local ranchers chowing down on hearty-looking sandwiches.

"It doesn't look as if the newlyweds regret their impulsive ceremony or intoxicated nuptials," Kayla noted, nodding toward a table where Will Clifton was sitting with his wife, Jordyn Leigh.

Trey had heard that the couple married on the Fourth of

July while under the influence of the wedding punch, but something about Kayla's choice of words struck a chord—as if he recognized the phrase *intoxicated nuptials* from somewhere.

"I heard a lot of people did crazy things under the influence of that punch," he said.

An elderly woman in a long, purple coat with an orange cap over her gray hair was standing ahead of them in line, and she turned back to face them now. "For some, the repercussions of that night are yet to be revealed."

Trey didn't know what to make of that cryptic comment, but Kayla's cheeks drained of all color.

"What was that about?" he whispered the question to her.

"I have no idea," she said.

"*Who* was that?"

"Winona Cobbs—a self-proclaimed psychic who moved here from Whitehorn a couple years back. Apparently, she used to run a place called the Stop 'N' Swap, but now she writes a nationally syndicated column, *Wisdom by Winona*."

"She's a little scary," he said. "Not just what she said, but the way she said it, as if she knows something that no one else does."

"Some people think she truly has a gift, others think she's a quack."

"What do you think?" he asked.

Kayla's expression was uneasy as she watched Winona settle at an empty table. "I think we should get our lunch to go."

"To go *where*?"

"We can eat in the park," she suggested.

"You want to eat outside?"

"It's a beautiful day," she pointed out.

"It's sunny," he acknowledged. "But the temperature is hovering just above freezing."

"I have a blanket in my car."

He'd been born and raised in Montana and was accustomed to working outside in various weather conditions, but even when the sun was shining, he didn't consider thirty-four degrees to be a beautiful day. But if Kayla could handle being outside, he wasn't going to wimp out.

He ordered a hot roast-beef sandwich platter with fries and slaw; Kayla opted for grilled turkey on a ciabatta bun with provolone and cranberry mayonnaise.

"To go," she told the server.

Trey glanced around the diner. "There are plenty of tables in here," he noted. "Are you sure you want to go to the park?"

"I'm sure."

He carried the bag of food and tray of hot drinks while she retrieved a thick wool blanket from her truck. It was a short walk to the park, where she spread the blanket over the bench seat for them, folding the end back across her lap when she was seated.

Maybe it wasn't exactly a beautiful day, but she looked beautiful in the sunlight. He didn't think she'd ever worn a lot of makeup, but she didn't need it. Those big blue eyes were mesmerizing even without any artificial enhancement; the soft, full lips naturally pink and tempting. She smelled sweet, like vanilla and brown sugar. The scent triggered a fresh wave of memories of the night they'd spent together and stirred his blood. Thankfully, his sheepskin-lined leather jacket was long enough to hide any evidence of his body's instinctive response.

He opened the bag and took out the food, unwrapping Kayla's sandwich so that she didn't have to take off her mittens before turning his attention to his own.

"Thanks."

"You're welcome."

That was the extent of their conversation for a few minutes while they both concentrated on eating. Trey had to admit, his roast beef was delicious. The meat was thinly sliced and piled high on a Kaiser then topped with gravy so piping hot, there was steam coming off his sandwich.

When the sandwich was gone, he turned his attention to the fries—thick wedges of crispy potato that were equally delicious. "Obviously, Daisy's Donuts has a lot more going for it than just donuts these days."

"I told you you'd find something you liked."

"So you did," he agreed.

A gust of wind blew her hair into her face. Kayla lifted a mittened hand to shove it away.

"Your hair looks different today," he noted.

"It's covered by a hat," she pointed out.

"Aside from that."

She shrugged. "I haven't had it cut in a while. It's probably longer than it was in the summer."

He wrapped a strand around his finger, tugged gently. "You wore it pinned up at the wedding."

She nodded.

He remembered taking the pins out of her hair and combing his fingers through the long, silky tresses. Of course, he didn't mention that part to her, because he knew that she was still a little embarrassed about what had happened that night.

"So you mentioned that your sister plays the part of Scrooge's fiancée in *A Christmas Carol*, but you didn't tell me what your role is."

"I work behind the scenes," she told him. "Helping out with costumes, scenery and props."

"So you don't have to be there for every performance?" he guessed.

"No. I usually work Wednesday and Thursday nights, and the occasional Saturday matinee."

"That's a pretty big commitment."

"Kristen does eight shows a week," she noted. "And Belle isn't a major part, but she's also the understudy for Mrs. Cratchit."

Once again, she'd deflected attention away from herself in favor of her twin. Trey noticed that she did that a lot. What he didn't know was if it was because she was proud of her sister or uncomfortable having any attention focused on herself.

Now that he thought about it, she'd always seemed content to hover in Kristen's shadow, but he didn't remember seeing much of her sister on the Fourth of July. "Was Kristen at the wedding?" he asked her now.

"Of course," Kayla responded. "Although she spent most of her time on the dance floor or with Ryan."

"I'm glad she was preoccupied," he said. "Because I don't think you would have approached me if you'd been hanging out with her."

"Probably not," she acknowledged. "But even without Kristen around, I wouldn't have approached you if I hadn't been drinking the spiked punch."

"Then I guess I should say thank you to whoever spiked the punch."

She narrowed her gaze on him, but the sparkle in her blue eyes assured him that she was only teasing when she said, "Maybe it was you."

"The police still haven't found the culprit?"

She shook her head. "No, and I'm not sure they ever will."

"What makes you say that?"

"It's been five months and there's no new evidence, no more leads to follow, no other witnesses to interview."

"What about Boyd Sullivan?" he asked, referring to the old man who had literally bet his ranch in a high-stakes poker game the night of the wedding.

"I'm sure they'd like to talk to him, if they could find him, but I doubt that he's responsible for spiking the punch when that's believed to be the reason he lost his home."

"Some pretty strange things happened that night," he acknowledged. "But it wasn't all bad, was it?"

Kayla knew he was asking about the time they'd spent together, and seeking reassurance that she had no regrets.

"No," she said in response to Trey's question. "It wasn't all bad."

But he didn't know that there were unexpected repercussions from that night, and she had to tell him. There probably wouldn't be a smoother segue into the topic or a more perfect opportunity. She opened her mouth to speak, but the words—those two simple words—stuck in her throat.

Because those two words would only be the beginning of their conversation. Once she told him about their baby, he'd have questions—*a lot* of questions. How could she explain to him how it had happened when she wasn't entirely sure herself? And how could she possibly justify remaining silent about the fact for so long?

"But you wish you hadn't gone back to my room with me?" he guessed.

"No. I just wish…"

"What do you wish?"

She shook her head. "I just want you to know that I don't usually do things like that. At least, I never have before."

He frowned. "You weren't a virgin."

She flushed. “I didn’t mean that. I only meant that I’ve never had a one-night stand before.”

“I didn’t invite you back to my room with the plan that we would only spend one night together,” he told her. “But the next morning, well, you know that I was a little hazy on the details. And you seemed to want to pretend it had never happened, so I decided to play along.”

“I thought *you* didn’t remember.”

“I wouldn’t—couldn’t—forget making love with you,” he told her.

“But you never even looked at me twice before that night.”

“That’s not true. The truth is, I was always careful not to get caught looking at you, because of my friendship with your brother.” He crumpled up his sandwich wrapper, dropped it into the bag. “The punch didn’t make me notice you—it only lessened my inhibitions around you.”

“Really?”

“Really.” He wiped his fingers on a paper napkin. “But maybe you only noticed me because of the punch.”

“You know that’s not true.”

“That’s right—the remnants of your high school crush meant I was irresistible to you,” he teased.

“Maybe it was the punch,” she teased back.

He grinned. “Well, now that you’re not under the influence, what do you say to the two of us spending some time together, getting to know one another better?”

Under other circumstances, she would have said “absolutely.” She wanted exactly what he was offering, but she knew any time they might have together was limited—not just because he would be returning to Thunder Canyon in the New Year, but because her baby bump was growing every day.

If you don’t tell him, I will.

With Kristen's voice echoing in the back of her mind, Kayla opened her mouth to finally confess her secret. "Before you decide that you want—"

"I'm sorry," Trey said, as his cell phone rang. He pulled it out of his pocket, glanced at the screen. "My cousin, Claire."

He looked at her, as if for permission.

"Go ahead," she said, grateful for the reprieve—and then feeling guilty about being grateful.

He connected the call. "Hey, Claire."

Whatever his cousin said on the other end made him wince. "TMI." He shook his head as he listened some more. "So why are you calling me?" Then he sighed. "Okay, text me the details—but that 'favorite cousin' card is wearing pretty thin."

"Problem?" Kayla asked, when he disconnected.

"She wants me to pick up diapers. Apparently, she bought a supersize package at the box store in Kalispell yesterday, but she left them in the car and Levi has the car at work, Grandma's out getting her hair done, she doesn't trust Grandpa to buy the right size and she needs diapers *now*."

"And you didn't even know diapers came in different sizes?" Kayla guessed.

"I never really thought about it," he admitted. "Except about two minutes ago and more in the context of 'thank God I don't have to think about stuff like that.'"

She frowned as she folded up the blanket. "Stuff like what?"

"Any and all of the paraphernalia associated with babies. I swear, you can hardly see the floor in Claire and Levi's room for all of the toys and crap strewn around."

Toys and crap.

Well, that was an enlightening turn of phrase. If she'd

been under any illusions that Trey might be excited about impending fatherhood, the phone call from his cousin had cleared them away.

Thank God I don't have to think about stuff like that.

His phone chimed and he glanced at the screen again. "She actually texted me a picture of the package, to make sure I get the right ones."

"Then I guess you'd better go get the diapers."

"I'm sorry," he said. "She really did sound desperate, although I'll spare you the details that she didn't spare me."

"I have to head over to the newspaper office, anyway," she reminded him. "Thanks for lunch."

"Wait." He caught her arm as she started to move away. "You were in the middle of saying something when Claire called."

She furrowed her brow, as if trying to remember, then shrugged. "I don't remember now."

Liar, liar.

She ignored the recriminations from her conscience as she headed back to her truck.

When she got to the newspaper office and glanced at her own phone, Kayla saw that she had three missed calls and four text messages—all from her sister.

She sat down behind her desk and finally called her back.

"What did he say?" Kristen demanded without preamble.

"Hi, Kristen. It's good to hear from you. I'm doing well, thanks for asking, and how are you?"

Her sister huffed out a breath. "We covered all of that when I talked to you earlier. Now tell me what he said."

"I didn't tell him," she admitted.

"How could you not tell him? Wasn't the whole purpose of your meeting with him today to tell him about your baby—*his* baby?"

"Yes, that was the purpose," she agreed. "And I was trying to come up with the right words to tell him what I needed to tell him."

"That you're pregnant with his child."

She sighed. "I'm aware of that fact."

"If you can't even say the words over the phone to me, there's no way you're going to be able to say them to Trey."

"I know," she admitted. "And those words are going to turn his whole world upside down."

"Probably a lot less than the baby that's going to come along in a few more months," Kristen pointed out reasonably.

"Not just a baby, but all the *toys and crap* that go along with a baby."

"What?"

She sighed. "Claire called and asked Trey to pick up diapers for her, and he went off on a little bit of a rant that made it pretty clear he isn't ready to be a father."

"Ready or not—he is going to be one."

"I know," she said again.

"The longer you wait, the harder it's going to be," her sister warned.

She knew it was true. And she knew that she'd already waited too long, but with Trey's disparaging remark ringing in her ears, the truth had lodged in her throat. So many times, she'd tried to imagine how he'd react to the news, but every time she played the scene out in her mind, the mental reel came to a dead stop after she told him about the baby. She simply could not imagine how he would respond. His comments today gave her a little bit of a hint, and not a good one.

"The baby's moving around a lot now," she admitted.

"The whole time I was with Trey today, I could feel little flutters, as if the baby was responding to the sound of his voice."

"Maybe he was," Kristen said. "Or maybe my nephew was kicking at you, reminding you to tell his father about his existence."

"I don't know if the baby's a boy or a girl," she reminded her sister.

"It's a boy," Kristen said. "And a little boy needs his father."

"What if…"

"What if what?"

But Kayla couldn't finish the thought. A single tear leaked out the corner of her eye—not that her sister could see, of course, but in true Kristen fashion, she didn't need to see her to know.

"Are you crying, sweetie?"

"No."

"Kayla," her sister prompted gently.

"One tear is not crying," she protested.

"It's going to be okay," Kristen said. "But only if you tell him."

"What if he doesn't want our baby?" she asked, her voice barely a whisper. "What if he hates me for getting pregnant?"

"You didn't get pregnant alone," her sister said indignantly. "And if he couldn't be responsible enough to make sure that didn't happen, he has to be responsible for the consequences."

RUST CREEK RAMBLINGS: BITS & BITES

The spectacularly refurbished Maverick Manor has been doing steady business since it opened its doors last December. Rumor has it the exquisite honeymoon suite is in particular demand and has already been booked for the wedding night of dashing detective Russ Campbell to Rust Creek Falls's sexy spitfire waitress, Lani Dalton.

In other news, a truckload of our neighbors from Thunder Canyon recently rode into town bringing Presents for Patriots. The group included DJ and Allaire Traub with their pint-size son, Alex; Shane and Gianna Roarke, who will obviously be adding to their family very soon; Clayton and Antonia Traub, with children Bennett and Lucy in tow; and Trey Strickland, who is apparently planning to spend the holidays with his grandparents. Take my advice, single ladies, and slip a sprig of mistletoe in your pocket just in case you're lucky enough to cross paths with the handsome bachelor while he's in Rust Creek Falls!

Gene folded his newspaper and set it aside. "Better watch out," he told his grandson. "The Rambler announced your return to all of the eligible women in town."

"As if the news hadn't spread farther and faster through the grapevine already," Trey noted.

"Something wrong?" Melba asked him.

"Why would you think that?"

"You've been pushing those eggs around on your plate for five minutes without taking a bite."

He lifted a forkful to his mouth and tried not to make a face as he swallowed the cold eggs.

"I heard about your lunch with Kayla Dalton on Monday," Melba said.

He didn't bother to ask where she'd heard. In a town the size of Rust Creek Falls, everyone knew everyone else's business.

"In the park," she continued, shaking her head. "Why on earth would you take the girl to the park in December?"

"The park was Kayla's idea," he told her.

Melba frowned at that. "Really?"

"And it was a nice day."

"Nice enough, for this time of year," his grandmother agreed. "But hardly nice enough for a picnic."

"You should take her to Kalispell," Gene said.

"Why would I take her to Kalispell?" he asked warily.

"For a proper date."

He looked across the table at his grandfather. "*You're* giving *me* dating advice?"

"Somebody apparently has to," Melba pointed out. "Because lunch in the park in December is *not* a date."

He didn't bother reminding her again that it had been Kayla's idea—clearly nothing he said was going to change her opinion.

"You should take her somewhere nice," his grandmother continued.

"Speaking of going places," he said. "I'm heading to Kalispell this afternoon to do some Christmas shopping. Do you need me to pick up anything for you?"

"I was there to get my groceries yesterday," Melba said. "You should ask Kayla to go with you."

"Grandma," he said, with more than a hint of exasperation in his tone.

She held her hands up in mock surrender. "It was just a suggestion."

And because it was one he was tempted to follow, he instead got up and cleared his plate from the table, then headed out the door.

Chapter Six

The following night Kayla had volunteered to help with the wrapping of Presents for Patriots at the community center. She wasn't surprised to see Trey was also in attendance, but she deliberately took an empty seat at the table closest to the doors—far away from where he was seated.

She wasn't exactly avoiding him, but after the way they'd parted at the conclusion of their lunch date, she wasn't sure of the status between them. She knew that nothing he'd said or done absolved her of the responsibility of telling him about their baby, but she couldn't summon up any enthusiasm to do so. Instead, she chose a gift from the box beside the table and selected paper covered with green holly and berries to wrap it. There was Christmas music playing softly in the background and steady traffic from the wrapping tables to the refreshment area. The mood was generally festive, with people chatting with their neighbors and friends while they worked.

Despite the activity all around her, Kayla was conscious of Trey's presence. Several times when her gaze slid across the room, she found him looking at her, and the heat in his eyes suggested that he was remembering the night they'd spent together.

She was remembering, too. Even before she'd learned that she was carrying his child—an undeniable reminder of that night—she hadn't been able to forget. She'd had only one cup of the spiked punch—or maybe it was two. Just enough to overcome her innate shyness and lessen her inhibitions, not enough to interfere with her memories of that night.

That evening had been the realization of a longtime fantasy. She'd had a secret crush on him all through high school, but she'd never let herself actually believe that he could want her, too. But for a few hours that night, she hadn't doubted for a moment that he did. The way he'd looked at her, the way he'd kissed her and touched her, had assured her that what was happening between them was mutual.

But the next day, he hadn't remembered any of it.

Or so she'd believed for five months.

Now she knew that he knew, but he was prepared to act as if nothing had ever happened. Unfortunately for Kayla, that wasn't really an option.

"Instead of staring at her from across the room, you could go over and talk to her."

Shane Roarke's suggestion forced Trey to tear his gaze away from Kayla. He pulled another piece of tape from the roll and resumed his wrapping.

"What?" he asked, as if he didn't know what—or rather whom—his friend was talking about.

Shane shook his head. "You're not fooling anyone, Trey."

"I don't know what you're talking about," he said.

But of course it was a lie. He'd noticed her the minute she'd walked through the door. He'd watched her come in, her nose and cheeks pink from the cold, and waited for her to come over and take the empty seat beside him. Her eyes had flicked in his direction, and his heart had pounded in anticipation. Then, much to his disappointment, she'd turned the other way.

"I'm talking about the pretty brunette across the room. The one with the big blue eyes and the shy smile who keeps looking over at you almost as much as you're looking at her."

"She's looking at me?"

Shane glanced at his wife and shook his head. "Was I ever this pathetic?"

"No," Gianna smiled indulgently. "You were worse."

Her husband chuckled. "I probably was," he acknowledged, reaching over to cover the hand that his wife had splayed over her enormous belly. "But look at us now."

Trey did look at them, and he was surprised by the little tug of envy he felt. He never thought he wanted what his friend had—certainly he wasn't looking to add a wife and a kid to his life just yet. But maybe, at some future time down the road.

For now, however, he couldn't stop thinking about Kayla. He'd told her that they could forget what happened between them on the Fourth of July, but it was a lie. He hadn't stopped thinking about her since that night, and now that he was back in Rust Creek Falls, he was eager to spend some time with her and to rekindle the chemistry that had sparked between them five months earlier.

"And look at his corners," Gianna said, interrupting his musing.

Trey followed her pointing finger to the package in front of him. "What's wrong with my corners?"

"They're lumpy."

"Shane's corners weren't so great, either, until you started helping him," he pointed out.

"That's true," Gianna agreed, pushing back her chair. She came around the table to his side. "Come on."

He eyed her warily. "Where are we going?"

"To get you some help."

He looked across the table at his friend and coworker; Shane just shrugged. Trey reluctantly rose to his feet and let Gianna lead him away. His steps faltered when he realized where she was leading, but she only grabbed his arm and tugged him along until they were standing by Kayla's table.

"You look like you know what you're doing," Gianna said to her. "Maybe you could help Trey with his wrapping?"

Kayla's pretty blue eyes shifted between them. "Help—how?"

"Show him how to fold the ends of the paper, for starters. He's making a mess of everything."

"You'd think a man who trains horses could handle a roll of paper," Kayla noted.

"You'd think," Gianna agreed. "But he can't."

"But I can hear," Trey pointed out. "And you're talking about me as if I'm not here."

"Sit," Gianna said, nudging him into a chair.

He sat.

"Good luck," she said to Kayla before she went back to her husband.

"I'm sorry about this," Trey said.

"About what?"

"Gianna dragging me over here."

"Why did she?"

He shrugged. "Partly because I was making a mess of everything. Mostly because I was paying more attention to you than my assigned task."

Her cheeks flushed prettily. "I'm sure you weren't making a mess of everything."

"You haven't seen me wrap anything yet," he warned her.

She handed him a box. "Give it a go."

He let his fingertips brush against hers in the exchange, and smiled when she drew away quickly. He laid the present on the paper and cut it to size, then wrapped the paper around the box. He was doing okay until he got to the ends, where he couldn't figure out how to fold it.

"You really do suck at this," she confirmed, amused by the fact.

"I'm not good with the paper," he admitted. "But I'm a tape master."

Her lips twitched, just a little, and her brows lifted. "A tape master?"

He demonstrated, tearing off four short, neat pieces of tape onto the tips of each of his fingers, and then transferring them one by one to secure the seams of the paper.

"Not too bad," she allowed.

"I have other talents," he told her.

"What kind of talents?"

He tipped his head closer to her and lowered his voice suggestively. "Why don't we go for a drive when we're finished here and…talk…about those talents?"

"I have a better idea," she said. "I'll cut and wrap, and you tape."

Her tone was prim but the pulse point at the base of her

jaw was racing. Satisfied by this proof that she wasn't as unaffected as she wanted him to believe, he backed off. "That'll work," he agreed. "For now."

The system of shared labor did work well, and they chatted while they wrapped. Their conversation was mostly easy and casual, but every once in a while, he'd allow his hand to brush against hers, or his knee to bump hers beneath the table. And every time they touched, her breath would catch and her gaze would slide away, reassuring him that the feelings churning inside him weren't entirely one-sided.

"I'm always impressed by the generosity of people at this time of year," he noted. "Even those folks who don't have a lot to give manage to make a contribution."

"You're right," Kayla agreed. "The year of the flood, when so many local families were struggling, Nina started the Tree of Hope to ensure that everyone in town had a holiday meal and presents under their tree. The response of the community was overwhelming."

"Nina Crawford?"

Kayla nodded. "Actually, she's Nina Traub now."

He'd grown up knowing about the feud between the Crawfords and the Traubs, although no one seemed to know for sure what had caused the rift between the families. Regardless of the origins, the animosity had endured through generations and escalated further when Nathan Crawford and Colin Traub both ran for the vacant mayoral seat after the flood. How Nathan's sister had ended up married to Colin's brother was a mystery to a lot of people, but their union showed promise of being the first step toward mending the rift between the families.

"The Tree of Hope is just one example of how the people of Rust Creek Falls look out for one another," she continued.

"I don't think I ever realized how much they did until I saw the way everyone pitched in and worked together after the flood."

"We had a lot of help from our Thunder Canyon neighbors, too," she reminded him. "And the money and publicity that Lissa brought in through Bootstraps was invaluable."

He nodded. "But looking around the town, I don't think anyone who wasn't here to see the devastation would ever guess how badly the town was hit."

"We're doing okay now."

"Better than okay, from what I've heard, since Maverick Manor opened its doors."

"Nate and Callie have big plans for their place, but I don't think the Thunder Canyon Resort needs to worry about its clientele heading this way."

"Have you ever been to the resort?" Trey asked.

She shook her head.

"You should come for a visit sometime."

Kayla wasn't sure if his statement was a general comment or an invitation, so she kept her response equally vague. "I've thought about it," she said. "In fact, I had considered doing some Christmas shopping that way."

"I wish you had come to Thunder Canyon," he said. "It would have been nice to spend some time with you without our every step being examined under the microscope of public opinion."

"Such is life in a small town," she said, glancing at the door to see Kristen and Ryan enter the hall.

"I didn't think you were going to make it," Kayla said to her sister.

"We didn't, either," Kristen admitted. "And I was exhausted after our final performance this week, but we both wanted to help out."

"There's no shortage of help," Trey said. "But still plenty

to do—especially if you have more wrapping experience than I do."

"How long have you guys been here?" Kristen asked.

"When I arrived, around seven-thirty, Trey was already here," Kayla told her.

"Which means you both must be ready for a break," Kristen decided. "Why don't Ryan and I take over for a little while so that you and Trey can take a walk to stretch your legs and get some fresh air?"

"Isn't it a little cold outside for an evening stroll?"

"Not if you bundle up," Kristen said.

Trey glanced from Kristen to her sister and back again. "Why do you want us to go for a walk?"

"Because Kayla needs to talk to you."

He looked at Kayla. "Can't we talk here?"

"No," Kristen said firmly, leaving her fiancé looking as confused as Trey felt. "Kayla needs to speak with you *privately*."

He looked at Kayla; she glared at her sister then offered him a halfhearted shrug.

"O-kay," he decided, pushing his chair away from the table.

Kayla did the same, sliding her arms into the sleeves of the ski jacket she'd draped over her chair.

It was frigid outside, and she shoved her hands into the pockets and tucked her chin into the collar of her jacket.

"It's going to snow," Trey said, pulling on his gloves.

"It's December in Montana," she agreed. "The odds are definitely in favor of more white stuff."

He chuckled at that. "So where are we walking to?"

"There's really nowhere to go."

"Then maybe you should just tell me why your sister was so determined to get us out of the community center so we could talk."

"Because she doesn't know how to mind her own business," Kayla grumbled.

But she knew her sister was right—Trey needed to know about the baby. And she needed to be the one to tell him.

"That's a little cryptic," he noted.

"I told you that Kristen knows what happened the night of the wedding," she reminded him.

He nodded.

"Well, she thought I should talk to you about…"

"About?" he prompted.

But her attention had been snagged by the approach of another couple. "I didn't know Forrest and Angie were in town."

Trey turned to follow the direction of her gaze. "They're very involved with Presents for Patriots."

Kayla wasn't surprised by this revelation. Forrest was one of six sons born to Bob and Ellie Traub but the only one who had opted for a career in the military rather than on the family ranch. Three years earlier, he'd returned from Iraq with a severely injured leg and PTSD. He'd gone to Thunder Canyon for treatment and therapy at the hospital there—although there was speculation that he'd wanted to escape all of the attention of being a hometown hero even more than he wanted to fix his leg. It was in Thunder Canyon that he'd met and fallen in love with Angie Anderson, and it warmed Kayla's heart to see how sincerely happy and content Forrest was now that he'd found the right woman to share his life.

They chatted with the war veteran and his wife for a few minutes before they continued into the hall. When the doors closed behind them, Kayla braced herself to speak once again. Then Bennett and Lucy Traub raced out of the community center, followed closely by their parents, Clay and Antonia.

"This isn't the easiest place to have a conversation, is it?" Trey asked when the Traubs had moved on.

"Not tonight," she agreed.

"So maybe we should try something different," he suggested, and lowered his head to touch his mouth to hers.

He caught her off guard.

Kayla had been so preoccupied thinking about the conversation they weren't having that she didn't realize his intention until he was kissing her. And then her brain shut down completely as her body melted against his.

Trey wrapped his arms around her, holding her as close as their bulky outerwear would allow. She lifted her arms to link them behind his head, holding on to him as the world spun beneath her feet.

It was funny—they couldn't seem to have a two-minute conversation without being interrupted, but the kiss they shared went on and on, blissfully, endlessly. When Trey finally eased his lips from hers, they were both breathless.

"I wondered," he said.

"What did you wonder?"

"If your lips would taste as I remembered."

"Do they?"

"No," he said. "They taste even better."

She felt her cheeks flush despite the chilly air. "I thought you wanted to forget about that night."

"I'm not sorry about what happened between us in the summer. I just wish we hadn't rushed into bed."

"I'd guess that had more to do with the punch than either of us," she said.

"Or the chemistry between us."

"I thought the alcohol was responsible for the chemistry."

"Have you been drinking tonight?"

She flushed. "Of course not."

"Because from where I'm standing, that kiss we just shared proves the sparks between us are real, and I'd like to spend some time with you while I'm in town over the holidays, so that we can get to know one another better, and maybe see where the chemistry leads us."

"But you're only going to be in town for a few weeks," she reminded him—reminded both of them.

"Thunder Canyon isn't that far away."

"And I'm sure there's no shortage of women there."

"There's not," he agreed. "But I haven't stopped thinking about you since July. I haven't been out with another woman in all that time because I didn't want to go out with anyone else."

His words stirred hope in her heart. If he really meant what he was saying, maybe they could build a relationship—except that anything they started to build now would be on a foundation of lies, or at least omission.

Her baby—their baby—kicked inside her belly, a not-so-subtle reminder of that omission.

"Trey..."

"Just give us a chance," he urged.

"I want to," she admitted. "But—"

He touched his fingers to her lips. "It's enough that you're willing to give us a chance."

She shook her head. "There are things you don't know. Things you need to know."

"We've got time to find out everything we need to know about one another," he told her. "I don't want to rush anything."

And she let herself be persuaded, because it was easier than telling him the truth.

Or so she thought until she considered having to go back inside and face her sister. Because she knew Kristen would take one look at her and immediately know that she'd failed in her assigned task.

"We should probably get back inside before people start whispering and my grandparents read about our disappearance from the gift-wrapping in Rust Creek Ramblings."

"They won't read anything in the paper," she told him.

His brows lifted. "How can you be so certain?"

Kayla wasn't quite sure how to respond to that.

"Is that what your sister wanted you to tell me?"

"What?"

"That you're the Rust Creek Rambler."

She gasped, shocked as much by his casual delivery as the statement itself. "Why would you think that?"

"The first clue was your assurance that Kristen wasn't the Rust Creek Rambler. It occurred to me that the only way you could be so certain was if you knew the true identity of the Rambler. And then, when we saw Will and Jordyn Leigh at the diner, you made reference to their *intoxicated nuptials*—which was, coincidentally, the same phrase that was used in the 'Ramblings' column."

She was surprised that he'd figured it out. She'd been writing the column for three and a half years with no one, aside from the paper's editor, being aware of her identity.

"You're right," she admitted softly. "But no one else in town has ever shown any suspicion about me being the author of the column."

"Maybe because no one else has been paying close attention to you."

"Are you mad?"

"Why would I be mad?"

"Because I kept it from you."

"And everyone else in town."

She nodded.

"Actually, I'm more baffled—especially when I think

about what was written in Ramblings about the two of us dancing together at the wedding."

She shrugged. "Several people saw us together. If I'd ignored that, it would have been suspicious. By mentioning it in the column, it deflected attention away from me as the possible author."

"Clever," he noted. "So tell me, is your copy editing job real or just a cover?"

"It's real, but only part of what I do."

"You are full of surprises," he told her. "But I'm not sure why it mattered so much to your sister that you tell me about your secret occupation."

"Kristen's a big fan of open communication," she told him. "But I wouldn't be able to do my job if everyone knew that I was the Rambler, so I'd appreciate it if you didn't out me to the whole community."

"I think, if I'm going to keep such a big secret for you, I'm going to need something in return."

"What kind of something?" she asked warily.

"Help with my Christmas shopping?" he suggested.

She smiled. "You've got a deal."

Kayla hadn't seen Trey since their gift-wrapping at the community center. She'd been lying low on purpose—not just because she still hadn't figured out how to tell him about the baby, but because she wanted to be able to tell her sister that she hadn't seen him and, therefore, hadn't had a chance to tell him.

Apparently, she was a liar *and* a coward. And while she wasn't particularly proud of her behavior, she consoled herself with the assurance that these were desperate times.

Thursday afternoon she went into the newspaper office again to work on the Sunday edition of the paper and polish her own column. Unfortunately, the onset of winter meant that many residents were hunkered down indoors rather than creating and disseminating juicy headlines.

There were rumors that Alistair Warren had spent several hours with the widow next door during a recent storm—"much longer than it would take to fill her firebox with wood" she'd heard from one source—but Kayla didn't have much more than that for her column.

She considered mentioning that Trey Strickland had recently been spotted at Crawford's buying diapers, but putting his name into any context with babies hit a little too close to the secret she was keeping—and knew she couldn't continue to keep for much longer.

Already her mother was looking at her with that calculating gleam in her eye, as if she knew her daughter was hiding something from her. Kayla's father—always preoccupied with ranch business—probably wouldn't notice if she sat down at the breakfast table with a ring through her nose, but her mother had always had an uncanny sense when it came to every one of her five children.

Kayla wanted to share the news of her baby with her family. She wasn't particularly proud of the circumstances surrounding the conception, but she wasn't ashamed of her baby. And the further she progressed in her pregnancy, the more she wanted to talk to her mother about being a mother, about the changes her body was going through and the confusing array of emotions she was experiencing. She wanted to share her thoughts and feelings with someone who had been through what she was going through right now.

Kristen had been great—aside from the constant pressure to tell Trey—but her sister was so caught up in the excitement of being in love and planning her wedding, she couldn't imagine the doubts and fears that overwhelmed Kayla.

She so desperately wanted to do right by her baby, to give her child the life he or she deserved. Of course, Kristen kept insisting the baby was a he, despite the fact that the ultrasound photo gave nothing away.

Kayla opened the zippered pocket inside her purse and carefully removed that photo now. At the time it was taken, her baby had measured about five inches long and weighed around seven ounces.

"About the size of a bell pepper," the technician had said, to help Kayla put the numbers into perspective.

She'd also reassured the mother-to-be that baby had all the requisite parts—although the baby's positioning didn't reveal whether there were boy parts or girl parts—but it was the rapid beating of the tiny heart on the monitor that snagged Kayla's attention and filled her own heart.

She'd marveled at the baby's movements on the screen, but she hadn't been able to feel any of those movements inside her. Not until almost three weeks later.

She was much more attuned to the tiny flutters and kicks now. Of course, the baby seemed most active when she was trying to sleep at night, but she didn't mind. Alone in her room, she would put her hands on her belly and let herself think about the tiny person growing inside her.

Her doctor had suggested that she start looking into childbirth classes. Kayla understood the wisdom of this advice, but she didn't dare register for classes in Rust Creek Falls and she didn't know that she'd be able to get to Kalispell every week to commit to classes there. Although Kalispell was a much bigger city than Rust Creek Falls, her encounter with Melba Strickland at the shopping mall had reminded her that she couldn't count on anonymity there. Instead, she'd been reading everything she could find and had even been taking online classes about pregnancy and childbirth.

As she traced the outline of her baby's shape with her fingertip, she hoped her efforts were enough. She was so afraid of doing something wrong, of somehow screwing up this tiny, fragile life that was growing inside her.

She wanted to show the picture to Trey; she wanted to talk about her hopes and dreams for their child and share her fears. Mostly, she wanted him to want to be part of their child's life, because she didn't want to raise their child alone. She wanted her baby to have two parents.

The beep of her phone interrupted her thoughts. She carefully tucked the photo away again before checking the message from her sister.

I want it!

She opened the attachment to see what *it* was, and smiled at the picture of a multi-tiered wedding cake. Each stacked layer was elaborately decorated with a different white-on-white design: silhouettes of bucking broncos, cowboy boots, cowboy hats and horseshoes.

Despite the Western motif, it was elegant and unique—totally Kristen.

She texted back,

Luv it

Because she did. She didn't have a clue where her sister would find someone in their small town capable of recreating such a work of art, but that was a practical worry for another day. Right now her sister was dreaming of her perfect day, and Kayla was happy to be drawn into the fantasy with her.

Kristen had asked Kayla to be her maid of honor, and she had, of course, accepted, but she needed to talk to her twin about the timing of the event and the likelihood that she would be a maid of *dis*honor. She didn't think Kristen would want to be upstaged on her wedding day by her hugely pregnant and unwed sister. As much as Kristen enjoyed the spotlight, Kayla didn't think she'd want the happiest day of her life tainted by that kind of scandal.

Upon receiving her reply, Kristen immediately called. "Are you sick and tired of hearing about the wedding?" she asked.

"Never," Kayla assured her sister.

"Then you won't mind if Mom and I drag you into Kalispell tomorrow to go shopping for my dress?"

"Are you kidding? I've been wondering when you'd finally get around to that." She knew that Ryan had offered to fly his fiancée out to California so that she could shop on Rodeo Drive in Beverly Hills, but the idea hadn't appealed to Kristen. Her twin was surprisingly traditional in a lot of ways—and very much a country girl.

"I've just been so busy with the play that I haven't had much free time," Kristen said now. "But June isn't that far away, so I figured I'd better make time to start preparing for the wedding."

"You've set a date, then?"

"June eleventh," her sister confirmed.

"Then I guess we'd better find you a dress."

Chapter Seven

When Trey saw Kayla's truck pull up in front of the boarding house, for a moment he thought—hoped—she had come into town to see him. When he saw her lift a small box out of the passenger seat of her vehicle, he was disappointed to realize she had another reason for being there.

He met her at the door and took the box from her. "What's this?"

"Your grandmother wanted a couple of jars of bread-and-butter pickles."

"She makes her own pickles."

Kayla shrugged. "Apparently, your grandfather was looking for something in the cellar and knocked over a shelf and she lost the last of hers."

He hadn't heard anything about such an incident—and he was pretty sure if his grandfather had truly engineered such a mishap, the whole town would have heard about it. More likely his grandmother had engineered the story to bring Kayla to the boarding house, and though he didn't approve of Melba's meddling, he wouldn't complain about the results.

"Did she happen to mention why she needed—" he glanced into the box "—half a dozen jars of pickles right now, today?"

"She spoke to my mother, not me. I'm just the delivery girl."

"Because I'm sure you didn't have anything better to do," he said dryly.

"Not according to my mother," she agreed.

"Do you have anything else on your schedule today?"

"No, but I figured, since I was coming into town, I would stop in at the newspaper office and try to get a head start on editing anything that has been submitted for the next edition."

"Or you could help me," he suggested.

"Help you with what?" she asked, a little warily.

"I've been tasked with finding the perfect Christmas tree for the main floor parlor."

"Perfect is a matter of interpretation when it comes to Christmas trees," she warned him.

"I figure as long as it's approximately the right height and shape, it's perfect."

Kayla *tsked* as she shook her head. "What kind of tree does your grandmother want?"

"A green one."

She laughed. "Well, that narrows your search to most of Montana."

He shrugged. "She didn't seem concerned about specifics so much as timing—it's only two weeks before Christmas, and she wants a tree in the parlor today."

"Where in the parlor?" Kayla pressed. "Does she want something slender that can be tucked into a corner? Or would she prefer a fuller shape that will become the centerpiece of the room?"

It was an effort to refrain from rolling his eyes. "I don't know. I just know that the tree is always in the corner—with stacks of presents piled underneath it on Christmas morning."

She smiled. "Everyone's a kid at Christmas, aren't they?"

"You don't get excited about presents?"

"Of course I do."

"So will you help me out with the tree?"

She pulled back the cuff of her jacket to look at the watch on her wrist. "Sure."

Twenty minutes later he pulled into the parking lot of a tree farm on the edge of town.

"I didn't expect it would be this busy in the middle of the day on a weekday," he commented.

"Two weeks," she reminded him.

However, most of the customers seemed to be examining precut trees, and although he knew that was the easier option, his grandmother had specifically requested a fresh-cut tree and had sent her husband out to the shed to get the bow saw for him.

They walked down the path, following the signs toward the "cut your own" section of the farm.

"Aside from green, what should I be looking for?" Trey asked Kayla.

"It depends on what matters most to you—scent, color, hardiness. Balsam fir smells lovely but they tend to be bulky around the bottom and take up a lot of space. The Scotch pine is probably the most common type of Christmas tree. Its bright green color is appealing, but the branches and needles tend to be quite stiff, making it more difficult—and painful—to decorate."

"You're not a fan," he guessed.

"They're pretty trees," she insisted. "But no, they wouldn't be my first choice."

"How do you know so much about Christmas trees?"

She shrugged. "Every year, from as far back as I can remember, we've trekked deep into the woods to cut down a tree, so I probably could have steered you in the right direction on the basis of that experience without necessarily knowing what was a spruce or a fir. The technical stuff I learned when I edited an article—'Choosing the Perfect Christmas Tree'—for the newspaper a couple of years back."

"You must get to read some interesting stuff in your job."

"I do," she agreed. "And not just in the "Ramblings" column."

"That doesn't count, anyway—you make that stuff up."

"I do not," she said indignantly. "I simply report facts that are brought to my attention."

"There's a fair amount of speculation in addition to the facts," he noted.

"Speculation about the facts, perhaps," she allowed.

He shook his head, but he was smiling when he paused beside a blue spruce. "What do you think of this one?"

She let her gaze run up the tall—extremely tall, in fact—trunk. "I think it's a beautiful tree for the town square but way too big for anyone's parlor."

He nodded in acknowledgment. "Who picks out the tree in your family?"

"Majority rules, but there's usually a lot of arguing before a final decision is made. My mom has a tendency to pick out a bigger tree than we have room for, which means my dad ends up muttering and cursing as he cuts down the trunk 'just another inch more' or trims some of the branches 'just on one side' so it'll end up sitting closer to the wall." She smiled a little at the memory. "My dad now carries a tape measure, so that he can show my mother that a tree isn't 'perfect' for an eight-foot room when it's actually eleven feet tall."

"I suspect my grandmother has had the opposite experience, because she made a point of telling me that the room has a twelve-foot ceiling and she doesn't want anything shorter than ten feet, preferably ten and a half."

"Did you bring a tape measure?"

He pulled it out of his pocket to show her.

"Did you bring a ladder so that you can measure up to ten feet?"

"It's in my other pocket."

She laughed.

He looked at her—at her cheeks pink from the cold, at the delicate white flakes of snow against her dark hair and at her eyes, as clear and blue as the sky, sparkling in the sun—and realized that he was in danger of falling hard and fast.

And in that moment, he didn't care.

He caught her hand, halting her in midstride. She tipped her head back to look up at him, and he lowered his head to touch his mouth to hers.

He kissed her softly, savoring the moment. He loved kissing her, loved the way her lips yielded and her body melted. He loved the quiet sounds she made deep in her throat.

But he wanted more than a few stolen kisses. He wanted to make love with her again, to enjoy not just the taste of her lips but the joining of their bodies. But he'd promised that they could take things slow this time, and he intended to keep that promise—even if it meant yet another cold shower when he got back to the boarding house.

When he finally eased his lips away, she looked as dazed as he felt. "What was that for?"

"Does there need to be a reason for me to kiss you?"

"I guess not," she admitted. "You just…surprised me."

He smiled at that. "You surprise me every time I see you."

"I do?"

"You do," he confirmed. "I always thought I knew you. You were Derek's sister, the shy twin, the quiet one. But I've realized there's a lot more to you than most people give you credit for."

"I am the shy twin, the quiet one."

He slid his arms around her, wanting to draw her nearer. "You're also smart and beautiful and passionate."

She put her hands on his chest, her arms locked to hold him at a distance. "Tree," she reminded him.

"They're not going anywhere," he noted.

"You say that now, but do you see that stump there?"

He followed the direction of her gaze. "Yeah."

"That might have been *your* perfect tree, but someone else got to it before you did."

"So I'll find another perfect tree."

"Do you think it will be that easy? That perfect trees just—"

"Grow like trees," he interjected drily.

Her lips curved. "Touché."

Half an hour later, they were headed back to the boarding house with a lovely tree tied down in the box of Trey's truck.

When they arrived, they found that Gene had carted out all of the decorations: lights and garland and ornaments.

"Looks like our work isn't done yet," he noted.

"I thought your grandmother usually let her guests help with the trimming of the tree."

"Apparently she stopped that a couple of years ago, when a three-year-old decided to throw some of her favorite ornaments rather than hang them. A few of them were mouth-blown glass that a cousin had brought back for her from Italy."

Kayla winced sympathetically.

"She has a story for every ornament on her tree," Trey told her. "And now a story for eight that aren't."

She tucked her hands behind her back. "Now I'm afraid to touch anything."

"You can touch me," Trey told her, with a suggestive wink. "I won't break."

Kayla laughed. "Let's focus on the tree," she responded, stepping out of his reach.

But Trey circled around the tree in the other direction and caught her against him. "Now I have to kiss you."

"Have to?" She lifted a brow. "Why?"

"Because you're standing under the mistletoe."

Kayla looked up, but there was no mistletoe hanging from the ceiling above her. There was, however, a sprig of the recognizable plant in Trey's hand, which he was holding above her head.

"That's cheating," she told him.

"I don't care," he said and touched his mouth to hers.

As Kayla melted into the kiss, her objections melted away.

The slamming of the back door returned her to her senses. "It's only two weeks until Christmas," she reminded him. "And your grandmother wants her tree up."

He sighed regretfully but released her so they could focus on the assigned task.

After leaving the boarding house, Kayla stopped at Crawford's to pick up a quart of milk for her mother. She was carrying the jug to the checkout counter when she saw Tara Jones, a third-grade teacher from the local elementary school.

"This is a lucky coincidence," the teacher said.

"Why's that?" she asked curiously.

"Our annual holiday pageant is in less than a week and we're way behind schedule with the costumes and scenery. I know it's a huge imposition," Tara said, "but we could really use your help."

"It's not an imposition at all," Kayla told her. "I'd be happy to pitch in."

"Thank you, thank you, thank you. We do have other volunteers who can assist you, but I think one of the biggest problems is that no one was willing to take the lead because they're not sure what they should be doing. But with your experience in the Kalispell theater, you should have them on track in no time."

"When do you need me?"

"Yesterday."

Kayla laughed.

"Okay, Monday would work," Tara relented. "Three o'clock?"

"I'll be there."

"And if you want to bring your beau, I'm sure no one would have any objections to an extra pair of hands."

She frowned. "What?"

"Come on, Kayla. Do you really think people haven't noticed that you've been spending a lot of time with Trey Strickland?"

"I wouldn't say it's a lot of time," she hedged.

"So you're not exclusive?"

She frowned at the question. "We're not even really dating—just hanging out together."

"Is that what you told the Rambler?"

"What?"

The other woman shrugged. "I just wondered how it is that everyone knows you and Trey have been hanging out, but that little tidbit has yet to make the gossip column of the local paper."

"Probably because it's not newsworthy."

"That's one theory," Tara agreed. "Another is that the Rambler is someone you know."

"Or maybe it's someone Trey knows," she countered.

"I guess that is another possibility. But you can bet if I was dating Trey Strickland, I'd shout it out from the headlines."

Trey was shoveling the walk that led to the steps of the boarding house when he heard someone say, "Hey, stranger."

He recognized his friend's voice before he turned and came face-to-face with Derek Dalton. The instinctive pleasure was quickly supplanted by guilt. Derek had been his best friend in high school and one of the first people he sought out whenever he returned to Rust Creek Falls, but he hadn't done so this time because he didn't know how to see Derek without feeling guilty about what had happened with Derek's sister. And now he had another reason to feel guilty, because he was dating Kayla behind her brother's back.

"What brings you into town?" Trey asked.

"I'm heading over to the Ace in the Hole for a beer and thought I'd see if you wanted to join me."

Trey had decided to tackle the shoveling while he waited for Kayla to respond to any of the three messages he'd left for her. Since that had yet to happen, he decided he'd look pretty pathetic sitting at home waiting for her to call.

"Let me finish up here and grab a quick shower," Trey said.

While he was doing that, Derek visited with Melba and

Gene, hanging out in their kitchen as he'd often done when he and Trey were teenagers.

Trey was quick in the shower, then he checked for messages on his phone again. *Nada.*

He pushed Kayla from his mind and headed out with her brother.

They climbed the rough-hewn wooden steps and opened the screen door beneath the oversize playing card—an ace of hearts—that blinked in neon red. Inside, a long wooden bar ran the length of one wall with a dozen bar stools facing the mirrored wall that reflected rows of glass bottles. Shania Twain was singing from the ancient Wurlitzer jukebox at the back of the room.

There was a small and rarely used dance floor in the middle of the room, surrounded by scarred wooden tables and ladder-back chairs. The floor was littered with peanut shells that crunched under their boots as they made their way to the bar, taking the last two empty stools. He nodded to Alex Monroe, foreman of the local lumber mill, who lifted his beer in acknowledgment.

Trey settled onto his stool and looked around. "This place hasn't changed at all, has it?"

"Isn't that part of its charm?"

"It has charm?"

Derek chuckled. "Don't let Rosey hear you say that."

"She still in charge of this place?"

"Claims it's the only relationship that ever worked out for her."

"Sounds like Rosey," Trey agreed.

The bartender delivered their drinks and they settled back, falling into familiar conversation about ranching and horses and life in Rust Creek Falls. They were on their second round of drinks when two girls in tight jeans and low-cut shirts squeezed up to the bar beside them on the pretext of wanting to order, but the flirtatious glances they sent toward Trey and Derek suggested they were looking for more than drinks.

The girls accepted their beverages from the bartender then headed toward an empty table, inviting Trey and Derek to join them.

"What do you say?" Derek asked, his gaze riveted on their swaying hips as the girls walked away.

Trey shook his head, not the least bit tempted.

"C'mon, buddy. You're supposed to be my wing man."

"Don't you ever get tired of women throwing themselves at you?"

Derek laughed. "That's funny."

Trey frowned.

"You weren't joking?"

"No," he said.

"You meet someone?"

"As a matter of fact, I did."

Derek obviously hadn't expected an affirmative response, but he shrugged it off, anyway. "So even if you've got a girl in Thunder Canyon, she wouldn't ever know about a meaningless hookup here."

He didn't correct his friend's assumption that he was seeing someone in Thunder Canyon. If he admitted that he was interested in a local girl, Derek would be full of questions—questions that Trey wasn't prepared to answer. So all he said was, "*I'd* know."

Derek shook his head. "She's really got her hooks into you, doesn't she?"

Trey frowned at the phrasing, but he'd recently started to admit—at least to himself—that it was probably true. "Your turn will come someday," he warned his friend.

"Maybe," Derek allowed, setting his empty bottle on the bar. "But that day is not today."

"Where are you going?" he demanded when Kayla's brother slid off his stool.

"When a girl gives me a 'come hither' glance, I come hither."

Trey just shook his head as he watched him walk away to join the two girls at the table they now occupied.

Even if Kayla did have her hooks in him, so to speak, he knew there were still obstacles to a relationship between them, and the geographical distance between Thunder Canyon and Rust Creek Falls was one of the biggest.

But that distance wasn't an issue right now, and he really wanted to see her. He slipped his phone out of his pocket and checked for messages. There were none.

He scrolled through his list of contacts, clicked on her name then the message icon. The blank white screen seemed blindingly bright in the dimly lit bar.

Just thinking abt u, wondering what u r doing…

There was no immediate reply. Of course not—whatever she was doing, she obviously wasn't sitting around waiting to hear from him.

He glanced over at the girls' table, where his friend was holding another bottle of beer. Derek caught his eye and waved him over, but Trey shook his head again. Then he tossed some money on the bar to pay for his drink and walked back to the boarding house.

Kayla didn't get Trey's message until the morning, and her heart fluttered inside her chest when she picked up her phone and saw his name on the screen. She clicked on the message icon.

Just thinking abt u, wondering what u r doing…

The time stamp indicated that he'd reached out to her at 10:28 pm.

Sorry—I was in the barn all night watching over a new litter of kittens.

He replied immediately.

Everything okay?

8 kittens, only 5 survived.

Tough night for you.

She hadn't expected his immediate and unquestioning understanding. It had been a tough night. Yeah, she'd grown up on a ranch and seen a lot of births and deaths, but it still hurt to lose an animal. She'd tried to keep the kittens warm with blankets and hot water bottles and her own body heat, but the three she'd lost had just been too small.

I'm sorry I didn't have a chance to call.

Me 2. I ended up @ the Ace with Derek.

She had enough secrets in her life, but she wasn't ready for the third degree from her family when they learned that she'd been hanging out with Trey Strickland, because they all knew that she'd had a huge crush on her brother's best friend in high school. And though she wasn't proud of her instinctive cringe, she had to ask.

You didn't say anything about us?

There r enough brawls there without giving your brother an excuse to hit me.

She exhaled a sigh of relief.

Good. I like your nose where it is.

Me 2. But now I'm wondering…r u ashamed of our relationship?

I'm just not sure what our relationship is.

Maybe we can work on figuring it out today.

Which was an undeniably tempting offer. She missed him more than she wanted to admit, conscious with each day that passed that he wasn't going to be in Rust Creek Falls for very long, and the time was quickly slipping away. Unfortunately, she knew that they wouldn't be able to figure out anything that day.

I'm on maid of honor duty today—looking for Kristen's wedding dress.

All day?

Knowing my sister, probably.

OK. I'll touch base with u 2morrow.

I'm at the theater 2morrow. But I'm free Tuesday.

Tuesday is too far away.

It was far away, and the fact that he thought so, too, put a smile on her face as she got ready to go shopping with the bride-to-be.

RUST CREEK RAMBLINGS: DECK THE COWBOY
Local cowboys have been showing their holiday spirit…or maybe it would be more accurate to say that Tommy Wheeler and Jared Winfree demonstrated the effect of imbibing *too many* holiday spirits after the men went a couple of rounds at the Ace in the Hole this past Friday night! Both were declared winners in the brawl and awarded a free night's accommodation in the sheriff's lockup as well as receiving a detailed bill for damages from everyone's favorite bar owner, Rosey Travern.

Chapter Eight

Kristen tried on at least a dozen different styles of wedding dresses—from long sleeves to strapless, slim-fitting to hoop skirts, simple taffeta to all-over lace decorated with tiny beads and crystals. And she looked stunning in each and every one. Even the layers and layers of ruffled organza that would have looked like an explosion of cotton candy on anyone else looked wonderful on Kristen.

"You must at least have a particular style in mind," Rita Dalton chided, when Kristen went back to the sample rack and selected four more completely different dresses again.

"I don't," the bride-to-be insisted. "But I think I'll know it when I see it."

But none of those four dresses seemed to be the right one, either. Rita moved away from the bridal gowns to peruse a more colorful rack of dresses.

"What do you think of this for your maid of honor?" she asked, lifting a hanger from the bar.

"Oh, I *love* the color," Kristen agreed, touching a hand

to the cornflower taffeta. "The blue is almost a perfect match to Kayla's eyes."

Kayla glanced at the dress. "It is pretty."

"You should try it on," Rita urged.

Her panicked gaze flew to her sister. Though Kristen understood the cause of her panic, she was at a loss to help her out of the sticky situation.

Rita looked at the tag. "This is a size six—perfect."

The dress wasn't only a size six, it was also very fitted, and there was no way Kayla could squeeze into the sample without revealing her baby bump.

"Today is about finding Kristen a dress," she reminded their mother.

"But if Kristen likes it and you like it, why can't we pick out your dress, too?"

"Because the bridesmaids' dresses should complement the bride's style—which means that there's no point in considering any options until she's chosen her dress."

"But look at this," Kristen said, coming to her rescue by holding up another outfit. "Doesn't it just scream 'mother-of-the-bride'?"

Rita glanced over, the irritated frown on her brow smoothing out when she saw the elegant sheath-style dress with bolero jacket that Kristen was holding.

Thank you, Kayla mouthed to her sister behind their mother's back.

"I'm not sure I want a dress that screams anything," Rita said. "But that is lovely."

Kristen shoved the dress into their mother's hands and steered her into the fitting room she'd recently vacated. They left the store thirty minutes later with a dress for the mother-of-the-bride but nothing for the bride herself.

"There's another bridal shop just down the street," Rita said.

"Can we go for lunch first?" Kristen asked. "I'm starving."

"Priorities," their mother chided. "June is only six months away, and you need a gown."

"I need to eat or I'm going to pass out in a puddle of taffeta."

Rita glanced at her watch. "All right—we'll go for a quick bite."

They found a familiar chain restaurant not too far away. Even before she looked at the menu, Kayla's mouth was watering for French fries and gravy, a lunchtime staple from high school that she hadn't craved in recent years—until she got pregnant. After a brief perusal of the menu, she set it aside.

"What are you having?" Kristen asked.

"The chicken club wrap and fries."

Her mother frowned. "French fries, Kayla?"

"What's wrong with French fries?" she asked, aware that she sounded more than a little defensive.

"Do you think I don't know the real reason you didn't want to try on that dress is that you're afraid you won't fit into a size six right now?"

"I've put on a few pounds," she admitted. "Not twenty." At least, not yet.

"It always starts with a few," her mother said, not unsympathetically.

"What starts with a few?"

"Emotional eating."

Kayla looked at Kristen, to see if her sister was having better luck following their mother's logic, but Kristen just shrugged.

"I understand that it's hard," Rita continued.

"What's hard?"

She glanced across the table at her other daughter. "You

and Kristen have always been close. You've always done so many things together. Now your sister is getting married, and you're afraid that you're going to be alone."

She opened her mouth to protest then decided that if that was the excuse her mother was willing to believe, why would she dissuade her?

"I'm going to wash up," Rita said. "If the server comes before I'm back, you can order the chicken Caesar for me."

"And people think I'm the only actress in the family," Kristen commented when their mother had gone.

"Am I really that pathetic?" Kayla wanted to know. "Do you think I'd ever be so devastated over the lack of a man in my life that I'd eat myself into a bigger dress size?"

"You're not pathetic at all," her sister said loyally. "And if Mom had seen you and Trey dancing at the wedding, she'd realize how far off base she is. Then again, if she'd seen you two dancing at the wedding, she might suspect the real reason you're craving French fries."

"She's right about the weight gain, though," Kayla admitted. "I'm up nine pounds already."

"And still wearing your skinny jeans." She lifted the hem of her sweater to show that the button was unfastened and the zipper half-undone.

"Wow—we're going to have to paint 'Goodyear' on you and float you up in the sky pretty soon."

"Sure, you're making jokes," Kayla said. "But at dinner Sunday night, when I said that yes, I would like some dessert, Mom cut me a sliver of lemon meringue pie that was so narrow, I could see through the filling."

"So tell her that you're pregnant," her sister advised. "I bet she'd let you have seconds of dessert if she knew you were eating for two."

"If she didn't drown the pie with her tears of disappointment and shame first. And then, of course, she'd demand to know who the father is—"

"And daddy would get out his shotgun," Kristen interjected.

She shook her head. "Definitely not a good scene."

"But probably inevitable," her sister said. "Which is why you have to tell Trey."

Kayla sighed. "I know."

The server came and they ordered their lunches—Kayla opting for a side salad rather than fries to appease her mother. Kristen chose the same sandwich as her sister but with the fries and gravy that Kayla wanted.

"When are you seeing Trey again?" Kristen asked when the waiter left them alone again.

"I don't know."

"You need to make a plan to see him," her sister insisted. "And you need to *tell him*."

"Tell who what?" Rita asked, returning to her seat at the table.

"I need to, uh, tell Derek that Midnight Shadow was favoring her right foreleg when I moved her out of her stall this morning."

"He won't be happy about that," their mother noted.

"Hopefully it isn't anything serious," Kristen said.

When their meals were delivered, talk shifted back to the wedding. Kayla ate her salad, silently promising the baby that she'd have something fatty and salty later, when she'd escaped from the eagle eye of her mother.

"What did you think of the dresses I tried on?" Kristen asked her sister, as she dragged a thick fry through the puddle of gravy on her plate. "And I want your honest opinion."

Kayla focused on her own plate and stabbed a cherry tomato with her fork. "I think they were all beautiful dresses and you looked stunning in each one."

"That's not very helpful," Kristen chided.

"Well, it's true. It's also true that I don't think any of them was the right dress for you."

"Why not?"

She chewed the tomato. "Because they were all too… designer."

Kristen wrinkled her nose. "What does that even mean?"

"It means that you're trying too hard to look like a Hollywood bride."

"Ryan lived and worked in Hollywood for a lot of years, surrounded by some of the world's most beautiful women," her sister pointed out. "I don't want to disappoint him on our wedding day."

"Think about what you just said," Kayla told her. "Yes, your fiancé was surrounded by beautiful women in Hollywood—but he didn't fall in love until he came to Montana and met *you*. So why would you want to be anything different than the woman he fell in love with?"

"I don't," Kristen said.

"Remember the first dress you looked at—the one you instinctively gravitated toward and then put back on the rack without trying it on because it was too simple?"

"The one with the little cap sleeves and the open back?"

Kayla nodded. "You need to go back and try it on."

"I will," Kristen decided, popping another French fry into her mouth. "Right after we finish lunch."

"How was shopping with your sister and your mother?" Trey asked Kayla, when he called the next morning.

She let out a deep sigh. "It was…an experience."

"Did Kristen find a dress?"

"I think it was about the thirty-fifth one she tried on, but yes, she finally found it."

"Does that mean you're free today?"

"It means I don't have to go shopping," she told him. "But I do have to bake Christmas cookies."

"Okay, what are you doing after that?"

"I'm probably going to be tied up in the kitchen most of the day," she told him.

He paused. "I was really hoping we could spend some time together."

She was hoping for the same thing, especially since she knew that Trey's time in Rust Creek Falls was limited. "Do you want to come over and help me make cookies?"

"I can't believe I'm actually saying this," he noted. "But yes, if that's the only way I can be with you, I do."

"You know where to find me."

"Will I find coffee there, too?"

"There will definitely be coffee," she assured him.

It wasn't until he pulled into the long drive of the Circle D Ranch that he considered the possible awkwardness of the situation if Derek was at the main house. Not that his friend's potential disapproval would have affected his decision to come, but he should have factored him into the equation and he hadn't. He hadn't thought about anything but how much he wanted to see Kayla.

When he got to the house, there was no sign of Derek—or anyone else other than Kayla. "Where is everyone?"

"My parents went to an equipment auction in Missoula, and my brothers are out doing whatever they do around the ranch."

"So no one will interrupt if I kiss you?"

"No one will interrupt," she promised.

He dipped his head toward her. "Mmm…you smell really good."

She laughed softly. "I think it's the cookies."

He nuzzled her throat, making her blood heat and her knees quiver. "No, it's definitely you."

"You smell good, too." She kissed him lightly. "And taste even better."

He drew her closer, kissed her longer and deeper—until the oven timer began to buzz.

Saved by the bell, Kayla thought, embarrassed to realize that she'd momentarily forgotten they were standing in the middle of her mother's kitchen, making out like teenagers.

"You said no one would interrupt," he reminded her.

"Mechanical timers excluded." She moved away from him to slide her hand into an oven mitt and take the pan out of the oven.

While she was doing that, he surveyed the ingredients, bowls and utensils spread out over the counter. "How many cookies do you plan to make?"

She gestured toward the counter. "The list is there."

He read aloud: "Pecan Sandies, Coconut Macaroons, Brownies, Peppermint Fudge, Sugar Cookies, Rocky Road Squares, Snowballs, Peanut Brittle, White Chocolate Chip Cookies with Macadamia Nuts and Dried Cherries." He glanced up. "You don't have a shorter name for that one?"

She shook her head.

"Well, I guess people would at least know what they're getting," he acknowledged. "As opposed to a snowball."

"Snowballs are one of my favorites," she told him. "Chopped dates, nuts and crispy rice cereal rolled in coconut."

"There's no gingerbread on the list."

"Kristen and I baked that last week."

"What are these?" he asked, pointing to a plate of cookies she'd baked earlier.

"Those are the Pecan Sandies."

"Can I try one?"

"Sure," she said.

He bit into the flaky pastry. "Mmm. This is good," he mumbled around a mouthful of cookie. "No wonder so many people put on weight over the holidays with these kinds of goodies to sample."

She froze with the spatula in hand, wondering if he was just making a casual comment or if he'd noticed the extra pounds she was carrying. She was wearing yoga pants and a shapeless top that disguised all of her curves, but especially the one of her belly.

"What can I do to help?" Trey asked. "Because if you don't give me a job, I'll just eat everything you make."

She chided herself for being paranoid and turned her attention back to the task at hand. "You can start by pouring yourself a cup of the coffee you wanted." She indicated the half-full carafe on the warmer. "Sugar is in the bowl above, milk and cream are in the fridge."

"Can I get you some?" he asked.

"No, I'm fine, thanks."

While he doctored his coffee, she measured out flour and sugar and cocoa powder.

"What are you making now?"

"Brownies."

"One of *my* favorites," he told her.

She laughed. "Did you skip breakfast?"

"As if my grandmother would let me," he chided, stealing another cookie.

She put a wooden spoon in his hand and steered him toward a pot on the stove containing the butter and chopped semisweet chocolate she'd measured earlier. She turned the burner on to medium-low. "Just keep stirring gently until the ingredients are melted and blended."

He sipped his coffee from one hand and stirred, as instructed, with the other. "I think I have a talent for this."

"Just so long as you keep your fingers out of it."

"I'll try to resist." He caught her as she moved past him and hauled her back for a quick kiss. "But only the chocolate."

"I'm going to have to send you out of the kitchen if you continue to distract me," she warned him.

"I like kissing you."

She felt her cheeks flush. "Stir."

He resumed stirring.

She had expected that Trey would end up being more of a hindrance than a help, but aside from stealing the occasional kiss at the most unexpected times, his presence really did help move things along quickly. He willingly measured, chopped and mixed as required and without complaint.

Rita called home just after two o'clock to tell Kayla that the auction was over and that they were going for dinner in Missoula and would be home late. It was only then that Kayla realized she hadn't given any thought to dinner—or lunch. She immediately apologized to Trey for not feeding him, which made him laugh, because he'd been steadily sampling the cookies and bars while they worked.

"But you're probably starving," he realized. "You haven't touched any of this."

"I had a brownie," she confessed.

"A whole brownie?"

"It's not that I'm not tempted," she admitted. "But most of this stuff would go straight to my hips."

His gaze slid over her body, slowly, appraisingly. "I don't think you need to worry."

Kayla half wished her mother could have been there to hear what he said, except that she wouldn't have invited him to help her with the baking if her mother had been home.

"But cookies probably aren't a very healthy dinner," he continued. "Do you want to go out to grab a bite?"

She should offer to cook something there so they could sit down and talk, but the truth was, after standing around in the kitchen most of the day, her feet and back were sore, and the idea of sitting down and letting someone else prepare a meal was irresistible. "I do," she decided.

Of course, going out with Trey meant giving up another opportunity to tell him about their baby, because she didn't dare whisper the word *pregnant* within earshot of anyone else in town. She might have control over what appeared in the Ramblings column, but the Rust Creek Falls grapevine had a life of its own.

They went to the Ace in the Hole. The bar wasn't one of Kayla's favorite places, but it did have a decent menu and wasn't usually too busy on a Sunday night.

It wasn't until they were seated in the restaurant that she thought to ask, "Your grandparents weren't expecting you home for dinner?"

"I called them while you were getting changed and told them that I was going out."

She didn't ask if he'd mentioned that he was going out with her—she wasn't sure she wanted to know. Whether or not Melba had deliberately called about the pickles to force her path to cross with Trey's, as he believed, she suspected it would be dangerous to encourage the older woman's matchmaking efforts.

Especially when she was worried enough about getting her own hopes up. Yes, she had to tell Trey about the baby, but she'd thought it might be easier if they knew one another a little better. But as they were getting to know one another, she was letting herself get caught up in the romance of being with him—talking and flirting and kissing. For a girl with extremely limited dating experience, he was a fantasy come to life. A fantasy that she knew would come crashing down around her when she told him that she was pregnant.

And she wasn't ready for that to happen. Not yet.

After their meal, Trey drove Kayla back to the Circle D.

He wasn't anxious to say good-night to her, but he could tell that she was tired. She'd been on her feet in the kitchen all day, having started her baking hours before he showed up, and was obviously ready for bed.

Of course, thinking about Kayla in bed stirred his memories and his blood and made him wish that she didn't still live in her parents' home—or that he wasn't staying with his grandparents.

He'd been back in town a little more than a week—barely nine days—but she'd been on his mind each and every one of those days. No one he knew would believe it if he told them that he'd spent the day in the kitchen with Kayla, but the truth was, he didn't care what they were doing so long as he was with her. And when he couldn't be with her, he was thinking about her.

Now that he knew her a little better, he wondered how he could have been so blind as to overlook her for so many years—even if she was his best friend's little sister. Because she was also a smart and interesting woman with hair as soft as the finest silk, eyes as blue as the Montana sky and a smile that could light up a room. And when she smiled at him, she made him feel like a superhero.

No other woman had ever made him feel that way. No other woman had ever made him feel as good as he felt when he was with her. He loved touching her and holding her and kissing her. In recent years he'd had a few relationships, but for some reason, those had been short on the simple things—like kissing and hand-holding.

He and Kayla had already made love, and he wanted to make love with her again, but for now, he was enjoying the kissing and hand-holding and just being with her.

He was also taking a lot of cold showers.

As enjoyable as it was to spend time with Kayla, she also got him stirred up. But he was determined not to rush into anything. Not this time. He wasn't a teenager anymore—or under the influence of spiked wedding punch—and he was determined to take things slow, to show Kayla that she was worth the time and effort.

Kayla didn't tell Trey that she'd been asked to help out at the elementary school, but when she showed up at the gymnasium at three o'clock, he was there, anyway. Of course, there were a lot of people there. With the pageant scheduled for the following weekend and much work still to do, the teachers had obviously tried to pull in as many extra hands as they could.

Apparently Trey had been asked to contribute his, as he was already hammering a set together, Natalie was working on costumes—and flirting with Gavin Everton, the new gym teacher—while Kayla was put to work painting scenery.

She felt perspiration bead on her face as she stretched to paint stars in the night sky. She was wearing leggings and an oversize flannel shirt, and while the bulky attire did a good job of disguising the extra pounds she was carrying, it also ratcheted up her internal temperature considerably.

She swiped a hand over her brow. "It's warm under these lights."

"Why don't you take off that flannel shirt?" Trey suggested.

"Because I'm only wearing a camisole underneath," Kayla told him.

He grinned. "And the problem?"

She waved her paintbrush at him. "Don't you have to go hammer something?"

He lifted the tool in acknowledgment and returned his attention to the set he was building.

On the pretext of retrieving a box of lace and ribbon, Natalie sidled over to her friend. "How do you resist jumping his bones?" she asked.

"It's not easy," Kayla admitted.

"So why don't you give in and share all the details with your friends who have no romantic prospects and need a vicarious thrill?"

"Because I want what Kristen has with Ryan," she admitted. "A happily-ever-after, not just a holiday fling."

"I want a happily-ever-after someday, too. But in the meantime, I'd settle for a little happy-right-now."

"Is that why you were chatting up the new gym teacher?"

Natalie's gaze shifted to the man in question. "He's cute," she acknowledged. "But not good fling material."

"How can you tell?"

"Residential address."

"What does that mean?"

"He lives in Rust Creek Falls, which means that a casual hookup could—and very likely would—result in awkward encounters after the fact."

"Or maybe a relationship," Kayla suggested.

Natalie shrugged. "Maybe. But the risk might be greater than the reward."

But when Gavin came over to ask Natalie for her help untangling the strings of candy garland that would line the path to the Land of Sweets, she happily walked away with him.

Over the next few hours, many more people came and went, giving a few hours of their time, including Paige Traub, Maggie Crawford, Cecelia Pritchett and Mallory Dalton. Both Paige and Maggie had young children, and as Kayla picked up on little bits and pieces of their conversation, she wished she didn't feel compelled to hide her pregnancy. She wanted to be free to join in their circle and listen to their experiences and advice.

Instead, she was on the outside, alone with her questions and fears. A soon-to-be single mother still afraid to tell even the father of her baby about the baby.

She capped the paint, dropped her brush into the bucket to be washed and wiped her hands on a rag.

Trey must have finished his assigned task, too, because he closed up the toolbox and made his way over to her. "My stomach's telling me that we worked past dinner."

"Your stomach would be right," she confirmed.

"Why don't we head over to the boarding house to see what my grandmother cooked up tonight?"

Kayla brushed her hands down the thighs of her paint-splattered pants and shook her head. "I'm not going anywhere dressed like this."

"I think you look beautiful."

She looked at him skeptically. "I think someone must have hit you in the head with your hammer."

He smiled as he wiped a smear of green paint off her cheek. "Do you really have no idea what you do to me?"

"What do I do to you?" she asked warily.

"You tangle me up in knots inside."

"I'm…sorry?" she said, uncertain how to respond to his admission.

"I don't need you to be sorry," he told her. "I need you to stop taking two steps back every time we take one step forward."

She frowned. "Is that what you think I'm doing?"

He looked pointedly at the floor so she could see that she had—literally—done exactly that.

He stepped forward again.

She forced herself to hold her ground.

"Good." He framed her face in his hands and, despite the presence of several other people still lingering in the gym, lowered his mouth to hers. "That's a start."

Chapter Nine

While Kayla seemed to be resisting Trey's efforts to get closer to her, he also knew she had a hard time saying no to anyone who asked for help. The elementary school production was a case in point. So instead of asking her if she wanted to take a trip into Kalispell to go shopping with him, an invitation that he suspected she would politely decline, he stopped by the ranch the next day and said to her, "I need your help."

Not surprisingly, she responded, "With what?"

"Christmas shopping."

"I'm sure you're perfectly capable of shopping."

"You'd think so," he acknowledged. "But the truth is, I suck at shopping even worse than I do at wrapping."

She managed a smile. "I'm not sure that's possible."

"It is," he insisted. "I never seem to know what to buy, and on the rare occasion that I have a good idea, I end up with the wrong size or color."

"That's why vendors introduced gift receipts."

"We had a deal," he said, reminding her of the bargain he'd extracted from her in exchange for keeping her identity as the Rust Creek Rambler a secret. Not that he would ever have betrayed her confidence, but he wasn't opposed to using the leverage she'd given him to spend more time with her. "And I'll buy you lunch."

She sighed. "You're right—we had a deal. You don't have to bribe me with lunch."

"You'll earn it," he promised, as she followed him out to his truck. "I have a couple of things for my grandparents, but I've just found out that Hadley and Tessa are coming to Rust Creek Falls for the holidays, and I don't have a clue where to start finding something for either of them."

"What about your parents and your brothers—are they coming, too?"

He shook his head. "Not this year."

"Isn't it strange, not being with your own parents for Christmas?"

"Not really," he said. "Because when we were kids, we were always at Grandma and Grandpa's. It would seem stranger to me not to be here."

"I guess that makes sense," she agreed. "Okay, tell me about the cousins you need to shop for."

"They're Claire's older sisters. Both of them live in Bozeman. Hadley is a twenty-nine-year-old veterinarian who never turns a stray away from her door. Tessa is a twenty-seven-year-old graphic designer and movie buff."

Half an hour later, they were at the shopping center. She moved with purpose and though she claimed not to have anything specific in mind, she assured him she would know when she found what she was looking for. Since he honestly didn't have a clue, he was content to let her lead the way.

For Hadley, she found a set of glass coasters with etched

paw prints that somehow managed to be both elegant and fun. For Tessa, she found a book of iconic movie posters that he knew his cousin would love. As they exited the bookstore, he couldn't help but be impressed by her efficiency.

"I bet you're one of those people who has all of her shopping and wrapping done by the first of December, aren't you?" Trey asked her.

"Not the first," she denied. "But I don't believe in leaving things to the last minute, either."

"It's still ten days before Christmas," he pointed out.

"Apparently, we have different opinions of what the last minute is."

"Apparently," he agreed. "So tell me—have you sent your letter to Santa yet?"

She shook her head. "I think the big guy's going to be kept busy enough meeting the demands of those under the age of ten."

"Is that how old you were when you stopped believing in Santa?"

"Who says I stopped believing in Santa?"

His brows lifted.

She shrugged. "Santa made Kristen's wish come true this year."

"Huh?"

So she told him about Ryan riding in the parade as Santa Claus and his subsequent proposal to her sister.

"My grandparents told me that she was engaged, but they didn't tell me how it happened."

"Well, that's how it happened," Kayla said.

"It was pretty quick, don't you think? I mean—they only met in the summer."

She shrugged. "I guess when you know, you know."

He wondered if that was true—if that was the real reason he hadn't stopped thinking about Kayla since the night they spent together. He'd never believed there was one woman who was the right woman for him—why would he want to narrow down his options when there were so many women in the world? But since the summer, he hadn't thought about anyone but Kayla; he hadn't wanted anyone but Kayla.

"Okay, so now that Hadley and Tessa are taken care of—what about Claire?"

"I've got that one covered," he told her. "Grandma and Grandpa have booked a weekend at the Thunder Canyon Resort for Claire and Levi, and I got Claire a gift certificate for the spa."

"She'll love that," Kayla said, sounding surprised by his insight and thoughtfulness.

"That's what my grandmother said when she suggested it."

She laughed, then stopped abruptly in front of the display window of a store called Christmas Memories. She tapped a finger on the glass. "Speaking of your grandmother."

His gaze followed to where she was pointing. "Um… that's a Christmas tree."

She rolled her eyes. "What's *on* the tree?" she prompted.

"Ornaments," he realized.

She nodded, already heading into the store.

There weren't just ornaments displayed on trees but boxes of them stacked high and baskets overflowing. There were classic ornaments and fun ornaments, sports-themed and movie-themed decorations, baubles that lit up or played music—or lit up *and* played music. And there was even a selection of imported mouth-blown glass ornaments.

She held up a delicate clear glass sphere with a gold angel figurine inside. "What do you think?"

"I think I'll be the favorite grandchild this Christmas," he told her, grinning. "She'll love it so much that she'll probably rearrange all of the other ornaments on the tree so that it's hanging front and center."

"I doubt she has that much time on her hands."

"You're right—she'll make my grandfather do it."

Kayla chuckled as he took the ornament to the register to pay for it.

"Now you're all done except for the wrapping," she told him, as they exited the store.

"Oh, yeah." He made a face. "I forgot about the wrapping part."

"Do you have paper? Bows?"

"My grandmother has all of that stuff."

"You can't wrap your grandmother's gift in paper that she bought," Kayla protested.

"Why not?"

"Because you can't."

"That's not a reason."

"Yes, it is," she insisted.

"Okay, so I'll pay for the gift-wrapping service down the hall for her gift and use her paper for the rest."

Kayla shook her head. "You can bring the gifts to the ranch and I'll help you wrap them."

"Really? You'll help me?"

"I'll fold your corners—you're in charge of the tape."

He didn't manage to avoid Derek at the Circle D later that day. When they got back from shopping, Kayla sent him to the kitchen to set up at the table while she went to get her wrapping supplies. His steps faltered when he saw his friend standing at the counter, filling his thermos with coffee from the carafe.

"What are you doing here?" Derek asked, his tone more curious than concerned.

He held up the bags of gifts in his hands. "Kayla offered to help me with my wrapping."

"When did she do that?"

"When we were shopping."

"My sister went shopping with you? How did that come about?"

"I asked her."

"Why?"

"Because I needed some help figuring out what to buy for my cousins." Although that was partly true, the real truth was that he'd used the shopping as an excuse to spend time with her, and he was deliberately tiptoeing around that fact. He didn't want to tiptoe around it—he didn't want to keep his relationship a secret from anyone, especially his best friend. "And because I like her."

Derek frowned. "What do you mean—you *like* her?"

"I mean she's smart and fun and I enjoy spending time with her."

"How much time have you been spending with her?" Kayla's brother wanted to know.

"As much as possible," he admitted.

"I thought you were seeing someone in Thunder Canyon."

"I only said I was seeing someone," Trey pointed out. "You assumed that someone was in Thunder Canyon."

Derek's scowl deepened. "Are you telling me that you're *dating* my sister?"

He nodded.

"Dammit, Trey. I thought we were friends."

"We are friends."

"You can't date a friend's sister—it makes everything awkward."

"I'm sorry."

"Sorry enough to back off?" Derek challenged.

"No," he replied without any hesitation.

"How long has this been going on?"

Trey thought back to the night of the wedding but decided that didn't count—or even if it did, he had no intention of mentioning it to Kayla's brother. "A couple of weeks."

Derek shook his head as he capped his thermos. "I suppose I should be glad you didn't hook up with the blonde that night we were at the bar," he said, and walked out the door.

"What blonde in the bar?"

He winced at the sound of Kayla's voice from behind him. "Heard that, did you?"

"And I'm still waiting for an explanation," she told him.

"I mentioned that I went to the Ace in the Hole with your brother last week," he reminded her.

She nodded.

"Well, there were a couple of girls who invited us to join them," he explained. "Derek went to their table. I went home."

"Why didn't you go to their table?" she asked, sounding—to his surprise—more curious than annoyed.

"Because," he said honestly, "I didn't—I don't—want to be with anyone but you."

Kayla was so confused.

Trey was saying and doing all of the right things to make her believe that he wanted a real relationship with her. He'd even told her brother that they were dating. But he was only in town for the holidays, after which he would be going back to Thunder Canyon, and he hadn't said a word about what would happen between them after that.

Did she want a long-distance relationship? Did long-distance relationships ever work or were they just extended breakups? What were their other options?

If Trey asked, she would move to Thunder Canyon to be with him. She wasn't a schoolgirl with a crush anymore but a woman with a woman's feelings and desires. And she wanted a life with Trey and their baby—the baby he still didn't know anything about.

"That didn't take as long as I thought," Trey said, when she'd affixed a bow to the final gift.

"Doesn't it feel good—to have your shopping and wrapping done?"

"I can think of something that would feel even better," he said, leaning across the table to brush his lips to hers. "Why don't we go down to the barn, saddle up a couple of horses and go for a ride?"

She wasn't sure whether she was relieved or disappointed by his suggestion. "Actually, I have to go into town."

"For what?"

"I've got some things to do at the newspaper office."

"We don't have to go out for very long," Trey said.

"I'm sorry, but I really don't know how much time I'm going to need. I probably should have gone into the office first thing, but I promised to help you."

"I didn't mean to impose on your time," he said, just a little stiffly.

"You didn't," she assured him, reaching across the table to touch his hand. "I *wanted* to help, but now I need to go into town."

She wasn't surprised that he looked disappointed. He was probably accustomed to spending several hours a day on horseback in addition to the several more that he spent training horses at the Thunder Canyon Resort, and he likely missed the exercise and the routine.

"But there's no reason you can't go down to the barn and ask Derek—or Eli—" she added, not certain of the status of things between her youngest brother and his friend "—to give you a mount to saddle up."

"I didn't want to ride as much as I wanted to ride with you," Trey told her.

"I'm sorry," she said again, and she meant it. Not just because she couldn't accept his invitation but because she couldn't tell him the real reason why.

"Okay, we'll do it another time," he said. "For today, why don't I give you a ride into town?"

"Then I'd need a ride back again," she pointed out.

"And I was hoping you wouldn't see through my nefarious plan."

"That was your nefarious plan? Don't you have better things to do than play chauffeur for me?"

"Actually, I don't," he said. "There's nothing I want more than to be with you."

"Then I will accept your offer," she agreed.

It didn't take her very long at all to read and edit the copy for the next edition of the paper, but Kayla lingered in the office to give credence to her claim that it was a major task. She felt guilty about lying to Trey—and she'd panicked when he mentioned riding.

She hadn't been on a horse in almost two months. She'd read a lot of conflicting advice about the safety of riding during pregnancy. Many doctors said a clear and unequivocal no. In Montana, though, where most kids were put on the back of a horse before they started kindergarten, doctors were a little less strict. Kayla's own doctor had assured her that while it was usually safe for a pregnant woman to ride during her first trimester, because the baby was small and adequately protected by the mother's pelvic bone, after twelve weeks, the risks to both mother and child were increased.

Kayla had decided that she wasn't willing to take the risk. She might not have planned to have a baby at this point in her life, but as soon as she became aware of the tiny life growing inside her, she'd been determined to do everything in her power to protect that life. Of course, it was a little awkward to invent new and credible excuses to explain why she wasn't participating in an activity she'd always loved, but the busyness of the holiday season had supplied her with many reasons.

She was sure she would love riding with Trey, because she enjoyed everything they did together. At the same time, it was hard to be with him with such a huge—and growing—secret between them. Contrary to what her sister believed, she *wanted* to tell him about their baby, but she knew that revelation would change everything. She was enjoying the flirting and kissing, and she wanted to bask in the glow of his attention just a little while longer.

Surely there wasn't anything wrong with that—was there?

"Did Grandma run out of coffee?" Trey asked, sitting down across from his grandfather at Daisy's Donuts.

"She wanted me out of the house," Gene said. "Something about a fancy tea for her girls. But what are you doing here?"

"I wasn't invited to the fancy tea for the girls, either."

His grandfather barked out a laugh. "I don't imagine you were—but I was more interested in why you aren't with a certain pretty lady who has been keeping you company of late."

Trey didn't see any point in pretending he didn't know who his grandfather was talking about. "Kayla had some things to do at the newspaper."

"I forgot she worked there," Gene said. "Things getting serious between you two?"

He tried not to squirm. "I don't know."

Gene's bushy white brows lifted. "What the hell kind of response is that?"

"An honest one," Trey told him.

"She's not the type of girl you toy with. She's the type you settle down with."

He shifted uneasily. "I'm not ready to settle down, Grandpa."

"Why not?"

"I'm only twenty-eight years old."

Gene nodded. "You're twenty-eight years old, you've got a good job and a solid future. Why wouldn't you want to add a wife and a family to that picture?"

"Because I like the picture exactly as it is right now."

"Sometimes we don't really know what we want until we've lost it," his grandfather warned.

"And sometimes people rush into things that they later regret," Trey countered. "Like Claire and Levi."

"What do you think they regret?"

"Getting married so young, having a baby so soon."

"Do you really think so?"

He couldn't believe his grandfather had to ask that question. "Claire was barely twenty-two when she got married, and then she had a baby less than a year after that."

"And she's thriving as a wife and mother."

"Was she thriving when she packed up her baby and left her husband?"

"She was frustrated," Gene acknowledged. "Being married isn't always easy, but even though they hit a rough patch, they're still together, aren't they? Not just committed to one another and the vows they exchanged, but actually happy together."

Trey couldn't deny that they seemed happy and devoted to one another and their little girl. But that didn't mean he was eager to head down the same path.

"And I couldn't help but notice that you seem happy with Kayla," his grandfather continued.

"I enjoy being with her," he agreed cautiously.

"What's going to happen when the holidays are over and you go back to Thunder Canyon?"

"I haven't thought that far ahead," he admitted.

"Well, maybe you should, because if you think a girl as pretty and sweet as Kayla Dalton will still be waiting around for you when you finally come back again next summer, you might find yourself in for a nasty surprise."

The possibility made him scowl. "If she finds someone else and wants to be with someone else, then that's her choice, isn't it?"

"It is," Gene agreed. "I just wanted to be sure that you could live with those consequences."

"Besides, she doesn't give the impression of a woman chomping at the bit for marriage."

"Maybe she's not. On the other hand, her twin sister just got engaged and is starting to plan her wedding. That kind of thing tends to make other women think about their own hopes and dreams." Gene pushed his empty cup away and stood up.

"Do you want a refill?" Trey asked.

His grandfather shook his head. "I'm going to head over to the feed store and catch up with the other old folks. You young people exasperate me."

Trey got himself another cup of coffee while he waited for Kayla to text him to say that she was finished at the newspaper. Daisy's seemed to do a pretty steady business throughout the day, and several people stopped by his table to say hi and exchange a few words. But mostly he was left alone, and he found himself thinking about what his grandfather had said.

If you think a girl as pretty and sweet as Kayla Dalton will still be waiting around for you...you might be in for a nasty surprise.

Gene was probably right. There wasn't any shortage of single men in Rust Creek Falls, and just because Kayla hadn't dated many of them in the past didn't mean that couldn't change. As a result of her naturally shy demeanor, she'd been overlooked by a lot of guys, but since he'd been spending time with her, he'd noticed the speculative looks she'd been getting from other cowboys. He suspected several of them were just waiting for Trey to go back to Thunder Canyon so they could make a move—and the thought of another man making a move on Kayla didn't sit well with him.

He'd never been the jealous type, but he hadn't exactly been thrilled to see Kayla hug some guy the night they were talking outside the community center. She'd introduced the guy as Dawson Landry and told Trey he'd worked in advertising at the *Gazette* before he moved to a bigger paper in Billings. Dawson then told her that he'd recently moved back to Rust Creek Falls and the *Gazette* because he realized he wasn't cut out for life in the big city.

It was a simple and indisputable fact that after his holidays were over, Trey would go back to Thunder Canyon. He had a job and a life there, and he was happy with both. But he was happier when he was with Kayla. And when he was gone, Dawson would still be around.

The realization made him uneasy. He'd meant what he'd said to his grandfather—there were a lot of things he wanted to see and do before he tied himself down. So why did the prospect of being tied to Kayla seem more intriguing than disconcerting?

RUST CREEK RAMBLINGS: MISSING IN ACTION...
OR GETTING SOME ACTION?
Architect Jonah Dalton and artist Vanessa Brent both seemed intent on putting down roots in this town when they married last year. But the happy couple, who lives in the stunning house built by Jonah himself on the Triple D Ranch, has dropped out of sight in recent days, fueling speculation about their whereabouts. Have they slipped out of town for a pre-holiday getaway? Or are they sticking closer to home and family—and working toward expanding their own? Only time will tell…unless the Rambler tells it first!

Chapter Ten

The Candlelight Walk was an event to which all the residents of Rust Creek Falls were invited, and most enjoyed taking part in at least some aspect of it. At one end of Main Street, members of city council distributed lighted candles that were then carried in a processional to the other end where a bonfire would be lit, refreshments served and carols sung.

"I don't remember this," Trey admitted as he walked beside Kayla, the flicker of hundreds of candles illuminating the dark night with a warm glow that moved slowly down the street toward the park.

"It's a fairly new Rust Creek Falls tradition," Kayla told him.

His brows lifted. "Isn't new tradition an oxymoron?"

"I guess it is," she agreed. "Maybe it would be more accurate to say it's a recent ceremonial event that the townspeople have embraced."

"The people of this town find more excuses to get together than anyone I've ever known."

She smiled as she looked around the crowd, recognizing so many familiar faces. "That's probably true. The flood was an eye-opener for all of us, a reminder that everything we take for granted can be taken away. Even those whose homes were spared weren't immune to the effects on the community. As a result, it brought everyone closer together."

He looked around, too, and saw Shane and Gianna heading in their direction. He lifted a hand to wave them over.

"I swear, Gianna looks more pregnant every time I see her," he commented to Kayla. His friend's wife was hugely pregnant—her baby bump plainly evident even beneath the heavy coat she wore.

"When is she due?"

"I have no idea."

"Don't you and Shane work together at the resort?"

"Sure, but I'm in the stables and he's in the kitchen, and guys don't talk about stuff like that."

She rolled her eyes as his friends drew nearer.

"I didn't realize you were still in town," Trey said. "Are you staying for Christmas?"

"We are," Shane confirmed. "With both my sister and brother here now, it seemed the easiest way to get the whole family together for the holidays. Even my parents are coming—they're flying in on the twenty-second and staying at Maverick Manor."

They talked some more about holiday plans, with Gianna admitting that she was already more excited about *next* Christmas, when they would be celebrating the occasion with their baby.

"Staying with Maggie and Jesse and witnessing first-hand the havoc a child can wreak, I'm not quite so eager," Shane admitted.

"Well, it's not as if you can change your mind now," his wife pointed out. Then, to Trey and Kayla. "Madeline has made both of us realize that you can't learn parenting from a book. No matter how much you think you know, a child will quickly prove you wrong."

"Of course, the child in question is my sister's daughter," Shane interjected. "Which might explain a lot."

Kayla smiled at that.

"You guys are going to be fabulous parents," Trey said.

"Do you think so?" Gianna asked, obviously seeking reassurance.

"Of course," he agreed.

"We're both so afraid that we're going to screw something up," she admitted.

"We're going to screw a lot of things up," Shane said. "We just have to hope that our child makes it to adulthood relatively unscathed."

His wife shook her head. "And he wonders why I worry."

"Right now I'm worried about getting you back to the house and off your feet."

"As if my belly wasn't big enough, my ankles are swelling, too," Gianna explained.

Kayla and Trey exchanged good-nights with the other couple, then moved away in the opposite direction.

"Are you okay?" Trey asked. "You seemed to get quiet all of a sudden."

"I was just thinking about Gianna and Shane," she told him.

"What about them?"

"Your assurance that they're going to be fabulous parents," she admitted. "Not that I disagree—I guess I'm just wondering how you can be so sure, how anyone can know how they'll deal with parenthood before they're actually faced with the reality of it."

"Maybe no one can know for sure, but the odds are in their favor because they love one another and their unborn baby."

She nodded, envying the other couple that. She agreed that their commitment and support were important factors in parenting—and wished that she could count on Trey for the same. Of course, she couldn't expect him to support her through the pregnancy and childbirth when he still didn't know that she was pregnant. "They're certainly excited about impending parenthood, notwithstanding the challenges," she noted.

"They've been married two and a half years and are ready to enter the next stage of their life together."

"Could you ever imagine yourself as excited about becoming a father as Shane is?" she asked, striving to keep her tone light and casual.

Trey's steps faltered anyway. "What kind of a question is that?"

She shrugged. "I'm just wondering whether you've ever thought about having kids of your own."

"Well, sure," he finally said. "Someday."

"Someday?"

"There's a lot I want to do before I'm hog-tied by the responsibilities of marriage and babies."

Hog-tied?

Kayla stopped in the middle of the street and turned to look at him. "Is that how you view a family—as something that ties you down and limits your opportunities?"

"I don't mean it as if it's a bad thing," he explained. "It's just not something I'm ready for right now. Especially when I look at my parents—married thirty-two years with five kids born within the first seven years of their marriage. No, I'm definitely not in any rush to go down that same path."

She nodded, pretending to understand, but inside she felt as if her fledgling hopes—and her fragile heart—had been crushed like a candy cane beneath the heel of his boot. There was no way she could be with a man who would feel tied down by her and their baby—no way she could even tell him about their baby now.

She'd had such high hopes for their relationship a few hours earlier. While they'd walked through the town, hand in hand, she'd let herself dream that they would always be together. When she saw Nate Crawford with Noelle perched on his shoulders, she'd imagined that would be Trey with their baby in a couple of years. But now that she knew how he really felt about the prospect of fatherhood, she knew she had to end their relationship before she got in any deeper.

"It's starting to snow," she noted. "Which means it's time for me to be heading home."

"It's only a few flakes," he pointed out. "And we haven't even roasted marshmallows on the bonfire yet."

"A few flakes is all it takes for my mother to worry."

"Well, we don't want that to happen," he said, guiding her to his truck.

She felt his hand on her back, even through the thick coat she wore, and felt tears sting her eyes as she accepted she would never feel his hands on her again. Whatever fantasies she'd spun about living happily-ever-after with this man and their baby weren't ever going to be.

He helped her up onto the passenger seat and she murmured her thanks.

"Are you sure everything's okay?" he asked her.

"I'm sure," she said. "I'm just really tired." And she was—not just physically but emotionally exhausted. Not eager to make any more conversation, she fiddled with the radio until she found a station playing Christmas music, then settled back in her seat, concentrating on the song and holding back the tears that burned her eyes.

Kayla jolted when the door opened and a blast of cold air slapped her face. "What—"

"You're home," Trey told her.

She blinked. "Did I fall asleep?"

"You did," he confirmed.

"I'm sorry."

"I should apologize to you for keeping you out past your bedtime."

She managed a wan smile. "It isn't really that late," she acknowledged. "I've just had so much on my mind—so many things still to be done before Christmas—that I probably haven't been getting enough sleep."

"Then I should let you get inside to bed," he said.

She nodded. "Thanks for the ride."

He didn't take the hint. Instead, he took her arm and guided her to the front door. "Will I see you tomorrow?"

"I don't know," she hedged, aware that she needed to start putting space between them. A lot of space. Three hundred miles would be a good start, but she knew that wouldn't happen until after Christmas.

And right now, Trey seemed more focused on eliminating the space between them. "I'll call you in the morning and we'll figure it out," he said.

Then he leaned in to kiss her, but before his lips touched hers, the porch light clicked on. He pulled back just as Rita Dalton poked her head out the front door.

"What are you two doing outside in this cold weather?" she chided. "Why don't you come on in for some of the hot chocolate I just took off the stove?"

"I'm sure Trey is anxious to get back to town before the snow gets any worse," Kayla told her mom.

"It's just a few flakes," he said again.

Rita smiled at him and stepped away from the door so that they could enter.

"It's so nice that you're here to spend the holidays with Melba and Gene," Rita commented to Trey, as she busied herself pouring the steaming liquid into mugs.

"There's nowhere I'd rather be," he admitted. "And spending time with Kayla has been an added bonus on this trip."

"I know she's been enjoying your company," Rita said. "Her happy glow has brightened up the whole house these past few days."

Kayla kept her gaze focused on the mug she held between her hands and resisted the urge to bang her head against the table.

Could her mother be any more obvious in her matchmaking efforts? And how would she react if Kayla told her that *happy glow* wasn't a consequence of Trey's company but his baby in her belly? Would her mother think the man sitting at her table and drinking hot chocolate was so wonderful if she knew he'd knocked up her daughter?

"Do you have any specific plans for tomorrow?" Rita asked him, setting a plate of cookies on the table.

"Not yet," Trey said, reaching over to touch Kayla's hand. "Although I was hoping to talk Kayla into taking a drive into Kalispell with me so we could go ice skating in Woodland Park."

"Oh, that sounds like fun—doesn't it, Kayla?"

"It does," she agreed. "But I've got to put the finishing touches on the sets for the elementary school holiday pageant tomorrow."

"But you've been working on those sets all week," her mother pointed out. "Surely you can take a day off."

"Actually, I can't. The pageant is tomorrow night."

"Well, maybe we can go skating the day after," Trey suggested.

"Maybe," she agreed.

Rita frowned at her daughter's noncommittal response before she turned her attention back to their guest. "Tell me about your plans for Christmas—is your grandmother cooking a big meal with all the trimmings?"

"Of course."

"She usually serves it around midday, doesn't she?"

"Everyone is expected to be seated at the table at one o'clock sharp," he confirmed.

"We don't eat until six," Rita said. "If you wanted to join us later in the day for another meal."

Kayla felt as if she was watching a train wreck in slow motion—she could see what was happening, but she was powerless to stop it. Not an hour after she'd vowed to put distance between herself and Trey as the first step toward ending their relationship, her mother had invited him to Christmas dinner. On the other hand, spending Christmas with a girlfriend's family was probably too much of a commitment, so she felt fairly confident that he would decline the invitation.

But just in case, she decided to nudge him in that direction. "Mom, you're talking about Christmas Day," she pointed out. "I'm sure whatever plans Trey has with his family will keep him busy throughout the afternoon."

"And if they don't, I'm just letting him know that he's welcome to come here," Rita replied.

"Thank you, Mrs. Dalton. I appreciate the invitation and I'll see what I can do."

"Well, I'll leave you two to finish your beverages," she said.

"Thanks for the hot chocolate and the cookies," Trey said.

Rita beamed at him. "Anytime, Trey."

The next night Kayla attended the holiday pageant at the elementary school. The night after that she was busy helping Nina and Natalie assign and wrap gifts from the Tree of Hope for the area's needy families. It was the day after that—Saturday—while Kayla was hiding out in her room after breakfast that her sister came in.

Kristen had been so busy with the theater and wedding plans that she hadn't been at the ranch very much over the past couple of weeks.

"Trey came to see me yesterday," Kristen announced without preamble.

Kayla's head whipped around in response to her sister's casual announcement. "Why?"

"Because he's trying to plan a special surprise for you and wanted my help."

"What kind of surprise?" she asked, both curious and wary.

Kristen rolled her eyes. "If I told you, it wouldn't be a surprise, would it?"

"Then why did you mention it?"

"Because he mentioned to me that you've been so busy he hasn't seen you since the night of the Candlelight Walk, and I know for a fact that you haven't been any busier than usual and certainly not too busy to spend time with Trey if you wanted to spend time with Trey."

"Okay, so I don't want to spend time with Trey," she acknowledged.

"I don't understand," Kristen said. "Everyone can see

that the man is head over heels for you, and I know how you feel about him, so why are you avoiding him now?"

"Because I finally realized that we want different things."

"What different things?"

"A family, for starters."

Kristen frowned.

So Kayla found herself telling her sister the whole story of that night, from the candle-lighting to their encounter with Gianna and Shane and Trey's subsequent denouncement of marriage and everything that went along with it.

"Wait a minute," Kristen said. "Are you telling me that Trey still doesn't know about the baby?"

"How could I tell him?"

"How could you not?" her sister demanded. "Kayla, the man has been spending every possible minute with you over the past couple of weeks—*everyone* knows he has feelings for you. Except, apparently, the Rust Creek Rambler."

Kayla's eyes filled with tears. "Even if he does have feelings for me, how can I be with a man who doesn't want our baby?"

Her sister was silent for a long moment. "You don't know that he doesn't want your baby," she finally said. "You're making an assumption based on his response to a vague and seemingly hypothetic question. You can't hold that response against him."

"He compared being married to being hog-tied."

"He's still the father of your baby." Kristen's tone was implacable. "And even if you think you can get through the holidays without him finding out about your pregnancy, what's going to happen afterward? What are you going to tell people when they want to know the identity of your baby's father? And even if you refuse to name him, what's going to happen when Trey comes back to Rust Creek Falls and sees you with a baby? Do you really believe he won't immediately know the child is his?"

"Maybe he won't," Kayla argued, albeit weakly. "Maybe he'll want to think it's someone else's baby so that he doesn't have to be tied down by the responsibilities of parenthood."

"There's no maybe," Kristen said. "Because you're going to tell him."

Kayla sighed, but she knew her sister was right.

And maybe her dreams had been crushed, but at least now she had no expectations. Trey had made his feelings clear, and she was going to tell him about the baby without any illusions that he would want to be part of their life, and she would make it clear that she didn't want or expect anything from him. She was simply doing him the courtesy of telling him that she was pregnant.

She was admittedly a little late with that courtesy, but she would tell him.

"Tonight?" Kristen prompted.

"I can't tonight," Kayla said. "Russell called this morning. He's down with the flu and asked me to fill in for him at the theater this afternoon."

"Then tomorrow," her sister said firmly.

"Tomorrow," she agreed.

But when the curtain fell after the matinee, Kayla found Trey waiting for her backstage, and her heart gave a jolt—of surprise and longing. And when he smiled at her, her knees went weak.

Despite what she'd said to her sister about their wanting different things, she couldn't deny that she still wanted Trey. She managed to smile back, though her stomach was a tangle of nerves and knots.

"What brings you to the Kalispell Theater?"

"I decided to take your advice and check out the play," he told her.

"What did you think?"

"I was impressed. I didn't expect a small theater production to be so good."

"The actors are all spectacular," Kayla agreed. "But Belle steals the show."

Trey chuckled. "Your sister does have a flair for the dramatic."

"Speaking of my sister, I'm supposed to meet her outside her dressing room. She's waiting to give me a ride home," she explained.

"Actually, she's not—Kristen knows that I'm here to kidnap you."

"Kidnap me?"

"Well, I'm not going to throw you over my shoulder and carry you off against your will, but I asked Kristen to help me figure out a way to spend some time with you, and this was the plan we came up with."

The *surprise* that her sister hadn't given her any details—or warning—about. "Are you going to tell me anything else about this plan?"

"You don't like surprises?" he guessed.

"I guess that would depend on the surprise."

"How does a romantic dinner and a luxury suite at a local B and B sound?"

"It sounds like you've thought of everything—except what I'm going to tell my parents about where I am."

"They think you're spending the night at your sister's place," he told her, taking her hand. "I just wanted us to have some time together—just the two of us—away from all of our well-meaning but nosy family and friends in Rust Creek Falls."

"It's a good plan," she said and resigned herself to the

fact that her promise to tell him about their baby *tomorrow* had been bumped forward to *tonight*.

Trey was having a hard time reading Kayla.

She was going through the motions, but her attention seemed to be a million miles away. The restaurant he took her to for dinner had been highly recommended for both its menu and ambience. The lighting was low, the music soft and the service impeccable. His meal was delicious, and Kayla assured him that hers was, too, but she pushed more food around on her plate than she ate, and although she responded appropriately, she didn't attempt to initiate any conversation.

Needless to say, by the time he pulled into the driveway of the bed-and-breakfast, he was certain that he'd made a mistake—he just wasn't sure where. Was it the surprise aspect that she objected to? Would she have preferred to be involved in the planning? Or was she worried about his expectations? Did she think that because he'd paid for the room and dinner he'd expect her to get naked to show her appreciation?

He suspected it might be the latter when he opened the door to their suite and she caught sight of the enormous bed that dominated the room. And yeah, when he'd made the reservation he'd hoped they might share that bed, but he knew there was a sofa bed in the sitting area if Kayla decided otherwise.

He guided her past the bed to the sofa and sat her down. "What's going on, Kayla? What did I do wrong? Because it seems obvious to me that there *was* something."

"You didn't do anything wrong," she said. "Not really. It's just that… I've come to the realization that we want different things."

"What are you talking about?"

"I want what Shane and Gianna have," she told him. "I want to fall in love and get married and have a family."

"So? I want those things, too."

"'Someday,'" she remembered.

"And when I think of that someday, I think I'd like it to be with you."

That announcement gave her pause. "You do?"

"I do," he assured her. "I'll admit the whole conversation threw me for a loop, and it's probably going to be a while before I'm ready for marriage and babies, but please don't give up on me—on us."

Then he held out his hand to her, and Kayla gasped when she saw her teardrop earring sparkling against his palm.

"Ohmygod. I can't believe..." Her words trailed off as her eyes filled with tears. "I thought I'd lost it forever."

"I've been carrying it around with me since July," he told her. "Waiting for the right time to give it back. I should have returned it sooner. I did plan to give it back to you the next day, but you seemed so embarrassed by what happened between us."

He'd been carrying it around with him? Why? Was it possible that night had meant as much to him as it had to her? Or was she reading too much into his words because she wanted his gesture to mean more than it did?

"I was embarrassed because I thought you didn't remember," she admitted.

"I was fuzzy on the details," he acknowledged. "But I knew it was your earring and how it ended up in my bed."

She lifted the delicate piece from his palm. "Thank you. It's not worth a lot of money, but it used to be my grandmother's and it means a lot to me."

"I have to admit, when I found it in my sheets, I felt a little bit like Prince Charming after the clock struck midnight—except I had an earring instead of a shoe."

She knew that accessories weren't the only difference between her life and that of the fairy-tale princess, and yet his claim of wanting a future with her gave her hope that her story with Trey might also have a happy ending. But she knew that wasn't possible until she was honest with him about what had happened at the beginning.

"Will you give me another chance?" he asked her.

She looked around the room, noting the flowers and candles, the bottle of champagne chilling on ice. He wouldn't have gone to so much effort if he didn't think she was worth it, but would he still think so if he knew the truth she'd kept from him for so long?

"There's something I have to tell you—something that's going to change everything."

"What are you talking about?"

"I should have told you a long time ago—I wanted to tell you. But I was afraid that it would change how you felt—"

"Nothing is going to change how I feel about you," Trey said. "I promise you that."

She shook her head. "Don't. Please, don't make promises you can't keep."

"I don't know what's going on here, but you're starting to scare me," he admitted. "So whatever it is, I wish you'd just tell me so that we can deal with it."

She buried her face in her hands. "I'm messing this up."

"What's wrong, Kayla? Are you—" He hesitated, as if he didn't even want to ask the question. "Are you sick?"

"No, I'm not sick." The words were little more than a whisper as she lifted tear-drenched eyes to his. "I'm pregnant."

Chapter Eleven

Trey took a step back. Actually, it was more of a stumble than a step, which probably wasn't surprising, considering that he felt as if the rug had been pulled right out from beneath him.

"What did you say?"

"I'm pregnant."

His gaze dropped to her stomach, hidden behind yet another oversize sweater. She smoothed a hand over the fabric to show the slight but unmistakable curve of her belly.

Holy crap—she really was pregnant.

His knees buckled, and he dropped to the edge of the sofa.

"When…how—" He shook his head at the ridiculousness of the latter question. "Is it…mine?"

She nodded.

His stomach tightened painfully. "So you're—" he mentally counted back to the wedding "—five months along?"

She nodded again.

"Five months," he said again, shock slowly giving way to fury. "You've kept your pregnancy from me for *five months*?"

Kayla winced at the anger in his tone. "I didn't realize I was pregnant until the beginning of October."

"October," he echoed. "So you've only kept it a secret for the past three months?"

"I haven't told anyone because I was waiting to tell you first."

"Really? Because I think if you wanted to tell me, you would have picked up a phone and called."

Her big blue eyes filled with tears. "You don't understand," she said, her tremulous voice imploring him to try.

"You're damn right I don't understand. If the baby you're carrying really is mine—"

She gasped. "How could you doubt it's true?"

"How can I doubt it?" he demanded incredulously. "How can I believe anything you've told me when you just admitted that you've deliberately kept your pregnancy a secret for three months?"

She lifted her chin. "You have every right to be angry, but you should know me well enough to know that I wouldn't lie about my baby's paternity. And I wouldn't have spent the past couple of weeks agonizing over how to tell you if the baby wasn't yours."

"I *am* angry," he confirmed. "And obviously I don't know you as well as I thought because I never would have imagined you'd keep something like this from me."

"Please, Trey," she said. "Listen to me. Give me a chance to explain."

"I'm listening," he said, but his tone was grim, and his attention was focused on the screen of the cell phone that he'd pulled out of his pocket. His thumbs moved rapidly over the keypad, then he skimmed through the information that appeared. "We can be married right away, without any waiting period required."

Her eyes widened. "You want to get married?"

"Under the circumstances, I can't see that what I want is relevant right now," he said.

"You don't *want* to get married," she realized, her gaze dropping away. "You're only trying to do the right thing."

"Of course I'm trying to do the right thing." He looked at his phone again. "Come on—there's an office in Kalispell where we can get a license."

"It's Saturday night, Trey."

"So?"

"So I doubt very much if the county clerk's office is open right now."

He scowled. "I didn't think about that."

"And even if it was open…I'm not going to marry you."

"Why not?" he demanded.

"Because it's not what you want."

"None of this is what I want," he admitted. "But we've only got a few more months until the baby is born, and there's no way any child of mine is going to be illegitimate."

"Illegitimate is only a label," she pointed out.

"And not a label I want applied to my child."

"I'm not going to marry you, Trey."

Something in her quiet but firm tone compelled him to look at her. The stubborn set of her shoulders and defiant tilt of her chin warned him that she was ready to battle over this, although he didn't understand why. "You don't have a choice in the matter."

"Of course I do," she countered. "You can't force me to marry you."

"Maybe I can't, but I'm willing to bet your father—and your brothers—can and will."

At that, some of her defiance faded, but she held firm. "They would probably encourage a legal union, under the circumstances," she acknowledged. "But they're hardly going to demand a shotgun wedding if it's not what I want."

"You're saying you don't want to marry me?"

Her gaze slid away, her eyes filling with fresh tears. "I don't want to marry you—not like this."

The words were like physical blows that left him reeling. He didn't understand why she was being so unreasonable. She was carrying his child, but she didn't want to marry him? Why the hell not? What had he done that she would deprive him of the opportunity to be a father to his child?

And how could he change her mind? Because he had no intention of accepting her decision as final. But he also knew that he couldn't talk to her about this anymore right now. There was no way they could have a rational conversation about anything when his emotions were so raw.

He turned blindly toward the door.

"Where are you going?"

"I don't know," he admitted.

"Please, Trey. Let's sit down and talk about this."

He shook his head, his fingers curling around the doorknob. "I can't talk right now. I need some time to try to get my head around this."

And then he was gone, and Kayla was alone.

She sank down onto the sofa, her heart aching, and put a hand on the curve of her belly. "I'm sorry, baby, but I guess it's just going to be you and me."

She wasn't really surprised. She'd always expected it would be like this. From the moment she'd realized she was pregnant, she'd anticipated that she would be on her own—a single mother raising her child alone.

Over the past couple of weeks, she'd let herself imagine that things could be different. Spending time with Trey, she'd got caught up in the fantasy, believing that they were a couple and, with their baby, could be a family.

Except that wasn't what he wanted. Not really. But he had asked her to marry him—and for one brief shining moment, the dream had been within her grasp.

And she'd let it slip through her fingers.

She heard the sound of his boots pounding on the steps, fading away as he moved farther away from her.

Would he have stayed if she'd agreed to marry him?

It was what she wanted, more than anything, to marry the man she loved, the father of her child. But she'd meant what she said—she couldn't do it. Not like this. Not because he was feeling responsible and trapped. Not without knowing that he loved her, too.

And right now she was pretty sure he hated her.

But she couldn't let him storm off with so much still unresolved between them. She understood that he needed time, that he needed to think. But she suspected that if she let him go now, she could lose him forever. No—it would be better for them to talk this through. It was her fault that they hadn't done so before now, but she wasn't willing to put off their conversation any longer.

She pushed herself off the sofa and turned quickly toward the door, determined to go after him.

But she'd barely risen to her feet when the room started to spin, then the floor rushed up to meet her.

Trey was beyond angry. He was thoroughly and sincerely pissed off—possibly at himself as much as at Kayla.

He felt like a complete idiot.

Pregnant.

Since *July.*

And she hadn't said a single word to him.

Not. One. Single. Word.

Worse—he'd been completely and frustratingly oblivious. Despite all the time he'd spent with her over the past few weeks, despite the numerous times he'd kissed her and the countless times he'd held her, he hadn't had a clue.

Her assurance that no one knew about her pregnancy didn't make him feel any less like an idiot. He should have wondered about her sudden preference for baggy clothes, her unwillingness to go horseback riding with him and her determination to keep him at a physical distance. But he hadn't, and the revelation of her pregnancy had completely blindsided him.

How was he going to share the happy news with his family? If it was, indeed, happy news. *A baby.* His head was still reeling, his mind trying to grasp not just the words but what they meant to him, to his life.

He yanked the steering wheel and pulled over to the side of the road. *Christ.* He was going to be a father. Him. And he was so completely unprepared for this his hands were shaking and his heart was pounding.

Have you ever thought about having kids?

Had it only been three days ago that she'd asked him that question, after they'd seen Shane and Gianna in town after the Candlelight Walk? At the time, he'd thought the question was out of the blue—now he knew differently. She'd been trying to figure out his feelings, anticipate his reaction to the news that he was going to be a father.

And what had he said? How had he responded to her question about whether he wanted to have kids? "Someday," he'd acknowledged. A lackluster response that he'd immediately followed with, "There's a lot I want to do before I'm hog-tied by the responsibilities of marriage and babies."

He dropped his head against the steering wheel.

He'd actually compared being married to being hog-tied—no wonder she hadn't replied with an announcement of her pregnancy and confetti in the air. He couldn't have screwed things up any worse if he'd actually tried.

And what was he supposed to do now?

He had no clue.

He was surprised by the sudden urge to want to talk to his father. Maybe that was normal for a man who'd just learned he was going to be a father himself, but he couldn't begin to imagine how that conversation might proceed. No doubt his father would be completely stunned—although perhaps not so much by the news of his impending fatherhood as the identity of the mommy-to-be. Because who would believe that sweet, shy Kayla Dalton had gotten naked with serial dater Trey Strickland?

When he thought about it, even he continued to be surprised by the events of that night. And especially the repercussions. Because one of his first clues that they'd done the deed was the condom wrapper he'd discovered on the floor beside the bed the next morning. Obviously they'd taken precautions to prevent exactly this scenario, and yet, it had happened. Condom companies advertised their product as ninety-eight percent effective, but the baby Kayla was now carrying proved that they'd beaten those odds.

Unless she was taking advantage of his memory lapse from that night to make him think—

No. As frustrated and angry and hurt as he was—and despite his own question to her—he knew that Kayla wouldn't lie about something like that. There was no doubt that she was pregnant or that it was his baby. She wouldn't have agonized over how and when to tell him if she was perpetrating some elaborate ruse.

She was pregnant.

More than five months pregnant.

With his child.

Nope—it didn't get any easier thinking it the second, third or even the tenth time, and he wasn't sure he'd be able to say it aloud to anyone else, especially his father. Would his parents be disappointed in him? He was sure they would accept and love their grandchild, but he didn't think they'd be particularly proud of his actions. Not in July and not now.

They would definitely expect him to do the right thing by his child—which meant marrying the child's mother. Surprisingly, the prospect of marriage didn't scare him half as much as impending fatherhood. But he knew Kayla was scared, too, and he realized that it really didn't matter who had said or done what on the Fourth of July or even in the time that had passed since then. What mattered was what they were going to do now—and they needed to figure that out together.

Now that he'd had a little bit of time to get his heart rate down to something approximating normal, he could acknowledge how difficult it must have been for her to face him and tell him that their impulsive actions that night had resulted in a pregnancy. Especially after he'd told her that he wasn't eager to be a father.

But was it really fair for her to judge him on a response he'd given when he'd assumed she was speaking hypothetically? Because the idea of a baby, without any context, would probably scare the hell out of any guy. Not that a real child was any less terrifying than a hypothetical one, but the idea of having a child with the woman he loved—because over the past couple of weeks, he'd gradually come to accept that he did love Kayla—was almost as exciting as it was terrifying.

Maybe he'd been a little high-handed in his assertion

that they needed to get married, but he did *want* to marry her. He *wanted* to be a father to their child.

Okay—there. He didn't feel like the vise around his chest was tightening. In fact, he could almost breathe again.

His first glimpse of that subtle curve beneath her sweater had thrown him for a loop, but the ability of the female body to grow and nurture another human being was amazing. And the realization that Kayla was carrying *his* baby was both awesome and humbling.

He wondered how big the baby was now, whether she could feel it moving. Would he be able to feel it kicking inside her? Suddenly, he wanted to.

He thought about his friend, Shane, how excited he was about his baby and how he was always touching his wife's swollen belly. Trey had been happy because his friend was happy, but he didn't really get it. Now—barely an hour after he'd learned that he was going to be a father—he finally did.

Gianna was due to give birth in early February which—Trey did a quick count on his fingers—was only a few months before what he estimated was Kayla's due date. It would be kind of cool for their kids to grow up together—except that might not happen if he wasn't able to convince Kayla to marry him.

Obviously, they still had a lot of details to work out. She had a home and a job in Rust Creek Falls, and he lived and worked in Thunder Canyon. If they were going to raise this child together—and he refused to consider any other possibility—they needed to be together.

The light snow that had been falling when he left the bed-and-breakfast had changed—the flakes were coming heavier and faster now, but he wasn't concerned. He had all-wheel drive and snow tires on his truck. What he didn't have was any particular destination in mind, so when he turned onto a street filled with shops, he decided to park and walk for a while.

He tucked his chin in the collar of his jacket and walked with his head down. The wind was sharp and cold but he didn't really notice—everything inside him felt numb. At the end of the block, he found himself standing outside a jewelry store, the front window display highlighting a selection of engagement rings.

He impulsively opened the door and stepped inside.

Apparently he wasn't the only one who had decided to ignore the inclement weather. There was a man about his own age looking at bangle-style bracelets, a woman browsing a selection of watches and an older gentleman perusing engagement rings with a much younger woman.

He found what he was looking for almost immediately. The vintage-style was similar to the earrings she'd been wearing the night of the wedding, and he knew the delicate design crusted with diamonds would suit her. The clerk, visibly pleased with the quick sale, wished him a Merry Christmas and happy engagement—Trey wasn't counting on either but he was going to give both his best effort.

The weight of the ring was heavy in his pocket as he considered how and when to propose to her again. He thought she would appreciate a traditional proposal, despite the fact—or maybe because—nothing else about their relationship had been traditional. From their first kiss at Braden and Jennifer's wedding, they'd followed their own timetable. They'd fallen into bed together before they'd even gone out on a date, and now she was pregnant and showed no indication of wanting to marry him. But he was determined to change her mind on that account.

He had to brush a couple of inches of snow off his windshield before he could pull out onto the road, which was also covered with snow. The driving wasn't difficult but it was slow, and he was eager to get back to the inn, back to Kayla.

He was ready to talk to her now, eager to tell her that he was happy about their baby. He was still scared, but he was excited, too, and he wanted to share all of his thoughts and feelings with her.

But when he got back to the bed-and-breakfast, she wasn't there.

He tried calling her cell, but there was no answer. He didn't know where she could have gone—she didn't have a vehicle. And he couldn't imagine that she would have ventured outside to go for a walk in this weather. He went back downstairs, to check with Jack and Eden Caffrey, the owners of the inn. It was then that he found their note.

Kayla had a little bit of a fainting spell, so we took her to the hospital to be checked out.

Now his heart was racing for a completely different reason.

"I really am fine," Kayla told Eden, who had been hovering over her since she found her guest sprawled on the floor of her third-floor guest room.

She'd tried to resist the woman's efforts to get her to go to the hospital, because she really did feel fine, but in the end, worry about her baby won out. Jack had driven the car while Eden sat in the back with Kayla, just to be sure everything was okay. And except for a few minutes while the doctor performed his exam and then to get Kayla a snack from the cafeteria, Eden had not left her side. Jack was there, too, but he was tucked into a chair in the corner, working in a crossword puzzle book he'd brought in from the car.

She glanced from Eden's worried face to the doctor's calm facade. "Please, Dr. Gaynor, tell them that I'm fine."

"She's fine." Her ob-gyn—who had conveniently been making rounds when Kayla was brought in to the hospital—echoed the words dutifully.

"And she can go home now," Kayla prompted hopefully.

The doctor smiled as she shook her head. "I'd prefer to keep an eye on you a little bit longer, just to ensure the slight cramping you experienced earlier has truly subsided."

She sighed as she turned her attention back to Eden. "I know you must be anxious to get back. Please don't feel as if you have to stay here with me. I can catch a cab back to the inn when the doctor finally okays it."

"We run a bed-and-breakfast," Eden reminded her. "And there are a lot of hours until breakfast."

"I'll be back to check on you in a little while," Dr. Gaynor said.

Trey entered the room as she was leaving.

Jack set his book and pencil aside and rose to his feet, offering his hand to the other man. "I see you got our note."

"I did," Trey confirmed. "Thank you for taking care of Kayla."

"Of course."

Kayla eyed Trey warily as he moved closer to the bed. He'd been so angry when he left, but she didn't hear any evidence of that in his voice now.

He touched his lips to her forehead, and the sweetness of the gesture made her throat tighten.

"How are you?"

She swallowed. "I'm okay."

"I'm so sorry I wasn't there."

"It's okay," she said, but she couldn't look at him when she said it. She understood why he'd been angry and upset, but she was still hurt by his abandonment of her. Reasonable or not, his walking away had felt like a rejection of not only her news but of herself and their child, too.

He turned to Eden and Jack again. "I'm so grateful you were there, and that you brought Kayla here."

"It's lucky that she knocked the lamp off the table when she fell, or we might not have known that she fainted."

"I'm not sure I really fainted," Kayla said. "I just felt dizzy for a minute."

"And didn't remember what had happened when I found you," Eden said. "Because you fainted."

"But I'm fine now," she insisted.

"The doctor wants to keep her a little longer, for observation," Eden told Trey, contradicting Kayla's statement.

"I'll stay with her," he told the couple.

"Then we'll get out of your way," Jack said.

"Any special requests for breakfast?" Eden asked Kayla.

She shook her head. "I'm sure whatever you have planned will be perfect."

"Drive safely," Trey said to Jack. "The snow is really blowing out there."

"My honey does everything slow and steady," Eden assured him, adding a saucy wink to punctuate her statement.

Jack shook his head. "We'll see you both in the morning," he said, putting his hand on his wife's back to guide her toward the door, quietly chiding her for "embarrassing the poor fellow."

"She did embarrass you, didn't she?" Kayla asked. "Your cheeks are actually red."

"It's cold and windy outside," he told her.

"They weren't that red when you walked in a few minutes ago."

"Okay," he acknowledged. "Now let's talk about you. Are you really okay?"

"How many times do I have to say it before people start believing it?"

"Maybe a hundred more."

She eyed him warily. "How are *you*?"

"I'm okay."

She lifted her brows; he smiled.

"What about…is the baby…okay?"

"The baby's fine. Apparently, he's well-cushioned in there."

"He?"

She shrugged. "Or she."

"You don't know?"

"I didn't want to know." She played with the plastic hospital bracelet on her wrist. "Do you want to know?"

"I don't mind being surprised."

Chapter Twelve

Kayla eyed him skeptically. "Really?"

"Okay—I know that's not what I was saying earlier," Trey acknowledged. "But I'm not sure I've ever been hit with a surprise of quite that magnitude before."

"I would hope not," she admitted, managing a small smile.

He reached for her hand, linked their fingers together. "I'm sorry."

She swallowed. "Sorry that I'm pregnant?"

"No." He squeezed her fingers. "I'm not sorry about the baby—I'm sorry that I was such an ass when you told me about the baby."

"And I'm sorry I waited so long to tell you."

"Why did you?"

"I was scared."

"Of me?"

She shook her head. "Of how you'd react."

"How did you think I'd react? Did you expect me to get mad and walk out?"

"That was one possible scenario—after you rejected the possibility that it was your baby."

He winced. "It was knee-jerk."

"I get that. But you should know that there wasn't any other possibility. What happened between us that night—I don't do things like that."

"I know."

Now it was her turn to wince. "I'm not sure if I should feel reassured or insulted."

He chuckled. "Rust Creek Falls is a small town," he reminded her. "You have a reputation for flying under the radar."

"Obviously, no one saw me do the walk of shame out of the boarding house the morning after Braden and Jennifer's wedding."

"Walk of shame? Because you spent the night with me?"

"Because I don't do things like that," she said again.

"I kind of hoped we'd do it again sometime."

"Like maybe this weekend?"

"Like maybe this weekend," he acknowledged. "But that isn't why I brought you here. I really did just want to spend some time with you away from all of the demands and distractions of our families."

"It was a sweet gesture."

He winced. "Sweet?"

She chuckled softly then sighed. "I really wanted to tell you," she insisted. "But every time I tried to lead into the conversation, something else came up."

"Nothing that was more important than what you weren't telling me," he pointed out.

She nodded, silently acknowledging his point. "The

first time was the day we had lunch—when Claire called and asked you to pick up diapers."

He did remember that his cousin's call had interrupted something Kayla started to say, and he winced when he remembered some of the things he'd said when he'd explained the errand request to Kayla. "Okay, I guess that one's on me."

"And then there was the night we were wrapping Presents for Patriots and you told me we had time to figure out everything we needed to know about one another."

"Only because I didn't know then that our time would be limited by the arrival of a bundle of joy."

"And then when we ran into Shane and Gianna after the Candlelight Walk."

"When I said that I wasn't looking to be a father anytime soon," he realized.

She nodded.

"You really should have just blurted out the news before I had a chance to make such an ass of myself."

"I'll keep that in mind if I ever find myself in this predicament again."

"You won't," he told her. "Our next baby—"

Whatever else he was going to say was interrupted by a knock at the door.

Kayla let out a breath—a sigh that was part relief and part frustration—when a technician pushed a trolley cart into the room.

"I'm Judy," she said. "Dr. Gaynor asked me to stop by so we could take a look at your baby."

Kayla's hand tightened on his. "Is something wrong?"

"There's no reason to think so," the technician assured her. "The doctor just wants to double-check before she releases you."

"Okay." But she didn't relinquish her viselike grip of Trey's hand.

Judy lifted the hem of Kayla's shirt and pushed down the top of her pants to expose the curve of her belly. She squirted the warm gel onto her tummy then spread it over her skin with the wand attached to the portable ultrasound machine.

A soft whooshing sounded, and the screen came to life, but Kayla found herself watching Trey, whose attention was riveted by the image that appeared.

"Is that…our baby?"

"That's our baby," she confirmed.

"It's…wow."

She understood exactly what he was feeling: the complete array of emotions that filled his heart. Awe. Joy. Fear.

She understood because it was the way she'd felt the first time she'd seen tangible evidence of the life growing inside her, not just the outline of the baby's head and torso or the little limbs flailing around, but the tiny heart inside her baby's chest that seemed to beat in tandem with her own.

"Everything looks great," Judy said. "Your baby is measuring right on target for twenty-four weeks."

"What does that mean?" Trey asked. "How big is he? Or she?" he hastened to add.

"Approximately eleven and a half inches long, probably weighing in at just under a pound—about the size of an ear of corn."

"Less than a pound?" Kayla wasn't happy. "I've gained more than ten, and you're telling me that less than one of that is my baby?"

The technician chuckled. "But all of it is necessary—there's also the placenta, amniotic fluid and various other factors that contribute to mother's weight gain during pregnancy."

"So it's not the hot chocolate with extra whipped cream?"

"It's not the hot chocolate," Judy promised. "Even with extra whipped cream." She continued to move the transducer over Kayla's belly. "You said 'he—or she'…did you want to know your baby's sex?"

Kayla looked at Trey. "Do you?"

"Do *you*?"

"I am a little curious," she admitted. "Especially because my sister seems convinced—on the basis of no scientific evidence whatsoever—that it's a boy."

Trey frowned at that but didn't comment, and Kayla realized he was probably unhappy to discover that her sister had known about the pregnancy before he did. But she wasn't going to explain or apologize—not in front of the ultrasound tech—and she was grateful that all he said to Judy was, "We'd like to know."

"The aunt-to-be is right," Judy told her. "It's a boy."

When Dr. Gaynor finally returned and approved Kayla's release, Trey insisted on bringing his truck right up to the exit doors of the hospital so that she didn't have to walk across the snowy ground to the parking lot. She appreciated his solicitousness, but she also knew his apparent acceptance of her pregnancy didn't mean anything was settled between them.

The earlier blizzard-like conditions had passed and the plows had already been out to clear the main roads, so the drive back to the bed-and-breakfast was quick and uneventful.

Throughout the short journey, her mind was so preoccupied with other things that she'd almost forgotten they weren't heading back to Rust Creek Falls. She knew that Trey would take her home if she asked, but she also knew that running away was a cowardly thing to do. They had to figure out their plans for the baby together so they could tell both of their families.

But back in their room at the inn, her gaze kept being drawn to the big bed at its center—the bed she'd hoped to share with Trey. The bed she still wanted to share with Trey, because apparently her active pregnancy hormones didn't care that there were unresolved issues so much as they remembered how much fun it had been to make a baby with this man and wanted to do the deed again.

She moved past the bed to the sitting area and lowered herself onto the edge of the sofa.

"Do you need anything?" Trey asked. "Are you hungry? You didn't eat very much at dinner."

She shook her head. "Eden got me some fries and gravy from the hospital cafeteria before you arrived."

"French fries and gravy?"

"Pregnant women have some strange cravings," she said, a little defensively.

"Anything else you've been wanting? Pickles? Ice cream? Pickles and ice cream?"

"No—at least, not at the same time," she assured him. "But if you're hungry, maybe Eden will let you sneak into the kitchen to make a sandwich."

She'd no sooner finished speaking when there was a knock on the door. Trey went to answer it and returned with a silver tray in his hands.

"Apparently Eden thought we might both be hungry," he said, setting down the tray set with a plate of cheeses and crackers, another of crudités and dip and a bowl of fresh fruit.

"They're both lovely people," Kayla said. "And this house is spectacular. How did you find it?"

He nodded. "Gage Christensen recommended it."

"You haven't stayed here before?"

"No." He selected a grape from the bowl, popped it into his mouth. "Did you think this was my usual rendezvous spot in Kalispell?"

She lifted a shoulder.

"I know I had a reputation in high school—and maybe for some years afterward—but I'm not that same guy anymore. And I didn't bring you here because there was a bed and none of our family within spitting distance. I brought you here because I wanted to give us a chance to reconnect without all the other craziness of our lives interfering."

"And the bed?" she prompted.

"I might have had hopes," he admitted. "But no expectations."

He plucked another grape from the bowl, offered it to her. She took the fruit from his fingertips, bit into it. The skin was crisp, the juice sweet. "Oh!"

"What is it?" Trey dropped the strawberry he'd selected. "What's wrong?"

"Nothing's wrong." She took his hand and laid it on the curve of her belly.

His brows drew together. "What…oh."

She knew then that he'd felt it, too, the subtle nudges against his palm that were evidence of their baby moving around inside her.

His lips curved and he shifted his hand to one side to make room for the other, splaying both of his palms against her belly. "Now I know why Shane's always touching Gianna's stomach."

The baby indulged him with a few moments of activity before settling again.

"It's fascinating," he said. "To know there's a tiny human being inside there. A baby. *Our* baby."

She smiled at the wonderment in his tone. "Our baby boy," she reminded him.

His hands moved from her belly to link with hers. "Do you know why I came back?"

"Hopefully because you didn't plan on returning to Rust Creek Falls with me stranded here."

"I didn't," he assured her. "But I meant why I came back when I did."

She shook her head. "Why did you come back when you did?"

"Because I realized that I love you."

For a moment, her heart actually stopped beating. Then it started racing. "You…what?"

"It kind of snuck up and surprised me, too," he admitted. "Maybe because I didn't ever expect to feel this way again. But it's true, Kayla. I love you."

She looked at their intertwined fingers and willed her heart to stop acting crazy for a minute so that she could think.

"This would be a great place to say that you love me, too," he prompted.

And she did love him. Maybe she always had. But she wasn't yet ready to put her heart on the line simply because he'd said the three little words she'd often dreamed he might one day say to her. Especially when she couldn't help but question the timing and his motives.

"I'm not sure that you're feeling what you think you're feeling," she said gently.

He scowled. "You don't believe I'm in love with you?"

"I think you *want* to believe you're in love with me because that would make the situation more acceptable to you."

"Kayla, there is nothing about this situation that is the least bit *un*acceptable to me."

"Six hours ago, the idea of being a husband and father totally freaked you out, and I understand that—"

"I'm not freaked out," he told her.

She lifted her brows.

"Okay, I *was* freaked out," he admitted. "Because the possibility that the one night we spent together might have created a baby never crossed my mind, and finding out not only that you were pregnant but more than five months pregnant was a little bit of a shock.

"But once I had some time to think about it—once my brain got past the holy-crap-I'm-going-to-be-a-father part and began to focus on the I'm-having-a-baby-with-Kayla part—I realized that I was okay with this."

"You're okay with it?" she echoed dubiously.

"I'm not explaining myself very well, am I?"

"I don't know," she admitted. "But if you're trying to reassure me, I'm not feeling very reassured."

"I wouldn't have planned for you to get pregnant that night," he said. "As I'm sure it wasn't in your plans, either."

"Definitely not," she agreed.

"But then I realized that if this had to happen—if a condom had to fail—I'm glad it was with you."

"That sounded…almost poetic," she decided, touched by the sincerity in his tone even more than his words.

"I want to be a father to our baby. I really do."

"I want that, too."

He was tempted to show her the ring right then and there, to prove how serious he was about wanting to be with her, but he suspected it was too soon to ask her again to marry him. If she needed some time to be sure of him and his feelings, he would give her that time.

Because the next time he proposed, he wasn't going to accept any answer but yes.

It wasn't really late, but it had been a long and emotionally draining day, and when Trey caught Kayla attempting to stifle a yawn, he said, "Why don't you go get changed and crawl into bed?"

"I don't have anything to change into," she realized.

"Your sister packed you a bag. I brought it up to the bedroom when I checked in before I went to the theater."

"I'm not sure I want to know what she packed for me," Kayla admitted, but she went into the other room to find out.

She was right to be suspicious. The silky short nightshirt and matching wrap certainly weren't from Kayla's closet, but since they were all she had, she put them on, then brushed her hair and cleaned her teeth.

When she was finished, she heard the television from the sitting area and saw that Trey was stretched out with his feet on the table and his eyes half-closed. She hesitated inside the doorway, and his eyes slowly opened and slid over her with a heated intensity that felt like a physical caress.

"I like what your sister packed," he murmured.

"This isn't mine," she blurted out.

"It looks good on you."

She tightened the belt around her waist, not realizing how the movement emphasized the curve of her belly until she saw his gaze drop and linger there.

"I think I understand your sudden affinity for shapeless clothing."

"I've gained ten and a half pounds already," she admitted.

"You're growing our baby."

"You didn't stumble over the words that time."

"I'm going to stumble," he told her. "This is all new territory for me."

"Me, too."

"But you've had a little bit more time to get used to the idea than me."

She didn't know if he'd intended the words as an accusation, but she couldn't help but interpret them as such, and she nodded in acknowledgment. "And more time to panic."

He'd been so shocked about the news of her pregnancy—and then so angry at her for keeping it from him—that he hadn't really considered how she'd felt, the gamut of emotions she must have experienced when she first suspected and then confirmed that she was going to have a baby. "Were you scared?"

"Terrified," she admitted without hesitation.

And she'd been alone.

But that had been her choice. She could have contacted him—could have shared her worries and her fears. Instead, she'd chosen to keep her pregnancy from everyone, including her baby's father.

"I didn't want to believe it was even possible," she said to him now. "I'd always thought I was so smart, that there really wasn't any such thing as an unplanned pregnancy anymore."

An understandable assumption considering that they'd taken precautions—and the reason for his own initial disbelief.

"I was so sure that my period was only late, but I went to a drugstore in Kalispell and bought a pregnancy test that I took into a public restroom. And I cried," she admitted softly. "I was so scared and confused. I couldn't do anything but cry."

He hated knowing that she'd been afraid and alone. Maybe she could have called him—*should* have called him—but he'd been three hundred miles away.

And maybe he should have shown some initiative and called her. Even if he'd had no reason to suspect there were any repercussions from the night they'd spent together, he should have kept in touch with her. By not doing so, he'd relegated their lovemaking to the status of a one-night stand.

"I'm sorry."

"I think we both need to stop saying that."

"I don't think I can say it enough," he said. "I totally screwed up. I should have—"

Determined to silence his self-recrimination, Kayla leaned forward and touched her lips to his.

Her kiss had the intended effect of halting his words, and the added benefit of clouding her own brain. Especially when he drew her closer and deepened the kiss, sliding his tongue between her lips to parry with her own.

Her hormones kicked into overdrive. She didn't know if it was a side effect of the pregnancy or just being with Trey, but she couldn't deny that she wanted him.

She slid her hands beneath his shirt, over the smooth skin and taut muscles. She felt his abs quiver beneath her touch. She wanted to feel his skin against hers, his body inside hers. She reached for the button of his jeans and was surprised—and disappointed—when he caught her wrist.

"I'm not sure that's a good idea," he told her.

"I disagree." She pressed her lips to his throat, just below his jaw, where his pulse was racing.

His hands gripped her hips. "You were just released from the hospital two hours ago."

"And when the doctor released me, she assured both of us that there were absolutely no restrictions on any physical activities."

"I'm sure she wasn't referring to..."

"To?" she prompted, amused by his inability to say the word *sex* aloud to her.

"Intimacy," he decided.

"I'm pretty sure she was," she countered. "Did you know that some women experience an increased sexual desire during pregnancy?"

"No, I...um...can't say that I did."

"And there are some women who become so hypersensitive they can't stand to be touched."

"I didn't...um...know that...either," he said, looking everywhere but at her.

"Of course, men have different responses to pregnancy, too. Some find their partners even more attractive and appealing...while others are completely turned off by the changes to her body," she said, attempting to withdraw from his embrace when he pointedly kept his gaze averted.

He let her pull back but not away. "And you think I'm turned off," he realized.

She shrugged. "You're not touching me."

"Only because I don't want to hurt you...or our baby."

"You won't," she assured him.

He drew her close again, so she couldn't possibly miss the evidence of his desire for her.

"I want you, Kayla. More than you could probably imagine."

"I don't know about that—I have a pretty good imagination," she told him. "And I want you, too."

"We were only naked together once before," he noted. "And as I recall, we were both fumbling around in the dark."

"I think we managed okay."

"This time, I want the lights on. I want to see you. And I want to take my time exploring every single inch of your sexy pregnant body," he told her.

"That sounds…promising."

"It is a promise."

Chapter Thirteen

He guided her through the doorway into the bedroom, over to the bed. He unfastened the knot at the front of her robe, parted the sides and then slid his hands over her belly and up. “Your breasts are fuller.”

“I should have figured you’d notice that.”

He grinned, unapologetic, as he brushed his thumbs over her nipples, through the silky fabric. She moaned softly.

“And more sensitive,” he realized.

“Yes, but in a good way. You don’t have to worry about touching me—I *want* you to touch me.”

“I want to touch you.” He pushed the robe off her shoulders, stroked his fingertips down her arms. “I am touching you.”

Then he lifted the hem of her nightshirt and lowered his head so that he was kissing her. First one breast, then the other, softly, almost reverently. After he kissed the hollow between them, his mouth moved lower, to the swell of her belly.

He pulled back the covers on the bed and eased her down onto the mattress, stripping her nightshirt away in the process. She was completely naked now, and suddenly very self-conscious.

She wasn't sure how he would respond to her belly unveiled. It was one thing to look at the curve beneath the fabric of the clothes she was wearing and quite another to see the skin stretched taut and all kinds of tiny blue veins visible beneath the surface. But he didn't seem put off at all.

He stripped away his own clothes and set a small square packet on the table beside the bed.

"That's a little like closing the barn door after the horse has escaped, don't you think?" she asked.

His brow furrowed. "I guess it is," he acknowledged. "I wasn't thinking. It's just a habit."

She nodded. "I'm relieved to know it is."

"But since we're not worried about you getting pregnant, there's nothing else you need to worry about, either. I have a clean bill of health and I haven't been with anyone else since we were together."

"You haven't been with anyone else in six months?"

"I didn't want to be with anyone else—because I couldn't stop thinking about you," he told her, trailing his fingertips along the insides of her thighs, upward from her knees, silently urging her legs to part.

"I couldn't stop thinking about you, either," she admitted.

"I'm happy to hear it."

The first time they'd made love, there hadn't been much foreplay. There hadn't been any need. They'd both wanted the same thing, and she had no regrets about what happened between them that night. But she had to admit their lovemaking had been a little…she wouldn't say disappointing so much as quick.

Trey made up for it now. He took his time learning his way around her body, exploring with his hands and his lips, touching and teasing until she was so aroused she could hardly stand it. Her heart was pounding, her blood was pulsing and her body was aching, desperately straining toward the ultimate pinnacle of pleasure.

She was already close, so close, but she wanted him there with her. She wanted to feel his hard length driving into her. She shifted restlessly, lifting her hips off the bed, wordlessly seeking the fulfillment she knew he could give her. When he eased back and pushed her knees farther apart, she thought, *Yes—finally, yes.*

But apparently he wasn't as eager as she was for their bodies to join together. Instead, he lowered his head and pressed his lips to the inside of one thigh, then the other. A whimper—a tangle of frustration and need—caught in her throat as his thumbs brushed the curls at the apex of her legs.

"Is this okay?" he asked.

"Only if you're trying to make me crazy."

"I'm trying to satisfy that raging sexual desire you were telling me about."

"I didn't say it was raging," she denied, just a little primly.

He chuckled softly, then his lips were on her, nibbling and teasing, his tongue gently probing her feminine core.

"Okay…now it's raging," she admitted breathlessly.

And then it was spinning out of control.

Finally, he lowered himself over her, into her.

She closed her eyes, sighing with satisfaction as he filled her. Then he began to move, slow, deep strokes that touched her very center. Her desire was definitely raging now. He'd already given her so much pleasure, but he held back, resisting his own release until he felt her body convulse around him.

Afterward, he brushed her hair away from her face and touched his lips to her temple. "I love you, Kayla. I understand that you might need some time to believe it's true, but I hope you won't need too much time, because I'm anxious for us to build a life together."

I love you, too.

The words—his and her own—filled her heart to overflowing, but the words stuck in her throat.

She *did* love him, but until she was certain that his feelings were real and the declaration wasn't prompted by some overblown sense of chivalrous responsibility, she wasn't going to let herself trust that they were true.

Trey wasn't surprised when Kayla suggested that he could drop her off at her sister's place rather than take her home, and considering that he'd manufactured her sleepover at Kristen's house to explain her absence from the Circle D, it wasn't an unreasonable request. However, now that he knew about their baby, he didn't want to keep the news of her pregnancy from either of their families a moment longer.

Her parents were at the table, having just finished their midday meal, when they arrived. Rita immediately offered to fix a couple more plates, but Trey assured her they'd already eaten. He didn't tell her that they'd had a late breakfast at the lovely little inn in Kalispell where he'd spent the night with her daughter.

"You just missed Derek and Eli," Rita told Trey. "They were here for lunch but headed out to check the fence on the northern boundary of the property."

"That's too bad," he said, though truthfully, he was grateful. He was prepared to face Kayla's parents and share the news of her pregnancy, but he wasn't eager to witness her brother's response. Derek had been unhappy enough to learn that Trey was dating his sister; he wasn't sure what his friend would do if he knew she was pregnant.

"I'm sure they'll both catch up with you soon," Kayla said, her words sounding like an ominous warning.

"In the meantime," Trey said, refusing to be sidetracked from his purpose, "we wanted to share some news with both of you."

Rita glanced from him to her daughter and back again, her expression one of polite confusion. "What news is that?"

He glanced at Kayla, indicating that it was her turn to talk, hoping that her parents would accept the news more easily if it came from her lips.

She drew in a deep breath and tried to smile, but her lips wobbled rather than curved. "We're going to have a baby."

There was silence for a long moment before Rita finally spoke.

"You mean you're planning to have a baby sometime in the future?" she asked, clearly trying to understand a statement that made no sense to her because she had no idea of the history between Kayla and Trey.

"No, I mean I'm pregnant."

Charles set his coffee mug down on the table, hard, his grip on the handle so tight his knuckles were white. "You're the father?" he demanded of Trey.

"Yes, sir."

"I don't understand," Rita said. "How is this possible? Trey's only been in town a couple of weeks…and the two of you just started dating."

"It happened in the summer," Kayla admitted. "The baby's due in April."

Her mother's eyes shimmered with moisture. "I knew something was up with you, but I never imagined…oh, Kayla."

Her eyes filled, too. He knew she felt guilty for keeping her pregnancy a secret, and she probably felt as if she'd disappointed her parents. Beneath the table, he reached for her hand and squeezed it reassuringly.

"When's the wedding?" Charles wanted to know.

"We're still trying to figure that out," Trey said.

"What's to figure? You call a minister and set a date, and if you haven't already done so, it just means you're dragging your heels and I—"

"Daddy," Kayla interrupted. "I'm the one dragging my heels."

Charles frowned at his daughter. "You don't want to marry the father of your baby?"

"I don't want to get married for the wrong reasons."

"A baby is never a wrong reason," he insisted. "And if you did the deed with a man you don't love, that's no one's fault but your own."

A single tear slid down Kayla's cheek; she swiped it away.

"Don't you think that's a little harsh?" Rita asked.

"Reality's harsh," her husband replied.

"What's done is done," Kayla's mother said, attempting to be a voice of reason. Then, to her daughter, "Have you been seeing a doctor?"

"Yes, I've been seeing a doctor," Kayla assured her.

"And everything's okay?"

She nodded. "Everything's fine."

"Everything except that she's unmarried and pregnant," Charles grumbled.

* * *

"That wasn't so bad, was it?" Trey asked her.

"It wasn't exactly a walk in the park."

"True, but I half expected to be leaving with my backside full of buckshot so, in comparison, it wasn't so bad."

"I'm sorry that my father is pressuring you to marry me."

"You seem to have forgotten that I asked you first—that I *want* to marry you."

"You want to do the right thing," she reminded him.

"Yes, I do," he confirmed. "Lucky for me that the right thing also gives me what I want—a life with you and our child."

Now that Kayla had told her parents, it was time for Trey to tell his. But since he wouldn't be seeing them until after the New Year, he decided to face his grandparents first.

He found his grandmother in the kitchen, preparing the evening meal.

"Where is everyone?"

"Claire and Levi took Bekka for a walk, and your grandfather is in the garage trying to find replacement bulbs for the Christmas lights that he insists are packed away somewhere."

"How long has he been digging around in there?"

"Let's just say it would have been quicker for him to drive into Kalispell to buy new replacement bulbs." She looked up from the potatoes she was peeling. "Something on your mind?"

His grandmother's instincts were uncanny as usual and since he couldn't imagine an appropriate segue, he just blurted it out. "Kayla's pregnant."

"I don't believe it," she said sternly. "And you shouldn't

be spreading gossip about matters that aren't any of your business."

"It is my business," Trey told her. "It's my baby."

His grandmother put a hand to her heart. "You're joking."

He shook his head. "She's due in April. April ninth."

Melba silently counted on her fingers.

"It happened when I was here in the summer," he admitted.

"What happened in the summer?" his grandfather asked, stomping into the kitchen.

His grandmother looked at him, because it was his news to tell.

"I slept with Kayla Dalton," he admitted.

Gene winced. "Why do I need to know this?"

"Because she's pregnant."

"Didn't your father give you the talk?"

"Yes, he gave me the talk," Trey confirmed. "And you gave me the talk. And we were careful."

"Obviously not careful enough." Gene nodded to thank his wife for the coffee she set in front of him. "You're going to marry her."

It wasn't a question but a statement; Trey nodded, anyway. "As soon as I can get Kayla to agree."

"What do you mean? Why wouldn't she agree?"

Melba rolled her eyes at her husband. "Because he probably said 'we better get married' without any attempt at romance."

"Don't you think the time for romance is past?" Gene asked.

"The time for romance is never past," his wife insisted.

"I can do romance," Trey interjected, attempting to shift the attention back to the subject at hand and away from the argument he could sense was brewing between his grandparents.

"Of course you can," Melba agreed.

"Start by buying a ring," Gene advised. "That's the most important thing."

"Telling her you love her is the most important thing," his grandmother countered. "But only if it's true."

"It is. And I did."

"Then you should buy a ring."

"I did that, too."

"And she still said no?"

"I didn't have the ring when I asked," he admitted. "And I didn't know how I felt about her when I asked."

"And now she'll think you only said those words because of the baby."

"That's the root of the problem," Gene spoke up again. "Thinking."

"I beg your pardon?" his wife said.

"Young women these days overthink everything—and young men don't know when to take action."

"What do you suggest I do?" Trey wanted to know. "Throw her over my shoulder and cart her off to the preacher?"

"I don't know that your actions need to be that drastic," his grandfather allowed. "But I've got an idea."

Later that night, Kayla tracked her mother down in the laundry room. "I know you're disappointed in me, and I'm sorry," she said softly.

"I'm mostly disappointed that you didn't tell us about the baby sooner," Rita said, measuring soap into the dispenser and setting the machine to wash. "It might have been a lot of years ago, but I still remember how anxious and worried I was during my first pregnancy—actually frantic and paranoid might be more accurate. I needed reassurance about everything I was thinking and feeling and doing, and I relied so much on my mother for that advice and support."

"I wanted to tell you." Kayla picked up a T-shirt, still warm from the dryer, and began to fold it. "But I didn't think it was fair to tell anyone about the baby until I told the baby's father."

"I can understand that," her mother allowed. "I can't understand why it took you five months to do that."

"Because Trey had gone back to Thunder Canyon and it wasn't the kind of news I felt comfortable sharing over the phone." Especially after a drunken one-night stand—but, of course, she didn't share *that* part with her mother.

"So when did you finally tell him?"

She set the folded shirt aside and picked up another. "Yesterday."

Rita matched up a pair of socks. "Yesterday?"

She nodded.

"The man's been in town for more than two weeks," her mother pointed out.

She nodded again.

"Well, I can't say I know how awkward and difficult it must have been to share the news," Rita admitted. "And that's between the two of you."

Kayla continued to fold her father's T-shirts.

"You know, I wouldn't have made a big deal about the French fries if I'd known you were pregnant."

She managed a laugh. "I know, Mom."

Rita matched another pair of socks. "Trey Strickland… I never would have guessed."

"I really am sorry," Kayla said.

"I don't want you to be sorry—I want you to be happy."

"I've screwed everything up so badly, I'm not sure that's possible. Trey is so angry…and hurt."

"He wouldn't be so angry and hurt if he didn't care about you deeply," Rita told her.

Kayla considered that for a minute, wanting to believe it could be true and, at the same time, afraid to let herself hope.

"Do you care about him?" her mother prompted.

There was no point in denying her feelings any longer. "I love him."

Rita smiled. "I thought you did."

"I'm not sure that's a good thing," she admitted. "I can't separate what I want from what's best for both of us and our baby."

"It *is* a good thing," her mother insisted. "Because with love, all things are possible."

RUST CREEK RAMBLINGS: BITS & BITES

Lovely Manhattan transplant, Lissa Christensen, has been spending time with fellow newcomer and nurse, Callie Crawford—at the local medical clinic. Are the two friends catching up on local gossip…or is it possible that the sexy sheriff's wife is "in the family way"?

Kayla was relieved when she woke up on Christmas morning because it was the one day she could be fairly certain that her family would be too busy with other things to pressure her about the situation with Trey.

She appreciated that they were thinking about what was best for her and the baby, but what they didn't seem to understand was that she *wanted* to marry Trey—she just needed to know that it was what he wanted, too, and she couldn't shake the feeling that he had only proposed out of duty and obligation. Until she could be sure that he really wanted them to be a family, she couldn't say yes.

The door flew open and Kristen leaped onto Kayla's bed. "Merry Christmas, Sleepyhead."

She smiled at her twin, who had opted to sleep in her old room the night before so the sisters could celebrate Christmas morning together one last time. "Merry Christmas, Earlybird."

Kristen fell back on the mattress, so their heads were side by side on the pillow. "It's the end of an era, isn't it?"

Kayla nodded. "Next year, you'll wake up with your husband on Christmas morning."

"And you'll be celebrating your baby's first Christmas."

She nodded again. Although it was a full year away, she couldn't help wondering what the day would look like—when she and Trey would have an eight-month-old baby with whom to celebrate the holiday. But where would they be? And would they be together? Or would their baby be shuffled from one house to another from one year to the next?

"I understand why you turned down Trey's proposal," Kristen said to her now. "You didn't want to marry him for the sake of your baby. But maybe you shouldn't have looked at it that way."

"How should I have looked at it?"

"You could have focused on the fact that the man you love was asking you to marry him."

"But I don't just want to marry the man I love—I want to marry a man who loves me, too."

"And he does," Kristen said.

But Kayla wasn't so sure. Since the day after she'd told him about the baby—and after they'd told their respective families about the baby—he hadn't said another word about marriage or even hinted about wanting a life with her and their baby.

"What does he have to do to prove to you that his feelings are real?" Kristen asked her now.

"I don't know," she admitted. "But I think I deserve something more than an impulsive and slightly panicked proposal."

"You definitely do," her sister agreed.

"Girls!" Rita called up to her daughters. "Breakfast is ready."

Kayla threw back the covers. "I'm starving."

Her sister laughed. "You're always starving these days."

She walked down the stairs beside Kristen, as she'd done every Christmas morning for as long as she could remember. But this year, Kayla wasn't thinking about presents from the jolly man in the red suit—she was preoccupied with thoughts of a different man…and hoping for a holiday miracle.

Chapter Fourteen

Breakfast was fruit and yogurt, pancakes, and bacon and eggs, and for once her mother didn't give Kayla a disapproving glance when she filled her plate.

She looked around the table as she ate—at her mother and her father, still solid after thirty-five years of marriage; her brother, Jonah, and his wife, Vanessa, still newlyweds; Kristen and her fiancé, blissfully in love and eager to start their life together. She wanted what they each had—the affection and commitment—and she wanted it with Trey.

After everyone had eaten their fill and the kitchen was cleaned up, the family moved into the living room to exchange gifts. Kayla hadn't yet sat down when there was a knock at the door. Her heart quickened.

Though Trey hadn't said anything more about her mother's invitation to join them on Christmas Day, she couldn't imagine who else it might be. Certainly there wasn't anyone else that she wanted to see today as much as she wanted to see him.

"I'll get it," she said, feigning a casualness she didn't feel as she tried not to race to the door.

It *was* Trey—and he looked so incredibly handsome in a black sweater and dark jeans with his leather jacket unzipped. He hadn't shaved, but she didn't mind the light growth of ginger stubble on his jaw. In fact, she thought it made him look even sexier than usual, and just a little bit dangerous.

Dangerous to your heart, she reminded herself, stepping away from the door so he could enter.

"Merry Christmas, Kayla." He took advantage of the fact that they were out of sight of everyone else to steal a quick kiss, touching his lips lightly to hers.

"Merry Christmas," she replied, feeling suddenly and inexplicably shy. After two days of no contact except through text messages, she wasn't sure what to say or how to act around him.

"Is it okay that I'm here?"

"My mother did invite you," she reminded him.

"I meant, is it okay with you?"

"Oh. Of course."

He tipped her chin up. "I've missed you."

"You have?"

"Yes, I have," he confirmed.

"I missed you, too," she admitted.

He smiled at that. "Did Santa bring you everything you wanted for Christmas?"

Everything she wanted was standing right in front of her, but she didn't know how Trey would respond to that kind of declaration. Instead she said, "I don't know yet—we're opening gifts in the front room now."

"Then I'm just in time," he said, holding up the bag of gifts he carried.

Kayla led him into the family room where a fire crackled in the hearth and the lights were lit on an enormous tree beneath which was a small mountain of presents. After greetings and holiday wishes were exchanged all around, Derek began to distribute gifts.

The mountain had been cut down to a moderate hill when her brother passed a heavy square box to her.

Kayla frowned at the tag. "It doesn't say who it's from."

Her family looked from one to the other, all of them shaking their heads. Trey did the same when the attention shifted in his direction.

"It doesn't matter who it's from," Kristen said. "It has your name on it."

So she undid the bow and tore open the paper, but the plain cardboard gave no hint as to its contents. She lifted the lid and found a bottle of something that looked suspiciously like moonshine, beneath which was a note in spidery handwriting.

"What does it say?" Rita asked.

She started to read aloud:

"Dear Ms. Rust Creek Ramblings,

"It didn't take people long to figure out that the wedding punch was doctored but no one knows who did it…or why. Now that you and Trey are together again, I'll fill you in on the story.

"What I saw on the Fourtth of July was more than just a happy couple ready to embark on a life together. I saw a lot of lonely people who needed a little push toward their own happiness. Or maybe more than a little push. Jordyn Leigh Cates, Levi Wyatt, Lani Dalton, Brad Crawford, your sister…and you. All of you sampled Homer Gilmore's Wedding Moonshine—and look at everyone now!

"My work is done. Sincerely, HG"

Kayla was stunned—and already thinking that this confession would make the perfect topic of her next column.

"Homer Gilmore?" Kristen said skeptically. "He doesn't strike me as the romantic type."

"Forget Homer Gilmore," Rita said. "The old coot's clearly off his rocker to think, for even a minute, that Kayla is the Rust Creek Rambler."

"Actually, that's something I need to talk to you all about," Kayla said, her gaze hesitantly shifting around the room from one family member to the next, briefly—and apologetically—encompassing them all.

Everyone was silent for a moment, stunned by the news that sweet, shy Kayla was the source of Rust Creek Falls's juiciest gossip.

Derek recovered his voice first. "Are you saying it's true?" he demanded.

"It's true," she admitted.

"You've been writing gossip for the paper about our friends?" her father asked, his voice heavy with disapproval.

"Not just our friends but our family," Kristen noted. "You wrote about *me*! And Jonah and Vanessa, too!"

"None of it was malicious or untrue," Kayla said defensively.

"Which just goes to prove that people aren't always what they seem," Derek said, looking pointedly from his sister to his high school pal.

"There's something written on the back," Trey noted, trying to deflect attention away from Kayla's revelation and back to Homer's confession.

She turned the page over.

"PS—It was Boyd Sullivan's idea to 'lose' the farm to Brad Crawford. His broken heart just couldn't mend here in Rust Creek Falls. Since he left, he's been living in upstate New York and may have found love again. I'll never regret buying him that train ticket."

"I still can't believe Homer Gilmore could mastermind such a plan," Rita said.

"I still can't believe our daughter is the Rust Creek Rambler," Charles grumbled.

"There's something else in the box," Kayla noted, lifting out a handful of ring boxes and a stack of extra marriage licenses with another note attached. *I didn't get to use them all—maybe one will come in handy for you someday.*

"I guess that answers the question of how Will and Jordyn Leigh were able to get married so easily," Eli noted.

"I guess I should be grateful that I didn't drink any of that punch," Derek muttered.

"If you had, and if you'd actually met someone, you might be a little less cranky," Kristen pointed out.

"There are still presents to be opened," Rita noted, eager to defuse the argument she could sense brewing between her children.

Derek resumed handing out gifts.

"I have one for Kayla," Trey said, then slipped back into the foyer. When he returned, he was carrying an enormous fluffy white teddy bear with a Santa hat on its head.

"It's adorable," Kayla said, hugging the bear to her chest. Then she hugged Trey. "Thank you."

"I think he was expecting a yes or no rather than thank you," Kristen said.

In response to Kayla's blank look, she pointed to the stocking that the bear held between its paws.

On the stocking was embroidered the words "Will you marry me?"

Kayla's breath caught in her throat. She looked from the bear to Trey, who dropped to one knee beside her.

"I promised to give you some time, so that you could be sure—and know that I was sure. And I am. I love you, and what I most want for Christmas is to be your husband and a father to our baby." He reached into the stocking that the bear was holding and pulled out a small box, then flipped open the lid to reveal a gorgeous vintage engagement ring. "So I'm asking now, Kayla Dalton, will you marry me?"

She was glad she was already sitting down, because her knees had turned to jelly. When they were in Kalispell together, it had been easy to disregard his impulsive proposal because she knew he was trying to do the right thing. The fact that he'd chosen to ask her again, putting his heart on the line not just in front of her but her whole family, too, made her realize that his motivation might be a little more complicated than she'd assumed.

What did she need to believe his feelings for her were real? Only this—exactly this.

"Yes, Trey Strickland, I will marry you."

He fumbled a little as he pulled the ring from the box. "I'm not nervous about marrying you," he said, his voice lowered so that only she could hear. "I'm just feeling a little nervous about doing this in front of your whole family."

"So why did you?"

"Because I wanted to prove to you that it wasn't an impulse or an obligation. And because I thought putting a ring on your finger would increase my chances of getting out of here without my backside full of buckshot."

"I can see why you'd be concerned," she told him. "It's a really nice backside."

His brows lifted. "You think so?" He finally slid the ring on her finger and then leaned forward to kiss her softly.

Kayla almost forgot they were in a room filled with her family until everyone applauded. Trey must have, too, because he eased back and smiled sheepishly.

"Now we need to set a date for the wedding," Rita said. "And I think the sooner, the better."

"I agree," Trey said. "In fact, I was thinking today would be perfect."

"Today?" Kayla echoed. "We can't get married today."

"Why not?"

"Because there's paperwork that needs to be filed and—"

"The paperwork's done," he told her. "My grandfather suggested I take care of the administrative details so that we could have a Christmas wedding."

"You're serious," she realized. "You want to get married today."

"I don't want to wait another minute to make you my wife."

"I love the idea," she admitted. "But we need more than a license to make it happen."

"The minister is just waiting for our call."

"But… I don't even have a dress."

"I do," Kristen interjected.

"You just happen to have a wedding dress hanging in your closet?" Kayla asked skeptically, because she knew the gown her sister had ordered for her own wedding wouldn't be ready for several weeks and wouldn't fit Kayla even if she did have it.

"The theater was getting rid of some costumes, including a vintage wedding dress, so I brought it home, certain it could be put to good use one day," Kristen explained.

Kayla laid a hand on her swollen tummy. "I can't imagine anything designed for the stage would fit me in this condition."

"It has an empire waist and a full skirt," Kristen said.

Still, she hesitated.

"You should at least try it," her mother suggested.

"What do you think?" she asked Trey.

"I think you're going to be the most beautiful bride ever, no matter what you're wearing."

She glanced down at the simple green tunic-style top that she had on over black leggings. "Well, I'd rather not be wearing this," she admitted.

Kristen took her hand and tugged her to her feet. "Let's go upstairs so you can try it on," she urged.

"While you're doing that, I'm going to call my grandparents to invite them to the wedding."

"Then I guess you'd better call the minister, too," Kayla said.

"I will," he promised.

Trey made the necessary phone calls, then went in search of his high school friend and soon-to-be brother-in-law. He found Derek brooding in the corner, a long-necked bottle in his hand and a dark expression on his face.

"You're pissed," Trey realized.

"Did you expect me to be thrilled to learn that my buddy knocked up my little sister?" Derek challenged.

Trey winced. "It really wasn't like that."

"You weren't drunk on Homer Gilmore's moonshine when you seduced her?"

"The wedding punch might have been a factor," he acknowledged. "But I don't regret what happened, because I love your sister and I'm looking forward to building a life and a family with her."

"You always did have a way with words—and with the ladies," Derek sneered.

"We both did," Trey reminded his friend. "And if you

remember that, you should also remember that when I make a commitment, I honor it. I could tell you that, from this day forward, there will be no one for me but Kayla. The truth is, there hasn't been anyone for me but Kayla since that night we spent together in July."

"The fact you spent that night with her still makes me want to take you out to the barn to go a few rounds," Kayla's brother warned. "The only reason I'm restraining myself is that I know my sister wouldn't forgive me if I was the reason her groom was sporting a black eye on their wedding day."

"I appreciate your restraint," Trey said. "And I'd appreciate it even more if you stood beside me as my best man when I marry her."

Derek considered the offer for a long moment before he finally nodded. "I could do that."

Trey offered his hand. "I'm going to do everything I can to make Kayla happy—to be a good husband to her and a good father to our baby."

"I know you will," his friend agreed grudgingly. "Because if you don't, you'll answer to me."

"I can't believe the theater was going to throw this away," Kayla said, trailing a hand down the lace sleeve of the dress her sister presented to her.

"Lots of costumes and limited storage space," Kristen said matter-of-factly.

"But this is…beautiful."

"It is," her sister agreed. "And it will look even more beautiful on you."

"I'm feeling a little guilty."

"Why?"

"Because you got engaged first but I'm getting married first."

"Actually, I'm happy it turned out this way," Kristen said. "Because after you're married and your baby is born, there will be no distractions from my big day."

Kayla chuckled. "Absolutely not," she promised.

With her sister's help, she stripped down and slipped into the vintage gown.

"Maybe it wasn't just a lack of storage space," Kristen allowed, as she worked on fastening the dozens of tiny buttons that ran down the back of the dress. "It could be that this dress isn't exactly conducive to quick costume changes."

But at last she finished, then turned Kayla around to face her. "Oh, it's perfect." Kristen's eyes misted. "You're perfect. Absolutely perfect."

"You think it's okay that I'm wearing white?"

"I think a bride should wear whatever she wants on her wedding day, but it's actually off-white, so you don't need to worry about anyone wagging a finger in your direction."

"No, it's more likely tongues will be wagging."

"The joys of living in a small town," her sister reminded her. "But at least you've mostly flown under the radar of the Rust Creek Rambler for the past few years."

"Not entirely, though," she pointed out.

"Yeah, there were occasional—and completely forgettable mentions—just enough to ensure that no one ever suspected you were the author of the column."

"I protected you, too," she pointed out.

"Which is probably why people *did* suspect me."

"I guess I didn't think that one through very well," she apologized, as she pinned her hair into a twist at the back of her head.

"It didn't bother me," Kristen assured her. Then, "You need earrings."

"You're right." Kayla lifted the lid of her jewelry box

and selected the sparkly teardrops that had belonged to their grandmother.

"I thought you lost one of those."

"I did," she admitted. "In Trey's bed."

Her sister's brows lifted. "It's a good thing he found it before his grandmother did."

"No kidding," she agreed.

"When did you get it back?"

"Just a few days ago. He said he'd been carrying it with him since that morning, waiting for the right time to return it to me."

Kristen laid a hand on her heart and sighed dramatically. "Just like Prince Charming with the glass slipper."

Kayla felt her cheeks flush. "I don't know if it was just like that, but it was pretty romantic."

There was a tap of knuckles on the door, then Rita peeked her head into her daughter's room. "Everyone is here so anytime— Oh, Kayla." Her mother's eyes filled with tears. "You look so beautiful." She drew in a breath and blinked away the moisture. "But you don't have any flowers."

"I didn't expect to even have a dress," she reminded her mother. "I'm not too worried about the flowers."

"But it's your wedding day. It should be perfect."

"I'm marrying the man I love—it already is perfect."

"You're right," Rita agreed. "And speaking of men, your father would like to give you away."

"I know—he tried to do that the day he found out about my pregnancy."

Her mother flushed.

Kayla touched a hand to her arm. "I'm kidding, Mom. I would very much like to have Dad walk me down the aisle."

"Actually, it's going to be the hall, not an aisle," Kristen pointed out.

"I'll go get him," Rita said, and slipped out of the room, closing the door softly behind her.

"Are you nervous?" Kristen asked.

Kayla shook her head. "Excited. Although I'm still not convinced this isn't all a dream."

"It is a dream," Kristen said. "It's *your* dream come true. Don't question it—just enjoy it."

"I've been in love with Trey since I was twelve years old."

"I know."

"I never thought he'd even notice me, never mind love me back."

"Well, he did and he does," her sister told her. "And right now, he's waiting downstairs to marry you."

Trey shifted from one foot to the other as he waited for Kayla to appear. His grandmother had positioned him in front of the Christmas tree—insisting it would be the best backdrop for pictures—and Derek stood beside him. The minister was there, too, smiling and chatting with guests, assuring them that it wasn't an imposition but a pleasure to be called out to perform a surprise wedding ceremony, even on Christmas Day.

Trey had been in agreement with the plan—the idea of a small family wedding suited him perfectly. But apparently it wasn't going to be as small as he'd anticipated. Not only had his grandparents picked up the minister on their way to the Circle D, they'd also brought Claire, Levi, Bekka, Hadley and Tessa. And while Kayla was doing whatever she was doing upstairs to get ready for the wedding, the mother of the bride had been busy on the phone, because before the bride descended the stairs again, the living room was practically bursting at the seams with people.

There were Kayla's siblings, of course. Jonah and his wife, Vanessa, Kristen's fiancé, Ryan Roarke, and Eli and Derek. Her aunt and uncle, Mary and Ben Dalton were also there, along with their unmarried children—Anderson, Travis and Lindsay. Also in attendance were Caleb and Mallory Dalton with their adopted daughter, Lily; Paige and Sutter Traub with their son, Carter; and Lani Dalton and Russ Campbell.

Then Kayla appeared and everyone else faded away.

He'd meant what he'd said when he'd told her she would look beautiful in whatever she was wearing, but in the white dress with her hair pinned up and a pair of familiar earrings dangling from her lobes, she was absolutely stunning.

He couldn't take his eyes off her while they exchanged their vows, and he didn't want to. A few short weeks earlier, he could not have imagined that he would be married before the end of the year—certainly and not be happy about it. But as Kayla returned his promise to love, honor and cherish "till death do us part," he realized that he was finally where he belonged. It didn't matter if they were in Rust Creek Falls or Thunder Canyon or even Timbuktu—what mattered was that they were together.

Finally, the minister invited the groom to kiss his bride.

Trey lowered his head to hers, pausing before his lips touched hers to whisper, "I love you, Mrs. Strickland."

"And I love you, Mr. Strickland," she whispered back.

He smiled and then—finally—he kissed his wife for the first time.

After that, flutes of champagne and sparkling grape juice were passed around so that guests could toast the newlyweds. Kayla surprised everyone by offering a toast of her own.

"I just want to thank our families and friends who have gathered here today—on very short notice—to celebrate this occasion with us. Christmas has always been my favorite time of the year but now for even more reasons. Because of Trey, I got everything I wanted this year—and more.

"But if I could have one more wish come true, it would be that all of our siblings and cousins and friends will someday be as lucky to share the same love and happiness that I've found with Trey."

Of course, there were many more toasts after that, and everyone wanted to kiss the bride and congratulate the groom. Trey didn't really mind, but he was anxious to be alone with Kayla, and it seemed like forever before they managed to extricate themselves from the crowd to head back to his room at the boarding house.

"Why do I feel like I'm returning to the scene of the crime?" Kayla asked, after Trey had parked his truck and came around to the passenger side to help her out.

"Maybe because you're whispering and tiptoeing," he suggested.

"I feel guilty," she acknowledged.

"Why would you feel guilty?"

"Because we violated your grandparents' rule prohibiting overnight visitors."

"That was five months ago," he reminded her. "Now we're lawfully married and there's no reason to feel guilty."

"I guess it's going to take me a little while to get used to that fact."

"You've got the rest of your life—the rest of our lives," he amended, unlocking the door to his room.

"I'm looking forward to every single day of it."

"Me, too," he said. "And I promise you, now that my ring is on your finger, if you ever try to sneak out in the middle of the night again, I will go after you."

"I guess I didn't handle that very well, did I?"

"You might have saved us some confusion and a lot of lost time if you hadn't disappeared before the sun came up."

"I'm not going anywhere this time," she assured him.

"You won't have a chance—I'm not going to let you out of my arms tonight."

She smiled. "Is that a promise?"

"That is very definitely a promise."

His gaze skimmed over her, slowly, appreciatively, from the top of her head to the toes of the shoes that peeked out beneath the hem of her gown. "Your sister made a good call on this dress," he said. "You look fabulous in it, but I suspect you're going to look even better out of it."

"I'm five-and-a-half months pregnant," she reminded him.

"I know."

"I've gained twelve pounds now."

He framed her face in his hands. "You were beautiful in July, you're beautiful now, and you'll be just as beautiful in April when you can't see your swollen ankles, and even more so when we're celebrating our fiftieth anniversary," he said sincerely.

"What did I ever do to deserve you?"

"You got drunk on Homer's punch." He turned her around and began to unfasten the buttons of her dress.

She laughed softly. "I wasn't drunk. I was in love. I've been in love with you since the day you climbed the big maple tree behind my parents' house to retrieve my favorite doll that Derek had thrown into the top branches."

"I can't say I loved you then," he admitted. "But I love you now. For now and forever."

Her heart sighed with contentment—and then Trey swore under his breath.

She glanced over her shoulder.

"I changed my mind about this dress," he grumbled. "How many damn buttons are on this thing?"

"I don't know," she admitted. "Kristen did it up for me."

He struggled for a few more minutes, then finally had the back opened up enough that he could push the dress off her shoulders and over her hips. He quickly stripped away her undergarments and dispensed with his own attire in record time.

Then he slowed everything down. His lips were patient, his hands gentle, as he aroused her tenderly and very thoroughly. When she was ready for him—almost begging for him—he finally, and again slowly, eased into her. The pressure built inside her the same way—slowly, but steadily, inexorably guiding her toward the culmination of pleasure.

She was close…so close. But she needed something more than what he was giving her, more than soft touches and gentle strokes.

"Trey, please. I need—"

He brushed his lips against hers. "I know."

But he didn't, because he continued at the same leisurely pace, and while it felt good—*really* good—it wasn't enough. She bit back a whimper of frustration as the pleasure continued to build inside her, gentle rolling waves of sensation that teased her with the promise of more.

And then, just when she thought that promise was beyond her reach, her body imploded, shattering into a million little pieces that scattered like stars into the far reaches of the galaxy before they drifted back to earth. Slowly.

It was a long time later before they were both able to breathe normally again, before Trey summoned the energy to tuck her close against him.

"Wow," she said softly.

With her head nestled against his shoulder, she couldn't see his face, but she heard the smile in his voice when he said, "I never thought I'd say this—but I think I'm going to have to thank Homer Gilmore for spiking the wedding punch."

"Maybe we should name our baby after him," Kayla suggested.

"I think we should stick to saying thanks," Trey countered.

She laughed softly. "Okay—we'll do that."

"Did you have any thoughts about names?"

"No, I've tried not to think too far ahead."

"It isn't so far now," he pointed out. "Less than four months."

She shifted so that she was on her side, facing him. "I'm sorry that I didn't tell you sooner, that you missed out on so much."

"I won't miss out next time."

Though she was touched by the confident assurance in his voice, she wanted to enjoy the present with him before scheduling their future. "Could we have this baby before you start planning for the next one?"

"Of course," he agreed. "But I do think we should practice our baby-making technique."

"Again?"

He shrugged. "We missed a lot of months together—and they do say practice makes perfect."

She lifted her arms to his shoulders and drew him down to her. "In that case, we should definitely practice."

Epilogue

When Trey returned to their room at the boarding house, he found his wife exactly where he'd left her: sitting at the desk, staring at the screen of her laptop computer.

"Are you *still* working on that?"

"Just finishing up."

He set down the tray of fruit and cheese he'd snagged from the kitchen along with the two crystal flute glasses he'd borrowed from his grandparents' cabinet, then reached into the mini-fridge for the bottle of nonalcoholic champagne he'd purchased for the occasion. "That's what you said half an hour ago."

"But now it's true," she told him, turning the computer so that he could see the screen.

His brows lifted. "You're giving me a sneak peek?"

"I want an unbiased second opinion before I send it to my editor."

"Then you shouldn't ask me," he pointed out. "How

can I be unbiased about anything written by the woman I love?"

She smiled, as she always did when he told her he loved her. "True, but I want you to read it, anyway."

He stood behind her chair, his hands on her shoulders, as he read her last column for the Rust Creek newspaper.

RUST CREEK RAMBLINGS: OUT WITH THE OLD, IN WITH THE NEW (YEAR) & MISCELLANEOUS OTHER THINGS

2015 was an eventful year for the residents of Rust Creek Falls. In addition to the usual weddings and funerals, engagements and reunions, there was the mystery of the wedding punch served at the Fourth of July nuptials of Braden Traub and Jennifer MacCallum. A mystery that was finally solved when Homer Gilmore confessed to spiking the punch with his homemade moonshine in an effort to help the lonely residents of our fair town find their bliss. On many accounts, he succeeded.

As the hours count down and the dawn of a New Year draws ever closer, one cannot help but wonder what events will make headlines in the months ahead. I'll look forward to reading about them rather than writing them myself, as I'm leaving Rust Creek Falls to make my home in Thunder Canyon with my new husband and the family we're going to have together. But don't worry, loyal readers, there is a new Rambler already in your midst, already keeping an ear to the ground and a notepad in hand.

Happy New Year to All!

Your (former) Rust Creek Rambler,
Kayla Dalton Strickland

"You put your name on it," Trey noted with surprise.

His wife nodded. "I thought it was time for the people of Rust Creek Falls to learn the identity of the Rambler."

"You mean that you wanted them to know your sister wasn't responsible for the column," he guessed.

"That, too," she agreed.

"Are you going to miss it?"

She shook her head. "I had a lot of fun with it, but I'm more than ready to move on, to focus on being a wife and—very soon—a mother."

"No regrets about leaving Rust Creek Falls?"

"None," she assured him. "Besides, Thunder Canyon isn't really that far away, and we'll come back to visit whenever we can."

"I'm sure we'll be pressured to come back even more often," Trey said. "Especially after the baby is born."

"And no doubt there will be a convoy from Rust Creek Falls to Thunder Canyon as soon as our families hear that the baby is on his way."

"You're probably right."

She clicked SEND to submit her final edition of "Ramblings" to the newspaper, then shut down the computer.

As Trey handed her a glass of nonalcoholic champagne, she could hear the rest of the family and boarding house guests talking and laughing in the main parlor.

"Are you sure you don't want to go downstairs to ring in the New Year with your cousins and your grandparents?"

"I'm sure," he said. "I want to celebrate our first New Year together with my bride."

"But what if I want to wear a sparkly crown and blow one of those noisy horns?"

He picked up a sparkly crown—pilfered from the box of party stuff his grandmother had amassed for the celebration—and settled it on her head. Then he handed her a noisemaker.

"Once again, you've thought of everything, haven't you?"

"I tried." He touched his lips to hers. "I love you, Kayla."

Her eyes filled with tears.

He pulled back. "What did I do? Why are you crying?"

She managed to laugh at his panicked tone. "Sorry—I'm pregnant and hormonal, and I'm crying because I'm happier than I ever thought possible."

Trey wrapped his arms around her. "That's lucky for us then, because I feel the same way—well, except for the pregnant, hormonal and crying parts."

Kayla laughed again, and as the guests downstairs began their countdown to midnight, she and Trey celebrated the birth of the New Year in their own way.

* * * * *

JOIN US ON SOCIAL MEDIA!

Stay up to date with our latest releases, author news and gossip, special offers and discounts, and all the behind-the-scenes action from Mills & Boon...

millsandboon

millsandboonuk

millsandboon

might just be true love...